Praise for Michael J. Sullivan

"Riyria has everything you could possibly wish for: the characters are some of the best I've ever encountered in fantasy literature, the writing is top notch, and the plotting is so tight you'd be hard-pressed to find a mouse hole in it."
— *B&N Sci-fi & Fantasy Blog*

"This epic fantasy showcases the arrival of a master storyteller."
— *Library Journal* on *Theft of Swords*

"A delightful, entertaining and page-turning read that reminds us just how enjoyable, and how good The Riyria Revelations series is. A must-buy for all fantasy lovers."
— *The Founding Fields* on *Rise of Empire*

"Heir of Novron is the conclusion to the Riyria Revelations, cementing it in a position as a new classic of modern fantasy: traditional in setting, but extremely unconventional in, well, everything else."
— *Drying Ink* on *Heir of Novron*

"Sullivan's ability to craft an engaging and captivating fantasy world surpasses most any other fantasy author out there, and puts him alongside names like Sanderson and Jordan."
— *Fantasy Book Review* on *Age of Swords*

The Disappearance of Winter's Daughter
Copyright © 2017 by Michael J. Sullivan
Cover illustration © 2017 Marc Simonetti
Cover design & maps © 2017 Michael J. Sullivan
All rights reserved.

978-1-943363-14-8 - Rare edition hardcover
978-1-943363-16-2 - Limited edition hardcover
978-1-943363-15-5 - Regular hardcover
978-1-943363-13-1 - Trade paperback
978-1-943363-11-7 - e-book

Learn more about Michael's writing at **www.riyria.com**.
To contact Michael, email him at michael@michaelsullivan-author.com

MICHAEL'S NOVELS INCLUDE:
The First Empire Series: Age of Myth • Age of Swords • Age of War • Age of Despair • Age of Hope • Age of Novron
The Riyria Revelations: Theft of Swords • Rise of Empire • Heir of Novron
The Riyria Chronicles: The Crown Tower • The Rose and the Thorn • The Death of Dulgath • The Disappearance of Winter's Daughter
Standalone Titles: Hollow World

Printed in the United States of America

Published by:

RIYRIA
ENTERPRISES

THE DISAPPEARANCE OF
WINTER'S
DAUGHTER

Leabharlanna Poiblí Chathair Baile Átha Cliath
Dublin City Public Libraries

WORKS BY MICHAEL J. SULLIVAN

NOVELS
The First Empire
Age of Myth • *Age of Swords* • *Age of War* (Spring 2018)
Age of Despair (Early 2019) • *Age of Hope* (Mid 2019)
Age of Novron (Early 2020)

The Riyria Revelations
Theft of Swords (The Crown Conspiracy and *Avempartha)*
Rise of Empire (Nyphron Rising and *The Emerald Storm)*
Heir of Novron (Wintertide and *Percepliquis)*

The Riyria Chronicles
The Crown Tower • *The Rose and the Thorn*
The Death of Dulgath • *The Disappearance of Winter's Daughter*

Standalone Novels
Hollow World

ANTHOLOGIES
Unfettered: The Jester
Unbound: The Game
Unfettered II: Little Wren and the Big Forest
Blackguards: Professional Integrity
The End: Visions of the Apocalypse: Burning Alexandria
Triumph Over Tragedy: Traditions
The Fantasy Faction Anthology: Autumn Mists

To Royce and Hadrian:
two thieves who stole hearts
and fulfilled dreams.

AUTHOR'S NOTE

It may seem odd to dedicate a book to two fictional characters, especially ones of my own creation, but the pair have taken on lives of their own, and these days, I'm a simple observer listening to their conversations and following their exploits. Watching the pair has fulfilled a dream, one that I once felt was forever beyond my reach. To understand why I felt this way, let me take you on a short (yes, Robin, I promise it will be brief) journey back in time.

In 2004, when I wrote the first Riyria book, The Crown Conspiracy (the first half of Theft of Swords), I never thought I would be where I am now. The book I had finished directly before that one was called A Burden to the Earth, and it was written in 1994, a full decade earlier. You haven't read it. I can count on one hand the number of people who have—it was the straw that broke my camel's back. You see, from 1975 to 1994, I wrote thirteen novels and four short stories, and all that work got me exactly nowhere.

The first eight books weren't meant for publication. They were practice tales created to teach myself how to write. Having spent a decade learning the craft, I spent the next eight years penning five books and riding the query-go-round. None of that effort produced a single offer of publication; its only product was the assemblage of heart-wrenching rejections, apparently a rite of passage for nearly all authors.

Eighteen years is a long time to delude oneself, and it finally sank in that I'd never be a writer. So, I did the only sane thing I could . . . I quit. A reasonable conclusion given what Albert Einstein said: "The definition of insanity is doing the same thing over and over and expecting different results."

I should note that during this time, my wife, Robin, was a saint of the highest order. I never had to juggle writing with a career; she was willing to be the single wage-earner and never once asked me to "quit this nonsense and get a real job." She knew that writing was my joy and my passion, and if doing it made me happy, that was good enough for her.

So, as I said, I finally wised up, and I left writing with dramatic flair. I saw myself as Scarlett O'Hara just before Gone with the Wind's intermission, but my declaration was "I shall never write creatively again!" I couldn't imagine anything that could make me break that vow—which brings me back to Royce and Hadrian.

During that decade's hiatus, I was able to prevent myself from typing stories, but I couldn't silence the voices in my head—most notably, the duo otherwise known as Riyria (it's elvish for two). After I'd listened to them for ten years, we had become close. You might say it was difficult for me to differentiate between where I left off and they began. As you already know, I finally relented, and the Riyria books came into being. The Disappearance of Winter's Daughter is the tenth novel starring the pair. I had no idea so many books would grow from the whisperings of these two characters, and I never dreamed that their world would spawn another six books (currently releasing as the Legends of the First Empire series). And it doesn't end there. I'm now writing a new series (code name: The Bridge Trilogy), which is set in the time period between Riyria and Legends. These books uncover the events precipitating the downfall of Novron's Empire.

All these books have allowed me to return Robin's gift, and she left her day job in 2011. And while she still works incredibly hard (all on my behalf and for the benefit of the readers), at least she can set her own schedule, she doesn't have to "dress for success," and her longest commute is from the bedroom to the porch where she spends the mornings watching the sun come up over the mountains of the Shenandoah Valley.

So, yes, I dedicated this book to Royce and Hadrian, for their constant whispering during that terrible decade when writing wasn't a part of my life, and for staying with me once I returned to the keyboard. Each time I sit down to write about the pair, it's like reuniting with old friends, and my work on The Disappearance of Winter's Daughter was no exception. If you enjoy reading it half as much as I enjoyed writing it, then you should have a very fun time indeed.

With that out of the way, I have a few housekeeping things to go over before I get on to the tale. First, if you are new to the Riyria stories, you certainly can start with this book. Yes, that sounds strange since it's the fourth book in the Riyria Chronicles and the tenth Riyria novel as a whole, so let me explain. I've continued the same technique as I used for The Death of Dulgath, which was also designed to stand on its own. I've received reader feedback from hundreds of people who've read only that book, and they confirm no prior knowledge was required. In addition, I sent The Disappearance of Winter's Daughter to another group (none of whom have read any of my novels) and each one confirmed the lack of Riyria familiarity wasn't a problem.

Second, in my more recent works, I've asked people to drop me a line if they feel inclined to do so, and I'm happy to say that many have taken me up on the offer . . . some of whom have never written an author before. Their emails often start out with, "I don't want to bother you, but . . . " Let me assure you, hearing from readers is never a bother. Writing is its own reward, but learning that my scribblings have been enjoyed by others takes a good thing and makes it even better. So, please, by all means, drop me a line. My address is michael@michaelsullivan-author. com.

Third, and this is last, but certainly not least: My eternal gratitude goes out to you, the readers, without whom my dream of being an author could never have been fully realized. Yes, I would still pen my tales (I won't be quitting again), but your generous support keeps me and Robin away from the dreaded "day jobs," and that means we have more time to create stories for you—a synergistic arrangement if ever there was one. So in conclusion, I want to say, "Thank you, thank you, thank you."

AUTHOR'S NOTE

I take your trust seriously and will always strive to put out the very best book that I'm capable of creating. I hope you find it worthy of your time.

Now turn the page, tap the screen, or adjust the volume. A new adventure awaits, and I'm glad you'll be along for the ride.

Michael J. Sullivan
October 2017

World Map

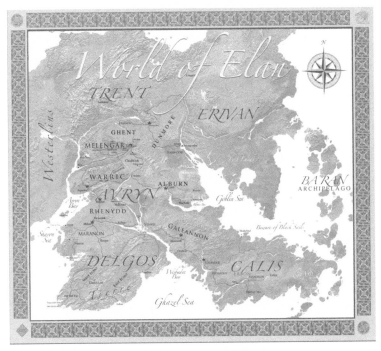

Detailed Map

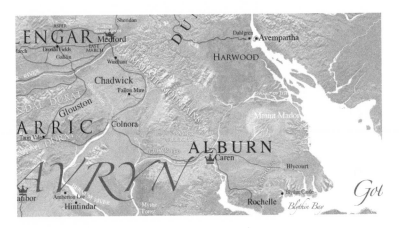

CONTENTS

CONTENTS

THE DISAPPEARANCE OF
WINTER'S DAUGHTER

By
MICHAEL J. SULLIVAN

RIYRIA
ENTERPRISES

CHAPTER ONE
VESTED INTEREST

Devon De Luda wondered, and not for the first time, if Genevieve Hargrave, the Duchess of Rochelle, was insane.

"Stop! Stop!" she shouted while hammering her fist against the roof of the carriage.

She shot a sharp look his way and commanded, "Make him stop!" Then she pushed her head out of the window and yelled up at the driver, "Rein in those beasts, for Maribor's sake. Now!"

The coachman must have assumed an emergency, halting the carriage so abruptly that Devon flew against the opposite bench. The moment the wheels stopped, even a bit before, the duchess launched herself out the door and raced away, skirts hiked, heels clacking.

Abandoned and dumbfounded, Devon nursed his banged knee. As ducal cofferer of Rochelle, Devon usually performed duties revolving around coins and notes. He didn't welcome his newfound responsibility of looking after such an impulsive whirlwind; he preferred an ordered, predictable existence. But nothing had been normal in the city since the new duchess's arrival.

Maybe she is, at least a touch, mad. It would explain so many things.

Devon considered simply waiting in the carriage, but if anything happened to her, he would be blamed. With a sigh of resignation, he climbed out of the carriage and followed the duchess.

Darkness had settled in early, the spring days still short; like prosperity, the season of rebirth had been slow to arrive in Alburn. The rain had stopped, but an evening mist crept in from the sea, ensuring that everything remained damp. Cobblestones glistened in the light of streetlamps, and the world beyond the carriage smelled of wood, smoke, and fish. A smattering of puddles created an obstacle course for Devon's new shoes, and as he picked his path through them, he tugged the collar of his coat more tightly around his neck. Inside the carriage, it hadn't been warm, but the evening's air was bitterly cold. They were on Vintage Avenue, both sides bordered by reputable three-story mercantile shops. On the curbs, dozens of carts lined the street, where migrants sold a circus of wares. Colorful scarves, embroidered saddles, and fresh-roasted pig were sold side by side. As always, a seedy crowd had gathered in the chaotic hive of commerce—few could afford to do much more than look at the scarves and smell the pig.

The duchess trotted down the line of merchants. She bustled through the crowd, most of whom stopped short and stared in wonderment at this heavyset lady in satin and pearls chugging down the thoroughfare, her heeled shoes clip-clopping as loudly as a horse.

"Milady!" De Luda chased after her. "Where are you going?"

The duchess didn't pause or slow until she reached a rickety cart holding up a rack of clothes. There she halted, panting, and stared up at the display.

"It's perfect." The duchess clapped. "That vest, the one with the satin front and floret pattern. You see it? It's not my taste at all, you understand, but Leo will love it. The print is so bold and vibrant. And it's blue! It'll be exactly what he needs for the Spring Feast. He'll definitely be noticed in that. No one could wear that vest without standing out."

Devon had no idea who she was talking to, and perhaps she didn't, either. With the duchess, it rarely mattered. While Devon spent more time with Her Ladyship than many, he hadn't seen her often. The duchess sought him out only when she required advice on ducal economics, which had brought them together only a few times—although more often lately as she had embarked on a new endeavor. Even so, a dozen summonses, a few carriage rides, and a talk or two hadn't provided him enough information to know, much less understand, the new duchess. Devon doubted even the duke understood the actions of his new wife.

"Hullo! You there!" she shouted to the merchant, a dark-skinned Calian with shifty eyes. They all had the same way about them as far as Devon was concerned. Calians were devious savages who dressed in the costumes of cultured society but fooled no one. "Hullo! How much for the vest? That blue one up there on the rack, the one with the shiny brass buttons."

The man beamed a lecherous grin. "For you, good lady, just two gold tenents." His voice was thick with an untrustworthy far-eastern accent, every bit what Devon expected—the sort of voice Deceit itself would use.

"Outrageous!" De Luda balked, shuffling up behind her. That was the trouble with these cart-shop merchants: They swindled the innocent and inexperienced. They talked as if unbelievable, once-in-a-lifetime deals were being offered, but later the swindled buyer would discover the diamond was quartz or the wine, vinegar.

"I'll give you seven silver tenents," the duchess replied. "Devon, give this man seven silver tenents and—"

The merchant frowned and shook his head. "For seven silver, I have a nice handkerchief for you. For a *gold* tenent *and* eight silver, I could part with the vest."

"Your Ladyship, it's unseemly for the Duchess of Rochelle to haggle in the street with a—" He scowled at the Calian merchant, who waited for the slur that didn't come. Normally, De Luda wasn't shy, but in the past three months, he had discovered that the duchess took issue when people were insulted in her presence, no matter how well deserved the remark.

"I don't care. Leo will be thrilled, and oh, how I can't wait to see him in that vest! Don't you think he'll look marvelous?" When the merchant lowered the garment from its hook, she spotted a bright-yellow coat that had been hidden behind. "Dear Maribor! Would you look at that jacket? It's even more divine!"

Grabbing Devon's arm, she shook it violently, overwhelmed with enthusiasm. This wasn't the first throttling at her hands, but he knew a firm jostle was infinitely better than a hug. Her hugs were notorious. The duchess passed them out so liberally, and so violently—even to the staff—that many an individual changed course after spotting her in the halls of the Estate.

"I must have them both. Leo's birthday is coming up, and that jacket will make him feel young again. He's turning forty, you know, and no one likes crossing that threshold. I nearly cried the morning I turned thirty. Time sneaks up on one, doesn't it? Pounces like a wicked cat from the shadows when you least expect it. And thirty is a ditch compared with the canyon that is forty. But I don't have to tell *you* that, do I? Leo *needs* the vest and will *love* that jacket. These are not the garments of a stodgy, no-account, forty-year-old duke; it's the attire of a young and handsome man whose star is rising." The duchess glared at the merchant. "One gold, no silver, for *both* jacket and vest."

The merchant laid out the vest out on the counter before them, shaking his head. "My dear lady, this is imported silk from eastern Calis, extraordinary workmanship. For months, it rode in a caravan through the panther- and cobra-infested jungles of the dreaded Gur Em." He accompanied his outlandish tale with hand gestures as if putting on a children's show, going so far as to reach out with claws when he mentioned the panther. "Many died delivering this rare and beautiful cloth. Only master seamstresses are granted access to such material, for one wrong snip or a misplaced cut could result in a devastating loss. You, of course, appreciate the skill required to create such a masterpiece, so I'll part with it for one gold, six silver for the vest, and an additional two gold for the coat."

The duchess ran a pudgy hand over the shimmering material. "I think not, but the bit about the master seamstresses was a nice touch." She gave him a friendly smile—the only sort she knew how to make. "This is common Vintu silk, farmed in the Calian lowlands along the southern coast of the Ghazel Sea. It sells in Dagastan for five silver dins per yard in any number of thrift shops. But sometimes, in spring mostly, you can find a bundle for four and some change. The parcel this came from was likely imported via the Vandon Spice Company and bought wholesale for three silver a yard and shipped here in less than two weeks as part of their usual rotation. Granted, the VSC likes to add exorbitant markups, and I'm sure that raised the price considerably, but there were no panthers, cobras, or deaths."

Devon was stunned. Duke Leopold's new wife, who insisted on being called Genny rather than the more formal Genevieve, was full of surprises—most of them disturbing and more than a little cringeworthy—but the duchess's command of the mercantile industry was undoubtedly vast.

Still, the Calian didn't lose a beat. He frowned, spread his hands apart, and shook his head. "I am but a poor merchant. Such a great lady as you won't even notice the loss of a few pitiful coins. Yet for me, this sale could feed my wife and poor children for weeks."

With those words, Devon was certain the Calian had won. The merchant had read the duchess correctly and properly spotted the weakness in her defense.

Genny took a step closer to the man, tilted her head down to eye him squarely, the ever-present smile growing sharper. "This isn't about money," she said with a glint in her eye. "We both know that. You're trying to cheat me, and I'm trying to undercut you. It's a game we both love. No one can convince you to sell for less than your minimum profit, and you can't force me to pay more than I'm willing. In this competition, we are equals. You don't even have a family, do you? If you did, they would be here helping to—"

A commotion cut through the crowd. A small boy, thin and dirty, darted through the throng of shoppers. The waif clutched a loaf of bread to his chest as he skillfully dodged through the forest of legs. The cry had alerted the city guard, and a pair of soldiers caught hold of the kid as he struggled to crawl toward a broken sewer grate. They hauled him up, his legs free and kicking, bare feet black as tar. No more than twelve, he was a wildcat: twisting, jerking, and biting. The guards beat the boy until he lay still on the cobblestone, quietly whimpering.

"Stop!" The duchess charged toward them, hands raised. Being a big woman in a large gown, the duchess was hard to miss, even on busy Vintage Avenue. "Leave that child alone! What are you thinking? You aren't, are you? No, not thinking at all! Of course not. You don't beat a starving child. What's wrong with you? Honestly!"

"He's a thief," one of the soldiers said, while the other pulled out a strap of leather and looped one end around the boy's left wrist. "He'll lose his hand for this."

"Let him go!" the duchess shouted, and, taking hold of the child, she wrenched his arm free of the soldier's loop. "I can't believe what I'm witnessing. Devon, do you see this? Is this what goes on? Outrageous! Brutalizing and butchering children just because they're hungry?"

"Yes, Your Ladyship," Devon answered, "the law states . . . your husband's law states that a thief forfeits the left hand for the first offense, the right for the second, and his head for the third."

The duchess stared at him with an expression that could only be described as flabbergasted. "Are you serious? Leo would never be so cruel. Surely the law doesn't apply to a child."

"I'm afraid so; there are no exceptions. These men are merely doing their jobs. You really should leave them to it."

The boy cowered into the skirt of her gown.

The guards reached out and took hold of the lad again.

"Wait!" The duchess stopped them as she spotted a man in a flour-covered apron. "Is this *your* bread?"

The baker nodded.

"Pay him, Devon."

"Excuse me?" Devon hesitated.

She planted a hand on her hip and set her jaw. Even though Devon had worked only sporadically with the duchess, he'd learned this meant: *You heard me!*

Devon sighed, and as he walked toward the baker, he opened his purse. "This doesn't change the fact that the boy broke the law."

The duchess pulled herself up to her full height—which was considerable for a man and astounding for a woman. "I asked this boy to fetch me a loaf of bread. He obviously lost the coin I gave him, and since he didn't want to fail in his assigned duties, he resorted to the only option available. I'm merely replacing the money he lost. Since he was acting on my request, your issue is with me, not him. Please feel free to submit any complaints you might have to the duke. I'm certain my dear husband will do the right thing."

The baker stared at her for a brief instant. His mouth opened to answer, but survival instincts beat back his tongue.

She looked around at the others. "Anyone else?" She glared at the guards. "No? Well then, good."

The soldiers scowled, then turned away. While Devon was paying the baker, he heard one of them mutter "Whiskey Wench." The words were said softly but not quietly enough. The soldier wanted her to hear.

The carriage rolled on again with the duchess slumped in her seat. Being a large woman and having little room in the coach, she couldn't slouch much before her knees pressed against the opposite bench. "Just a child. Can't they see that? Of course they can, but do they care? Brutes, that's what they are. They would have cut off that boy's hand—chopped it off right there on the silk merchant's stool I suppose. That's the type of barbarity doled out in this city? Children are crippled because they are starving? That's no way to run a duchy, and I'm sure Leo doesn't realize how inappropriately his edicts are being measured out. I'll talk to him, and he'll clarify the law. With stupidity like this, it's no wonder Rochelle is floundering. Such punishment only inflames dissent among a populace. Will the boy be a better citizen with one less hand?"

"Not a boy," Devon said, rocking beside her as the carriage rolled and the horse's hooves clattered.

"How's that?"

"The thief wasn't a boy, not human, I mean. He's a mir. Didn't you notice his pointed ears? He's likely a member of some criminal organization. That's how they operate, a colony of rats that haul their catch back to a central nest."

"We have mir in Colnora, too, Devon. The boy's heritage doesn't change a thing. He's still a destitute, starving child. It's as simple as that."

"Simple, you say?" Devon struggled to keep as civil a tongue as the baker had. He would have preferred to point out that it was *she* who was being a simpleton, but that would be going too far. The duchess often rubbed his fur the wrong way, and as a result, he usually said too much. Fortunately, he'd gotten away with comments that most people in her position would find disrespectful. With anyone else, he might have lost his tongue by now, and it was not without a sense of irony that Devon realized the same attitude which had saved the mir child had worked in his favor as well. "You haven't been with us very long, Your Ladyship. You don't understand Rochelle. How things work, I mean. This isn't Colnora. Nothing is simple here. We have the problems of any major city, but we're packed closely together, and this is home to four separate and distinct races."

"The Calians aren't another race, just another nationality."

"Regardless, Rochelle is unique in its collision of diversity, and added to that are the rigid trappings and traditions of a bygone era. This city is resentful of changes that have occurred over the centuries. We are a lake with layers of sediment. At the bottom are the mir, and they're down there for a reason."

"You disapprove of my intervention on behalf of that child?"

"That *mir*."

She frowned. "I guess you don't think I should have added the pork and cheese, either? Would you have preferred that I send him on his way with a pat and a wave? Better yet, I should have just let him be mutilated, yes? You believe that because the mir are unattractive and unsophisticated . . . because they don't fit in . . . that they should be shunned? Is that it?"

The duchess wasn't speaking about the child anymore, and Devon wasn't about to step into her trap. "I think you should have just bought that horrible vest and given it to your husband."

The duchess folded her arms across her massive bosom and let out a *humph*. "Why? Why was saving a child so wrong?"

Devon shook his head. "Mir aren't like us, my lady, and neither are the dwarves or Calians. They're creations of different gods, lesser gods, and it's wrong to grant them the same privileges enjoyed by the blessed of Maribor and his son Novron."

"You're wrong; they are the future of this city!" she declared with conviction. "If golden wheat grew wild on your farm, you'd cultivate it in the hope of profiting from a natural crop. That's just common sense. When one is desperate as we are, one must leverage every asset . . . not merely the pretty ones." She scowled so that her lips appeared squeezed by full cheeks. "So, I'm guessing you also don't approve of what I just told the merchant guild. A little late to make your opinion known,

Devon. Care to weigh in on my marriage to Leo? It's only been three months; perhaps you will change his mind, and he'll ask the bishop for an annulment."

De Luda sighed and rubbed his temples. "I'm simply trying to point out that you are inexperienced and naïve."

"Inexperienced? Naïve?" The duchess let out a deep chuckle. "I've hammered out deals on a pirate ship in a storm while downing shots of Black Dog. Back in Colnora, I have a neighbor who is one of the most renowned thieves in the world, a man rumored to toss rivals off Amber Falls during summer barbecues. But he's also an excellent customer, and the people he invites to dine aren't innocent, so I overlook his transgressions. As for naïve, do I look like a rosy-cheeked debutante?" She waited, but he said nothing. "Of course not. I'm a heifer too old to milk and too tough to butcher. Do you think I got where I am by being blind? I'm not pretty, nor polished, definitely not *quality stock* as people tend to say. I'm the Whiskey Wench. That's what the soldier called me, isn't it? That's what everyone says, right? I know what they think. I'm not oblivious to the whispers about why Leo chose me. Well, I've heard worse, believe me. I'm a woman. We always hear worse. The starched-shirt-and-tight-hosed dandies around here are dandelion tufts next to what I'm used to dealing with."

Devon took a deep breath, then another. "I merely meant that you are too naïve about the ways of Alburn, and Rochelle in particular. Ours is a complex and dangerous city. Your Colnora is a free and open municipality where merchants flaunt their independence. Rochelle is old, congested, and choked by tradition and bureaucracy. This city is filled with hidden places and dark secrets. Too many secrets, and it's unforgiving of mistakes. We still believe in the traditional ways and in ancient-world monsters. I assume from your interest in the *blue* vest that you've heard about our murdering ghost."

"My hometown has its fair share of bogeymen, as well, Devon. I've personally lived a whole summer in a city terrorized by gruesome murders that took low- and highborn alike."

"The murderer was a man?"

"What else?"

Devon nodded. "In many places, paying heed to superstition is merely a habit. For instance, in Colnora, when someone tosses salt over their shoulder after an accidental spill, they don't actually expect to fend off a demon creeping up behind them."

"Are you trying to tell me that Rochelle has *literal demons* stalking people?" She raised her eyebrows and displayed a lopsided smile. "Do they have fangs and bat wings? Do they spit fire?"

"I'm saying wise people stay indoors at night and dress their children in bright blue to ward off evil. And despite that, citizens of this city are mutilated—a great many as of late. Myths are too often rooted in truth, and we—"

The carriage came to an abrupt halt. They hadn't yet crossed the bridge leading to the Estate. "Why are we—"

The door on Devon's side ripped open. Cold air rushed in, damp and clammy. In the dark, he saw a pair of cruel eyes, malevolent and evil. He recoiled, pushing away and fighting to retreat, but there was nowhere to go. He died with the duchess's screams ringing in his ears.

CHAPTER TWO
THE RETURN OF VIRGIL PUCK

R oyce *knew* what was coming.

Hadrian had glanced back at their prisoner more than a dozen times, even though nothing had changed. Virgil Puck continued to walk behind Royce and Hadrian's horses, still tethered with one end of a rope tied tightly around his wrists and the other end fastened to the horn of Hadrian's saddle. Nevertheless, the interval between the glimpses shortened, and the length of each look grew at a measurable rate. If Royce had a means of calculating time in small increments, he thought it possible to determine the exact moment when—

"What if he's telling the truth?" Hadrian asked.

Royce frowned, feeling cheated. He expected it would've taken longer. Hadrian hadn't changed as much as Royce had hoped. "He's not."

"But it sounds like he might be."

The Return of Virgil Puck

"Yes, I am," Puck said, his voice rising above the shuffle of his own feet—the walk of the reluctant.

"He's no different from anyone accused of a crime. Everyone proclaims their innocence." Royce didn't bother looking back. Everything he needed to know was revealed through the tautness of the rope. From it, he could tell Puck was still tethered; beyond that, Royce didn't care.

The three made leisurely progress along the rural portion of the King's Road, just north of the city of Medford. The day was warm, and while most of that year's snow had finally melted, runoff was still making its way to lakes and rivers. All around, Royce could hear the trickle of water. Each season had its own distinct sounds: the drone of insects in summer, the honk of geese in autumn, the wind in winter. In spring, it was birdsong and running water.

"He's no criminal, not a murderer or even a thief. I mean, technically, he's accused of giving rather than taking."

Royce raised a brow. "Lord Hildebrandt would disagree. Virtue and chastity, these are the things that have been taken from his daughter."

"Oh please!" Puck erupted. "Don't be ridiculous. Have either of you seen Lady Hildebrandt? She didn't receive the name *Bliss* from her lovers, I can assure you of that. She's forty-three going on eighty-nine, with the face of a savagely carved jack-o'-lantern and the figure of a two-ball snowman. And don't get me started on her acidic personality and that grotesque cackle of a laugh. I'm absolutely positive she retains her virtue the same way a bruised and rotting melon avoids being eaten. No one who has actually met Bliss Hildebrandt of Sansbury could possibly imagine crawling into bed with her. I'd personally rather curl up with a diseased monkfish. *Maybe* if there had been a knife at my throat, I might . . ."

His pause caused Royce to look back.

Virgil Puck's misshapen nose was off center and sported a bulbous tip like the knob on the end of a walking stick. Beyond that, the man was tall, thin, and endowed with long, curly blond hair, the sort to evoke sighs from women of every rank and class. He wore only a heavy tunic, breeches, and boots. The tunic was covered in vertical white-and-blue stripes, and the boots were yellow as a canary's breast. Hadrian was right about one thing. Virgil didn't have the look of a normal run-of-the-mill criminal.

But criminal *is such a relative term, and what is normal, anyway?*

Puck looked at the ground, shaking his head with a grimace. "No, no, I can truthfully say not even that would be enough. I'm telling you for the third time, you have the wrong man. The true culprit must be either deaf and blind or depraved to the point of utter insanity."

Hadrian turned around, shifting the tip of the sword strapped to his back and resting a hand on the rump of his mount. "Are you noble?"

"If you mean, do I have highborn blood in my veins, the answer is no. Why do you ask?"

"The way you talk is . . . clever . . . complicated. You use odd words like *culprit* and *depraved.*"

"That's because I'm a poet," Puck declared with dramatic flair. He tried to follow the remark with a sweeping bow, but there wasn't enough slack in the rope to execute it successfully. "I make my living going from great house to great house entertaining my hosts with songs and stories. Tales of woo and woe. From the epic love affair of Persephone and Novron to the tragic courtship of Lady Masquerade and Sir Whimsy. I make them laugh; I make them cry; I inspire, educate, and—"

"Seduce?" Royce provided. "Women have a weakness for poets. Did you beguile Bliss Hildebrandt with words?"

Puck expressed his indignation by stopping, and he was jerked forward by Hadrian's horse. "You aren't listening. I didn't seduce her. I wouldn't do that for all the gold in Avryn. I'd rather fornicate with a rabid ferret. I'm telling you, when we get back to Sansbury, you'll see her and understand. And I hope she gives you both hugs and wet kisses for your efforts. Then you'll realize the true depths of your mistake. She's like an ugly old hound that still thinks it's a puppy, even while drooling those long elastic strands of goo. And when she opens her mouth to thank you, you'll see her tongue, an organ that's far too long for any reasonable living thing."

"Lady Hildebrandt is with child," Royce said. "Had to happen somehow."

Puck smirked. "I've seen baby porcupines, too—don't know how that happens, either."

"He just sounds so . . ." Hadrian struggled. "You know, sincere."

"By all the gods! That's because I'm telling the truth!" Puck shouted to the sky. "The two of you are . . . you're . . . what exactly? I have no idea. Sheriffs? Bounty hunters? No matter, whatever your profession, you must do this often, right? You've surely captured dozens of suspected wrongdoers and brought them to justice. You must know what nefarious men are like.

How they act. When you dragged me out of that tavern in East March, did I act guilty? I'm assuming most criminals run, isn't that so? Did I? Did I resist at all? No, I didn't. What did I do instead?"

"You called for a sheriff," Hadrian replied, and glanced at Royce with a tiny nod of acknowledgment.

"Yes! Yes! I did that because I thought you were accosting me. Only thugs would drag a person out of a public house and tie him up. And if a sheriff had heard, it would be the two of you on the end of a rope—and a shorter one than this, I suspect."

Hadrian shifted his sight between Puck and Royce with a ruminating expression.

"Doesn't matter," Royce interjected, attempting to preempt the thought forming in his partner's head.

"But if he's innocent, should we really be turning him over to Lord Hildebrandt? If he's convicted, he won't have the shield of noble blood. The baron will kill him."

"Doesn't matter."

"It certainly matters to me," Virgil chimed in.

"Why? Why doesn't it matter?" Hadrian asked.

"All I care about is the eight gold Hildebrandt is paying us."

"That's cold, Royce," Hadrian said.

"No, that's life. Don't complain to me. Take it up with Maribor, or the universe, or nature. The same rules that starve a sparrow in winter will see Puck hang for a crime . . . even if he didn't commit it. But that's not our problem. We don't have anything to do with that."

"Excuse me?" Puck spoke up. "I feel obligated to point out that it's *you* who tied this rope to my wrists, and it's *you* who is dragging me incessantly toward a fate I don't deserve. It's *your* horse, not Maribor's, not the universe's, not nature's, and it certainly has nothing to do with any ruddy, bloody sparrow!"

"Eight gold tenents." Royce looked hard at Hadrian. "Say those three words out loud. Repeat them over and over until it drowns out the little ferret bugger behind us."

Hadrian didn't look convinced.

"Okay, how's this. Remember that we promised . . . we gave our *word* to Lord Hildebrandt that we would fetch Puck and bring him back." Royce struggled to get the words out with a straight face.

When Hadrian replied with a solemn nod, Royce had to bite the inside of his lip to keep from laughing. The two had been together for three years, two working officially as the rogues-for-hire enterprise called Riyria—and still Hadrian thought a promise was something that must be kept. Hadrian was young, in his early twenties, but the man had been to war more than once, and it baffled Royce how he could remain so unworldly.

Puck focused his attention on Royce. "So, that's all my life is worth? Just a few gold coins? What if I offer you more than Lord Hildebrandt is willing to pay? Would that balance the scales in your maladjusted world, a place where you claim to play no part even though you hold the leash?"

Royce frowned. "You don't have that kind of money. If you did, we would've reached a deal back in East March."

"I could get it."

"No, you can't. You're a poet. Poets make little money, and they certainly don't save for a rainy day. You throw your coin away on ridiculous things—your clothes, for example."

"True enough, but I wasn't talking about *my* money," Puck said. "While I swear I never touched Bliss, I have dallied with a few ladies in my time. Some of them are quite fond of me. I'm sure Lady Martel would pay ten to save my life."

"Lady Martel? Are you referring to Lord Hemley's wife?" Royce asked.

"The very same."

Royce smirked. "I doubt your prowess between the sheets could possibly be worth ten gold."

"You misunderstand me. My relationship with Martel Hemley isn't like that. I mean, I *could* have slept with her. She's no great looker, either, but at least she's intellectually stimulating, and she finds me equally so. I'm sure ten gold would seem like a small price to ensure our continued conversations. Our kinship is based on a mutual love of the written word. Why, just last summer I spent a whole night, in her bedroom no less, doing nothing but drinking and exploring her library."

"Is that a euphemism, or are you *actually* talking about books?" Royce asked.

"Oh, so you've heard of them! Yes, books. The woman has a wide range of interests and has a little library right off her private chambers. She has copies of the *Song of Beringer* and *The Pilgrim's Tales,* which is impressive but not atypical. The most interesting thing on her shelves is a bizarre little diary."

Royce reined his horse to a stop and pivoted in the saddle. "She showed you her diary?"

Puck looked up, concerned. Royce hadn't intended to be threatening, but it was an attribute difficult to control.

"Well, yes, but it wasn't *her* diary. The memoir belonged to a fellow named Falkirk de something, who had excellent penmanship and an archaic writing style. Lady Martel mentioned she stole it, although I doubt that. I mean, who ever heard of a noble thief? She was fairly drunk at the time, so I didn't take what she said seriously."

"Did she mention where she met this Falkirk guy?" Royce asked.

"Oh no, she didn't get it from him. Lady Martel obtained the diary from a monk she'd been having a tryst with. One night while he slept, she came upon the diary and took it because she wanted to learn about his true feelings toward her. Wasn't until later that she realized it was the writings of this Falkirk fellow. She tried to return it, but the monk had disappeared before she could. She never saw him again."

"You said the style was archaic. So, you read it?"

Puck nodded. "Tried to. To be honest, it bored me. Why are you so interested?"

When Royce didn't answer, Hadrian said, "We do odd jobs for people. One was getting that diary from Lady Martel. After we did, she claimed it hadn't been taken. Things like that needle Royce; he sees conspiracies and nefarious intent wherever he looks."

Royce focused on Virgil. "What can—"

The sound of horses drew Royce's attention. Eight men rode toward them, white tabards covering chainmail shirts, swords clapping thighs. They slowed upon approach but showed no signs of aggression. Royce and company had passed, or been passed, by a dozen groups of travelers that morning: farmers, tradesmen, merchants. These were the first with swords, and the tabards looked official. Usually, a patrol like this signaled trouble, but for once Royce and Hadrian weren't breaking any law. They were acting in service of a respected baron of Melengar. And yet Royce still tensed.

"Pardon our intrusion," the lead rider said, bringing his mount to a stop. The man's helm was off, only a single day's growth of beard on his face, and he was smiling. Royce didn't know what to make of him. The rider continued, "Might I ask your names and inquire as to why you are dragging this man along the King's Road?"

Royce hesitated for a dozen reasons, not one of which he could pin down as good or even sensible. He just didn't like being stopped. He liked answering questions even less.

In that momentary vacuum, his partner jumped in. "My name is Hadrian. How are you?"

"I'm great," the man replied. "What's this fella's name?" He pointed at the prisoner.

"My name is Virgil."

"Is it?" The rider nodded and climbed down off his mount to face Puck. "Got a last name?"

"Puck. Perhaps you gentlemen can offer me some assistance. These two fellows seem to be under a misconception. They accuse me of taking advantage of Lady Bliss Hildebrandt—which I *absolutely did not do*. I've been wrongfully charged. If you could—"

Without warning, the tabard-clad man pulled out his dagger and stabbed Puck in the chest. Virgil didn't even have time to cry out before falling to the ground.

Royce and Hadrian drew back, their horses shuffling and nickering. They each pulled weapons. Hadrian produced his bastard sword, and Royce freed his white dagger, Alverstone. The shift in Hadrian's horse dragged Puck's bleeding body away from his attacker, leaving a bloody trail. The man who'd stabbed Virgil showed no signs of concern. He merely took out a handkerchief and wiped the mess of blood off himself and his blade.

Virgil gasped, gurgled, and convulsed for only a few seconds. The poet was dead the moment the blade hit his heart, but it took a little time for the message to reach all quarters of his twitching body.

Royce and Hadrian waited, but none of the others so much as touched their weapons. The man who had killed Puck put his dagger away and climbed back up on his horse.

"Why did you do that?" Hadrian demanded, holding his sword at the ready.

"King's orders," the killer replied matter-of-factly. He wore an amused smile as he noticed Hadrian's sword. "Nothing to do with either of you."

Hadrian shot a look at Royce, and then he looked back at the patrol. "King Amrath ordered the death of Virgil Puck?"

The man looked down at the sad crumpled body on the side of the road still tethered to Hadrian's saddle. He shrugged. "Sure. Why not?" Then he kicked his horse and the entire troop rode away.

Royce and Hadrian arrived back on Wayward Street just before dark.

They would have returned sooner, but Hadrian had insisted on arranging for Puck's burial. Royce, who had littered and in some cases *decorated* many a landscape with corpses, had difficulty following the logic. Puck wasn't their mess to clean up. His body—once it had been disconnected from Hadrian's horse—was nature's problem. They had nothing to do with his death, so why waste time, let alone money, to dispose of the remains? But Hadrian and logic weren't always on a first-name basis, or perhaps it was more accurate to say that Hadrian had his own *version* of logic. Royce didn't understand it, and after three years, he'd given up trying.

Wayward Street was still a muddy mire festooned with a dozen stagnant pools and scarred with the deep tracks from wagon wheels. A filthy patch of stubborn gray snow remained clutched in the shadowy armpit between the tanner's shop and The Rose and the Thorn tavern. But the roofs were clear, and like a spring flower, Medford House blossomed with fresh blue paint. The last rays of sunlight illuminated the front porch of the grand house of prostitution, which was looking more like a luxurious inn as of late.

"Not much on patience, is she?" Hadrian said. "Thought she was going to wait for warmer weather."

The front door opened, and Gwen DeLancy stepped onto the porch. She was wearing her blue dress, and the color very nearly matched the paint on the house. Royce guessed that was the point. He'd always liked that dress, and the color had nothing to do with it. Gwen smiled and extended her arms in proud presentation. "Well? What do you think? They just started today. Didn't get too far, just this one wall, but isn't the color wonderful?"

"It's blue," Hadrian said. "Wouldn't a different color be better for business? Shouldn't it be pink or something?"

"Of course it's blue!" she scolded. "Medford House was always going to be blue. Just took me a while to raise the funds."

Hadrian nodded. "Looks expensive."

The two climbed down. They didn't bother tying up their horses. The animals knew the routine and patiently waited to be unloaded.

"It *is* expensive." Gwen pulled her arms in tight and half spun to admire the place she'd built. The skirt of her dress flared with the movement and her shoulders squeezed close to her neck, battling the chilly breeze. She was barefoot, one leg bent, her weight on the other, a hip tilted.

Royce stared and cursed time for insisting on moving.

"Royce?" Hadrian said.

"What?"

"Your pack."

"What about it?"

"You set it down in the mud. It's getting filthy."

Royce looked around. His bag had somehow found its way into the slurry that was known to be a mixture of manure and sludge. "Gah!" he uttered his disgust, grabbing it and hoisting it to the steps. "How did that get there?" He glared at Hadrian accusingly.

"Don't look at me. That was all your doing."

"Don't be ridiculous. Why would I do that?"

"I was thinking the same thing. Kinda why I mentioned it."

Royce scowled at the pack as if it were somehow responsible.

"Maybe you were distracted by how beautiful the new color is," Gwen said, turning back. Her skirt did that flaring thing again. The sunlight caught her face and highlighted eyes outlined in dark paint. Her lips glistened, pulled up in a modest smile.

Hadrian snorted. "Yeah, that must have been it." He placed his own saddlebags on the porch steps and took Royce's reins. "Go on in. I'll take the horses over."

Gwen shook her head. "Don't bother. I'll have Dixon take care of them. Albert's waiting inside."

"Is he?" Hadrian exchanged a look of confusion with Royce.

Gwen nodded. "He's all smiles. Says you got paid."

"Paid? For what?" Royce asked.

Gwen shrugged, rolling mostly bare shoulders, making Royce want to ask *For what?* again. "The job you just finished, I would expect."

"That doesn't make any sense." Royce turned to Hadrian. "Does that make sense to you?"

"Maybe you should talk to Albert," Gwen coaxed.

Hadrian started up the steps, but Royce didn't move. Days had passed since he'd seen Gwen, and he just wanted to look at *her*—to *be* with her. Such behavior wasn't normal, not like him at all. Royce felt awkward and uncomfortable. Gwen, it seemed, was a much better thief. She'd managed to steal an entire person; She'd pinched his old self, stealing it away like a poorly guarded purse. When she was around, everything was different. Mostly, it was confusing, both exciting and peaceful, which left Royce pondering the change. Was he better off or crippled? Had he lost his way or found a better one?

"You should go inside," Gwen said. "It's getting cold out here, and Albert probably wants to talk to both of you."

The Return of Virgil Puck

Eight. Eight gold tenents. Royce eyed the pale yellow disks with the embossed image of Amrath, or maybe it was the king's father. Apparently, the two looked similar, or perhaps they didn't and the kingdom's treasurer got lazy and had the minter make only slight modifications to the previous molds. Didn't matter. The fact remained that they were genuine, and there were eight. Royce, Hadrian, and Albert were in the Dark Room, a moniker bestowed due to its lack of windows as well as the shady business conducted there. Albert had dumped the coins on the table, then sat back in the chair nearest the fireplace to put his stocking feet up on the hearth. He had a self-satisfied smile on his face.

"I don't understand," Royce said.

"No mystery; we got paid." Albert gestured at the money with an overly dramatic flourish. The viscount had lost everything except his title before becoming Royce and Hadrian's liaison to the nobility. He retained a lofty air and that easygoing attitude that comes from living without fear of any natural predator.

Hadrian set his bags down and took a seat by the fire. "We didn't finish the job. Didn't even get Puck back to Sansbury. A troop of men killed him on the King's Road."

Albert swished his lips back and forth in momentary thought, then waved his hands dismissively. "Clearly Lord Hildebrandt was pleased with how things turned out. Likely he planned to execute the poor fellow as it was. You merely saved him the effort."

Hadrian dragged over a chair and sat down beside Albert and the table of coins. He plucked one up, turning it over in his fingers. "How could he have . . ." He looked at Royce. "He can't possibly know Virgil is dead."

"Of course he can." Albert sat forward, an annoyed scowl forming on his face, as if the objections were a condemnation of his efforts. He fluffed the lace cuffs of his ruffled sleeves like a preening peacock. "The men who killed him probably worked for Hildebrandt. They must have ridden back, reported the deed done, and—"

"Puck died just north of here, not far from where the South Road splits from the King's Road. That's twenty-five miles from Sansbury." Royce, who had remained standing, shook his head. "Someone would have had to ride amazingly fast to reach there by now. And then it would take time for them to . . . Albert, when were you paid?"

"Early this morning."

Royce and Hadrian looked to each other for answers but found only reflected confusion.

"This morning?" Hadrian said. "Puck was *alive* this morning. We were all enjoying a pleasant little walk from East March."

Albert's brows rose as the truth finally dawned. "Well, that . . . that is quite odd, isn't it?"

"Who paid you, Albert?" Royce asked.

The viscount sat up, pulled his feet back under him, and straightened his vest by tugging on the bottom. "Lady Constance. We had a meeting this morning at Tilden's Tea Room in Gentry Square. Wonderful little place right next to the bakery, so they get—"

"Constance?" Royce said the word aloud. Something clicked, and he felt the way a hound might when taking a second sniff at a footprint. "I've heard that name before."

Hadrian nodded. "Me, too. Albert's mentioned her a few times."

"Of course I have. I get most of our jobs through Lady Constance. She makes social butterflies look like shut-in moths. The woman knows everyone, and everyone knows her. She's native to Warric, has connections in Maranon, but prefers the parties here in Melengar."

"Wasn't she the one who hired us for the Hemley job? The one with Lady Martel's diary?" Royce asked.

Albert nodded.

"But she wasn't procuring the diary for herself, right?"

"I believe that's so. Just as I represent you, Lady Constance acts as a liaison for her people . . . er, clients . . . um, friends . . . however you want to refer to them. She's never said anything, but I assume she adds a surcharge and pays us the difference. She has to make a living somehow."

"Isn't she a noble?"

"Yeah, well, given the straits you found me in, you should know that not all nobles are rich. She was married to Baron Linder of Maranon. Why, I don't think even she could say. He had no lands, wasn't wealthy, and not even particularly attractive."

"*Wasn't?* Is he dead?"

"Yes, in addition to his other shortcomings, he apparently lacked skill with a lance; he was killed by Sir Gilbert of Lyle in a Wintertide joust just six months after they married. How she manages to maintain such a lavish lifestyle is a mystery to everyone at court and a topic of much speculation." He paused in thought. "I wonder what rumors circulate about me." He waved the question away. "Anyhoo, I'm guessing she's made herself as useful to her acquaintances as I've been to you."

"You never asked her about it?"

Albert looked shocked and insulted at the same time. "Oh, dear Maribor, no! And she has never asked me about my affairs. We have a perfectly wonderful lack of curiosity about each other, which makes working together not only possible but delightful as well."

"You slept with her," Hadrian said, his tone neither critical nor approving. He was merely stating a conclusion.

Albert let slip a mischievous grin. "Along with our lack of curiosity, we share an obvious absence of morals and a mutual aversion to cumbersome attachments. But filling that void is a healthy appetite for lust. It's a wonderful arrangement, two peas in a pod are we."

Royce, whose tiring hand reminded him that he was still holding his pack, looked around for a place to set it down. Mindful that the bottom was still wet with muck, he placed it on the hearth near the crackling fire. "So, you have no idea who actually hired us to steal that diary?"

"Nope, can't say that I do."

"And Virgil Puck?"

"Well, that's a different matter, now isn't it? Of course it was Lord Hildebrandt; otherwise it would be terribly awkward when you arrived with him and . . ." Albert's eyes shifted as he fit the puzzle pieces together.

The Return of Virgil Puck

Albert was a fine intermediary. He'd a handsome face that polished up well, and he knew all the finer points of etiquette required to sail the dangerous waters of the Avryn aristocracy. He was competent and well spoken but suffered the illness of all nobles, a dulling of the senses due to privilege. Pets suffered from the same disorder. Having grown up in a household, a dog couldn't be expected to live in the wild, any more than a cow or chicken. Domesticated creatures lacked basic situational awareness, that fearful ever-present state of expected catastrophe that kept the less pampered alive. Watching Albert, Royce saw him questioning his foundations and knew what was running through his head: *No . . . that sort of thing happens to other people, not me.*

"So, Puck was telling the truth. He didn't have anything to do with Bliss Hildebrandt. Guess I'm a better judge of people than you on this one." Hadrian beamed a smile, which didn't last long. Royce guessed it faded just as soon as his partner realized he had helped kill an innocent man.

Royce knew better. Puck wasn't innocent; no one was. He'd done something to someone, and the only thing Royce wanted to know was whether that something was going to rub off on him.

"So, who killed Virgil and why?" Hadrian asked.

"Won't ever find out," Royce replied. "It's a double blind. Quadruple if you add in Albert and Constance. We apprehended the poet under trumped-up allegations, nothing dire enough to arouse suspicion—even from someone like me. Then, a second group was hired to do the killing, and probably they were told an entirely different story. All of which makes it incredibly difficult to trace the responsible party or determine the actual motive."

"Well, not to be insensitive to Mister Puck and his demise, but"—Albert looked over at the coins—"I'm in dire need of a new doublet and breeches. It's important to keep up appearances you know, and—"

"Go ahead." Royce nodded. "Take a tenent, but the new outfit will have to wait. We still need to pay Gwen for the use of the room and catch up on our late stable fees."

"Well then, we're in luck because I already have another job lined up."

"Not through Lady Constance, I hope. I'd prefer something a little more straightforward. A job where I know what I'm getting into *before* I step in."

"Ah—no, this one didn't come from Constance, but it's . . ." Albert paused. "Unusual."

Royce folded his arms. He'd had his fill of unusual. "How so?"

"Well, normally I have to poke around and look for work, but this fellow came to me, or rather he came looking for you." Albert looked pointedly at Royce.

"Me?" This *unusual* was sounding worse by the second.

Albert nodded. "He's staying in the Gentry Quarter. Wouldn't give me a name or even tell me what it was about. He said he'd know when you returned, and he'd stop by then."

"He would know?"

Albert nodded. "That's what he said."

"Well, doesn't that just make me feel all warm and cozy. Did he mention how he knew I was living in Melengar, or how he knew me, period?"

"Nope, only said he was up from Colnora and was looking for . . ." Albert paused to think. "It was a strange name, one that made me think of a cleaning service. He didn't mention Riyria, but when I did, he recognized the word. Hmm, I wish I could remember what it was." Albert furrowed his brow further in concentration.

"Don't worry about it," Royce told him and wished he could take the same advice, but he knew all too well that the stranger from Colnora had called him Duster.

CHAPTER THREE
THE WHISKEY BARON

It took only a few hours for the mystery man to show up at The Rose and the Thorn. They had time for baths and a hot meal. Hadrian was able to down two tankards of beer, but Royce wanted to stay clearheaded. Normally he unwound after a job with a glass or two of Montemorcey, and he was annoyed that the wine would have to wait. Albert had Gwen seat the potential client in the Diamond Room, which had been kept empty of other patrons to give them privacy.

He sat in the back, an elderly man with gray hair and a face as salty and rugged as a seaside cliff. He wasn't tall; if he stood, Royce suspected they might be the same height. He was, however, big. More than stocky, and even larger than portly, the man eclipsed the chair in which he sat and strained the seams of his traveling clothes. The tunic he wore had double stitching and metal studs, which decorated the floral designs across his chest. A heavy cloak lay tossed over the back of the chair beside him. Made of a thick two-ply wool, the wrap looked new. He had gloves, too, expensive calfskin. They rested on the table near the cloak. Each had the same floral design as his tunic. *A matched set,* Royce thought.

The visitor watched Royce and Hadrian enter as if studying them for later recall. He didn't bother getting up or offer to shake hands. He patiently waited as Royce and Hadrian took their seats on the stools opposite him, not saying a word.

He focused on Royce. "Is it you? Are you Dust—"

Royce cut him off with a raised hand. "I don't use that name anymore."

The man nodded. "Fair enough. What *should* I call you, then?"

"Royce will do, and the big fella is Hadrian."

Each gave a nod of acknowledgment.

"Who are you?" Royce asked.

"I'm a man who lived in Colnora during the Year of Fear."

Royce let his hand slip off the table. Beside him, Hadrian placed both feet flat on the floor to either side of his stool. The old man didn't appear formidable in any sense, but the look in his eyes was unmistakable: revenge. He wanted it, and he'd come to get it.

"Name's Gabriel Winter."

Royce knew the name but had yet to make the connection. And as far as he could recall, he'd never tangled with anyone named Winter.

"You terrorized Colnora. The entire city was paralyzed from the horror you wrought. Pushcart people, street sweepers, shop owners, business barons, everyone right up to the magistrate was terrified. Even brave Count Simon fled to Aquesta that summer. That did a lot for morale, I can tell you." The fat of the man's neck quivered as he spoke, but his eyes never wavered, and his voice remained steady and calm. Both hands stayed in plain sight, ten pudgy fingers, palms on the table beside the empty gloves and half-melted candle. Nothing else lay between Royce and Winter but the tabletop.

No cup or mug—he hadn't ordered a drink.

The Diamond Room was quiet. Not part of the original inn, the room had been recently built to accommodate the tavern's growing popularity. The addition filled the oblong space between The Rose and the Thorn and Medford House and gave the place its diamond shape. The only sounds came from two barmaids cleaning mugs in the other room.

"What do you want?" Royce asked as his fingers entered the front fold of his cloak and slipped around the handle of Alverstone.

"I want to hire you."

It shouldn't have surprised Royce. Albert had described the man as a potential client. But so much about the meeting was worrisome. "Hire me?"

"Yes," the man replied with curt candor, a hint of a smile on his lips, as if he knew a secret or the punch line to a joke that had yet to be revealed.

"To do what?"

"Exactly what you did in Colnora. Only this time I want you to make the city of Rochelle bleed."

Hadrian shifted in his seat, his feet coming off poised footings. "Why?"

The Whiskey Baron

The man pushed back from the table, folding his arms across his chest as if contemplating what to say next, or maybe just working himself up to say it. Some things didn't come easy. Royce understood that well enough, and from the miserable expression on the man's face, he guessed that whatever he was about to say, this might be the first time he'd put it into words.

"My wife died ten years ago. Just been me and my daughter since then. Good girl, my Genny, faithful, loyal, a hard worker, quick as a whip, and tough as leather. We did well together, the two of us. She got me through the tough times, and there were plenty of those. But less than four months back she went off with a nobleman from Rochelle. Fella named Leo Hargrave."

Hadrian leaned forward. "Leopold Hargrave?"

"That's him."

Royce raised a questioning brow at Hadrian.

"He's the *Duke* of Rochelle. It's in Alburn, southeast of here. I was in King Reinhold's army down that way before I shipped off to Calis."

"Reinhold is dead," Winter said.

"The king of Alburn has died?"

"Him and his whole family. Bishop Tynewell is going to crown a new king come the Spring Festival. Genny wrote me all about it. She wrote me three days a week ever since the wedding, then nothing." The man frowned, his sight falling to the surface of the table where he scraped at a worn spot with his thumbnail, trying to tear back a splinter.

Royce nodded. "So, what? You think she's dead?"

"I know she is."

"Because she's late in sending letters?" Hadrian said. "The woman just got married; she's in a new city, a very different city, and she's a duchess now. Might be a tad busy. Or maybe she sent letters and the courier was lost in the snows. It's not spring yet, and those mountain passes can be treacherous. You're jumping to conclusions."

Gabriel Winter looked into Hadrian's eyes. "I did receive a letter, but not from my Genny. Hargrave wrote to say she's disappeared."

"Oh, well, disappeared is . . . it's not good, but it doesn't mean she's dead."

"Yes, it does." His stare was cold and harder than granite. "I told her what would happen. She just wouldn't listen. The only reason Hargrave married Genny was for her dowry. He doesn't love her. Never did. But Genny, she loves him, see. From the top of her head to the tip of her toes she does. Don't know why. She's always been so sensible in the past, and this Hargrave . . . well, the man is noble, that should have told her everything right there. I tried to stop her, but how could I? He's all she ever wanted. That's what she told me. My Genny, she's not what you would call pretty. Even as wealthy as we are, no one ever came knocking on her door. She was getting up there in age, will be thirty-three in the fall, and, well, when the duke asked for her hand it was like offering the gift of flight to a chicken. She couldn't see past the dream. Hargrave killed her all right, him and his ilk. That was his plan from the start. I saw it in the man's eyes. He was using her." Gabriel turned to Royce. "I'd go there myself, but—" He spread his arms. "I'm old and fat, and never was that good with a knife. What could I do to avenge my darling daughter? Nothing. As a father, I'm incapable of doing the deed myself, but as a businessman"—he pointed at Royce—"I have the means to pay others to be my hands."

Businessman! That clicked the tumbler, and Royce finally knew who he was talking to, and how the man knew where to find him. "Winter's Whiskey."

"That's me."

It was Hadrian's turn to raise a questioning brow.

Royce clarified, "One of the business barons of Colnora, the ones who actually run the city. Nobles appointed by the king of Warric are supposed to administrate, but they rule like a barnacle commands a ship. The real control resides in the hands of the magnates who live in the Hill District: men like the DeLurs, the Bocants, and Gabriel Winter, purveyor of fine liquors and quality spirits."

"My neighbor is Cosmos DeLur. He was kind enough to provide me with your change of address."

"I guessed as much."

"My money has bought me all manner of comforts, but right now the only thing I want is revenge."

"Have you tried contacting the duke?" Hadrian asked.

"Of course I have."

"What did he say?"

"His *scribe* wrote that Hargrave was 'investigating the matter.' *Investigating the matter!* Oh, I'm sure he's looking real hard, given he's the one who killed her!"

"You know that for a fact?" Hadrian stared in shock.

"I know it as well as you're sitting here. I told Genny he only wanted her money. Guess he didn't need my girl once his debts were paid. No reason to keep her. Nobles aren't like you and me. No loyalty, no civility. They behave all righteous and proper, but it's just an act."

Gabriel turned to Royce. "Will you make them suffer the way you did in Colnora?"

"Expensive," Royce said.

"You know who I am. What street I live on. I can afford it, and I want blood. I'll give you fifty gold for your time and another twenty-five for every life you take, double if they suffer."

Hadrian dragged a hand down his face. "All this talk of blood and bodies; she could still be alive." Gabriel started to speak, and Hadrian put a hand up to stop him. "Granted, it doesn't look good, and it does sound like something bad has happened to her, but she might not be *dead*. Could be she's locked up somewhere. Killing a duchess is dangerous, even if she's new to the family."

Gabriel thought about this for a moment. "Fine. I'll pay one hundred and fifty yellow stamped with Ethelred's ugly head if you find, rescue, and bring Genny back alive. But if she's dead, my original offer stands."

"Depending on the extent of involvement, this job might prove costly, even for you."

Gabriel Winter's rage returned. He made fists on the table. "I have a lot of money, but only one daughter. And if she's gone, what need have I for gold?" He wiped his eyes. "Make that goddamn duke and all those working for him bleed. Turn the Roche River red for me, for me and my Genny."

"How far is it?" Royce asked.

Hadrian stuffed the round of fresh bread in the small sack tied around the horn of Dancer's saddle. This was his quick-access bag where he kept his travel essentials for riding: gloves, some peanuts, three strips of jerky, a rag, a few apples, cedar grease to keep the bugs away, a tinder kit, and a needle and thread. The loaf was fresh out of the oven and still warm. Though he'd just finished a fine breakfast, Hadrian knew the odds of the loaf surviving even the short distance to the Gateway Bridge were slim. He considered stuffing it into the big leather bags behind his saddle, but the loaf would be crushed there, and that was no way to treat a gift from Gwen.

"To Rochelle?" he asked. "I dunno, five, six days maybe, assuming the mountain pass is clear, which it should be since Gabriel Winter has been getting letters from there. We'll have to cross to the eastern side of the Majestics."

"And we'll need to skirt around Colnora," Royce reminded while he finished tying down the last of his gear across the rump of his horse. "Will it be hot down there?"

Hadrian considered this. Rochelle was nearly as far south as Dulgath, but the regions didn't share the same climate. Dulgath had the most magnificent weather of anywhere he'd been. In contrast, Alburn, as he remembered, was a cold, wet place. "Bring your heavy cloak and boots."

"Already have them."

"When do you think you'll be back?" Gwen asked. She stood on the porch of Medford House along with Jollin, Abby, and Mae, all out to see them off. The sun was just rising, and, except for Gwen, the girls were still in their nightgowns and wrapped in blankets. Behind them, painters set up scaffolding to continue turning The Medford House blue.

"Might be a while," Royce said, his voice soft, regretful.

Gwen met him in the street, and the two stood an arm's length apart. Hadrian watched and waited, as did the girls.

"This job could be more complicated than the one we did in Maranon, more . . . well, I don't know, just more." Royce held on to the lead of his horse, the distance between him and Gwen remaining undiminished. "Don't get worried if we aren't back for . . . I don't know, could take several weeks. Let's just say that, okay?"

Gwen nodded. "We'll say that, then."

"Right." Royce didn't move, just stared at her.

A moment, maybe two, went by and Hadrian considered whether Royce would ever move, wondered if he could. Hadrian couldn't understand what prevented his partner from hugging and kissing her goodbye. Then he remembered this was Royce he was watching, and it all made sense.

"Right," Royce said again, and nodded. He then led his horse down Wayward Street, and Hadrian followed.

The trip was quiet. Hadrian didn't even attempt to chat.

Over the last three years, they'd gone through various conversational stages. Initially, Hadrian sought to draw Royce out, mistaking silence for social awkwardness. This served only to irritate Royce, who refused to be manipulated into doing anything, even talking. Hadrian then tried pretending Royce was a *normal person* who simply couldn't speak. Thus, Hadrian took it upon himself to fill the many hours of slow travel with his own meanderings, and, when needed, he would supply both sides of a conversation. Royce had silently endured this. Given that Hadrian felt some of his musings were insightful, even entertaining, his companion's muted reaction irked him. Once, Hadrian had performed an improvisational debate between a work-obsessed honeybee and a flighty dandelion that ought to have resulted in a stirrup-standing ovation, but Royce had ignored it completely, which caused Hadrian to wonder: *Why am I doing all the work?*

Several hours after setting out for Rochelle, Hadrian finally concluded that it wasn't his job to entertain Royce. If the thief was too self-absorbed to participate in a simple conversation, then fine. They would ride in silence. Hadrian hung back, nibbling bread, waving to the milkmaids, and making silly faces at the boys herding sheep. He sewed up a hole in the thumb of his glove, and after he spotted a hawk that failed to catch a field mouse on its third attempt, he managed to stop himself from commenting on the bird's need for spectacles. And so it was that they rode the entire day without a word between them.

For the most part, they followed the Old South Road, which was also called the Colnora or Medford Road, depending on where one lived. As far as roads went, this was one of the best. Wide, firm, and mostly straight, it ran through a dignified countryside of respectable forests and friendly fields. Farms and small villages appeared, with names like Windham and Fallon Mire, places not unlike where Hadrian was born.

Just before sunset, Royce led them off the road and into a small stand of trees without saying a word. Silently, he tied his horse, unsaddled her, and removed his gear. Hadrian waited for the thief to say something, anything, but once his gear was in place, Royce went off on his usual security-patrol-and-wood-gathering ritual.

"It's like he's forgotten we're here," Hadrian whispered to Dancer as he tethered her to a branch. "Do you think he's mad at me?"

Hadrian shook out his bedroll and laid it on what looked to be a soft patch of grass, still matted from winter's recent retreat. While the surface looked dry, he discovered the ground was actually quite wet, so he went back for the tar-covered canvas to lay beneath his blankets. "Do you know anything I might have done?" he whispered to Dancer as he scanned the trees, looking for Royce. "Quiet is one thing, but it's like we're on our way to the Crown Tower again." He clapped the horse on the neck. "We left you tethered in a field, and Royce was unconscious while I floated down an ice-cold river. Not a good time for any of us, was it?"

When Royce returned with an armful of wood, he sported his usual miserable expression. The light was nearly gone, the camp set, and Royce still hadn't said a word. Hadrian wondered just how long the silence would last. *He's going to have to say something eventually. Maybe he'll ask where the bread is.* While Hadrian had saved half the loaf for Royce, he planned to respond that he'd eaten it all because Royce hadn't said he wanted any.

After lighting the fire, Royce sat down on his blankets and watched the flames.

I'm not making a meal until he says something. He's going to have to ask. He's going to have to open his mouth and say, 'Well, are you going to make something or what?'

He didn't. Royce continued to sit and stare as if he'd never seen fire before.

Oh, for the love of Maribor! Hadrian got up and dug through the food bag. *I can't believe he's—*

"I'm not mad at you," Royce said.

Hadrian glanced at Dancer, showing her a guilty expression. *He heard that?* Royce's hearing was unusually acute, but Hadrian hadn't known it was that good.

"Why so quiet then?"

Royce shrugged, which Hadrian knew was a lie.

"Is it the job?"

Royce shook his head. "Best we've had in ages."

"Are you upset this Cosmos person knows you're in Medford?"

"No. I would have been shocked if he didn't know."

"So, what is it?"

Another lying shoulder roll was followed by an unnecessary adjustment of his blanket.

Hadrian gave up and set the pot on the fire. Then he searched for the lump of lard, which always managed to find its way to the bottom of the pack.

"Do you think she likes me?" Royce asked.

"Gwen?"

"Yeah."

His arm still in the pack, Hadrian looked over. "Is this a trick question? Is there more than one Gwen?"

"I know she likes *us,* but she likes everyone, doesn't she? Even Roy the Sewer." Royce got to his feet and threw a stick at the fire with enough force to burst forth a cloud of sparks. "Roy traded the trousers she'd given him for a bottle, then nearly froze in the street, but she still smiles at him, still gives him free food. She's a nice person, obviously, but—"

"She likes you, Royce. And yes, more than Roy the Sewer." Hadrian rolled his eyes at the absurdity.

Royce stared back, his brow knitted tighter than a miser's purse.

"Are you serious?" Hadrian asked.

"Do I look like I'm joking?"

Hadrian had to admit his friend did appear grave, even more than usual.

"She's always so nice, makes me feel . . ."

Hadrian waited, shocked that Royce might finish such a sentence. He didn't.

"It's just that most people consider me . . . well, you know. If Medford took a vote for the person to avoid the most, it'd be a toss-up between me and old Roy the Pantless Wonder."

"Wait." Hadrian forgot the lard and walked back around the fire. "I always assumed . . . but . . . what are you saying? I mean, you two have kissed, haven't you?"

"Kissed?" Royce glared. "No! By Mar, are you insane? What kind of question is that? Gwen is . . . she's . . ."

"She's a woman who'd probably like you to kiss her."

Royce sat back down on his bedding, his eyes tense, angry. His hands clenched with unconscious energy.

"So, you two haven't done *anything?*"

"What do you mean by *anything?*"

"I mean—"

"I've hugged her," Royce declared proudly.

"That wasn't what I meant, but have you? Have you *really?* Or did she hug you, and you didn't cringe? Because that's not the same thing, you know."

"Look, just because you're quick to—"

"This isn't about me, and it isn't about Roy the Sewer, either. The woman's in love with you, Royce. And don't tell me you don't feel the same." Hadrian shook his head. "You can't stand leaving her and can't wait to get back. The two of you act as if you're already married—still in that honeymoon phase, too. I just don't understand it. You're normally so—" He paused. "Oh! That's why you're so quiet. You're not mad at *me;* you're angry with *her.*"

"I'm not."

"Yes, you are. You're angry at Gwen because she ruined your perfect little world. Everything was so neat and orderly, all painted the same color of black. Now she's gone and made a mess by spilling hope and sunshine all over the place. You're in love with her and it's killing you, isn't it?"

Royce didn't answer.

"Admit it, you love Gwen, and it scares you. You're terrified because you've never loved anyone before."

The hood came up, as it always did.

"That's not an answer, you know."

"Yes, it is."

CHAPTER FOUR
ROCHELLE

R olling hills and quaint farms disappeared as Royce and Hadrian headed into the Majestic Mountains. The jagged snow-swept peaks that ran from the Senon Uplands to Amber Heights divided Warric from Alburn, west from east, new from old. As always, Royce left the road to avoid the city of Colnora, maintaining his truce with the Black Diamond Thieves' Guild. They found the byway again near the Gula River and followed it into Alburn rather than risk the snows of the Amber Heights pass. Crossing to the far side of the Majestics, they entered a different world. The landscape reflected the transition. Rolling green hills turned into jagged mountains, river gorges, and ocean cliffs. Oaks and maples became pines and junipers. Snow reappeared at the higher elevations and dense fog hugged the seaside. The population was isolated in pockets—*valley villages,* they were called—and Royce and Hadrian had passed through several of these hamlets without stopping. The local folk didn't seem to like strangers.

"Is that it?" Royce asked as the two sat astride their mounts looking at a city clutched in a river valley below. Although the town wasn't as sprawling as Colnora; the buildings were packed tighter and appeared taller. Hadrian and Royce were still miles away, and from that distance and at that height, the place looked peaceful. Surrounded on three sides by snowy peaks and the open ocean on the fourth, it looked idyllic.

"I think so," Hadrian replied. "I haven't actually been there, but that's definitely the Roche River, and the city of Rochelle is supposed to be where it meets the sea, or the bay, I guess. The Goblin Sea is farther east. I think this—" he pointed to the cliff beside them, which dropped to an ocean inlet where waves announced the incoming tide—"is called Blythin Bay. At least it was six years ago, and I don't know why they would have changed the name."

By then, the two had been on the road for five days, always camping and avoiding cities or towns. The trip had been warm and dry, but according to the sky, all that was about to change.

The hood tilted upward, scanning the darkening sky. "Bad weather on the way. Best get down there. What do you know of this place?"

"I never came to Rochelle. I was only in Alburn for a few months. That was when I served in the military for King Reinhold. Most of that time I was bivouacked up on Amber Heights. I spent my days watching Chadwick's First Regiment, waiting for them to invade."

"Why just a few months?"

"Because less than a year before, I was *in* that same regiment. Lord Belstrad, the commander, gave me a medal for my part in the Second Battle of Vilan Hills. I knew all those men. Several were my friends, and everyone knew old Clovis was itching to attack Alburn and take the heights. So, I left. Disappeared in the middle of the night." Hadrian looked east across the inlet to where he could just make out the far coast, a thin green line fading in a rising mist. "I shipped over to Galeannon and kept right on going, all the way to Calis. Amber Heights wasn't the first time I faced the prospect of fighting past friends. So, I figured if I went far enough away, it couldn't happen again."

"Did it?"

"No." Hadrian sighed. "Instead, I only slaughtered strangers."

Hadrian expected a quip from Royce or at least a snide comment. The hood was silent.

"So, I can't say I know much about Alburn, even less about Rochelle. As a whole, about the only thing I remember is it being odd."

"Odd?"

"Unfriendly, secretive, and above all, superstitious. The east is different. Those who live in the sunset shadow of the Majestic Mountains are peculiar, and not in a good way. You'll see. None of my memories of Alburn are good ones, but . . . well, I can't say as I recall much that was good from those years. Maybe I'm biased."

"Good to hear you don't have fond memories, given the nature of this job."

"What do you mean?"

"We're not here for a social call. None of this helping to save people or advising nobles. We're here to hunt. Been a while since I did wet work. There's a certain . . . *clarity* that comes with executions."

"We're not here to kill anyone," Hadrian said. "We've come to rescue the duchess."

Royce drew back his hood to look at Hadrian, or maybe it was merely so Hadrian could see the mocking smile. "You understand Winter's daughter is dead, right?"

Hadrian shook his head. "No, I don't."

Royce's eyes widened. "The Duke of Rochelle married her for her money, then arranged a convenient accident to rid himself of the excess baggage. He's probably done it before, and he'll likely do it again with another rich daughter or perhaps an elderly widow."

"You don't know that."

They reached a ridge where the trail twisted down a narrow pass, which was steep enough that the rocks kicked by the horses' hooves started a tiny cascade. Seabirds cried overhead, and the wind coming off the water howled.

"Of course I do. Gabriel Winter was right. Dukes don't marry middle-aged, ugly merchant's daughters for love. He wanted the money. That's how the world works. People are motivated by money, power, security, and . . . well, that's pretty much it. Actually, when you think about it, they're all variations on the same theme."

"So, you don't believe in love?"

"*Love* is another word for lust or dependence. People confuse it with all sorts of other things, fantasies and wishful thinking, mostly."

"Oh really?" Hadrian urged his horse to catch up, as Royce's mare had a tendency to inch ahead. "Then tell me, O wise one, was it lust or dependence that caused you to risk your life to rescue Gwen from prison? And what fantasy or wishful thinking drove Gwen to hide and nurse us back to health despite the danger?"

Royce urged his horse ahead.

"Oh, and tell me, Sir Genius, why is it you can't remember your own name when she's around, but you haven't dared to kiss her?"

The hood came up again.

"That's still not an answer."

The city of Rochelle proved to be a congested hive of activity. Carts, wagons, and carriages packed cobblestone streets trapped between tall buildings. The soaring stone architecture, with its pointed arches and ornate façades, made Hadrian feel small, and not merely in size. Like the cathedral in Medford, the grandeur here left him feeling unworthy and unwanted, which was one of the reasons Hadrian never had much interest in religion.

The sun hadn't quite set, and yet the shadows of the buildings created a premature night on the streets below. Crowds moved through pools of radiance cast by illuminated shop windows. Among the men with walking sticks and ladies in gowns strolling the sidewalks, Hadrian spotted dark-skinned laborers in eastern garb and dwarven crafters bustling along the gutters. A man on stilts and a boy with a spitting torch cut through the mob, lighting streetlamps. A lady in a lavish cloak walked a tiny pug-nosed dog on a leash, making Hadrian think of Lady Martel and Mister Hipple. A pair of men in red-and-blue military uniforms moved casually up the street while a matching pair moved down the other side, eyes watchful and suspicious.

The smell of woodsmoke, roasting meats, and baked pies filled the air. Throngs stopped to peer into the bright shop windows or surrounded peddlers' carts, waving hands over their heads to catch the merchants' attention. Horses' tacks jingled; hooves clapped stone; bells rang; fiddlers played jaunty tunes; and barkers shouted about cheap shoes and shows about to start. *"Come see the lizard-man shed his skin on stage!"* Conversations poured over one another such that words were lost in the exchange, and yet Hadrian still managed to notice the accent. More lyrical and sophisticated than western dialects, the sound of the east was one of music and mystery. All of it served to remind him of a time he'd rather forget. He'd found such sights and sounds intoxicating as a youth, back when he was arrogant and stupid. Royce would argue he still was stupid, but his partner didn't know the pre-Calian Haddy, the boy-soldier with the skill of a man. What a cruel and absurd joke: The more ignorant you realize you are, the smarter you become.

He glanced at Royce, whose hood panned left and right as he struggled to take everything in. Being overwhelmed was a common reaction for those who hadn't traveled in these parts. When it came to the east, there was always too much—too much and yet never enough.

A light rain began to fall as they entered the city—more a nuisance than a problem, but Hadrian suspected that might change as the drops multiplied, the sun set, and the air turned colder. This was something else he remembered: The weather was as unpredictable as the people. According to the stars, spring was less than a week away, but the cool air had a different opinion. Pulling his own hood up, Hadrian tightened the collar as he and Royce waited atop their horses, caught in the traffic of a busy street.

"Any idea where we should go?" Royce asked as the two waited side by side just to the rear of a carriage, which was stopped behind a wagon being unloaded.

"I'm thinking an inn or at least a tavern of some sort. I don't know about you, but I'm hungry."

"A lot of these stands sell food," Royce pointed out. "That one is selling lamb, I think."

"It's nearly spring, most vendors will have lamb, but let's get indoors. I'd prefer not to get soaked on a night that's already turning cold."

Hadrian looked down the street at signs for potential havens: ABERNATHY'S ANTIQUE APOTHECARY; BOOTHMAN & FULLER GLASS; HINKEL'S HEART-STOPPING HATS; FISKE & PINE TALISMANS, AMULETS, AND WARDS. "Lots of shops, but no inns that I can see."

The wagon finished its delivery and rolled on. With no clear idea where to go, Royce and Hadrian followed the flow of traffic, trusting it the same way they sometimes relied on their horses to lead them to water. Much to Hadrian's amazement, the streets became even more congested as they reached a stone bridge. Wide as it was, the span across the Roche River was choked with traffic. Off to their right, a forest of ships' masts marked the location of the city's harbor, while ahead and up on a hill stood a grand estate behind a wall. Crossing the bridge, they discovered they were on an island. Traffic urged them around the walled manor and to another bridge. Crossing this second one, they found a large plaza bordered by a huge cathedral and more shops. Although it didn't seem possible, this plaza was even more packed with people. A sea of heads bobbed along in a slow-flowing current.

The architecture throughout the city was unusual and more pronounced near the center. Most buildings were constructed from stone and elegantly designed. Not only were they taller than the houses at the edge of town, but they had a grand quality expressed in the many subtle flourishes and unnecessary accoutrements: cupolas were numerous, as were spires. Even the smaller shops had an excess of fanciful gables. Doors were elaborately carved, as were supporting structures and the borders around windows. In towns like Medford, decorations of this sort would depict grapevines or flowers, but in Rochelle, grotesque, twisted faces peered out. Ornamental rainspouts were fashioned so that fantastic monsters, monkeys, lions, and nightmarish creatures belched forth the rain that ran from the slate-tiled roofs. Everything appeared ancient, worn, and weathered from centuries of storms. And everywhere was statuary.

One statue literally stood head and shoulders above the rest. In the grand plaza on the far bank of the Roche River, a monumental figure of a man loomed. Chiseled of pristine white marble, it stood seventeen feet tall and was as perfect a specimen of humanity as any Hadrian had ever seen. Lean, muscled, and youthful, the figure was carved with one shoulder down and a knee locked—a casual stance so life-like it could have been a giant covered in flour. The bare-chested man grasped a sword, point down, in his right hand. *Novron,* Hadrian guessed and it wasn't a particularly difficult conclusion seeing as how the statue was positioned directly in front of a massive cathedral. The figure sported all the traditional tropes of the demi-god: long hair, perfect physique, and the unmistakable sword. If it wasn't Novron, the Rochelle chapter of the Church of Nyphron had some explaining to do.

"There!" Royce pointed to a signboard: BLACK SWAN HOSTELRY.

They steered to the side, working their way out of the flow of people. Hadrian waited with the animals while Royce went in. He came back out only a few minutes later. "No vacancy. Place is packed."

They moved on to the Gray Fox Inn and then the Hound's Tooth, and finally The Iron Crown. Every room was taken.

"They have a waiting list," Royce explained after returning with the bad news. "A bunch of people are hoping that someone might leave." Royce climbed back aboard his saddle and in a quiet voice said, "Fella inside told me our best bet is a place called the Dirty Tankard. Says it's up this way."

Having drifted out of the more populated areas, Hadrian was both pleased and dismayed—happy to be away from the press of the crowd but uneasy as options ran out. He'd hoped to find someplace soon, especially since the rain was coming down harder. Crossing another smaller and less distinguished bridge, the two entered a neighborhood of equally narrow but darker streets. Shops were scarce, barkers and vendor carts completely absent. The Dirty Tankard lived up to its name: a dingy shack that reminded Hadrian of The Hideous Head before Gwen took it over and turned it into the much-improved Rose and the Thorn. Despite the Tankard's run-down appearance, a line of people stretched out the door and wound down an oily street.

Dismounting, Royce tied their mounts as Hadrian took a place in line. He could hear the rain on the inn's roof growing louder.

"Is de festival," the woman in front said to the man ahead of her. She pronounced the word *fest-e-vole,* forcing Hadrian to puzzle it out. "Always busy dis time o' year."

"Yes, but dis is a special year, taint it? Every-von coming."

"Don't know why. Not going to make no difference to most of dees folks here, now is it?"

"Why you here?"

"Same as you. To see how much a difference it doesn't make."

Royce rushed up, his hood taking on the shine it did when wet.

"When is the festival?" Hadrian asked the group ahead of him.

The woman turned. Middle-aged and dark-skinned, she had bright almond eyes. She gave the pair a puzzled look as she studied their clothes. She glanced at the horses tied to the nearby post. "You looking for a place to stay?"

Hadrian and Royce both nodded.

"You don't want dis place." She spoke with the same conviction as if they were all waiting in line before an executioner's block.

More heads turned. Hadrian saw the face of the man she had been speaking to and another woman looking back—all Calians. Ahead of them stood a pair of dwarves in traveling clothes holding satchels over their shoulders.

"She's right, you don't belong here," one of the dwarves said. "You should be in the Merchant District or Old Town. This place—" the dwarf hooked a thumb at the Dirty Tankard—"is awful."

"We tried," Hadrian replied. "They're all full."

"There's a room on Mill Street." The person who said this wasn't in line. She sat on the side of the road, her back up against the wall, wrapped in a sheet of worn sail canvas. She looked young, and Hadrian might have considered her a girl except that in her lap lay a bundled child. Hadrian hadn't even noticed her until she spoke.

"Oh, I'm sorry. Were you in line?" Hadrian apologized.

"No," she replied. "I'm not in line." She said the words hesitantly, as if unsure whether he had been making a joke.

"Where is that room?" Royce pressed.

She pointed. "An old woman lets it out. There's no sign, but it's available. Down there. The one with blue shutters and matching door, just up the hill from the bookbindery, back toward the Merchant District."

Royce looked the way she gestured. "If you know about this place, why are you sitting in the rain?" He glanced at the child. "Why don't you take it? Is it expensive?"

This made several people in line laugh.

"Where you two from?" the Calian ahead of them asked.

"Not from here," Royce said pointedly.

"Of course not. Wouldn't be talking to her if you were. Or me, I suppose."

"Wouldn't be waiting to get into the Tankard, either," one of the dwarves said.

"The lady who lets out the room on Mill Street *is* from here," the mother with the baby said, as if this explained everything. When she saw it didn't, she added, "I could knock on her door all day, and she'd never open for the likes of me."

"Why not?" Hadrian asked.

The woman pulled back the sail canvas she'd used as a hood, revealing a pair of ears that narrowed dramatically at the top. "No place in this city would rent me a room." She put a hand on the back of her sleeping child. "Not even the *Dirty Tankard*. Their bedbugs are too good for us." She said this last part as a joke; she even laughed a little.

A man came out of the shack waving his arms over his head to get everyone's attention. "We're full!" he shouted. "Go look someplace else."

The line let out a communal groan as they broke formation.

"And it's gonna be a wet one tonight," the dwarf grumbled.

"And cold," said the Calian woman.

Royce looked at Hadrian, who shrugged. "What's this woman's name on Mill Street?"

"Dunno," the mother said, pulling her sailcloth back over her head, covering her ears. "Husband used to be a tax collector, which didn't make her popular. He died a few years back. Now she lets out the room. Not a friendly sort."

"That makes two of us," Royce said.

Mill Street was a narrow paved track with a series of brick-and-stone buildings so closely butted together that they formed an irregular pair of walls. Narrow balconies cast shadows on cobblestone where rainwater had been trained to hug the curb. No trees, bushes, or grass broke the uniformity. This was a serious street; a proper humorless precinct that didn't simply frown, it scowled. Even in that crowded city, Mill Street was vacant, an empty stretch of blinds and closed doors. Only one building had blue shutters. Near the center of the block, it stood three stories high and had a pair of narrow framed windows marking three floors, each endowed with a barren flower box, painted blue. An old-fashioned black iron candle-lantern illuminated the front door, which had also been painted the same sapphire hue. A brass knocker in the shape of a woodpecker perched in the center above a large grated window, its beak pressed against a plate.

Just as the mother had mentioned, there was no indication of a room for rent.

"You should let me do the talking," Hadrian said as he grasped the woodpecker. It made a surprisingly loud *clack! clack! clack!*

"You? You're an awful negotiator," Royce replied, using the stoop to scrape mud off the edge of his boots. "And far too generous. You'll let this old hag fleece us out of every copper."

"See, that's just the sort of thing I think we ought to avoid. 'Old hag' isn't the best way to approach a woman who might be willing to share her home with us."

Royce frowned. "I wasn't going to say it to her face."

"But that's what you're thinking."

"She can't hear my thoughts."

"Actually, it's sorta in your tone."

"I don't have *a tone*." Royce directed his attention to the woodpecker. His hood was still up, and rain beaded on the surface, glistening with the lamplight. "Besides, I'm a professional thief. I make a living by lying convincingly."

"You scare people," Hadrian said. "This old widow lives alone. She's not going to take chances renting to anyone who frightens her. She—"

The door itself didn't open, but the brass-grated security window slid back. Behind, a thin and withered gray-haired woman appeared, her lips pursed. She clutched the collar of a shawl about her neck and peered out with trepidation. She spotted Royce first.

He studied her for only a moment, then sighed and stepped aside, granting Hadrian the audience.

"By the Unholy Twins," the old woman cursed. She glared at both of them. Her eyes were large—sunken and bulbous— accentuated by arching brows that glared in judgment. "If you're looking for handouts, this isn't the door. If you're selling something, the Merchant District is in the city center. If you're spreading news, I assure you I've already heard it. If you're dispensing trouble . . . believe me, I've all I need, stocked full, I say."

Hadrian blinked, stunned.

"Oh, my apologies," she softened her voice, her brows drooping in understanding. "I see. You're nothing but a pair of idiots. Off you go. Play in the rain. Leave the pretty bird on my door alone. It's not real; it can't fly." She shooed at them with frail fingers. "The river is that way. If you fall in, odds are good that all your troubles will be over in short order. Goodnight and goodbye." With a smile, she clapped the little window grate shut.

"We're here for the room," Hadrian shouted, his voice descending in volume with each word, accepting the defeat.

"Well done," Royce said. He clapped slowly. "I must admit she didn't appear the least bit frightened."

The entire door jerked back, making the woodpecker clack. "Did you say you want to rent my room?"

"Ah, yes," Hadrian replied. "We heard you have one to let. Is that true?"

"It is." She looked them over anew, and a frown developed. "Do you have *any* money?"

Royce sneered at her.

"We do," Hadrian said, and followed this with a big smile. He poured all his charm into it.

"I see," she said, still frowning. Her eyes adding a cloud of disappointment to the mix. She promptly turned to address Royce. "I charge four silver a night—that's *tenents,* mind you."

Royce narrowed his eyes. "Unless this room comes with running water and its own staff, you're dreaming. I'll give you three silver dins."

The woman sniffed. "Forgive me, did I say four silver? I meant five. And I only deal in tenents. I'll have nothing to do with that worthless *din* fiddle-faddle. That funny money is nothing but painted metal. And the room comes with a pot and a bed. I, young man, comprise the entire staff, but don't expect me to lift a finger on your behalf."

Royce shook his head. "We'll pay three silver."

"No, if you want to stay here, you'll pay six."

"Six? But . . ." Royce glanced at Hadrian, perplexed and irritated. The thief had never shown much capacity for patience with children or the elderly, or indeed any living thing. "You're supposed to *reduce* your price. It's called *haggling*."

"And you're supposed to be polite to your elders. I'm not a *hag*."

Royce sighed. "That's not what *haggling* means."

"No, it isn't." She glared at him with a look that could wither the most resilient weed.

"I think she was listening earlier," Hadrian explained.

Royce glowered. "Yeah, I got that."

"The price is six silver. Would you like to try for seven?" The old woman folded her arms stiffly, her lips pursing into a sour expression. And while she and Royce were close to the same height, she somehow managed to look down on him, waiting for the inevitable answer that her face declared she knew all along.

"You drive a hard bargain for a non-hag."

"It's also raining, and the city is packed." She held her hand out, palm up. "You pay in advance. I'll kick you out with no refund if you don't obey my rules."

"Which are?"

"You be quiet, respectful, and clean up after yourself. No women. No animals. No drinking. No smoking. No nonsense.

Breakfast is at dawn. There is *no* dinner. Do *not* be late for breakfast. I don't like wasting food."

Hadrian pulled the coins out of his purse, and the woman took and inspected each in the light of the candle-lantern.

"We may want to stay more than one night," Hadrian said, and dipped his fingers into his bag for more coins.

She held up a hand stopping him. "Let's just see how the first night goes, shall we? Now—what are your names?"

"Baldwin and Grim," Royce said.

She clamped the coins in a fist and stepped to one side, granting them entrance. "Well then, Mister Baldwin and Mister Grim, you're at the top of the stairs on the left. My name is Evelyn Hemsworth."

CHAPTER FIVE
MERCATOR

Mercator Sikara shivered in the cold rain, pulling the thin shawl tighter to her neck. A wind blew up Vintage Avenue the way it often did that time of year, coming off the bay to deliver its damp, salty slap. The squall had a clear path funneling between Grom Galimus and the Imperial Gallery, the two biggest buildings on Darius Square, creating a piercing blast that coursed along the river. The spiderweb-thin shawl was poor defense against such an onslaught, and the pelting rain added insult to injury. "And look at you without even a wrap," she said to the great statue of Novron as she watched the rain drizzling down the marble. "But then, I suppose demi-gods don't get cold, do they?"

The weather has been terrible, so much worse than last year. Mercator vaguely remembered feeling the same way the previous spring and wondered if she'd thought the same thing each year. If so, then it might be because that was the natural progression, a downward spiral. *Or maybe I'm just old. Too old to appreciate the charm of a late winter's rain. The young look at snow and marvel at its beauty. Old folk look at it and think about the danger of falling. Am I that old? I mean, I am—but, not really. Or am I?*

She supposed a stranger wouldn't guess her to be beyond forty. She was. Mercator was *well* beyond forty, and not even the very young would find pleasure in such a cold rain. Her hypothesis was confirmed by those around her. Everyone braced themselves as best they could against the winter's spiteful bite. All along the riverfront, vendors and customers alike bowed their heads, clutched cloaks, and hunched up their shoulders like hedgehogs in a hurricane.

Why is misery easier to bear in groups? Unlike the changing state of the weather, this thought seemed to be an irrefutable truth. There was strength in numbers; any anthill proved that. Still, a million ants working in perfect harmony couldn't stop the wind or halt the rain. And if they could, there was always the question of whether it would be wise to try.

Mercator trudged with her burden up the street to the Calian dealer and his rickety wagon filled with scarves, cheap jewelry, and a rack of clothes. Erasmus wasn't a *real* merchant, in that he wasn't a member of the Rochelle Merchants' Guild—wasn't allowed to be. He was Calian, and while he was prominent among his people, he wasn't permitted to engage in commerce in any substantial, permanent, or professional way. Every transaction he completed was illegal, but a transient cart could be overlooked. The illicit nature of his trades had to be one of the all-time cosmic absurdities: One of the world's greatest tradesmen was barred from his practice in one of the largest trading ports in the world. But the city—all of Alburn, really—was home to many of life's most profound absurdities. Mercator knew this all too well because on that same list there was a line reserved specifically for her.

"Evening, Mister Nym," she greeted the Calian, dropping her bags at his feet. The man, whom she'd known for decades, ignored Mercator, pretending to straighten his counter of baubles. The rain drizzled off his tiny red-and-white-striped awning. "I have more dyed wool: double-ply bolts, thread, and yarn. This batch came out particularly well: very deep, extremely even."

Erasmus sniffed and wiped his nose, looking at her only from the corner of his eye, still pretending she wasn't there. "Too early," he grumbled, slurring his words as he attempted to move his lips as little as possible. His hands busied themselves with the stock. "You shouldn't be here. People will see."

He was absolutely correct in that she was there much earlier than usual, but . . . "Mister Nym, it's pouring, and it's cold, and it's only going to get worse as the night goes on. No one is watching. I need money. Eating is a habit that, once started, is hard to break." She paused, then added, "Or so I've heard, at least."

This forced a smile onto the Calian's grim face. He looked up and down the street. As she'd said, no one was paying attention to them. She wouldn't have approached otherwise. Mercator knew the rules, and she wouldn't do anything to jeopardize

Erasmus's tenuous hold on his street corner. He was one of the few who bought her dyed wool, and he was a friend.

"I can't buy any now." There was a sympathy in his eyes.

Erasmus Nym was a good man, braver than most. He'd often risked his life and livelihood to help her. She couldn't ask for more than that, and she offered him a nod.

As she bent to pick up her bundles, he stopped her. "Hold on."

Erasmus pulled back some scarves and retrieved a small purse. He poured out a few coins and set them on the countertop, pushing them in her direction.

"What's that for?"

"I owe for the last batch."

"No, you don't."

"Maybe the one before, then. Just take it."

"But I—"

Erasmus reached up, pulled down a beautiful blue vest, and dropped it onto Mercator's bundles of dyed wool. "Here, you might as well take this. Can't sell it. Everyone thinks it's cursed now. I should have sold it to the duchess straightaway."

"Why didn't you?"

"Habit." He sniffed. The Calian was coming down with a cold. Spring colds were a curse. "Couldn't help myself. It's in our blood, you know."

Mercator's brows went up. This was the first time in forty years he'd ever suggested, even vaguely, that the two of them shared the same blood. Then she realized he hadn't. Erasmus Nym was merely referring to himself and other Calians; he hadn't intended to include her in the term *our*. Sometimes

Mercator heard what she desired. Not that she wanted to be seen as Calian; that wasn't the point. Her skin and his were the same color, but she wasn't Calian. And even though Erasmus Nym had long claimed some kind of noble ancestry, his people were the dirt on the streets of Rochelle. Mercator's ilk was the manure that even the Calians stepped around. And Mercator herself was—

"Your head!" Erasmus was waving a hand over his own in an urgent motion. "Cover your head!"

Mercator noticed a carriage rolling toward them. She quickly lifted her sopping shawl and covered her ears. Erasmus turned away, pretending to adjust stock in the rafters of the awning as the coach passed by.

"They weren't even looking," she said. "The curtains were closed."

"Doesn't matter. If anyone sees your ears, if anyone thinks I'm dealing with a mir . . ." He gave her a look of exasperation. "Take the coins and go."

Did he set the coins on the cart because he didn't want anyone to see him giving me money, or because he didn't want to accidentally touch my hand? Sometimes Mercator also saw what she didn't desire.

She couldn't tell which was more likely or which was better.

"Before I go, I need to know. Has there been any word? Any hint about the duke taking action?"

This was her real reason for coming. She needed the money, but the necessity for hope was even more demanding.

He shook his head, an angry scowl on his face. He, too, was running out of patience. They all were, and that was bad. That was dangerous. Erasmus turned toward the sound of another carriage and glared at her.

The Disappearance of Winter's Daughter

She took the coins, snatched up the vest and her bundles, and left.

Tucked between the old open-air sewers and river spillway, the derelict Rochelle neighborhood—known as Melrah by the inhabitants, and the Rookery by everyone else—lacked paved streets, and the rain turned the narrow paths of dirt, ash, and night soil to slop. Most of the buildings in that part of Rochelle had long been abandoned. Since the residents had no means or right to repair them, roofs and walls collapsed as support beams rotted. Mercator's people used the timber remnants as firewood on cold nights, gutting their shelters for warmth. The old forest encroached on Melrah as it sought to take back what had long ago been stolen. Cutting firewood wouldn't have been difficult, except they weren't allowed to down trees. Technically, they weren't allowed to burn the fallen walls and stairs. The grand total of what the inhabitants of the Rookery weren't allowed to do seemed endless. Still, Mercator counted her blessings. There was still one thing left off that list: The mir were allowed to live.

But is this really living?

Mercator stepped around those bundled in rags, who huddled in every windbreak and dry patch. She made for the light of the little fire where half a dozen mir still warmed themselves beneath the surviving roof of the old mill. Seton was the first to spot her, and a smile stretched the girl's face. *Girl.* This was another absurdity. She should have considered her a *gyn,* but even in her own mind the old language was being replaced. A *girl* was a human female child, not an eighty-three-year-old mir who had so little human blood that she possessed the traditional blond hair and blue eyes of the ancient Instarya and looked to be just beyond adolescence. But just as with the shattered homes, they worked with what they had. And, at least compared with Mercator, Seton *was* a child.

"You're back!" Seton called and left the warmth of the fireside to hug Mercator.

The hug was a surprise. Mercator hadn't expected it, and the open expression of affection overwhelmed her. Feeling the unabashed arms of the girl, who ignored Mercator's soaked clothes to squeeze her tightly, made the old mir tear up. She thanked the rain for hiding it.

"Has there been any word?" Seton asked.

"It's been two weeks," Vymir said. "Something must have happened by now. It's nearly spring."

Mercator shook her head, and their happy expressions deflated. "No," she said, and then pulled out the coins. "But we have this." She moved around the fire's circle and dropped a coin into each person's hand.

When she got to Seton, the girl refused to lift her palm. "It's your money."

"You helped me gather the plants for the dye."

"But that's all," Seton protested. "If you let me, I would—"

Mercator took the girl's hand and forced the money into it. "Unlike you, I don't need to look pretty."

Seton's face darkened. "Beauty has always been a curse for me. You know that. Would have been better if I had been born a twisted wretch. If it hadn't been for the rasa . . ."

"That was years ago."

"Still haunts me. Besides, what good are looks when I'm a mir, a *filthy elf* that—"

"You're beautiful," Mercator said firmly. "We all are, even Vymir." She gave him a wink. "Don't let the opinions of the ignorant convince you truth is a lie."

Seton scowled, looking down at the mud on her own feet. "An eight-year-old boy threw a rock at me today. I was in the street—just walking, for Ferrol's sake!—and he threw a chicken-egg-sized rock—one that his mother had given him. When he missed, she gave him another. After a while, it's hard not to see yourself as they see you."

"After a while?" Mercator smiled while still holding tight to the girl's pale hands with her own bluish-black fingers. "I'm a hundred and twenty-three years old, and let me tell you something. *After a while,* you learn the truth about *people,* which is *people* don't know anything. People are dumber than spooked cattle chasing one another off a cliff. It's *persons* you need to listen to."

Seton's eyes narrowed in confusion.

"Look," Mercator told her. "You can talk to a person. You can reason with an individual. Usually. But *people,* that's another thing altogether. In a group is where they lose their way. Doesn't matter if it's humans, dwarves, or mir, if you put three or more in a room, they'll manufacture stupid like it was spun gold. They're like honeybees that way, except the product is never sweet. Don't listen to *them.* Listen to *me.* Don't listen to *people,* listen to a *person.*"

MERCATOR

Mercator bent down to lock eyes with Seton, offering a reassuring smile. "Things will improve. I'm going to make it better. That's my responsibility as matriarch of the Sikara. I owe that to my grandfather and his father before him."

"It's been this way for centuries," the girl said.

"Yes, it has, but spring is coming. Trust me. Spring *is* coming."

Seton sighed and nodded, but she clearly didn't believe.

Mercator couldn't blame her. She had a hard time believing it herself. "Good. Now take that coin to the Calian Precinct tomorrow and buy something nice to eat."

Mercator turned to leave.

"We have food," Estrya announced to her gaily.

"You do?" Mercator turned back.

They all nodded proudly.

Estrya pointed to the black pot on the fire. "Vymir and Bista found mushrooms growing in the alley under a crate. You'll stay, won't you? It's the least we can do."

Mercator shook her head. "I don't have to lift that pot's lid to know you don't have enough to feed three mouths, much less seven. Besides, I need to get back. I've been gone too long as it is."

"Where is it you go?" Seton asked.

Mercator smiled wryly. "It's a secret."

"You can't tell me?" Seton looked shocked.

"Not even you."

Her expression turned pained. "You don't trust me?"

"It's not a matter of trust; it's a matter of responsibility. I'm matriarch, so the unpleasant tasks fall to me." Mercator raised her arms, letting the sleeves fall back, revealing the blue skin that ran up to her elbows. "See? Perfect example. Some things leave marks that cannot be erased, and what I have to do is another one of those things." She turned away from the fire. "Enjoy your meal. Soon it will be better. I promise."

With a final wave, Mercator walked back out into the cold rain.

CHAPTER SIX
OVER LAMB AND SMALL BEER

R oyce was stunned when they reached the top of the stairs and opened the door. The room was the very definition of cozy. A large, elaborately carved dark-wood chimney breast framed the fireplace and dominated one wall, a fire already crackling behind a brass screen. A figurine of a boy skating on a pond adorned one side of the mantel and a candelabra the other. Deep-burgundy paper covered the walls, heavy drapes framed the tall windows, and a plush Calian rug lay on the hardwood floor. Soft chairs, dressers, and tables made a pleasant sitting area near the fire; a big bed all but filled an adjoining room. Paintings hung on the walls, and a bellows rested in a basket beside a full set of hearth tools. The chamber was bedecked with lamps, pillows, and a mirror. Even paper and pen lay upon a desk.

Hadrian dropped his bags near the door. "This is the nicest room I've ever been in." He looked down at his dirty boots. "I'm afraid to move."

Royce eyed the place, confused. He made a quick tour, peering behind the wardrobe, checking the backside of the drapes. In most places they stayed, he would find dry rot, mildew, rat droppings, and sometimes blood. Here, he found pristine wood and polished glass. "No wonder she didn't dicker."

Hadrian crossed to the dry sink. "Hey, there's soap next to the wash basin—and towels embroidered with the name Hemsworth."

Royce looked over, nodding. "Makes them harder to sell after stealing. You have to pay for the thread to be removed. No name on the rug, though." He studied the intricate floral design. "How much do you think the carpet would fetch? A fortune, right? We could drop it out the window. Wouldn't make much of a sound when it hit the street."

Hadrian looked up from the towels and shook his head. "We aren't stealing from a widow."

Royce looked affectionately at the rug. "An apparently rich widow."

"We're here to do a job, remember?"

Royce faced the windows, assessing the logistics. They were too narrow to climb through, but a carpet could slip out just fine. Assuming they weren't painted shut, he could roll the rug up and shove it out while Hadrian waited below. They could throw the thing over the back of one of their horses easily enough. The hard part was knowing where to sell it. That was always the challenge of working in an unknown town.

Hadrian snapped his fingers, gaining Royce's attention. "Hello. Focus. You said you like the current job. Can we concentrate on that? You might get to kill people, remember?"

Royce looked up. "True." He stared back at the carpet longingly. "We can empty this place later. No sense doing it now and losing the room."

Hadrian sat down in one of the upholstered chairs, appearing as comfortable as if he were sitting on blown glass. He stared at the cushioned stool in front of him but made no move to put his feet up. "What's our first move?"

Royce stepped to the window and, barely moving the drapes, peered out at the street below. The rain was coming down harder, and the cobblestones were slick. Their horses, left out front, were getting a cold bath. "Need to quarter our animals, find some food, and gather some information. As soon as the rain lets up a bit, we'll visit the news center."

"Huh? What makes you think Rochelle has such a thing?"

"Every city does."

"A tavern?"

Royce shook his head. "A brothel."

The rain never entirely stopped, and while they did find a place for their horses, they failed to spot a single brothel after almost two hours of searching. In a city as heavily populated as Rochelle, that was just strange. As far as Royce could determine, Rochelle was only a bit smaller than Colnora, which supported no less than thirty-two houses of comfort—three more than the number of certified taverns, eight more than the number of inns. Even Medford—a provincial village in comparison—provided twelve. Yet after crisscrossing both sides of the river, they found nothing of the sort.

Hunger, the wet, and the smell of cooking meat finally proved irresistible, and Hadrian dragged him into something called The Meat House—a small, smoky, congested shack off one of the narrower side streets. The weather-warped shack sold one-pound chunks of lamb or pork on small planks of grease-stained wood. "Freshest meat in the city. We get it from the slaughterhouse next door," the cook told them. They each bought a slab of lamb from the man who worked the spit. Then, helping themselves to a pair of pre-poured beers lined up on the counter, they elbowed spots at the long, narrow shelf that served as a communal table. With a row of men standing and chewing on steaming meat while staring at a wood wall decorated with years of grease splatter, the Meat House had all the ambience of a bovine food trough. The only light came from the open spit as drools of grease hit the coals and set off brilliant flares. Still, awful as it appeared, the no-nonsense eatery was warm and dry, and the meat—if nothing else—was hot.

A beefy, bald-headed thug dressed in a stained blue work shirt, smelling of fish and lacking so much as a scarf to shield him against the cold, struggled to rip a mouthful of meat free from the bone without burning his fingers.

"Might want to let it cool," Royce offered.

The bald man barely turned his head, just shifted his eyes to focus suspiciously on Royce. Dogs did that, too, when eating.

"Only got a few minutes before the next trawler comes in," the man said, and licked his fingers. "I can work with burnt hands, but not an empty stomach."

"Ugly night to be working outdoors."

"Any night's a good night if you're getting paid."

Royce didn't like the prospect of blisters, so he used Alverstone to cut a bite-size chunk. Popping it into his mouth, he still needed to suck in air or risk burning his tongue. He was shocked to find the meat tender and flavorful, but Royce, of all people, ought to know better than to judge anything based on appearance.

Hadrian stood on his left, talking quietly with a small fellow in a gray hood. Royce had a keen sense of hearing, but at times it worked against him. With so many conversations, it was difficult to focus on just one. He and Hadrian needed information, but while Hadrian was friendly and liked to talk, he was also likely to give out unnecessary details. Believing the job would eventually take a violent and unlawful turn, Royce preferred to monitor his friend's conversation. Best to make certain Hadrian didn't advertise their real names, where they came from, or the fact that they were very likely going to murder the Duke of Rochelle.

After a while, Royce relaxed. Despite Royce's many comments to the contrary, Hadrian wasn't an idiot. They wouldn't still be together if that were the case. While his friend might retain the asinine belief that most people were basically good, he had at least learned not to trust everyone who smiled his way. Because two hooks in the water could catch more fish than one, Royce turned his back to Hadrian and focused on the bald man to his right.

Adopting the local manner, Royce slumped against the shelf, resting on his elbows, and asked, "If a fella was looking for something to keep him warm tonight besides a blanket, any idea where he might look?"

"You want whiskey?"

Denser than expected.

Royce shook his head. "I was thinking more along the lines of a woman, the sort you pay for."

The bald man's face turned toward him. Lit by the fire, it glistened with a thick coat of slathered grease. "Ain't got that here. Illegal." He tore another mouthful of lamb from the bone, actually ripping it with a turn of his head, then chewed with his mouth open. "Church don't approve."

"Church doesn't approve of a lot of things," Royce said. "That doesn't mean they don't exist."

"Don't exist here."

"Where you two from?" asked a lean, swarthy fellow on the far side of the bald man, who also had grease dripping from his chin.

"Maranon," Royce answered. "Little place called Dulgath."

"Un-huh." The dark man nodded, displaying what Royce had hoped for: total ignorance. "Well, Tom's right. Don't know how they do things in *Dul-gath,* but Rochelle is a pious place." He said the word *pie-us* as if demanding a dessert.

"Moral and pure as the season's first snowflake," Tom added through a mouthful of meat.

Then both men snickered. Hearing each other, the two grease-stained geniuses laughed harder until the bald guy nearly choked to death on a chunk of lamb. He coughed, spit some gristle into his hand, looked at it doubtfully, and stuffed it back into his mouth.

Royce took a swig from his mug and discovered it was small. The term didn't refer to its size, which in this case was far more than Royce was willing to consume, but rather the amount of alcohol. Small beer was a poor man's brew, similar to the watered-down wine used in church services. The drink was designed to quench rather than intoxicate. Royce wasn't thirsty, but he wanted to keep up appearances. "You're both from around here then, is that right?"

"Born on the docks," the baldheaded one said. "Took over my father's job unloading the fish trawlers. Which is why I run all the way here on my break. By bloody Mar, I can't stand fish."

"I'm originally from Blycourt," the other said. "That's down east, closer to Blythin Castle. You probably heard of it. But my family moved here when I was young. Spent most of my life in Little Gur Em." He pointed out the door as if this held some meaning.

"Glad to meet some locals." Royce forced himself to talk with his mouth full and let grease drip to his chin. "Maybe you can tell me a bit about the city. What to look out for, where not to go."

The swarthy gent jumped to answer so quickly that he nearly lost the food in his mouth, and he had to pop a hand to his face to trap it. "You in town for the Spring Festival?"

"Yep, though it doesn't feel much like spring. More crowded than I would have thought."

The local man nodded. "Bishop proclaimed anybody seeking the crown has to be here for the feast, else they ain't eligible to be king. It's bringing noble folk from all over. Some, a lot actually, think he plans to hold a contest, and the winner gets the crown."

"That explains a lot. Had trouble finding a place to stay. Any clue who's going to be picked?"

"Most likely it will be Floret Killian, the Duke of Quarters," Tom put in.

"What about Leopold Hargrave? He's the duke here, right?" Royce asked.

"Old Leo's got no children. A king needs heirs."

"Just got married, didn't he?'" Royce asked. "He could still have kids, although . . . I heard something about his wife going missing, is that true?"

Like candles blown out by Royce's words, the gleeful smiles on both men's faces vanished.

They shot nervous looks at each other, then scanned the shack as the fire flared and shadows hit the walls.

"I got to get back. Trawler is likely in by now." The bald man chugged his remaining beer and wiped his face with his sleeve. Before pushing his way out, he fixed Royce with a suspicious glare.

The swarthy man continued to stare from across the gap that was left behind by the bald man's hasty departure. He studied Royce from boots to hood. "You looking for the duchess?" His words reached out slowly like fingers in the dark.

"I didn't say that. Just making conversation."

"Why are you here . . . Mister . . . ah . . . what did you say your name was?"

"His name is Grim, and I'm Baldwin," Hadrian jumped in, shoving his extended palm past Royce. "And you would be?"

The man looked at Hadrian's hand as if it were a hissing snake. "Leaving, I think." He backed away, pulling a blue kerchief from his neck and wiping his hands. Without another word, he shoved past and headed out the door.

Royce and Hadrian shared a puzzled look.

"Curious," Royce muttered.

"I told the fella I was talking to that my name was Baldwin," Hadrian whispered. "Didn't want you picking the same name."

Royce looked for the guy in the gray hood. "Where *is* the fellow you were talking to?"

"I mentioned the duchess, and he remembered he had to feed his cat."

Royce looked around the Meat House. Smoke filled the space where a row of men leaned on the shelf, guzzling beer and tearing seared flesh. Too many eyes looked their way. *More than before?*

"Maybe *we* should—"

"Not be here?" Hadrian smiled. "Was thinking the same thing." He swallowed the last of his beer, and together they moved back to the street.

The Meat House was in a run-down section a few blocks from the city's harbor. Royce led the way uphill, heading back toward their rented room while steering away from the crowds. The route threaded them through ever-narrower streets lined with walls of brick, places where rodents darted in the shadows. Rain was still falling, drizzling down walls, pouring off roofs, and creating a stream that threatened to back up the open-grate sewers.

"I take it you didn't learn anything useful?" Royce asked.

"You mean beside the fact that a monster stalks the city streets and rips people's hearts out?"

"Cute, but—"

"I'm not joking. That's what he actually told me."

"The one with the cat?"

Hadrian nodded. "Had the same kind of ears as the mother who told us about the room for rent. He was trying to hide them, but you could see the points when he turned."

"They're called "mir"—part human, part elven."

"Is mir an elven term? In Calis, they're called *kaz*."

Royce nodded. "I think so, but don't know what kaz means, besides 'universally hated,' that is."

They reached the crest of a little hill. The street veered right, and, trying to stay on track, Royce took a side lane to the left. He didn't know for certain, but hoped it went through to something bigger. If nothing else, it afforded a quieter, darker path, and he felt the need to disappear. They hadn't been in town a full night and already he felt they'd made a misstep, one he couldn't even blame on Hadrian.

"How about you?" Hadrian asked. "Any luck?"

"Some. I know why it's so crowded. Apparently, you have to be at the Spring Feast to be chosen king. Every noble in Alburn must be here, and the lowborn have come to see who gets picked. Oh, and maybe Leo didn't marry Genny for *just* her money."

"What makes you say that?"

"Candidates need to produce an heir."

Hadrian smiled. "Which means . . ."

"Yeah, yeah. I guess it's doubtful the duke killed her, but that doesn't mean she's alive. She could have been murdered by a rival."

Hadrian nodded. "But she *could* be alive. She doesn't have to be dead to prevent the bishop from picking her husband. Maybe she's being held captive until after the new king is crowned."

The two skirted a puddle. The present road, which was so narrow it felt more like an alley, lacked the precision engineering of Mill Street. Sewers were still in use—Royce saw the grates at regular intervals—but the water didn't drain into them. Instead, the runoff chose to gather in low pockets and holes that the road menders had neglected.

"Hmm," Hadrian mused.

"What?"

"Don't you find it suspicious?"

"I find everything suspicious. Can you be more specific?"

"Well, Gabriel Winter said Reinhold *and* his whole family were dead. I saw him once when he reviewed the troops. That old guy had enough children to be an honorary rabbit. And none of his heirs are alive? Seems odd. His death and Genny's *disappearance* might be related. Could be we've stumbled into something more than the disappearance of a wealthy woman. We should find out what happened to the previous king. I suppose we could ask Evelyn Hemsworth. She might know."

Royce made a face.

"Did you just shudder?" Hadrian began to chuckle. "You shuddered, didn't you? The infamous Mister Grim quivers at the thought of talking to an old woman?"

"Oh, and I suppose you're eager to have breakfast with her in the morning? Won't that be grand! Assuming the shriveled shut-in biddy eats food. I'm betting she gets by on blood she sucks from goats."

"She's not that bad."

Royce stopped walking and faced Hadrian straight-on.

Hadrian's shoulders slumped. "Okay, so she's as irritating as rough wool to a sunburn, but she has to have the finest—"

From behind them, a loud noise cut through the drumming rain.

The two spun.

They were alone on a dark street. A moment before, Royce had considered the lack of light as a bonus, but now he had cause to reconsider. Seedier neighborhoods settled for oil lanterns; some got by with torches, and many made do with nothing at all. But even in the worst areas, there was light from windows, except where they now stood. This street had none. No doors, either. Three-story brick walls hemmed them in.

The clatter was unmistakable: horses running, headed their way.

"Is that what I think it is?" Hadrian asked.

From behind, a wagon—one of the big ones with high sides used to haul livestock—came thundering their way, pulled by a pair of black draft horses racing at full tilt. The street was so narrow the wheels scraped the walls, first one side, then the other. Even in the dark, Royce could see the lathered sweat on the animals, their ears back, eyes wide and wild. The steeds were in a panic.

"Run!" Royce shouted.

Together, they sprinted up the street, but Royce knew they wouldn't reach the end of the block.

"Here!" He led Hadrian to a sewer grate.

The two dropped to their knees and together wrenched the square of iron bars free, revealing an uninviting hole. Sparks flared and illuminated the dark alley as the left wheel of the wild wagon scraped the end of its metal axle across the face of one brick wall. Royce didn't search for a ladder. No time to even look below. Anything was better than death by trampling. This was a lie, of course. He admitted it to himself even as he leapt in. There were many things worse, Royce just didn't think he'd find any on that list at the bottom of a sewer. For the most part, Royce liked sewers. He'd grown up in one.

The fall wasn't far, and the water at the bottom was deeper than he expected, which initially seemed like a good thing. Royce always believed it was better to hit water than rock when leaping into a dark hole of unknown depth. After the inaugural splash and obligatory gasp for air, he had a second to realize the water was chest high. A second after that, he discovered the amount of water wasn't insignificant when combined with the rainwater surge. A powerful current dragged him and Hadrian off their feet and hurtled the two through a lightless tunnel that scraped their legs and elbows across stone walls too slick from slime to grasp.

The darkness was broken by intermittent columns of light entering through other sewer grates. The flashes gave Royce a sense of how fast they were going. *Slower than a trotting horse, but not by much.* The sensation was odd and eerie. Bobbing weightless in the dark, the patches of pale light—set at near-regular intervals—rushed by, the only marker of time and distance. The hard stone walls echoed every noise, magnifying drips, splashes, and the water's rush.

"This isn't good!" Hadrian shouted.

His voice bounced around the tunnel, making it impossible for Royce to tell his partner's location—*behind, maybe?* "What was your first clue?"

"Where do you think this goes?"

"Best guess? The bay."

They swept around a sharp curve that had Royce reaching for a handhold as he skidded along another wall. His fingers came up with fists of muck.

"How much you wanna bet this doesn't pour out on a nice soft beach?" Hadrian yelled.

They passed more lighted grates. In the flash, Royce looked behind him. Hadrian was there, just back and off to the left. The current held the two in near-perfect synchronicity. Kicking and stroking as best he could, Royce broke the distance, moving closer until he latched on to Hadrian's foot. When he did, Hadrian kicked.

"Stop it, you fool!" Royce yelled.

"Was that you?"

"Yes, it's me. Hold still!"

Royce caught Hadrian's foot again and pulled, docking them together. He grabbed hold of Hadrian's belt to ensure they stayed that way.

"I thought . . ." Hadrian paused. "I don't know. I mean, we're in a big sewer, aren't we? Could be anything down here."

"Use your sword," Royce said. "The big one. See if you can catch it on anything."

He felt Hadrian twist, then heard the sound of metal scraping, but he sensed no noticeable decrease in speed.

They came near the wall again. Hadrian stretched and twisted. More scraping. A series of jerks, and there it was, the force of water surging against them. The force was too much for whatever grip Hadrian had managed, and they were off again.

"Wall and ground are too smooth," Hadrian reported. "Need something to catch the blade on."

"There!" Royce pointed at the next grating. "See the light."

"Too high. I can't—"

"Not the grate, next to it! Stairs!"

In the dim light, Royce could see a set of stone steps descending into the sewer. He realized it was likely too dark for Hadrian to see. "Trust me. Right in front of that next shaft of light. On the left. Kick!"

They both swam as hard as they could, which did little to alter their course. The current liked to keep them and everything else trapped in the center.

Not going to make it, Royce realized as once more the light revealed their speed and the lack of sideways movement.

"Hang on!" Hadrian shouted as they came close to the grating. His head dipped below the water. A moment later Royce nearly lost his grip on Hadrian's belt as the bigger man shoved off the bottom of the sewer, propelling himself toward the steps. Holding the long blade with one hand on the pommel and another on the flange, Hadrian caught the corner where passing sewage frothed against the wall. Grunting loudly, Hadrian drew them to the side. The current grew weaker the farther away from the center they moved; still, Hadrian's arms shook with the strain to keep them stationary as water frothed in his face.

"Go! Go! Go!" Hadrian shouted.

Royce clawed up Hadrian's body, and caught the edge of the steps. Then reaching back, he pulled Hadrian to the stairs. The two scrambled onto the bottom step and collapsed, panting in the dark, listening to the rush of water. A loud clank echoed as Hadrian set the big spadone blade down on the stone. Unable to lie down, Hadrian pushed his back against the wall and stretched out his legs along the step's length. His head was back, and he groaned while laboring to breathe. Royce crouched, head between his knees, spitting sewer swill from his mouth and swiping his hair back.

"That was refreshing," Hadrian said between breaths. His voice quavered.

A faint light spilled down from an opening at the top of the stairs, providing just enough illumination for Royce to see his partner's face. Hadrian's breath was misting, his body shaking. The night had always been cold, but walking in the rain had been one thing; being soaked to the bone was another. No wind at least, but that would change the moment they went topside. Royce gritted his teeth in anticipation.

"What just happened?" Hadrian asked. "I'd like to believe a horse was accidentally spooked and ran in our direction."

"Down an otherwise deserted street?" Royce said, sounding skeptical. "A street that lacks windows and doors?"

"I said I'd *like* to believe that."

Together they pushed to their feet and climbed up a few steps, where they paused to wring out the worst of the wet.

"Someone just tried to kill us, didn't they?" Hadrian asked.

"Sure seems like it."

Hadrian returned the spadone to its place on his back. "But we just got here."

"I know. Doesn't seem fair, does it?" Royce squeezed his cloak, letting the water drizzle down the steps. "You might be right. I think we got ourselves into something bigger than a simple case of a man killing his wife for her money."

"But why would anyone—I mean, how could anyone even know what we're doing here? Or do you think they treat all visitors this way. Hey, welcome to town. Here, have a scalding-hot mouthful of lamb, some incredibly weak beer, and don't forget your free runaway cart!"

"We asked about the duchess."

"We asked about . . . wait . . . are you serious? This is because of that?"

Royce nodded. He looked up at the damp, dripping walls of the sewer. "This city reminds me a lot of Ratibor—a lot more crowded, far more embellished, and no brothels, but it harbors the same mentality. Bald dockworker and company didn't run away from us, they ran to someone, maybe several someones."

"But why did those someones try to kill us? All we did was—"

"I'm guessing they don't want people inquiring about the duchess."

"Because she's dead?" Hadrian asked. "Or because she's alive?"

Royce pondered this and realized he didn't have the slightest clue. After nearly an entire night in the city, he had more questions than when he'd arrived.

CHAPTER SEVEN
BREAKFAST

R oyce and Hadrian were on time for breakfast.
      Evelyn Hemsworth presided at a table covered in three
cloths—blue upon yellow, with pristine white on top—and on
this lay a vast collection of tableware. Porcelain creamers, cups,
plates, and spice towers had been placed with such precision
that Hadrian wondered if the woman had used plumb lines and
T-squares. Crystal glasses lorded over the silver forks and knives,
which guarded napkin-covered plates. Great silver serving trays
with ornate lids were set with equal precision in a circle around
a two-foot silver sculpture of a palm tree, at the base of which
three men in turbans and Calian garb stood holding candelabras.
While no food was visible, the entire house smelled of fresh
pastries and sizzling bacon.

      At the head of the table, Evelyn sat. She looked exactly as
she had the night before: hair in a bun, formal dress, high tight

collar that made Hadrian swallow in sympathy. She stared at the two of them with large piercing eyes and judgmental brows, her lips drawn up like a tight purse.

Royce looked at Hadrian, who stared back, both unsure what to do next: sit, offer a morning greeting, or ask permission to join her?

"Good morning," Hadrian ventured as lightheartedly as he could.

"You're late," she said.

Hadrian glanced at the window. The morning sun had only just pierced the glass, replacing the illumination of the diminishing fire and making the crystal stemware sparkle in rainbow hues. "You said dawn."

"I did. Dawn was eight minutes ago."

"But the sun—"

"The sun doesn't reach this house until eight minutes after dawn because Lardner's Cabinet and Wardrobe Shop, on the hill at the intersection of Cross and Howell, is a full four stories tall and traps my home in shadow."

Hadrian opened his mouth to speak, but he had nothing to say.

"Sit," she ordered.

They both complied. Hadrian sat in the middle. Royce took the seat farthest away.

"It smells wonderful," Hadrian said, reaching out to peek under the silver lid directly before him.

"Tut, tut!" Evelyn said, and clapped her hands sharply, stopping him. "What's wrong with you people?" She glared accusingly.

Once more Hadrian glanced at Royce, mystified. The truth was he could answer that question a dozen different ways.

"Have you no sense of propriety? No piety?"

Hadrian still hadn't a clue what she was getting at, and apparently it showed. She frowned his way.

"We need to give thanks to Our Lord, Novron, for this meal."

"Oh," Hadrian replied.

"Oh?" Evelyn intensified the disappointment in her eyes. "What sort of comment is that?"

Fearful of another verbal blunder, Hadrian shrugged.

"Now he's acting like a monkey," she said to Royce, as if he would understand and agree. Royce sat rigidly, staring back. Hadrian imagined he was entertaining himself ticking through all the ways he planned to kill her, mentally trying each out.

Evelyn turned to Hadrian, waiting. A long minute passed, and her brows rose with the passage of time. "Well?"

"Well what?" Hadrian asked.

Evelyn looked dumbfounded. "Are you telling me that you . . . am I correct in my assumption that you've *never* offered thanks to Novron for your good fortune? How is that possible? Were the two of you hatched in a cave somewhere such that you don't understand the basic concepts of civilization and devotion to our god?"

Hadrian looked to Royce for help, and he wasn't surprised to see his partner lifting his hood.

"We *do not* wear hoods at the table." Evelyn's words were so firm that the declaration came out as an indisputable fact.

Royce froze like a raccoon caught in a trash bin.

"Honestly, the two of you . . . it's like living with animals."

"I'm sorry," Hadrian said. "We're not from around here."

"Obviously. The two of you live in a forest, most likely in some worm-filled burrow."

"If it'll get us closer to eating, we're all for whatever thanks giving you have planned. Right?" Hadrian looked at Royce, who remained stationary with his hood partway up, watching Evelyn with a menacing fixation.

"Fine." Evelyn sighed with abundant disappointment. Then she bowed her head. "We thank you, Lord Novron, for the food before us. May we prove worthy of your kindness." She lifted her head and looked at Hadrian.

"Am I supposed to say that now, too?"

Evelyn gave an exasperated shake of her head. "Just—just eat. Please."

Lifting the lids, they found a steaming feast of eggs, pork, cheese, whitefish, shellfish, honey, almonds, pastries, and whey. For a moment, Hadrian was overwhelmed. "Did . . . did you prepare this all yourself?"

"Of course not. Didn't you see the army of fairy-cooks that filed out while you were insulting Our Lord? I particularly like their tiny aprons, don't you?"

"I—" Hadrian wasn't certain she was mocking him.

"Eat," she ordered.

They passed trays, loading up plates. Hadrian felt horribly selfish and decadent while piling up so much, but Evelyn insisted she'd cooked it for them and they had best eat it.

"I don't recall hearing you come in last night," Evelyn said, pouring herself tea from an elaborate pot made in the shape of an elephant.

To Evelyn Hemsworth and Royce, the pot was likely the whimsical design of a creative artist, but Hadrian had firsthand experience with the animals. He'd seen them during his years in Calis, where they were used as both beasts of burden and war machines. Much of the tableware setting was inspired by, or likely came from, Calis. The port of Rochelle was perhaps the first stop in the trans–Goblin Sea trade route. Even the spice shakers had monkeys on them.

"But I noticed you left quite a puddle on my rug and a nasty trail of wet up the stairs. I'll ask you to please remove your boots in the future. I'm an old woman and have more than enough to do. I don't need you providing me with extra work. And be aware, I lock the door promptly with the third chime of the bell tower after sunset." She reached for the sugar and paused. "You're not up to anything shady, are you? I won't stand for any higgery-jiggery or jiggery-pokery for that matter. Not in this house. Understand? While you're here, I'll expect the both of you to conduct yourselves properly. And you"—she indicated Royce with a tilt of her head and the raise of a brow—"don't wear a cloak to the meal table. And wash your hands before coming down. Who were your parents? That's what I'd like to know."

They ate for several minutes in silence. The food was wonderful, but Evelyn didn't eat much at all.

"Might I ask, what became of King Reinhold?" Hadrian ventured and received an apprehensive look from Royce.

BREAKFAST

Both of them visibly cringed in anticipation of the response. Talking to Evelyn was like searching for wayward eggs in a dark henhouse.

Evelyn sighed.

"I'm sorry if that's not a polite thing to discuss over breakfast," Hadrian added.

"What? Oh, no, that's fine, but well, His Majesty . . ." Evelyn frowned over her plate, which consisted of only a single small roll and a slice of orange cheese. "It was quite the tragedy, you understand. His ship, the *Eternal Empire,* sank in a storm off Blythin Point about five months ago. The entire royal family was aboard, along with most of the royal court. That's why stewardship of the kingdom has fallen to Bishop Tynewell."

"Why the bishop?" Hadrian asked.

"Tradition mostly. When the last emperor of the Novronian Empire died, the Bishop of Percepliquis was the one who assumed the mantle of steward to the empire." She peered at both of them for a moment expectantly. "Neither of you has any clue what I'm talking about, do you?"

"Not really," Hadrian said.

She sighed. "It's like talking to children. You're like a pair of five-year-olds dressed up in big people's clothes. I'm afraid to let the two of you wander the streets alone. You might accept candy from strangers and be whisked off to darkest Calis."

"He would." Royce pointed at Hadrian.

"Don't point," she said. "It's not polite."

Royce rolled his eyes.

"Watch yourself, young man. You're treading on thin ice, you are."

Royce smiled at her malevolently. "I'm actually quite good at that."

Hadrian didn't like the look in his friend's eye, which had changed from *surprised raccoon* to *hungry panther*. "I think you were going to tell us more about the death of King Reinhold?"

"Actually, no. I was explaining common history, of which you and your friend are as stunningly ignorant as you are lacking in suitable personal hygiene and proper manners."

"Right," Hadrian said. "That was it. Go on."

"Oh, yes, well, history is something of a passion in Alburn, you understand. The people here are quite proud of their heritage—we are, you see, unique in the world. It's our claim to the past that defines us as a people. Which is why it's so disappointing to encounter the likes of you two, who appear so nescient of that which is so important to us." She paused either to take a breath or to allow Hadrian the opportunity to prove her point, perhaps by asking what *nescient* meant. He didn't take the bait.

"Well, what I was going to impart was that after the death of the last emperor, his family, and the destruction of the capital city of Percepliquis, Bishop Venlin stepped in and took over. It was the bishop who officially moved the empire from somewhere in the west to here. At that time, this was the Imperial Province of Alburnia. The bishop—that's what the patriarch was back then—actually ruled the remains of the empire out of Blythin Castle until he finished his cathedral." She gestured, but didn't point, toward the east. "Even back then, Rochelle was a thriving port city. You need to understand that at that time, everywhere west of the Majestic Mountains was locked in complete and utter chaos because petty warlords were grabbing land and power."

Hadrian wanted to point out that not much had changed, but he wasn't about to interrupt. He hoped that Evelyn's ramblings would shed some light on more recent events. Royce didn't appear to be listening at all as he scraped eggs off his plate with a knife.

"Everyone loyal to the emperor's banner came here. The Calders, the Killians, the Hargraves—they had all been prominent families in the court of the last emperor. Alburn became home of the empire in exile. Everything that could be salvaged was brought here for safekeeping: artifacts, books, statues, paintings. So you see, Alburn in general, and Rochelle in particular, has very strong links with the traditions of the Novronian Empire. So when the king and his entire family sank in the Goblin Sea, the bishop naturally stepped in to act as steward. Simple as that."

"That was simple?" Royce asked and licked his knife clean.

"It's called thinking, dear," Evelyn told him. "If you work at it, the mind gets stronger."

Royce shifted his grip on the knife, taking hold of the blade.

"So what happened?" Hadrian quickly asked. "Why isn't this still the empire in exile? Why isn't the patriarch still here? How did Reinhold become king? He isn't a Calder, Killian, or Hargrave, is he?"

"No. That was all Glenmorgan's doing. He was the big winner of the monarch sweepstakes. The biggest thug of the west, if you will. When Glenmorgan invaded Alburnia, the patriarch avoided being sacked by anointing him the almost-emperor, otherwise known as a steward. Then when Glenmorgan set himself up at Ervanon in the north, the patriarch was obliged to join him. Still, while the church's head may have gone to Ghent, its heart remains here. For example, the Seret Knights are still headquartered in Blythin Castle, just as they always have been."

"And Reinhold?"

"His great-great-great-grandfather, or something, was appointed governor of Alburn by Glenmorgan. He set up his government at the westernmost city, Caren—as far away from all the traditional imperialists as he could. After good old Glenny the Third was executed at Blythin, the governor—by then it was his son—just kept on running things, but now as king."

"Because they were all lost at sea, there are no more descendants of that bloodline. Is that right?" Hadrian asked.

"Indeed, and the bishop will be making his choice during the Spring Feast." Evelyn looked down her nose at Royce and scowled. "You're not eating. For Novron's sake, you're thin as a brittle bit of last year's grass. That's why you wear that big cloak, isn't it? You're embarrassed at how little you are. Well, eat. You won't grow big and strong like your friend unless you do."

"We need to find a new place to stay," Royce said the moment they were clear of the house and moving with unusual speed down the street.

The rain had stopped, the weather warmer, and aside from a bit of fog and some puddles, it was a relatively pleasant day.

"There isn't any other place. Remember?" Hadrian replied, stretching his legs to keep up with Royce, who was practically trotting. "We spent forever searching yesterday."

"We looked for a couple of hours." Royce gave his third glance back, as if Evelyn Hemsworth were fast on their heels.

Mill Street was alive with activity. Carriages rolled by; a girl sold early spring flowers from a handcart; a man with a wagon delivered milk and cheese door-to-door; a tiny dog with a pug nose begged for scraps; and pedestrians with canes and overcloaks dodged street traffic, standing puddles, and one another. Everything was so different from the night before.

"What are you griping about?" Hadrian said. "Do you remember what the Dirty Tankard looked like? The Hemsworth house is *really* nice. And the food! That may have been the best meal I've ever had."

"The woman is insane."

"I actually kind of like her."

Royce stopped walking. He stood in the middle of the street between two separate but equally sized piles of horse droppings, glaring at his partner with a shocked expression that bordered on disturbed.

Hadrian continued walking two steps before noticing. "What?" He looked back with equal parts innocence and guilt. "She's nice . . . in an authoritarian, priggish, self-important sort of way. Think of her as the mother you never had."

Royce made a bitter face. "If my mother was anything like that, I'm glad I never knew her."

They resumed walking, moving clear of the milk wagon coming their way. The flat bed of the dray was laden with a half a dozen barrel-sized covered pails that cried white tears.

"She's right, you know," Hadrian said. "You should eat more if you want to grow up to be big and strong like me." He grinned.

Royce pulled up his hood. "Don't talk to me."

They climbed a hill that granted an expansive view of the city, most of it dominated by roofs and smoking chimneys. Yet with the rain gone and the fog restricting itself to the area around the harbor, Hadrian was finally able to form a mental map of the place. Rochelle straddled the Roche River as it poured into Blythin Bay—most of which was lost to the fog. Split in two as it was by the waterway, the city had been built with one half on either bank, the big harbor dominating the mouth of the river. In the middle of the Roche, a long thin island was joined to the two banks by a pair of stone bridges.

The island, aside from its role as the only means of traversing the river from one bank to the other, appeared to be reserved entirely for the duke. This was evident by the imposing wall that ringed the palatial estate. The areas nearest the bridges on both banks were the most affluent. The farther away from the river, the more destitute and neglected things became. The area just on the east side included the cathedral and its huge plaza. Hadrian suspected this was what people referred to as Old Town. Just east of there was another square surrounded by shops. Hadrian guessed it was the Merchant District—although the far side of the river had just as many shops, so he couldn't be sure.

Royce headed south toward the foggy bay and into narrower, dirtier streets. Hadrian remembered the area from the night before, and daylight only made the neighborhood worse. The Meat House was just ahead on the right.

"What are we doing back here? We just ate."

"Not looking for food this time. Need to find . . . there!" Royce pointed at the building next to the Meat House.

A ghastly looking two-story structure of gray mottled wood was fashioned in the general shape of a barn. A tall double door was stained with red handprints near the edge and along the latch. A row of wagons was parked in a line out front. They rocked and jiggled from hosts of restless passengers—mostly pigs that snorted and squealed.

"It's a slaughterhouse."

Royce nodded. "The cook said they got their supply fresh from next door. The wagon that nearly killed us yesterday was a livestock wagon, just like those."

"Royce, I'm sure there are hundreds of wagons like these in and around the city."

"But none as conveniently available to someone who overheard our conversation."

Royce approached the wagons and began walking up and down the row, studying them. They were old and worn. The sides were tall and bleached by the sun. The big spoked wheels had manure and straw stuck to the rims. Hadrian imagined what it might have felt like having one, or perhaps two, roll over him.

Death by slaughterhouse wagon wasn't on his list of best ways to go.

"Is there a problem with my wagons?" A man came out of the building wearing a blood-splattered apron and a dingy leather skullcap. He held a bloody rag in one hand and a dripping hatchet in the other.

"Yes," Royce said. "I think there is." He pointed to the third in line. "That one's axle hub—see it? The metal looks raw, like it was recently filed, or perhaps scraped against a brick wall."

The butcher didn't bother to look. "That's not a problem."

"It is for me." Royce took a single step toward the man. "Was it stolen? Did it disappear last night? Did you have to search for it this morning?"

The butcher mused a moment with his lips then spit on the ground between them. "Nope. Been there all night. Hasn't moved. How is that a problem for you?"

"You're right. It's not." Royce smiled as he took another step closer. "But it just became a problem for you."

Hadrian was fascinated by just how catlike Royce became when preparing to kill; his eyes became dilated, his pupils growing with his excitement. Hadrian didn't know for certain if Royce would kill the butcher. He generally didn't murder in plain sight on a busy street in daylight, but the body language was unmistakable.

"Someone tried to kill me with that wagon last night, and since it wasn't stolen"—Royce took another step—"I'll have to assume it was you."

While the butcher processed the accusation, Royce rushed forward.

BREAKFAST

With Royce, half seconds mattered. Luckily Hadrian had seen the attack coming even if the butcher was oblivious, and he stepped between the two. The butcher finally realized his peril and shuffled backward.

"Out of my way!" Royce snapped as Hadrian extended his arms, blocking the thief from dodging around him.

"Keep him away from me!" the butcher shouted. "That guy is crazy. I didn't do anything."

"He's not crazy," Hadrian tried to explain. "He thinks you tried to kill him . . . err . . . *us,* actually."

"Help! Help!" the butcher shouted, backing up.

Royce shifted left then right, but Hadrian blocked him both times. To the butcher—to anyone watching—it would have appeared that Royce was doing his best to get past. He wasn't. Royce could dance with an angry rattlesnake and never get bitten. He once boasted about his ability to dodge arrows; Hadrian had never seen him do that but believed he could. If Royce *really* wanted to get around, Hadrian probably couldn't stop his lithe partner.

"Step aside," Royce snapped. "I'm going to kill him."

The butcher's eyes widened, and his pleas became frantic, "Somebody . . . anybody . . . help me!"

"Calm down, both of you," Hadrian said.

A number of people on the street had stopped and were staring. An elderly man and two women took the most interest but posed no danger. Two laborers stacking bags of feed farther up the street, on the other hand, were worth keeping an eye on. They, too, had paused and turned. At that moment, everyone's expressions displayed puzzlement, but it wouldn't take long for that to change.

Hadrian addressed the butcher, "Look, we just want to know who tried to run us down last night."

"It was him," Royce insisted, and, reaching into his cloak, he drew out Alverstone. "And I'm going to treat him like one of his pigs. Time for the slaughter, you rat-tailed sow!"

The butcher looked at the gleaming white dagger, and with a squeak, which sounded a bit like the squeal of a pig, he turned to flee.

Hadrian tripped him. "Don't run! Whatever you do, don't run! He really will kill you then. Your only hope is to stay near me."

This was only partially a lie. Royce was intentionally scaring the man in the hope of getting information, but Royce was still Royce, and the cat analogy was a little too perfect. There was a good chance this man had been involved in the attack, and if he proved unhelpful, if he stopped being a potential lead . . .

"Help! I didn't do anything," the butcher cried from the ground where he lay on his back. He dropped the meat cleaver and rag, both hands up to fend off the expected attack. "I don't know how the wagon got like that. I didn't watch the thing all night. I was asleep. Maybe someone did take it. Maybe they took it and put it back. I don't know. But *I* didn't do anything!"

"Hold! In the name of the duke!" Running up the street were a trio of men in chainmail and blue-colored tabards—city guards.

BREAKFAST

Hadrian frowned as he realized that Royce's theatrics had taken a potentially serious turn. He had seen the guards around the city, but previously only in pairs. The reason there were three became instantly apparent. The lead man wore a helmet with the yellow horsehair crest of an officer, his face vaguely familiar.

"What's going on?" the officer demanded while trotting up. He spotted Royce's dagger, and his hand moved to a sword. His fellow soldiers followed suit.

Royce dropped into a full crouch, the ruse ended. The thief was poised to fight.

"Roland Wyberg?" Hadrian asked. "By Mar! Is that really you?"

No one moved.

The officer's eyes narrowed as he stared. His mouth opened in shock. "Blackwater?"

Then to the utter amazement of everyone, including the spectators on the street, the two clasped hands.

"You're still alive." Hadrian clapped the officer's back. "Who would have thought."

"Me? You're the one who disappeared. I expected—well, everyone thought you were dead. Rumors said you were knifed by a Warric patrol."

"Excuse me!" the butcher shouted from where he still lay on the ground. He pointed at Royce. "This man is about to kill me."

Roland glanced from Hadrian to Royce. "Friend of yours?"

"He is." Hadrian nodded. "We think the butcher might have tried to kill us last night."

"No," Royce said, putting his dagger away. "He's just an idiot."

"You saw him. He was going to kill me." The butcher pointed at Royce.

In a fair imitation of Evelyn Hemsworth, Royce said, *"It's not polite to point."*

"What's this all about?" Wyberg asked.

"Someone tried to run us down with a slaughterhouse wagon," Hadrian replied. "That one over there."

The officer studied the wagons for a moment, eyes narrowed in contemplation. "Sure it wasn't just an accident?" He focused on Hadrian with a new scrutiny. "Is there some reason why someone would want you dead? What exactly are you doing here, Blackwater? And for that matter, what made you disappear in the first place?"

Royce nodded at the crowd, which, despite the diminished chance of violence, had grown. A dozen people stood in the street, and more were arriving. "Is it possible to continue this conversation somewhere less public? The central square, perhaps? A community stage, maybe?"

Roland looked around and frowned at the audience. "There's a guard post just up the street." He hooked a thumb at the two other soldiers with him. "I was checking up on these two when we heard the shouts. I can offer you some coffee, not allowed to have anything stronger."

"Aren't you going to arrest them?" the butcher asked, still lying on the ground as if unable to get up.

"For scaring you?"

BREAKFAST

That made the butcher huff dramatically.

The officer pointed to the Meat House as they passed by. "If you're hungry, we could grab something to eat. Doesn't look like much, but the food is good."

"No!" Royce and Hadrian said together.

CHAPTER EIGHT
A TALE OF TWO SOLDIERS

The kid Hadrian remembered was a lean seventeen-year-old with deep dimples that attracted women like a bowl of candy drew children. He hadn't seen Wyberg in six years, not since Hadrian had left the service of King Reinhold. He didn't look much different. Heavier, but Roland had always needed a few pounds. The slender boy had become a solid man, but the dimples were still there, and in his eyes, Hadrian saw a vague reflection of another young soldier whom time had also changed.

The guard post was a typical one-room shack. Nothing more than a place to check in, store shackles and weapons, and provide a little warmth when it got cold. Much of the room was given over to stacks of wood, but there was an ink-stained desk in the corner on which was laid a stack of mangled parchments held down by a horseshoe. The floor creaked when stepped on, the fire hissed, and the whole place smelled of smoke and damp wood.

"So, Blackwater, what happened to you?" Roland snapped off his chin guard and tossed the big helmet on the desk, where the weight of the horsehair brush caused it to roll halfway to the edge.

"Went to Calis." Hadrian took a seat on a crude bench that looked to have been banged together from two unsplit logs and a wide board. Royce showed him an uncomfortable face before sitting alongside, enveloping himself in his cloak the way a proper woman might check the skirt of her dress.

Roland moved to the fire, where a blackened metal kettle sat on a wrought-iron grate, forming a bridge over glowing coals. "Why?"

"You probably don't remember, but I came to Alburn from Warric. Had friends serving in Chadwick's First Regiment. Didn't want to be here to welcome them and couldn't get a transfer, so . . ." Hadrian didn't bother finishing.

Roland lifted the kettle's lid. He shook his head and scowled. "No one ever puts a new one on after draining it." He took the pot outside, filled it with water from the rain barrel, struggled to latch the door, then set the pot back on the fire. He was still fussing with the lid when he said, "You were right. They attacked. A few weeks after you vanished. Nasty battle." Roland reached up to a shelf at the left of the desk and took down a large tin box. "Richard, Brick, and Mel were all killed. You remember Mel, don't you?"

"Swell Mel? Sure." Mel had been an older fellow who cut his hair short and made a habit of helping new recruits and adopting stray animals.

"The First Regiment hit us from two sides." With difficulty, Roland popped the top of the tin off. Some of the coffee beans fell to the floor. He poured a small pile onto the desk. "Captain Stowe and most of the officers died. Warric crippled us in short order." He took a hammer that hung from a peg and proceeded to smash the beans. "I sent Brady on a horse to Caren. Told him to ride his ass off and get help," he said in between hammer strikes. "The rest of us fell back to the Narrows. We held them there. Lost almost everyone doing it. We were four hundred when the sun came up, forty-two when it set. Afterward, I got a promotion and my choice of station. Picked Rochelle. Had my fill of fighting." Roland scooped up the crushed coffee and dropped handfuls into three cups, then checked the water and scowled. He looked back. "How was Calis?"

"Bloody." Hadrian left it at that.

Roland looked over. Their eyes met, and he nodded. "Guess we both woke up with hangovers."

Royce kept his attention on the single window that faced the street. The interior pane was covered in flies that relentlessly butted the glass. A large number of them were dead on the sill.

Roland took a pair of split logs off the stack and placed them among the coals beneath the grate. Damp stains indicated they had been left out in the rain, and the logs hissed. Smoke escaped the draft, and Roland cracked the door a couple of inches to allow it an escape.

"And who is this?" Roland nodded toward Royce.

"My partner in crime," Hadrian said with a smile that garnered a look from Royce, who otherwise hadn't moved.

"We've been working out west. Taking odd jobs as we could find them."

Roland spun the desk chair around and sat. "Is that why you're here? An odd job?"

Hadrian glanced at Royce, who provided no help. Discussing an assignment with the city guard was as likely as a pair of mice consulting a house cat about dinner options. But Roland was a friend, a decent man, in a position to help, and Royce's methods had failed to turn up anything except a near-death experience. Knowing he'd hear about it later, Hadrian took the gamble. "Yeah," he said. "We were hired to find a woman named Genny."

Royce shifted on the bench.

Roland, who was just about to peek under the lid of the kettle again, stopped. "You mean Genevieve? The duchess who married old Leopold?"

Hadrian nodded.

"Who hired you?"

Royce coughed into his hand. "Sorry. Think I'm getting a cold."

Hadrian felt Royce looking at him, but he didn't turn to verify. He'd already committed himself to the path. "Her father."

Hadrian imagined Royce to be mentally screaming at him, or gasping in horror, but the reaction of Roland was anticlimactic. He turned back to the pot with a sniff.

"Her father seems to think she's dead, although a note said she's only missing."

"We've looked for her. Tore the town apart, really. The duke had us going door-to-door, searching shops and private homes. But . . ."

"But what?"

"She's been missing for two weeks. No one has seen or heard anything about her." He nodded. "I think her father has cause for concern."

Roland dipped his pinkie into the kettle and jerked it back. Then he poured steaming water into three cups. "This is one of the best perks of this post. We get great coffee shipped over from Calis. Be sure to wait until the floating bits settle before you drink." He handed them the cups.

"Well then," Hadrian said, cheerily, "it's a good thing we arrived. Maybe we can help. Can you tell us what happened? How'd she disappear?"

"Not much to tell. She and the ducal cofferer, a fellow named Devon De Luda, were returning from a meeting with the city's merchant guild. On their way back to the Estate—that's the duke's residence—the carriage was attacked. De Luda was killed on the spot, and the duchess was dragged off."

"Where'd this happen?" Royce asked.

"Just before the bridge to the Estate, on the far side of Central Plaza. That's the big one with the cathedral."

"Seems like a pretty public setting for a murder," Royce noted.

"Usually is, but that night it was deserted."

"Deserted? A little odd, isn't it?"

"Not really. The town is filled with folk right now because of the festival. Two weeks ago, things were quieter. And Rochelle residents are a superstitious lot, tend to stay in at night."

"So, no talk, no rumors?"

"Plenty. Always are. But that's just gossip and ghost stories. No mysterious monster killed the duchess, if that's what you're getting at."

Hadrian glanced at Royce, puzzled. "Okay . . . I wasn't, but I guess that's good to know. Do you *usually* suspect monsters?"

"No, but that doesn't stop the tongues from wagging. De Luda was stabbed, plain and simple. His heart was in his chest, and he still had a face."

Hadrian opened his mouth but didn't quite know what to say.

Roland sighed. "I'm just saying it wasn't a monster, okay?"

Hadrian nodded. He glanced at Royce, who stared at Roland with a concerned look.

"Okay, so lately we've been finding mutilated children, most of them mir. Kids with their chests torn open and hearts ripped out. But their faces have been fine. No one's lost a face in years—if they ever really did."

"What a quaint city you have here," Royce quietly remarked.

"Yeah, well, no place is perfect. I think all the talk about the carriage being attacked by a monster is just people finding what they expect to see. Like I said, De Luda's body wasn't like the other corpses. My personal theory—about the duchess, I mean—is that she was dragged into the shadows, her throat slit, and her body dumped in the river."

"Why?" Royce asked.

"You've probably heard about what's going on during the Spring Feast, right?"

"Yeah, Alburn's going to get a new king."

"Well, a lot of people think there's some significance to the anointing ceremony being held here in Rochelle rather than in Caren. Folks think Leopold is the front-runner. They also believe it's why the forty-year-old duke suddenly took a wife. The theory is the bishop offered him the crown on the condition he got married first. If that's true, I bet there are plenty of nobles who would like to spoil that plan and make the bishop pick someone else."

"So, why not just kill Leopold?" Royce asked.

"Duke doesn't leave the Estate often; the duchess is always running around town. And it's easier to kill a strange, imported merchant's daughter than a man who you know, possibly like, and could even be related to. You might not want him dead, just don't want him to be king."

"Okay, but why wasn't her body next to that De Luda guy? Why go to the trouble of dragging her away before killing her?" Hadrian asked.

"I wondered about that, too." Roland grinned like the boy who knew the answer to the riddle. "But I realized if she were dead, the duke could just pick another wife, marry her quick, and nothing would change. But with her missing . . . well, he can't remarry. Not for a while. Not if there's a chance she's still alive. It's the not-knowing that lowered his chances. The bishop will pick a less risky candidate. Unfortunately, that means it could be any of a hundred or so nobles."

"But you have a favorite?"

Roland nodded. "I'd lay money on Floret Killian, Duke of Quarters. He's popular and powerful and the sort to do whatever it takes. But I can't make any accusation without proof, and I don't have any."

"You mentioned the duchess was coming back from a meeting with the merchant guild. Do you know what that was about?" Royce asked.

"Stirring up trouble is what I hear. She'd been sticking her nose in stuff a woman shouldn't be involved in. But I guess things are different in Colnora. That's where she came from. I suppose you already know that. She didn't fit in all that well around here. Rochelle has particular ways of doing things. People have roles, and I guess she didn't like hers much." Roland put another log on the fire.

"What about the driver?" Royce asked. "Was he killed, too?"

Roland hesitated. "Driver?"

"You mentioned that the duchess and De Luda were in a carriage. So what happened to their driver?"

Roland's eyes shifted back and forth. "Only De Luda's body was found. Guess the driver ran off."

"Where's the carriage now? Is it back at the duke's estate?"

Roland shook his head. "Just down the street. They took it to Woffington's shop to be cleaned. Everything was covered in blood."

He took another sip. "I'm sorry, but it looks like the two of you came a long way for nothing. Still, I hope you'll stick around a few days. I've been busy as a hummingbird on the last day of summer, but we could have a drink when I'm off duty. Maybe I can lure Hadrian back to Alburn now that we aren't at odds with Warric anymore."

"Oh, I think we'll be staying awhile," Royce said with a friendly smile that sent chills up Hadrian's back.

Woffington & Sons was located not far from the river, in an area where everything, even the carriage shop, was built of old stone, a material normally reserved for castles or churches. Royce felt certain it hadn't always been used for building coaches. The architecture was too sophisticated, too decorative for a business, even one that catered to nobles. Fluted pillars held up an arched, engraved transom, and over the big door crouched one of the town's many stone gargoyles. This one was endowed with a barbed tail curled around its feet as it perched vulture-like, peering down menacingly on all who entered.

Hadrian had followed Royce without a word, hanging back a step, and Royce was still deciding whether to admonish him. The problem stemmed from the fact that Hadrian might not have made a mistake. On a purely objective level, his partner had committed a monumental blunder. They were there to commit murder, probably more than one, and he'd just declared their association with the events to come—to a high-ranking officer of the city guard, no less. As ridiculous as that was, though, Royce had to admit Hadrian's direct approach had resulted in a bounty of information that might have required weeks to obtain by less direct methods, and Royce was starting to suspect that time might be a factor. And there was also one more restraint on Royce's rebuke, one more reason to suspect that Hadrian's knack for dumb luck might have turned out okay, but he needed more information to be sure.

The shop wasn't far from the plaza, so it was obvious why the carriage had been brought there. From the shop's entrance, Royce could see the cathedral. The massive edifice with its soaring bell towers dominated the eastern bank. Central Plaza itself hosted numerous shops, statues, and fountains. The river's early-morning fog had yet to burn off, but the square was already filling with pedestrians and hawkers.

That's where it happened.

Despite Captain Wyberg's assurances about the habits of Rochelle's residents, Royce found it an odd locale for a murder. Killing in a place so conspicuous generally meant the perpetrator was trying to send a message.

That's what I would do. He caught himself. *Have done.* He thought again. *More than once.*

This realization was both intriguing and disturbing, leaving Royce as curious as he was concerned.

Who are we dealing with?

A kid that Royce guessed to be about thirteen spotted the pair lingering at the shop's open doors. Brushing himself free of sawdust, he trotted over. A wide belt with tools hanging from loops, most of them chisels and wooden mallets, hung from his waist. "Can I help you, gentlemen?" Over the boy's shoulder, Royce spotted four men working in a large open space held up by old stacked-stone pillars. Suspended from the ceiling or piled on shelves was a plethora of wheels, raw lumber, and metal poles. Royce counted eight carriages in various states of production.

"Officer Roland Wyberg of the city guard informs me that this is where the duke's carriage is being repaired," Royce said with a dash of aggressiveness.

The boy straightened up. "Oh, ah, yes, sir. Are you from the Estate, sir?"

Royce folded his arms slowly, studying the boy with a dismissive expression that wasn't too difficult for him to conjure up. The kid was fresh-faced enough to have been a spring lamb. "I'm investigating the events of that night. Let's just say that, shall we?" He gave the boy a sly smile. "You'd be one of the Woffington sons, is that right?"

"Ah, yes, I'm Brian Woffington, sir."

"And, Brian, are you working on the carriage?"

"My father and brother Steven are, but they're not here just now. They went to get material for the interior. They're over at Handon's place on the west bank."

"That's fine; we don't need to talk to them. We only want to take a look at the coach. Can you take me to it?"

"Um, yes, sir."

Brian led them around tables, racks, bolts of leather, and massive spools of thread. The other sons looked over, but no one said anything.

"Working on a lot of wagons," Hadrian mentioned. "Business must be good."

"Rochelle has over three hundred carriages for hire," the kid told them. "Keeping them in good order sometimes requires replacing the whole rig."

They dodged around a few more tables, and in the back of the shop, Royce and Hadrian came across the gaudiest coach they had ever seen. It appeared to be made entirely of gold, right down to its wheels. The door panels were the only exception. There, the surface had been painted to depict a man on a rearing horse, his mantle flying in the wind as a beautiful woman watched in awe. The interior was gutted, the seats removed and lying on the shop's floor, their skin stripped bare, revealing the wooden frames. Royce went over to the window and peered in for a closer look. Tufts of padding, and the remains of regularly placed tacks, indicated the carriage had once been upholstered from floor to ceiling. All that remained was the skeleton of bare wood.

Royce stepped back and continued examining the carriage's exterior.

"Mind if I . . ." Royce pointed toward the driver's berth.

"Hmm? Oh, go ahead," Brian replied. "It's not real gold, by the way. Just painted to look like it. If it were real, the horses would die trying to pull it. Oh, and we'd need a troop of soldiers to guard the shop at night." The boy laughed.

Royce hopped up and made a quick study of the seat. "Has this bench been repaired?"

Brian shook his head. "No, sir. Didn't touch nothing. Weren't no damage. The bloodstains were inside."

As on most coaches, the footboard was adjustable. Royce positioned himself on the bench as if he was driving, and with his feet on the board, his knees came to his chest. "No one changed anything up here? Adjusted the seat?"

"Nope."

"When they brought the carriage over, someone must have driven it, right?"

Brian shook his head again. "Happened just down by the river, not far at all. The horse was led."

"Did you know who was driving the carriage the night of the attack?"

"Driving?" the boy asked, and thought for a moment before shaking his head. "Probably Ickard Wimbly."

"Probably? You don't know?"

"He's the duke's coachman. So, I *think* it was him. I can't remember exactly if—"

"Wasn't Wimbly," one of the other sons of Woffington paused in his work to chime in. This son was at least a couple of years older than Brian, having the start of a narrow beard. "He *never* drives the duchess. Steven has been down there a lot. Talks to Wimbly all the time. The man refused to drive *her*. Called the duchess the Whiskey Wench."

Hadrian gave them both a skeptical look. "How does the duke's coachman refuse to drive the duke's wife?"

"And how did he still have a job after calling her a wench?" Royce added.

"Wimbly used to drive the duke's father. He's a fixture at the Estate and very well respected. And he's not the only one who felt that way, trust me. The duchess wasn't exactly admired."

"And the duke put up with it?"

All of the sons of Woffington exchanged looks of agreement. "Not sure if he actually knew, but don't know how he couldn't."

"So who drove?"

The sons all either shook their heads or shrugged. "Wimbly's not picky when it comes to finding someone to drive *her,* so it coulda been anyone at the Estate."

"And it happened at night, yes?" Royce turned back to Brian.

"Yep, was dark."

"And do you know which route the carriage took from the Merchants' Guild?"

"Went right by this shop down the hill, past Grom Galimus, then over toward the bridge."

Grom Galimus? Royce wasn't an expert in languages, but knew a fair amount of Old Speech, elvish, and even a handful of dwarven words learned from Merrick, who had taught Royce to read and write. Of course, a lot of the elvish, and all the dwarfish terms, were various forms of profanity. Grom galimus was Old Speech, or elven, Royce couldn't remember which, but he did recall what it meant: *his glory.*

The kid nodded. "That's where it happened. That's where she was killed."

"You think the duchess is dead?"

"Of course. Nobody survives a Morgan attack. My guess is she got scared and tried to run. Big mistake. When they find her body, it'll be a mess. The Morgan has been busy these days. Just the other night a little elven boy was ripped apart, and a Calian girl was found the same way near the harbor."

"What makes you think the duchess ran?" Hadrian asked.

"'Cuz she would've been safe if she just stayed inside. But the duchess is new to these parts and probably didn't know."

"Didn't know what?"

"That monsters are repelled by the color blue, the color of purity, like the clear sky or clean water. Can't tell now, but the whole inside of the carriage was covered in plush blue velvet. If the duchess knew that color drove away evil spirits, she would have known that she'd be safe as long as she stayed inside."

Royce nodded, pretending to agree, but he was certain that the duchess's fate would have been the same no matter the color of the carriage's upholstery.

"No one ever notices the driver," Royce told Hadrian as they walked downhill toward the bridge, and Woffington & Sons became just one of many doors along a stone edifice. "I discovered that years ago. Servants are invisible except to one another. A baron can always tell you his horse's name, but he rarely knows the name of the groomsman who cares for it. They're the perfect blind spot for attacking the aristocracy. You saw how well it worked with Lord Exeter."

Royce was speaking quickly. He wasn't the sort to think out loud, but he was onto something. Wheels were turning, and he was either bouncing ideas off Hadrian to gauge their accuracy or educating him in the finer points of intrigue. Most of their lengthier conversations were along one of those lines. Hadrian rarely knew which was which and suspected Royce didn't, either.

"So you think the driver was involved?"

"If he wasn't, he'd have been found dead next to De Luda."

"Maybe he was dragged off like the duchess."

"Taking *her* is one thing, but there'd be no reason to go to the extra trouble for a no-account driver. If all the bodies were missing, you might have a point. But since De Luda was left behind, the killer or killers weren't concerned about cleaning up after themselves. No, the driver isn't dead."

They were entering the plaza, which turned out to be an attractive circle of decorative paving stones that highlighted the area between the mouth of the bridge and the massive doors of the cathedral. The last time they'd passed this way, it had been night and the whole square had been a mass of people jostling to push through a bottleneck, making it impossible to see the giant church's doors, much less the paving stones. Now the plaza served as a vast open space providing a stunning view of the cathedral's grandeur.

"His glory," Royce said.

"What?" Hadrian asked.

"It's the translation of the cathedral's name. Grom Galimus means 'his glory.' I'm guessing *his* refers to Novron." Royce pointed at the sculpture in front.

The statue of the first emperor looked bigger, more impressive in the absence of human clutter, though even at that early hour a few people knelt at its stairs, heads down, praying. Around them, carters were still setting up. The various vendors were busy putting out displays or propping up awnings, although some of the carts had permanent roofs. A flight of pigeons burst skyward as the clang of Grom Galimus's bells marked the hour, an event that, annoyingly, occurred all day and night.

"So, you're not mad at me for being so forthcoming with Roland?" Hadrian asked as they passed a bakery where the owner was setting wares out in display cases.

The smell of baking bread came two steps later. Then a breeze blew it away, replacing warmth and comfort with the fishy scent of the river, which wasn't bad, but the two odors clashed, opposites of each other. One was home and hearth, the other exploration and adventure. Hadrian felt a sense of loss without knowing why. Such was the mysterious nature of smells and memories.

"Thought about it," Royce replied.

"That's all? I expected you'd be ranting and throwing a fit the moment we left. I was thinking about excuses to tell passersby."

"What'd you come up with?"

"Best one was that you were stung by a bee. Although I thought it would be fun to say you were a snake charmer and one got loose in your pant leg."

Royce shook his head, frowning. "You really are terrible at lying. Need to work on that. In our profession, that's a serious handicap."

"So, why didn't you berate me?"

"Because, as usual, your luck held out."

Hadrian's brows rose. "In what way?"

The last of the fog was lifting. The soft white wisps hovered over the water, the morning reluctant to cast off its bedcovers. When it parted, an uncompromised view of the water and the series of stone arches that made up the bridge emerged. Sunlight glinted on the river.

"I think there's a good chance we won't need to go on a killing spree." Royce sounded almost sad.

A TALE OF TWO SOLDIERS

Hadrian had never planned on a spree of any kind, but he saw no reason to interrupt a current flowing in his direction. "So, you think she's still alive?"

Royce nodded. "Starting to look that way."

"I say she might be alive, and you think I'm crazy. The captain of the city guard and a kid at the local carriage shop tell you she is likely dead, and you think she's alive. Why do you always insist on taking the opposite of anyone's opinion?"

"Because most people are idiots. But in this case, lack of a body makes a compelling argument. To hear your friend tell it, corpses pop up all over the place, but there's no sign of the duchess's? When I thought her husband did her in, I figured she was in a hole under the Estate or, more likely, chained to a boulder under the bay, but now it looks like he's not involved."

"Do you think it was the *Morgan?*"

Royce frowned. "Of course not. There's no such thing as a monster that stalks city streets and mutilates people."

Hadrian's brows rose.

Royce frowned. "You know what I mean: monsters that *fear the color blue*. The carriage had to be reupholstered because of the cofferer's blood, which means Devon De Luda was attacked while still inside. That the kid missed such a hole in his logic demonstrates how people are willing to overlook the obvious if it doesn't fit their beliefs. We'll know more once we find the driver."

"How we going to do that? The guy's practically invisible. No one has any clue who he is."

"I do. And I know enough to be sure I'm not going to like him."

Hadrian laughed. "That narrows the search to nearly everyone on the face of Elan."

Royce started to respond, then stopped and nodded. "Okay, sure, but I'm *really* not going to like *this* guy."

CHAPTER NINE
THE GOLD EATER

Genny Hargrave scraped the silver coin across the stone floor. She paused frequently to check the sharpness of the edge, and to listen.

She didn't hear anyone outside the door or walls. No one to *see,* either. The door to the little cell, while solid enough to keep her imprisoned, had gaps aplenty. She'd found a handful of spy holes, and at that moment they all agreed: Her captors had left, and she was alone. Genny made the best use of her time by sharpening the edge of the coin, but each scrape chilled her.

What if he *comes back while* she's *gone? What if he discovers what I'm doing?*

He was Villar, and although a last name had been mentioned, it wasn't clear enough to catch. *She* was a significant improvement over the mad dog that was Villar. Mad, that's how

Genny thought about him, like a snarling rabid animal. He had a kind of caustic hatred doled out to everyone, for any reason.

Genny knew the type. She hadn't transformed from illegally distilling and distributing liquor on the black market to a key player in Winter's Whiskey of Colnora by attending cordial dinners with dignified aristocrats. In the same way, this wasn't the first cold, filthy bucket Genny had sat on. Men like Villar were mean, unpredictable, dangerous, and sadly plentiful. Her father had been one. She liked to think she'd tamed the madness out of the man, that the money, power, and respect had quieted the demons unchained by his wife's death. But she knew *quieted* wasn't *gone* and the mania would always be there, watchful and looking for a reason to return.

What if neither comes back at all?

Genny still didn't know where she was, couldn't even be positive how long she'd been there. More than two but less than three weeks was her best estimation. Early on, she hadn't bothered keeping track of the days. She had expected to die, and that one thought filled her mind to the exclusion of all else. Then, as time went on she had been forced to reevaluate. *No sense keeping me alive just to kill me later,* she reasoned, but had to admit a bias in her conclusion. The same could be said about her expectation of rescue. Her husband was the duke, and he controlled a full contingent of city guards. With such resources, could a rescue be far away? Apparently it could. As the days dragged on, she began to wonder if something had happened to Leo.

In all that time, Genny learned little about her prison. Didn't even know what sort of place it was. The stone was marred with pockmarks, lichen, and ivy, which made her suspect she was outside the main gates. She hadn't seen much beyond the Estate and the Merchant District since her arrival in the city. Parts of Rochelle might be deep in jungles—how would she know? There might even be a *ruined quarter* that she had yet to discover. Still, her little square of the world was unusually quiet. All she ever heard was birdsong. No sound of carriages, barkers, blows of hammers, or cries of babies. She'd never found a part of her new city—or any city—that was this quiet. Most important, she never heard the chimes of Grom Galimus.

They took me to the surrounding countryside, but where and why?

She tried to remember the night Villar grabbed her. So much of it remained muddled, like a nightmare recalled hours after waking. She'd witnessed Devon's death. Villar had wanted her to see, but it wasn't a matter of pride. The man wasn't a professional, no expertly slit throat or precisely inserted blade. It'd been brutal and bloody. Villar had stabbed Devon repeatedly with a small knife. The violence and gore paralyzed her. Genny was no pampered debutante, and before becoming the newest member of the nobility, she often enjoyed gambling at cards and impressing men with her capacity for holding hard liquor, but she'd never been exposed to anything like that. Watching a man butchered close enough to feel the spray of his blood was more than enough to horrify. She couldn't move, couldn't think. The hood came next, a bag placed over her head and cinched tightly. Then she was shoved into a cart, covered with rough blankets, and off they went.

Too afraid to scream or cry, she cowered, something she hadn't done since she was eight. At any moment, she was certain she'd be killed. If she'd been thinking, she might have taken note of the trip's length, turns, bumps, or accompanying sounds, but all she could think of was the way the knife had sounded when plunging over and over into Devon's chest. That and the gasping gurgle that came from his mouth. He'd been trying to say something, and Genny thought it might have been *please stop,* but she couldn't be sure. When the cart had finally halted, she was carried quite a distance before being dropped into the cell. A metal collar was fastened around her neck, and a chain secured her to a wall. A door slammed, and she heard a lock click. *A lock, not a bolt.* She took note of that. While lying on cold stone with the bag still over her head, she heard her assailants talking, their voices muffled by the door. The memory of the quarrel was so vivid because it had provided hope. Genny could recall it word for word.

"Where did the blood come from?" the woman had asked, her tone full of fear.

"She wasn't alone," Villar replied.

"Who did you kill?" The woman's tone had changed to anger.

"I have no idea, a courtier of some kind."

"No one was supposed to get hurt!" she shouted.

"No one was supposed to be with her, either. He saw me. Did you want a witness?"

"This is bad."

"It's what it is. Deal with it."

Genny clung to the most important line from that argument: No one was supposed to get hurt. If that was true, her death wasn't inevitable; it might even be unlikely.

THE GOLD EATER

That first night, she had waited for hours, until certain she was alone, before finding the knots, untying the string, and pulling the hood off. She found herself in the small stone room, no window and only one door. Light from a small fire on the far side seeped underneath and around it, as did an awful vinegar odor. The door was new and very sturdy. The freshly cut wood still smelled of the forest, and sap dripped from knotholes. The collar around Genny's neck was closed and fastened to the chain by a large iron padlock that hung on her chest like the gaudy pendant of a horrid necklace. The other end of the chain was bolted to the wall opposite the door. The restraint granted her full range of the room, but nothing more. There had been a pile of straw, which she assumed was meant to serve as her bed, but it had since been scattered and matted. She scooped it into a pile each night, but each morning it was strewn about, which made her wonder about her dreams. She couldn't recall them, but was sure they weren't pleasant. She had the bucket, the straw, and two surprisingly thick wool blankets. She lay on one; the other she wrapped around herself, tucking the corners down under her legs and shoulders. The cell was cold but, thanks to the blankets, not unbearable. She was able to sleep, and that was something.

She hadn't been hurt, and nothing was taken from her. Not that Genny had much when pulled from the carriage, just the dress she wore, her shoes, and a tiny wrist bag. She was surprised they hadn't taken the purse. Not that it had much money in it, only a few silver—emergency coins—she called them, but why had they abducted her if not for money? The purse also had one other item, the key to her traveling trunk. She'd used the big sea chest as luggage when she moved to Rochelle and continued to keep it in her room as the one personal space she reserved for herself. It held nothing of value to anyone but her. The trunk was filled only with memories and mementos. She had a bottle of whiskey from "the old days," and a diary, and her mother's rings that were too small for Genny, and letters from her father. She kept those in the chest because she didn't want Leo reading how much Gabriel hated him for "stealing" his daughter. The trunk couldn't help her now, nor could her dress or shoes, but the coins and key were treasures. She had long since hidden them in her cell, in the stone's cracks, fearful her captors would finally notice the purse and take it. She couldn't afford to lose her treasures.

Most of the time, Genny was left alone in her cell. She was pleased that Villar was rarely there. When he did appear, his visits were mercifully brief. Erratic and berating, he would argue with the woman, insult Genny, or rant about the misdeeds of others. He usually left in a huff. Genny preferred the other warden. She was quiet, reserved, and respectful.

A noise outside the door caused Genny to stop in mid-stroke. She stashed the coin, went to the door, and quickly pressed her cheek to peer through the crack in the slats. She was relieved it wasn't Villar. Standing near the entrance and shaking the rain out of her soaked shawl was the woman, the one Villar called Mercator Sikara.

Mercator pulled off her soaked dress and dropped it on the floor. Long ago she'd given up trying to save her kirtle.

Surrendering to the inevitable, she'd dyed the whole thing, but it didn't help. The front and sleeves were darker by several shades. Still, the garment fared better than her skin. The creamy white cloth had turned blue, but Mercator's brown skin became a blackish purple. Standing naked in the faint light, she looked like one great bruise.

On the bright side, I have to be the safest person in Rochelle.

She dried off and wrapped up in one of her blankets. Soft, thick, and warm, it ought to sell for close to a gold tenent, considering the ridiculous amounts nobles paid for anything blue. Mercator bought raw material from Calian weavers who either didn't know or, like Erasmus, didn't care she was a mir. Mercator had an excellent eye for quality, and made good deals buying cloth for five to eight copper. When able, she sold the blankets to merchants like Erasmus for double. The blue dye made all the difference. After more than a century, Mercator knew how to cultivate and harvest woad, a genial flowering plant that produced a less-than-effective blue dye. To compensate, she had to soak and dry each woven cloth or bolt of yarn, then repeat the process a dozen times. The process was time consuming, but she couldn't possibly afford to purchase indigo, a rare imported plant that was exceedingly expensive. The source of the dye wasn't what mattered; the only thing people cared about was the deep-blue color. Her process, while time consuming, produced the desired result. If she weren't mir, she would've been rich.

Mercator put the kettle on, stoked the fire, and then checked her work. Popping the lid on a clay pot marked with the blue handprint, she fished out the cloth, held it up, and let it drip while she studied the shade. It looked perfect, which meant it would be too light when dry—once the excess dye was removed.

With a disappointed sigh, Mercator submerged the cloth in the pot again. She had close to a dozen of the old clay vessels, which were found in the belly of the ruined church. At least she thought it was a church, but from the outside it was hard to tell it was even a building. Tall grass and bushes grew all around. If not for the arched doorway, the place could easily be mistaken for a stony hill.

The pots were huge old urns, a good three feet in height and beautifully crafted. Mercator almost hated employing them. Still, she had to use something, and these were ideal for her purposes. Mercator spent the late summer and fall gathering woad. She fermented the leaves in a tub of water mixed with a bit of lime. In the spring, she planted seeds that she'd meticulously salvaged, only a fraction of which would take root.

In winter, she spent most of her days dunking cloth in the blue dye just as she would do that day. She wrung out her soaked dress as best she could, dressed, and went back to work. Crossing to the last pot, the one she'd been working on the longest, she submerged her arms up to her elbows. Mercator held the wool under as if drowning a small animal, squeezing the material as hard as she could, wringing the cloth below the surface to help infuse the dye more completely into the material.

Dye! Dye, you miserable woolly lamb! She tried to smile, amazed at the insanity she indulged in to keep from going mad.

It wasn't working.

Not-thinking was her best hope. Work kept her mind occupied, but she was running out of cloth, and after speaking to Erasmus Nym, it was becoming impossible not to—

"Any chance you're thinking of feeding me in the near future?" The duchess's voice came from the other room. Even muffled by the only door in the ruin, the duchess was loud. And she talked a lot. "I know I could stand to eat a bit less, but there is a difference between a diet and starvation."

Mercator pulled up the cloth, let it drip, and studied it carefully.

Good enough.

Once upon a time, *good enough* was never acceptable. Mercator used to fuss about such things, but once upon a time she'd been younger. Age, she realized with some regret, had diluted her need for perfection. *Passion,* they called it. Everyone placed such high value on an intensity of spirit, but it was like the dye: valuable when focused, limited, and used properly. She looked down at herself—*but what good is anything when randomly splattered?* The young were fountains of energy and vigor, running blind sprints into imagined lands. Mercator was done with races.

I'm also done with this cloth.

She dropped it into a vinegar bath.

One more thing that makes this place smell so grand.

"In case you forgot, food is a plant or animal that can be consumed," the woman bellowed through the locked door. "It's required to live. Did you know that? Some people even enjoy the process of eating. They do it every day. More than once, even."

"Salt," Mercator said.

"What? What did you say? Did you say *salt?*"

"Yes, salt. It's a rock, a mineral. Neither plant nor animal and it must be consumed to live. It's the only rock you *can* eat, and you have to consume it in order to survive."

"True enough, but it doesn't quite fill the belly like a good roasted leg of lamb, now does it? People eat all kinds of things that aren't filling. You can eat gold, too."

"Gold is a metal and definitely not required to sustain life. No one would ever eat that."

"I have."

Mercator was wiping her hands and arms on the blue-stained towel she kept near the pots. She stopped and stared at the closed door that separated the outer room from the little chamber where they kept the woman. She had tried to refrain from speaking to the prisoner. At first, it was important that the duchess know as little about them as possible. As the days dragged into weeks, trying to avoid the woman was just pointless. "You're joking, right?"

"No, I'm not. Chefs make it very thin and lay it on top of chocolate cakes."

"You disgust me."

"Well, I can't say it's my favorite, but when it's served at the dinner of an important potential partner, one shouldn't insult the host by turning up one's nose, now should one?"

"People are starving all over the world, and rich people eat gold?"

"I know, I know! It's a ridiculous thing to do. I can assure you it wouldn't be my first choice. I'd much rather dine on a fine steak or perhaps a goose. Oh yes, what I wouldn't give for a roasted goose, one where the skin has been crisped to a caramel brown. Perhaps some oysters and mussels in a butter-wine sauce. You know, there are easier ways to kill me than starvation."

"You're not starving. It takes more than a month to die from lack of food. Being a person who consumes gold, I would expect you to be more learned."

Mercator took the cloth out of the vinegar rinse and hung it up on the line that ran the length of the area under the dome. A curious choice for a roof, it was the dome that made Mercator assume the little ruin had once been a church because the only other dome she'd seen was the one over the altar of the grand cathedral of Rochelle. This little dome above Mercator's dye industry was made of crude interlocking stones the same as the walls. While the ruins were ideal as a hidden workshop, the site also dripped with ancient mystery. All of Alburn was that way, and Rochelle was its graveyard of inconvenient secrets.

The duchess was one of those, and becoming more inconvenient by the minute. "And why do such a thing?" Mercator asked. "Why eat gold at all? What's the point? It doesn't benefit you, and it can't taste good. So why?"

"Same reason people live in houses with too many rooms, have more clothes than they can wear, and ride down the block in a horse-drawn carriage rather than walk. Only the very rich can afford such things, so they use these extravagances to demonstrate to others the height of their status."

"But everyone already knows you're rich."

"You'd think that, but there is one very important person that everyone wishes to impress. Someone who rarely gets the message of a person's true worth. People will go to any lengths, like eating gold, to convince this person that they have value."

"And who is that?"

"Why, ourselves, dear."

Such an odd woman.

They had abducted her in a desperate gamble to change things. But it didn't seem to be working. And if something didn't happen soon, everything would fall apart. So many depended on Mercator, and she felt like she was letting them all down.

Things will improve. I'm going to make it better. That's my responsibility as matriarch of the Sikara. I owe that to my grandfather and his father before him.

She had told Seton that spring was coming, but Mercator had failed to explain what that could mean. *Villar will have his way, all because I . . . because I . . .*

This isn't helping.

She took a deep breath and tried to calm down. She felt weak, even a little dizzy. Her stomach ached. She looked at the duchess's door and frowned. Maybe it *was* time to eat.

At first, Genny believed the poor quality and extremely small portions of food had been a tool to weaken her, make her more pliable and easier to control. She had since revised that theory. *They're doing it out of spite.*

They had a noble duchess at their mercy, and they were torturing her for entertainment. They fed her gruel as humiliation. That was their plan, to beat her down, starve, degrade, and intimidate her. When she was desperate, perhaps they would give her dead rats and laugh, goading her to eat them. It was possible that the poor treatment was part of some clever plan, but Genny had come to believe that it was merely for sport. How grand it must be to embarrass her, what hoots, what laughs they must share. How wonderful to finally make one of *them* suffer.

Only I'm not one of them. *Not really.* She grimaced at the worn wooden bowl and remembered a similar one she had eaten from as a child. *I'm not one of anything. The masses see me as privileged, and the nobles see me as the unwashed.*

If Duchess Dederia, Duke Floret's wife, had been abducted, she wouldn't have survived the first hour. The moment they stuffed Dederia's head into that smelly bag, she would have dropped dead.

They're fortunate they got me instead. Lucky on the one hand, not so fortunate on the other.

Genny was done playing nice.

No one got anywhere by being timid. No one advanced through whispers. This was a lesson she'd learned early.

Genny had observed that successful men were bold and acted confident, even when they weren't. They declared they were right, insisted it was so, and, amazingly, people who ought to know better, believed. Even if they were wrong half of the time, they were right the other half. After a while, the mistakes were forgotten, but the victories never were—the men made a point of reminding everyone of those. Genny had seen this, learned from it, and practiced what she had dubbed the Art of Bluster. She'd always had a big mouth, literally and metaphorically. And she was smarter than she looked, which at first was a hindrance, but later had become a weapon.

Peering out through one of the cracks in the door, Genny wanted to make certain there was an audience for the tirade she was about to unleash. Mercator was at the cook fire, dishing out her own meal. She poured the same dismal slop into an identical wooden bowl. Not a bit of fruit, nut, syrup, or berry was added. There was no meat, no bread, no cider or beer. Genny watched, baffled. She'd been certain her captives served themselves a different meal. *Who would willingly eat such miserable food?*

She stared as Mercator drained the last of the porridge into a bowl. That's when Genny realized the most remarkable thing of all. After pouring out the remnants, Mercator had significantly less in her bowl than what Genny had been served.

Is this really what she lives on?

Mercator sat down on the floor, crossed her legs, and ate that half serving of porridge, lifting the bowl to her mouth and drinking it in like soup. Even at their poorest, the Winter family never ate this badly.

Genny knelt at the reach of her chain, staring out the gap in the door, studying her captor. Mercator was a miserable sight. She was thin and ragged, her skin dark—reddish brown like an acorn—except her arms, of course. She was small and more than lithe. Mercator looked like a deer in late winter. Stick-like legs, a long slender neck, high, hollow cheeks, and the infamous oblong ears that declared the woman's elven heritage. Mercator was a mir, and all the mir Genny had ever seen were thin.

THE GOLD EATER

Are all mir in want of food?

Genny had already identified the need to empower the Calians and dwarves, but it turned out she had a blind spot—the mir. They were, as always, invisible. That was before Genny came to know one. Before she was forced to watch Mercator struggle to survive. Before she saw her eat the mouse's share of the porridge. Before she saw a person where there wasn't supposed to be one.

Mercator stopped eating. Her head bowed over the remains of her miserable meal, and with raised knees, she rocked in a regular rhythm. Try as she might to be quiet, Genny could still hear the sobs.

"What's wrong?" the duchess asked.

After a gasp and sniffle, the mir lifted her head, brushed her hair back, and surprised Genny with an answer. "Your husband isn't doing anything. He's not trying to save you."

"Leo? What do you mean?"

Mercator shook her damp hair. "When Villar grabbed you, he left our demands in the carriage—a simple set of instructions. Once they were followed, you'd be set free." Her lower lip shook as her mouth pulled into a deep frown, the sort attempted in the hope of restraining emotion—an effort that never worked. "We didn't even ask for much. Hardly anything at all. But rather than agree, or even make a counterproposal, he's refused to bargain."

"Demands?" Genny said mostly to herself. "You asked for money? A ransom? Is that what this is about?"

Mercator made a loud disgusted sound. "We aren't thieves. We just want . . . a chance to live." She sniffled again. "All we ask is to have the same opportunities as everyone else. For no known reason, Calians are denied the privilege to open their own shops. Dwarves are forbidden to engage in any trading, why is anyone's guess. And my people, the mir, are banned from everything, labeled outlaws at birth. Our crime is existing."

"Surely you exaggerate. You make and sell dyed cloth."

"Illegally. And if I'm caught, or if those who risk doing business with me are apprehended, we both face mutilation or death depending on the whims of the city guard who discovers the offense. The punishments are capricious and subjective." She shook her head and toggled a finger between them. "This right here, my talking to you, is against the law."

"What do you mean?"

"A mir isn't allowed to speak to a citizen of the city. Doing so will result in a beating. Technically, I can't even look you in the eye. That, too, is forbidden, although rarely enforced. We can't take water from wells or fountains, can't fish or hunt for food. We can't beg. Renting property is prohibited; so is sleeping on the streets or in alleys. We are banned from the bathhouses and denied the ability to clean ourselves in the river or bay. We mustn't start fires to warm ourselves, have to speak in whispers so as to not disturb *the better folk,* and are forbidden to teach our children to read, write, or learn numbers."

"How do you live?"

"That's just it, we aren't supposed to."

"What did you ask of my husband? What did you demand."

"We *begged* for the privilege to work, to buy and sell, and to rent land the same as anyone else. We asked to be made citizens of the city and be granted the same privileges, opportunities, and security granted to everyone else."

"That's all?"

"Yes. Your husband could fix everything with a signature, but when it comes to granting even basic dignity to the Pitifuls, even the life of his new wife isn't enough to make him do what is right."

"I can't believe that."

"Neither can I, but here we are."

Mercator hated crying. Knowing the duchess was peering out, seeing her moment of weakness, made it worse. At this point, all she had was her dignity, and the duchess was stripping away even that.

"You know you're being foolish," the duchess said. "Kidnapping me was about as stupid a thing as a person could do."

"So is calling me stupid if you ever want to eat again."

"You don't understand. I was trying to help you."

"By calling me stupid?"

"Don't be silly."

"Silly and stupid, I guess you really don't like food, do you?" Mercator picked up a rag and wiped her face.

"You misunderstand. Let me explain. The night you abducted me, do you know what I was doing? Where I was coming from?"

"I heard you were on a shopping spree. Checking out a blue vest to give to your husband."

"That was a momentary stop on my way back from a meeting with the Merchants' Guild."

"Merchants' Guild?" Mercator stared at the closed door. She couldn't see the duchess but guessed the woman was peering through the slats the way Mercator often did when trying to tell if the duchess was asleep. "What business does a duchess have with the guild? Are they not importing the fashions you desire?"

"I was trying to persuade them to grant membership to the Calians."

Mercator let out an absurd laugh. "Why would you do that? Because you anticipated being kidnapped and thought it might be a good way to—"

"Because this city is a financial mess!" the duchess burst out with enough indignation to overpower the bells of Grom Galimus.

She sounded so sincere that Mercator forgot her sarcasm. She forgot her indifference as well, her shield against sympathy. Instead, she listened.

"An absolute disaster and I'm just the woman to fix it. I wasn't always a duchess, you understand. Before coming here, I was a merchant. I helped run one of the most profitable businesses in the most successful mercantile city in the world. I may not know why the sun circles Elan, but I know how to make money. When you look like I do, it's a necessity. Believe me when I say I love Leo, but the man knows nothing about finances. I asked to see his books and he showed me his library of poetry! Ha! Can you believe it? This city possesses tremendous untapped potential. Most people don't see the downtrodden as valuable, but then they don't think much of me, either, and I helped turn an illegal moonshine operation into a respected distillery. Other people's ignorance is always a moneymaker, remember that."

Mercator wasn't certain she'd be capable of accurately remembering any of the duchess's ramblings but didn't doubt the truth of what she said.

"We are a port city with unique access to the exotic eastern trade routes, but we refuse to embrace our best resources. Instead, we force them to deal illegally, which not only denies the duchy tax on their profits, but it also lowers the income of legitimate businesses, depriving us of even more income."

Genny's blood was obviously up; Mercator could hear her walking back and forth in her little cell. "The situation is even more dire with the dwarves. Their neighborhood of Littleton should be a gold mine for this city. Raw goods arriving from Calis and Galeannon should be shaped into works of art by their hands. The results would be triple the profit when those finished goods are exported. With its wealth of natural talent and geographic position, Rochelle should be the crown jewel of the east, the powerhouse producer of Alburn. Instead, we flounder in debt."

She paused, perhaps to catch her breath, then went on, "This is why I screamed at all those pasty-faced shopkeepers who were too locked in their traditions and too blinded by intolerance and idiocy to see that they would stand to double their profit as well. A rising sea lifts all boats. I demanded they grant acceptance to all Calians interested in doing business in our city, or I would triple their taxes—for the good of the people, you understand."

"That's why De Luda was with you."

"Yes. While he didn't agree with my ideas, he was obligated to make the introductions. Ironically, he was murdered by the very people who would have benefited from his continued assistance."

CHAPTER TEN
VENLIN IS STANDING

Bishop Maurice Saldur of Medford stared in awe at the ceiling of the grand chapel inside Grom Galimus. The overhead fresco had been painted by famed imperial artist Elijah Handel. The beauty, the depth, the vividness of color displayed in the image of Novron receiving the Rhelacan from Maribor was the very definition of mastery. Several of the paintings on the walls of the cathedral were also created by Handel, who had been commissioned by Bishop Venlin in the years that directly followed the fall of Percepliquis. Venlin was famously quoted as saying, "Novron spared you from the destruction of the capital, Elijah, so you could decorate the new one." What wasn't painted was carved in marble. Three of the greatest sculptors of all time had worked on the cathedral: Burke Thatcher, who in his youth studied at the Art Academy of Percepliquis; his son

Alrick Thatcher, who surpassed his father; and the greatest of all, Marley Layton, who was best known for creating the massive statue of Novron that graced the plaza outside.

"Amazing, isn't it?" Tynewell said. The bishop mirrored Saldur's upward stare. "This is the closest thing we have to a piece of Novron's empire."

"It's magnificent," Saldur agreed.

"And this is my home," he said with a self-satisfied smile, the sort a man displays after making a pig of himself at a feast.

This was a source of irritation to Saldur that he knew full well was pure jealousy, but he couldn't help himself. *Who could?* Grom Galimus was easily the most sacred place in Elan. Why the patriarch and archbishop chose to dwell in that remote remnant of a castle built by that impious barbarian, Glenmorgan, who literally destroyed the last vestiges of the imperium, was beyond Saldur. Even so, the Crown Tower was a blessed relic compared with Mares Cathedral. Saldur was relegated to a cheap imitation of Grom Galimus built by childish thugs in the cultural desert otherwise known as Melengar. His church had been hastily erected with all the artistry of a blind cow with paint on her tail, and manifested all the sanctity of a whitewashed brothel. *This,* Saldur thought with a sigh while looking up at the marble and gold, *is what religion is all about.*

Catching Tynewell grinning at him, Saldur scowled and said, "Will we be dining here, or should we go out?"

"Rochelle does, indeed, boast numerous cafés and public houses that are a delight." Tynewell was grinding it in now, twisting the dagger, relishing Saldur's envious drool. "But I took the liberty of having meat and bread brought to my office. I felt that in private we could speak more candidly."

Maurice Saldur had hoped for a meal at the pretty coffeehouse across the plaza that he'd passed on the way in. They didn't have such places in Medford, not even in Colnora, but in Rochelle they were everywhere. While he preferred a good brandy to dark coffee, it wasn't seemly for a bishop to linger in a local tavern. Coffee shops were a different matter. In the cultured east, they were seen as sites of intellectual discourse where a learned bishop was a welcome visitor. While Saldur didn't savor the idea of chewing stringy meat across a battered desk in a cramped closet, he nevertheless resigned himself to accept his host's decision. He followed as Tynewell led the way through an intricately carved mahogany door into the Bishop of Alburn's private office.

The moment the door opened, Saldur was dumbfounded. This was just an office the same way Grom Galimus was just a church.

Tynewell led him into a series of rooms every bit as opulent as the cathedral proper. More frescoes, very likely created by Handel, adorned a ceiling never meant to be seen by the general public. They walked right by Tynewell's meticulously polished desk and into a separate suite with plush furniture arranged in a semicircle before a massive marble hearth where a trio of giant logs burned brightly. One wall was a towering stained-glass window; the other another fresco, this one of Novron laughing, with a silver flagon in hand. He was seated in a chair speaking with an elderly man in suspiciously modern church robes. The background was a perfect extension of the room they were in.

The illusion was amazing, and Saldur felt he could walk right through and into that other space.

"Venlin." Tynewell pointed at the older figure in the painting. "He had Handel put Our Lord in his office and him in the picture. This is the most candid image of Novron you'll find. It borders on the obscene, but no one ever sees it except the bishops. The story goes that Venlin ordered its commission to show Novron's human side, and that here, in the sanctity of this behind-the-scenes refuge, we, too, can relax and be human." The bishop sniffed contemptuously. "Personally, I think Venlin was an egotistical narcissist. I'm told that in his old age he thought Novron actually spoke to him." Tynewell stared at the painting that ran from floor to ceiling, making Venlin and Novron life-sized. "Can you imagine His Holiness, the self-proclaimed patriarch, sitting in this room and talking to himself while believing he was speaking to Novron? Astounding, don't you think?" He gestured at the couch. "Please, have a seat."

Only then did Saldur notice there was a banquet of venison and quail on the table before them.

"You live well," Saldur said, sitting and digging in.

"Venlin lived well," Tynewell corrected as he proceeded to close and lock the doors. "I benefit from his legacy." The Bishop of Alburn took a seat across from Saldur, reclining back, crossing his legs, and throwing a long arm out over the cushions. "Did the patriarch send you?"

Saldur ripped the leg off a quail. "Yes, well, not directly, that is. I didn't actually chat with the patriarch. I've never seen the man." He gestured at the painting with the drumstick. "This is the closest I've come to meeting a patriarch of the church. I sometimes wonder if he exists. Maybe Nilnev died a decade ago and the archbishop hasn't told anyone. Seems like something Galien would do, and who would be the wiser? But the archbishop did give me a message that he said came from Nilnev's hand." He pulled a sealed letter from a pocket of his robe and handed it to Tynewell.

The Bishop of Alburn broke the seal, read the note, and smiled.

"Do you mind?" Saldur asked, holding out his hand.

Tynewell shook his head and gave him the letter.

Saldur skimmed the contents quickly. "Well, this is quite an honor. The patriarch has left the selection of the new king up to you. Makes sense. You know your kingdom and can best judge the candidates." Saldur swallowed an excellent mouthful of well-seasoned quail, then reached for the jug of what he hoped would contain wine. "May I?"

"Of course."

Saldur filled a goblet with what sadly turned out to be mead. He wasn't a fan. He raised a greasy finger. "Just remember to pick someone who will be willing to relinquish power when the day comes."

"Will that day come?" Tynewell asked.

Saldur raised his brows. Such a question was tantamount to heresy, but then so was the painting behind him, which was commissioned by the founder of the Church of Nyphron. *This is why we have laws against such things. Exposure to temptation leads to mistakes.*

"I certainly hope so," Saldur said. "Otherwise I murdered an entire royal family and a dozen bureaucrats for nothing."

Tynewell sat up. "The sinking of the *Eternal Empire* was your work?"

Saldur nodded.

"That's not . . . wait . . . how could you possibly arrange for a storm?"

"There wasn't one. That was just the story we circulated, and because we told everyone about a terrible storm several days before the *Eternal Empire* was due to arrive, no one thought it strange that she might have been lost in it."

"So, how did the ship sink?"

"The *Eternal Empire* was an excellent vessel. Brand-new, top-of-the-line three-masted, four-decked frigate, even had a pretty figurehead of a woman with golden wings. Reinhold spared no expense. I couldn't waste something the future empire might one day need."

"It didn't sink?"

"Right now, that ship is in Aquesta harbor being stripped of all identifying marks. We added pretty green pennants and renamed it the *Emerald Storm*. Poetic, don't you think?"

"So, what happened to the royal family?"

"They were allowed to go free." Saldur grinned as his statement produced the expected reaction of shock. Tynewell was so very smug with his grand home, but his majestic life was as precarious as anyone's. Until the day the new empire was established, they were all little more than shadows hiding from the light.

"But . . . but . . ."

Saldur stopped Tynewell with the rise of another greasy hand. "They were out at sea, several miles away from land at the time . . . with their wrists tied."

"Oh."

Saldur found the bread and tore off a chunk. "So, who will you pick?"

"How's that?" Tynewell asked, his eyes shifting, no doubt still imagining the scene of the royal family, their cousins, and all the royal administrators thrown overboard.

"Rumors say you're going to hold a contest, is that so? I honestly think that isn't a good idea."

Isn't a good idea was the understatement of the century. Of course, matters could be framed in such a way that the desired candidate would prove victorious, but what if something unexpected happened? Then you would have the wrong person ruling, and another *accident* would have to be arranged. Too many *accidents* would arouse suspicion. No, contests were too fraught with danger due to random chance.

Tynewell returned a wry smile.

Saldur wasn't amused. "This isn't a game. We don't do this for our own entertainment."

"You handle your succession your way, leave me to mine."

This less-than-artful dig at Saldur's failure in Melengar felt like a slap, one Saldur didn't feel he deserved. He had aided Tynewell with the removal of Alburn's monarchist king—always the hardest part—and his fellow bishop should be more appreciative of Saldur's help. "Personally, I'd choose Armand Calder."

"Calder? Are you serious? In Alburn's family tree, he's one of the smaller roots. Not very accomplished, and not well connected. Also, I hear he neglected to bring his family, as I so particularly instructed. I don't care if his sons are sick with fevers. That was no reason to ignore my edict and leave behind his wife and daughter, not to mention his sons."

Tynewell shook his head, but Saldur pressed on. "Armand is a lesser-known earl, but he also has a smaller ego, a trait that could prove most useful when . . ."

Saldur stopped talking; Tynewell wasn't listening. He was looking at the painting of Venlin with a distant focus in his eyes.

"Are you going to eat any of this?" Saldur asked, waving a hand over the feast. "I feel like a glutton."

"Huh? Oh, I'm not hungry."

"Really? If I had food like this back in Medford, I'd be four hundred pounds by now." His host still wasn't paying attention. "Is there something wrong?"

"Hmm?" Tynewell looked up as if from a dream. "Oh, no. Nothing . . ."

"You aren't considering Leopold Hargrave, are you? I mean, he's pliable enough, but the man is a terrible administrator. Putting him in charge would no doubt create a fiscal disaster."

Tynewell's attention had finally returned to the conversation, and he nodded in agreement. "Leo is old-fashioned. His family descends from the Imperial Council. Rochelle is home to three of the most prominent families to survive the fall: the Hargraves, Calders, and Killians. Floret Killian even claims to be a direct descendant of Persephone's brother. These families, along with Lord Darius Seret, built this province that later became a kingdom. Leo believes in the old codes, the virtues once practiced by the Teshlor Knights of the old imperium. We don't need his kind of trouble."

"Good point. Well, whoever you pick, best to keep in mind that they actually have to rule a kingdom, you know?"

Tynewell focused on Saldur, and he smiled. "Yes, yes, of course. That's it exactly. This . . . this is such a big decision. I need to consider my choices carefully."

"Yes, but also expeditiously. The feast is what, three days from now?"

He continued to nod. "You're absolutely right. I just . . ."

"What?"

Tynewell bit his lower lip and hung onto it for a moment. "I want the patriarch to approve of my choice."

Saldur raised his hands. "He's given you the power, so I don't see how he can complain with the results."

Tynewell smiled. "Yes, that's true. That's very true. Maybe I will have something to eat after all." He plucked a slice of bread and proceeded to cover it with meat, then paused as his eyes went back to the painting. "Don't you think it's odd?"

"What?"

"That Venlin is standing."

Saldur turned and looked back at the fresco.

"Look at him. The patriarch is in the presence of Novron himself, but he doesn't kneel, doesn't prostrate himself in the slightest. If anything, he's standing more upright. It's as if he felt he was an equal to Our Lord. Where does confidence like that come from?"

"I would think ruling what was left of the empire would have something to do with it."

"I think you might be right."

CHAPTER ELEVEN
LITTLE GUR EM

The chimes of Grom Galimus rang out the midday bells as Royce led Hadrian past the harbor where dozens of sail-stripped masts looked like a forest in winter. They had spent the morning walking around the city. Royce had moved with the speed of intent, which kept Hadrian from asking questions. Royce never cared for them, and Hadrian assumed everything would reveal itself in time. Hours passed, marked neatly by the cathedral bells, as they cut through crowds crossing the bridges to the west side of the city, then circled back. Returning to the plaza, which by then had filled up with its usual crowd, Royce led the way south along the river, taking what appeared to be a nonsensical route that zigzagged streets to the harbor.

"Where are we going?" Hadrian finally asked as they passed between a pair of giant elephant tusks that made a gateway into a neighborhood of narrow streets.

"Hmm?" Royce murmured, glancing back as if he hadn't heard exactly what Hadrian had said, which was a sure sign something was up.

The blocks past the elephant tusks were so tightly packed that clotheslines stretched between buildings created a complex crisscrossed webbing. Those not covered with drying clothes were decorated with colorful flags or flower-laden garlands. The passage was jammed with people who edged around the obstacles of vendor stands where merchants purposely placed their carts in the way of traffic and shouted at customers in more than one language. From some unseen place, rhythmic drums pounded an addictive beat.

"Are you heading somewhere or just wandering?" Hadrian shouted as he dodged around a dark-skinned woman carrying two caged chickens that fluttered and squawked. "Are you looking for the driver in the crowds?"

"Oh, no." Royce shook his head. "I know where the driver is, but there's no sense in going after him until tonight."

Royce made an elegant spin, dodging around a wagon of firewood, his cloak sweeping behind. Trying to keep up, Hadrian nearly plowed into a mother holding the hands of two children, but halted at the brink. All three looked up at him and smiled. He smiled back, concluding a silent but clear conversation that included understanding, forgiveness, and a bit of humor. Slipping past, and around the wagon, Hadrian struggled to catch Royce as he darted and wove from one hole to the next—holes that all too often fit only Royce.

Is he trying to lose me?

They broke out of the narrows and merged into a broader marketplace, where Hadrian was able to use his long legs to cut the distance. "So . . . what? We're sightseeing?"

Royce glanced back to show the irritation on his face.

"What, then?"

"I'm looking for another place to lodge. Another boardinghouse. Figure there has to be something else. We didn't look everywhere. Maybe in the less affluent areas we'll find something. I'd rather share a room with rats than have another breakfast with that woman."

"Are you serious? The city is booked, and the room we have is fantastic."

"Our room is being let out by a crazy person."

"She's nice."

"She's demented and will likely knife us in our sleep."

"Evelyn Hemsworth? You can't be serious."

"No, I'm not. I'm obviously speaking metaphorically. It is far more likely that she'll poison us with tomorrow's breakfast. That's how her type usually works."

"Her type? What do you mean, *her type?*"

Royce didn't answer. He was moving again and once more eluded Hadrian. This time he cut around a group who gawked at a veil-draped young woman dancing with zills on her fingers. At her slippered feet lay a cloth hat littered with a few copper coins. If Hadrian weren't concerned about losing Royce in the crowd, he would have lingered a bit.

They were in the heart of the neighborhood dominated by colorful pottery, flatbreads, bright clothes, baskets, wood carvings, and exotic spices. Several signs denoted the location as Little Gur Em, a reference to the jungles of Calis, which were both dense and dangerous. To Hadrian, who had spent time in the real Gur Em, it seemed like a slur, but the residents appeared to have embraced the name, adding it to their carts. LITTLE GUR EM OILS AND SERUMS, one plaque read, GUR EM JUNGLE TEAS, another.

All around, dark-skinned Calians spoke in accents or in the harsh jungle tongue of the Tenkin language. Old wrinkled men in loose wraps clustered at open-air tables, playing games of Heker, drinking coffee, and smoking from tall brass water pipes. Hadrian recalled the salt and pepper shakers on Evelyn's table and realized that immigrants spilling into Alburn had brought all the flavors of home. The music, the smells, the voices and faces all threatened to unlock mental doors Hadrian preferred to keep closed. Moving down that street, he wasn't pushing through a crowd so much as through a thicket of thorny memories. This was an era of his life he'd walked away from. One he had vowed never to return to. He struggled to ignore the street and focused on Royce.

"Evelyn isn't crazy," Hadrian said. "She's normal. That's your problem with her. You don't know how to deal with normal."

"She's *not* normal."

"Sure she is. The woman is upstanding and decent. You can't even recognize it anymore because you're so . . . so higgery-jiggery."

Royce stopped and looked back at him. The thief wanted to scowl, to show his anger and disdain, but he was having trouble. Royce looked like a person trying not to sneeze, but that wasn't what he was holding back. He fought down an unwanted smile.

"Don't be absurd," he snapped. "A person can't *be* higgery-jiggery. Higgery-jiggery is something a person *does*."

Hadrian chuckled. "Oh, so you speak fluent Evelyn Hemsworth now?"

They had ended up in front of a pushcart painted with a landscape of a jungle waterfall. The picture offered an impressive display of carvings in wood and polished stone. The man behind it, a short, thin fellow with a white beard and big teeth, eagerly jumped to his feet. "You need a gift to settle a dispute with your girlfriend, yes?" he said to Royce.

The thief looked at the Calian cart worker, aghast.

"Ah yes, it is clear from the look of distress on your face. You have had a squabble and now you must make up with a present!" the merchant declared. "That is the only way to properly resolve these setbacks with a sweetheart."

"She's *not* my sweetheart."

"My apologies, good sir!" The merchant smiled and clasped his hands before him, revealing long thin fingers. "And I can see the problem clearly now. Oh, yes! It is a bickering feud with your *wife* that brings you to my cart. Ah, yes, a far more serious state of affairs than a mere misunderstanding with a trollop. Never a good thing when the wife suspects you of higgery-jiggery!" He grinned. "But better than jiggery-pokery, yes?" He followed this with a wink that left Royce staring at the man as if he had three heads.

"Now, what you need is a peace offering." He rubbed his hands together then flexed his fingers as if he were about to perform a magic trick. "A fine bit of artistry to make her forget your transgressions." The man snatched up a figurine of a man and woman in a passionate embrace. He held up the finely carved sculpture. "This—*this* will make her remember why she married you, yes? Hand-carved in Dagastan by a ninety-year-old blind shepherd who was rumored to have once been a pirate. And because you are in such a dire state, I will sell it to you for only a single pair of silver tenents. The answers to your prayers, yes?"

"No!" Royce snapped.

"Are you sure, Royce?" Hadrian grinned. "The little missus might forgive you when she sees that."

Royce didn't respond except to draw up his hood as he started to walk away; then he stopped. His sight fixed on one of the other figurines in the back. "That one," he said, pointing at a hefty sculpture of a man standing triumphantly with one foot on a defeated foe.

"So your wife is a devotee of the arena games?" the happy cart man asked, lifting the figurine up with some difficulty. This was no lightweight bauble. "And not a better choice will you find should you look the world over."

"He's not looking for a gift for his wife." Hadrian pushed abruptly forward. "He isn't even married. We aren't looking to buy anything. C'mon, Royce. We should probably find something to eat. Maybe we can—"

Hadrian stepped away, but Royce didn't follow.

"What's the story with this one?" Royce asked. "Why does the man have *three* swords?"

"Ah!" The merchant grinned at them both, and Hadrian noticed how all his teeth were yellow and crooked. "This carving is a beautiful work of art created to commemorate the greatest warrior in the world: Galenti, the Tiger of Mandalin, the Hero of Calis, the Courtier of the Queen, and the Bane of the Ba Ran Ghazel."

"I'm hungry. Aren't you hungry?" Hadrian clapped his palm to his stomach. "I think there's a place that sells meat on a stick over there. Smells great. Ever have meat on a stick?"

"Greatest warrior in the world, eh?" Royce asked. "That's hard to believe."

"Only to those who have never seen him fight, I would imagine. He was already well-known for his battles against the Ghazel when he arrived in Mandalin. But it was his victories in the arena that brought about his conquest of the queen."

"Is that so?" Royce took down his hood and smiled at Hadrian. "And who *is* this queen?"

The man turned and plucked another figurine from his inventory—this one of a beautiful, sultry woman with slanted eyes painted in decorative outlines. She had a round, doll-like face with a small pouting mouth accentuated by brilliant red lips. She wore a hat with pheasant feathers and a silken dress that appeared no more than paint on the figure. "Rea Rhys Ramsey, the illegitimate daughter of the king of Calis. Her half brother, Lemuel Ramsey, ordered her death, but Rea Rhys escaped and retreated to the one place she knew her brother would never look—the east. She followed the Estee River into the ancient Erbon region in the center of the country. There, she rediscovered the ruins of Urlineus. She claimed the ancient imperial city as her own and renamed it Mandalin. Her restoration of the old arena and resumption of the games made her quite popular. Now she rules Eastern Calis, while her brother rules the west from Rolandue."

"Oh, so she's still alive?"

"Very much so. Rea Rhys is notorious. Living on the fringe of civilization, she manipulates Tenkin warlords by day and battles the Ba Ran Ghazel at night. She has the beguiling beauty of a starry constellation and is as seductive and dangerous as a viper. For nearly two years, Galenti was her paramour and she his patron. The two swam in lakes of liquor, beds of tulan leaves, and pools of blood until his last fight." He pointed at the other statue. "They call Galenti the Tiger of Mandalin because he battled against a great striped cat."

"Last fight? That statue shows him victorious. Did the beast eventually kill him?"

The merchant laughed. "No, no, Galenti could never be defeated. Like all good legends, he simply disappeared." The man made a flamboyant show of throwing his hands up, as if releasing a dove to the heavens. Then he halted as he looked at Hadrian. The vendor's eyes narrowed as they shifted focus from one sword to the next.

Royce turned to Hadrian. "What do you think? Maybe *my missus* would like this one. Should I get it?"

Hadrian frowned and walked away. "I'm getting something to eat."

Royce didn't buy either statue. This didn't surprise Hadrian. There was no way Royce would walk around with a one-foot figurine under his arm. Nor could he see him riding back to Melengar with it strapped to the back of his saddle. Thus, Hadrian didn't find it odd when Royce joined him at the

Erbonese Teahouse without either *gift for the missus*," but he was surprised when Royce's only question was, "What do they serve here?"

Partially in the street and on the edge of the traffic flow, the café provided a grand view of the city's human parade. The two sat at one of a dozen wobbly tables, which were nestled under an outdoor thatch-covered pavilion. The structure did little to block the wind or sun. The proprietor was a native Alburnian, but all he did was greet the customers. The ones doing the work were Calian immigrants.

"If it's authentic fare," Hadrian replied, "rice and tea. Although if you're adventurous, you could try Hohura. That's a Calian liquor. If you're absolutely insane, you could get a mug of Gurlin Bog, goblin liquor that hisses and tastes like something a campfire vomited."

"I think I'll avoid intoxicants for the time being."

"Then you'll want to steer clear of anything with grenesta in it, and they tend to put the herb in everything. I once had a fabulous stew; ten minutes later I passed out."

Royce peered at him with a grimace. "You're making me long for the Meat House."

"But this place has chairs and a better view."

Few areas of the city had thus far matched Little Gur Em for activity and interest, and Hadrian revised his assumption that the name was derogatory. Perhaps it began that way, as the real Gur Em was as universally cherished as Black Fever— which was often contracted in the selfsame jungle. Still, the Gur Em was wild, colorful, fragrant, and bursting with life. In this way, it was mirrored by the Calian district of Rochelle. Hadrian remembered Calis as overwhelming to the senses, grand bazaars and vast markets set in old cities on the ocean coast, or vibrant villages in the dense brush, but here the experience was jammed into a tiny urban neighborhood of stone buildings and cobbled walkways. It was indeed a jungle of sorts.

Without a word, a barefoot man in a long, unadorned tunic delivered a communal bowl of rice and vegetables, which was accompanied by a plate of piled flatbread and dark tea. The food was so hot it steamed. Hadrian knew the dish as fried kenase. Royce sniffed it dubiously then waited until Hadrian took a bite before joining in.

"How come you didn't ask me about Mandalin?"

"You mean all that stuff the guy said about the queen and a tiger and arena fights?"

"Yeah."

"The truth?" Royce asked.

"Sure."

"Not interested."

"Really?" Hadrian set down his tea, surprised. "A man tells you this fantastic story about bloody battles and a notorious queen of Calis, and you aren't even mildly curious?"

"If our pasts aren't our present, there's likely a reason."

"So you won't ask me, and I shouldn't ask you?"

"Something like that. Besides, I'm sure in a contest of bygone horrors, I've got you beat."

Hadrian peered across the lip of his steaming cup. "You think so?"

"You don't?" Royce appeared genuinely surprised. "A whole city still has nightmares about me."

Hadrian nodded, then hooked a thumb back in the direction of the merchant. "You weren't paying attention. An entire country knows about my murderous past."

"Maybe. But they *like* you. No one is making carvings of me."

"In Calis, they also craft the likenesses of Death and Pestilence. They're an odd people."

"He didn't talk about you like you were a scourge."

"Because all he knows is the myth. Have you ever wondered how a soldier of fortune could be so . . ." Hadrian paused to take a sip of his tea.

"Naïve?" Royce offered.

Hadrian swallowed. "I was going to say optimistic."

"Really? I suppose it *could* be described like that. Yeah, I've puzzled over that one for some time. Most mercenaries are a bit more—"

"Jaded and cynical?" Hadrian offered.

"I was going to say realistic and practical."

"Really? I suppose it *could* be described like that. But what you might not be considering is that maybe I'm on the return trip."

"Huh?"

"Do you have nightmares of people you killed?"

"No."

"There you go."

"There I go, what?"

Hadrian took the clay pot left on their table and poured tea into his cup until it overflowed. "Every cup is different, but each can only hold so much. Eventually you either stop pouring or make an awful mess. Make a big enough mess and you have to clean up; you have to change." Hadrian looked at the pool of tea dripping through the slats of the wobbly table. "I made a really big mess, and it wasn't tea I spilled."

They were both looking at the puddle of tea when the screaming started.

CHAPTER TWELVE
UNICORNS AND POLKA DOTS

Up the street where an alley divided a makeshift livestock shelter from an old stone building, a crowd began to form.

The animal pen was nothing more than rope strung between driven stakes hemming in a score of sheep. Out front, alongside a hastily assembled stage, was a hand-painted sign that read: SUNSET AUCTION. With its white marble blocks and pillars, the three-story stone building opposite the alley gave the impression of having once been a place of importance—a counting house or a court. Now the upper windows were laden with drying clothes, and the balconies brimmed with spinning wheels, jugs, baskets, and pots. A number of families roosted in the vacuum of cracked-marble neglect. Most of them had rushed to balconies and peered down; several pointed at the alley below.

Hadrian swallowed the last of his kenase and stood up. His height allowed him to see over the crowd but granted him no further insight.

"What's going on?" Royce asked, not bothering to stand.

"Dunno. Something happening in the alley."

"Nothing good, by the sound of it."

The screams had stopped but were replaced by a chorus of wailing.

"Where are you going?" Royce asked as Hadrian pushed forward.

"To see what happened."

"Whatever it is, they have plenty of people to deal with it. And screams and cries are never portents of good fortune. I'd stay away."

"Of course *you* would."

What ability Hadrian lacked in deftly dodging his way through a shifting populace, he more than made up for in cutting through a dense crowd. People moved clear for a man of his size. Those who didn't, he could move. Any resistance to a gentle push was instantly stifled when they spotted his swords. The city's residents didn't carry steel. Most couldn't afford it, and few had the need. Farmers, merchants, and tradesmen rarely faced violence beyond the occasional drunken fistfight. Theirs was a life of endless repetition, where if they stayed in their place and hoed their given row, nothing of great note ever happened. Men of steel were different. A man with a trowel and hod sought to lay bricks; a man with a sword sought to lay men low; a man with three swords—you quickly avoided. It was in this manner that Hadrian worked his way forward until he was at the mouth of the alley. That was where the crowd stopped. While everyone was eager to see what the noise was about, few cared to get close. Content to view from a distance, the mob hung back, leaving a corridor open.

In a city as congested as Rochelle, the refuse needed to go somewhere. In the finer districts, waste was deposited into the Roche River, which carried it out to the bay and then the Goblin Sea. Poor neighborhoods like Little Gur Um made do by jamming their rubbish behind the buildings in alleys. So, finding a vast mound of garbage at the end of the alley wasn't a surprise. Broken crates, torn cloth, rotting food, animal waste, and bones were all piled high, but in this case, a handful of kneeling women wailed before the heap. A smaller number of men stood nearby looking aghast and bewildered as they stared down at what appeared to be trash being dragged from the pile.

For the most part, it was. A little cascade of rubbish had been formed where someone had been digging. People did that. Hadrian knew that even men and women of means went treasure hunting in trash piles for a lark. Stories always circulated about someone finding gold earrings or an overlooked sack of silver, but the best prize Hadrian personally knew to have been found was a torn leather belt long enough to be repurposed for a thinner man. This time, someone had apparently found more than they bargained for. No one likes to pick up a discarded shoe and find a foot inside.

The women wailed over the body of a child. A little girl, no older than six or seven, was dead. Hadrian knew dead bodies. He'd walked the aftermath of too many battlefields not to know the child had died only hours ago, certainly less than a day. But there was more than just death involved with this body.

Unicorns and Polka Dots

As Hadrian approached, as he reached the scene and took his place beside the other befuddled men, he understood the problem. The little girl hadn't been murdered, she'd been torn apart. Her face was fine, her mouth partially open, her eyes thankfully closed. He had killed more men than he could remember and been in battles where women and children had died. He'd lost his squeamishness to gore long ago but never grew accustomed to the sight of open-eyed dead children. The girl's rib cage had been broken into, its contents rifled through. Without needing to get closer, Hadrian could tell something was missing: The child's heart was gone.

"We should go," Royce whispered. The thief was behind him, motioning with a hand for them to retreat. "Soldiers coming."

His warning came too late.

"You really need to listen to me more often," Royce told Hadrian as the two sat in the guard post.

This was a different station house than where they had chatted with Roland, but the interiors were identical. Same one-room shack with a desk, weapons, stacks of wood, and a small fire. An identical horseshoe held down similar parchments. The military was nothing if not consistent. At least the shackles remained on the wall rather than on their wrists. The guardsmen had confiscated Hadrian's swords, missed Royce's dagger on the pat-down, and after some preliminary questions, ordered them to wait.

"We're not in trouble," Hadrian said. "The truth is, we've done nothing wrong."

Royce closed his eyes and shook his head. "By Mar, the way you think. It's . . . it's . . . I honestly don't know if there's a word for it. You realize the truth is rarely important, right?"

"Soldiers are people, too," Hadrian replied. "I know. I was one."

"I wasn't limiting the observation to soldiers. Most *people* don't care about the truth."

"Look, they have no reason to do anything to us. We're innocent. They just picked us up because we're strangers and didn't belong in that alley. They're just double-checking."

"Reason, truth, innocence"—Royce sat back against the wall and folded his arms—"unicorns, pixies, and dragons; you're not *that* young to believe in such things. How is it that you fancy yourself a resident of a make-believe world."

"I told you. At this point, it's a choice."

"It's not. It's fooling yourself. I can decide between eating fish or pork, but I can only *pretend* to eat unicorn meat. I can't *actually* eat a unicorn. The world is the world, and you live in it with open eyes or choose to be blind. It's all the same to me, but don't stand there pretending you're right."

Hadrian grimaced. "There are so many things wrong with that statement." Only Royce could think of a unicorn-eating metaphor. *Where do thoughts like that bubble up from? Why a unicorn? Who thinks of eating a symbol of purity and grace?* Maybe that was his point. Perhaps Royce was making an argument within an argument, but Hadrian wasn't about to be sucked down some obscure sewer where only Royce knew the way. Hadrian had a point of his own. "You always wear black and gray. That's a choice, too, and it says a lot about you."

"It says I don't like to be seen at night."

UNICORNS AND POLKA DOTS

"It says you like to hide, and people who like to hide are usually up to no good. That's a message you declare to everyone you meet, and people receive it as you might expect. Then when others don't trust you, when they avoid you, hurt or arrest you for doing nothing, your worldview is justified. So, you're right; you can't eat unicorns in your world because they don't exist, but they do in mine—probably because in my world we don't eat them."

Royce furrowed his brow, his mouth partially open as if he was hearing a sound he couldn't understand.

"Honestly, I think you should try wearing purple and yellow," Hadrian said. "Something bright and happy—polka dots maybe. And you should smile more. People would treat you differently. You might find the world a brighter place."

"Tell me you aren't serious."

Hadrian chuckled. "About the yellow polka dots? Of course not. You'd look ridiculous, and you might attract children, which would be a mistake on an epic level."

"And the unicorn stuff?"

"*You* brought unicorns into this. I have no idea where that came from. It's like you have a demented recipe book or something. Which if you do, please don't tell me."

"Are you two always like this?" The guard behind the desk had stopped his scribbling and was staring at them with an expression of utter bewilderment.

"He is," they both said in unison.

"You're hilarious." The guard smiled. "I sure hope you're not guilty. I'd hate to have to hang the two of you."

"Good," Hadrian said. "At least, we can agree on something."

"Sounds like unicorn-believer talk to me." The guard grinned. "Personally, I'm with dark-clothes guy. Living is anguish and then you die."

"Wow, that's uplifting," Hadrian said. "You should start your own church."

He shook his head. "Not the religious type."

"There's a surprise."

"The problem with the world," the guard went on, "is that too many people don't see it like it is. They want it to be something it just isn't. I think everything would be better if folks stopped believing in fantasies and dealt with the way things are. We might actually improve things then. I mean, there aren't any unicorns, or fairies, and there certainly isn't an Heir of Novron who's going to appear and save us all. That's just stupid."

"I couldn't have said it better myself." Royce pointed at the guard. "I really hope you don't try to hang me. I'd hate to have to kill you."

The guard looked confused again, then, assuming Royce was making a joke, he laughed.

Royce laughed, too.

Hadrian didn't, and this served to remind him he didn't have his swords. They were by the door. He could see them, and that made him feel better because the *truth* was that Royce and the guard had a point. Sometimes things didn't work out the way they should. They certainly hadn't for that little girl in the alley.

The door to the guard post opened, and a familiar face entered.

"Blackwater?" Roland asked, puzzled. "My, aren't you making the rounds." He looked to the desk guard. "Drake, what are they doing here?"

Unicorns and Polka Dots

"We picked them up in the alley where the mir was killed," the soldier said with a salute. "The big one had those three swords, and the other looked, well . . . suspicious."

"It's the color of his clothes," Hadrian offered. "Makes him look sinister."

"You know them, sir?"

"Yes. This is Hadrian Blackwater, an old friend. Not the sort to murder children, believe me." Roland turned his gaze on Royce but hesitated to add any clarification.

"Apparently, I need to wear polka dots," Royce said.

"What were you two doing in Little Gur Em?"

"Having our midday meal," Hadrian said. "I was introducing Royce here to Calian cuisine. We were at an outdoor café when we heard the shouts and went over to investigate."

"Still the soldier, eh?" Roland chuckled. He turned to the guard. "Is that really all you have on them, Drake? They were there and looked suspicious?"

The guard nodded. "Pretty much."

"Give them back their belongings, then."

The guard moved to the door and gathered Hadrian's swords.

"Sorry for the inconvenience," Roland told them. He glanced down at the desk, pivoted the top page so he could read it. "Looks like we'll have to add this one to the pile."

"What's that mean?" Hadrian asked, taking the spadone first and slinging it over his shoulder.

Roland, who didn't appear to have had time to shave in a week, scrubbed his growing beard and sighed. "I told you about the murders we've been having. Mir tend to be the targets,

177

and we can be thankful for that. If it had been the child of a citizen—a guild merchant or tradesman or, Novron forbid, a noble—I'd have the constable crawling all over me."

"But because it was a mir, you'll ignore it?" Royce asked.

"No, not ignore. There's really nothing I can do in any case. But there would be more pressure." Roland looked to the guard, who handed Hadrian's other two swords over. "No witnesses, right?"

The soldier shook his head. "As usual, no one knows anything."

"It's always the same," Roland said. "No one sees them. No one knows a thing. Then the next victim turns up in the river, or pit, or an alley—each one ripped open, heart missing."

Roland checked on the contents of the pot near the fire and grunted when he found it empty.

"Don't you think that's a little odd?" Royce asked.

"You'd think that, wouldn't you? But no, not anymore. I may have mentioned that life is cheap down here on the east side. Even cheaper next door in the Rookery, which is where most of the killings have occurred."

"But to rip out the hearts of children?" Hadrian asked. This made him think of Royce roasting unicorns, only this was the real-world form of that idea. *Could there be a purer example of evil? Why would anyone do such a thing? And how? How does a person kill and crack open a rib cage without anyone seeing or hearing it?*

"Probably selling them on the black market," Roland said with enough callousness to make Hadrian wonder what had happened to the young man he once knew. "Some of these Calians use them to make youth potions or healing balms.

UNICORNS AND POLKA DOTS

Spreading a little powdered baby heart on your face will keep you looking young, or so people have been told. Rich merchants' wives are their market. We try to stop it, but there's not much we can do. Usually, they use calf or lamb hearts, but someone is obviously making an extra effort. If people think they're getting the real thing, the price goes up. When news of a death spreads, the demand is higher."

Dealing with frequent loss of children's hearts and the indifference of bystanders has driven the unicorns out of Roland's world, as well, Hadrian realized. Such beliefs made sense and were difficult to debate. After all, horrors had a way of grabbing the limelight and diminishing everything else. *How can anyone believe that people are basically good when faced with such blatant evidence to the contrary?* What Hadrian couldn't make Roland, Drake the guard, or least of all Royce understand was that a life barren of unicorns was existence without purpose. Hadrian had visited that dark land once. He'd lived as a glutton of selfishness, reclining on the luxury of visible truths. He'd drowned himself in wine and blood, but the more he consumed, the emptier he felt. What was the point if, as Drake so eloquently put it: *living is anguish and then you die?* Hearing those words convinced Hadrian of the importance of unicorns. Even if there weren't any, it was absolutely necessary to believe they existed. What's more, he needed to try to find them. It wasn't much. Chasing fantasies was a thin thread to justify a life, and yet how many wonders had been wrought by people who did exactly that—those who believed in crazy dreams.

"Sorry for the mistake," Roland said. "I'd buy you both a drink, but I have the night shift the rest of this week, and the duke frowns on drunk officers."

"Ah, yes, the life of an honest soldier," Hadrian mused, feigning envy.

"How about you two? Still looking for the duchess? Heard you stopped by the carriage shop. Find anything?"

"Nothing yet."

"Let me know if you do. I'm pretty sure she's dead, but if she isn't . . ."

"What?"

Roland hesitated, and his face changed. The tough façade, the soldier's stare, dimmed, and for a moment, Hadrian once more saw the lad he had once known. "Everyone calls her the Whiskey Wench. No one showed her a lick of respect. I didn't, either. Guards are supposed to bow when she goes by. None of us did. We all said how she wasn't a real noble. That she was fake because she wasn't born one, and wasn't even from Alburn. I guess the feeling came from a kind of envy, as if she was getting away with something and didn't deserve respect. Then, well, she gave me a new pair of boots. My old ones had holes in them. My feet used to get soaked, and I nearly got frostbitten more than once. I hardly ever saw the woman. It's not like I was her bodyguard, but she must have noticed. Why she bothered, I don't know. Told myself she didn't like seeing a guard captain in a shoddy uniform, except . . . city guards are required to wear *black* boots, thin leather that looks nice, but doesn't do anything when you're out patrolling in the cold." He lifted his foot to show Hadrian his pair of brown, fur-lined footwear. "Nicest boots I've ever owned. Real warm. Hardly noticed the snows the rest of the winter." He put his foot down. "If she's alive, I want to know. And if she's not and you discover who did it, I want to know that, too."

UNICORNS AND POLKA DOTS

Hadrian nodded and, checking his weapons, pushed the short sword down on his hip and lifted the bastard sword higher and back a tad. "Well, thanks for helping us out." Hadrian took two steps toward the door, but stopped when he realized Royce wasn't following.

Across the roadway stood a busy countinghouse. Like many of the important buildings, it was constructed of stone that had grown dingy.

Seeing it, Royce turned back and caught Roland's attention. "Can you answer a question for me?" He pointed at one of the sculpted decorative faces on the building across the street. "Why are these things everywhere? They crouch under steps, frame windows, perch on ledges, and hold up everything from bridges to balconies. Even some of the cobblestones have tiny grotesque faces carved into them. Why is that?"

Roland dipped his head to see beyond the doorframe. "You mean the gargoyles?"

Royce nodded. "I've seen them before. They're used to channel rainwater off big churches, like the cathedral in Medford. But here, they're all over. Most don't even serve any real function, only a few are being used to divert runoff."

Roland pushed up his lower lip. "Just decorations, I suppose."

"There's no story behind them?"

Roland rolled his shoulders. "Sure. There's multiple stories, but they're all nonsense."

"Humor me."

"The most popular one has a priest who slays a dragon with the help of a condemned man. They burn the beast afterward, but the head isn't affected. You know, on account of it being able to breathe fire and all. So, the local bishop decides to mount the thing on his cathedral to scare off evil spirits. Seemed like a good idea, so stonemasons were asked to add them from that time on."

"Ah-huh," Royce said, dissatisfied.

"Well, there's another one about the town's founding. A crazy architect by the name of Bradford Crumin was commissioned to lay out the city. He chose the place for the Estate, Grom Galimus, and most of the old buildings. He was brilliant but also insane. He claimed to hear voices—ghosts, he called them— and the only way he could shut them up was to scare the spirits away. Apparently, they were terrified by scary faces, so he put all these grotesque creatures around."

Royce didn't say anything, just folded his arms.

"Okay, so there's another one. Seems they never used to be here. The city went up and all the buildings were plain, but functional. Then one day this swarm of creatures swooped down and overran the place. The town was swamped, and everyone was afraid to go outside. Didn't know where they came from, but a few days after the invasion, an old wizard comes hobbling along. He agreed to rid the town of the creatures for a price. The city agreed, and he turned them into stone, but—"

"But the town didn't pay," Royce said.

"You've heard this?"

Royce shook his head. "No, but stories are all the same, aren't they?"

Roland thought a second, then shrugged. "Anyway, you were right; they refused to pay. Since the creatures were all dead, their problem was solved."

"Let me guess: The wizard does something nasty."

Roland nodded. "He cursed the town. Now every night, usually in the dark of a new moon, the stone creatures come alive and exact revenge."

Royce frowned. "Never mind, I was expecting something awful, but also believable."

"We're talking monstrous faces, here. What would be believable?"

"How about, the stone carvers charged by the hour?"

�

"Why the sudden interest in architecture?" Hadrian asked as he once more followed Royce back into Little Gur Em.

"Didn't you notice?" Royce was once more moving quickly, nearly trotting, retracing their earlier trip back to the scene of the crime.

"Notice what?"

They came upon the same square where they'd spilled the tea, and Royce pointed up at the building near where the girl's body was found.

"What about it?"

"See the gargoyles lining the ledge up there?"

The old building was adorned with regularly spaced creepy monkey-like statuettes along the third-floor exterior. They weren't really gargoyles, not in the traditional sense. These didn't funnel rainwater; they were merely decorations.

"So?"

Royce frowned. "See the gap?"

The row of hunched, fanged monkeys leaned forward, holding up the top balcony with their shoulders, but Royce was right, one was missing. The rogue stone-monkey monster second from the left had abandoned his post, leaving the other little monsters to do all the work.

Such a massive weight hitting the ground from that height would have produced a lot of damage, not to mention debris, but the street below didn't show any signs of an impact. Hadrian's next thought was that it had been removed, perhaps in need of repair. But doing so would have required scaffolding and a hoist, neither of which was present. And the empty place showed no evidence of excavation, just a space for a carving that wasn't there. The statue looked to have simply flown away. The most sensible answer, and the one he concluded with, was that the gargoyle had never been installed in the first place. Maybe the builders had been short a figure. Likely, there was some story that went along with it. The kind of tale that people shared to show off their knowledge of local lore. *Oh, yeah, Grimbold the Carver dropped over dead when working on it, and out of tribute to him no replacement was ever made.* Or maybe something like, *Someone miscalculated the number of statues for that wall, and ol' Pete started installing from the right and Bradford from the left. It wasn't until they were done that they realized they were short by one. Funds were low, so the missing gargoyle wasn't made.*

UNICORNS AND POLKA DOTS

The problem with these neat and sensible explanations was the bare spot—bright and pristine. Like a sun-bleached carpet with a square of vivid color where a cabinet had once stood, the wall bore a clean silhouette where a statue should have been. Something *had* been there, but now it *wasn't*.

Royce looked at Hadrian and asked. "Why is one missing?"

CHAPTER THIRTEEN
GROM GALIMUS

Villar Orphe waited where he usually did, on top of a roof. He had several favorites, but that evening he sat on the peak of the Trio Vestments Building, where a tailor, a haberdasher, and a cobbler came up with the idea of a one-stop shop for men's clothing. Villar had never seen the inside of the Trio V, but he was quite familiar with the roof, which hid his home. Tucked in a hidden niche formed by hips and gables, his abode was less a house and more a tented nest built of canvas and discarded wood that he had dragged up at night like a giant owl. His tiny shelter was filled with the few things he valued: a salifan plant that he kept alive in a wooden cup, a torn bit of tapestry, and a sword left to him by his grandfather. That last item he mounted under the eave, so even if someone found his nest, they might not see it. He also had some food reserves—roots, nuts, and berries that he'd gathered on the outskirts of town. The berries were just starting to appear on the warm, sunny hillsides, and he'd found some mushrooms, as well. He had also hauled in a few treasures uncovered in the trash on Governor's Isle. Someone down there didn't like salted fish.

The sun was still up, which kept Villar's head down. He didn't like moving about in the daylight. He was blessed with the distinctly beautiful features of his people and refused to cover his ears or hide his eyes from the world. He was proud of his heritage; the rest of the world should be ashamed. Villar's list of *shoulds* was long. He *should* be able to walk into Trio V's and buy a new suit of clothes. He *should* be able to wear his grandfather's sword on his hip in public. He *should* be able to live in a house with four walls and have an honest-to-Ferrol pot for his salifan plant. What *should* be and what *was,* however, remained widely divergent, and this kept him hunkered down with his back against the cupola where the pointing-well-dressed-man weather vane proclaimed an easterly wind.

He often mused on what would happen if he dared wear the sword. It wasn't illegal. He'd heard that some rulers disallowed blades and bows inside city limits, except for those worn by knights, nobles, and city guards. Rochelle didn't have a weapons law, but then there was no edict against a mir walking into the Trio V, either. Some rules didn't need to be written down or enforced by the guard. If he was seen with the sword brazenly clapping his thigh, he'd draw looks. Then a crowd would form, and unless he was willing to use the weapon, they would beat him and rip it away. If he used it—if he acted like any other self-respecting person—the city guard would come. While wearing a sword wasn't illegal, wounding and killing people most certainly was. Villar knew from experience that the guards didn't like dwarves, barely tolerated Calians, but absolutely *hated* mir. Villar had no illusions of being able to fight off a squad of trained soldiers. He had no training with a blade, and he'd never been in a fight. He didn't consider being beaten the same as being in a fight. So, while being a mir was reason enough for a beating, being a mir with a sword was guaranteed suicide.

Looking down between his feet, he could see the river and the setting sun as it turned gold. Carriages rolled across the distant bridges. Smoke rose from countless chimneys. Crowds crawled along the canyon-streets, flowing like some viscous slime that oiled the workings of the city. He was literally above it all, but soon he'd add a more figurative aspect to that idea.

The bells of Grom Galimus began to play their lonesome melody, marking the end of the day. He should be going. The bishop wouldn't appreciate him being late. He started to rise, then paused. He heard the scraping again. Tiny claws on wood.

The rat is back.

Villar looked to his pile of possessions in time to see the black-and-white spotted rodent scurry into a crack in the roofing. The thief was at it again. This time he had gotten the box open.

Villar fished the old wooden container out of his pile and, in a panic, he searched the contents while guarding against any mischief that the demon wind might be plotting. Everything that had been there appeared safe. He drew out his most cherished possession: a small portion torn from a tapestry that was at least a thousand years old. According to the story his grandfather told, the tapestry had belonged to the Orphe family and had once been the size of a three-story wall. This two-foot scrap was all that remained. The rest had been confiscated and burned by the church—for obvious reasons. Even Villar's little scrap showed the detailed image of pointed-eared heroes in armor, riding horses and holding swords aloft. This, his grandfather had told him, was a depiction of the Fall of Merredydd. The image commemorated the battles against barbarians that eventually brought low the ancient and magnificent imperial province. A place that had once been ruled *by* mir *for* mir.

Villar spread the bit of tapestry across his thighs and lovingly caressed the fine needlework.

A mir had ruled a province.

He stared into the thread-woven eyes of the faces and made them a promise. "If Ferrol is willing, another one will yet rule a kingdom."

Seeing the sun touch the distant mountains, Villar lifted the cloth to his lips and kissed the image, then folded it and put the torn corner back.

Time was growing short, and he had much to do.

Villar took his usual rooftop highway route to the cathedral, dropping down in the shadow of the alley. With the workday over, the mass migration of weary people slogged home. Shoulders slumped, heads bowed, few looked up. Even if they had, even if they saw him, no one would have noticed, or cared about, another mir on the street.

The sun was dipping behind the Estate, most of its face gone, its power fading. A host of shadows crept out of the low places and claimed dominion over the world. The coin of chance was flipping. At last tails was coming up.

His kind couldn't safely enter most shops, but a few proprietors were sympathetic and looked the other way when a mir slipped in. Those rare merchants would only sell to mir if no one else was in the store. Common practice was to wait and watch for a lull in traffic then slip in, buy what was needed, and hurry back out before anyone saw. If someone did see, the mir would be turned away. The Crow Tavern on the east side went a step further. Each night, they threw bones and unwanted leftovers on the street for the mir from the nearby Rookery to grab. A crowd gathered religiously and fell to their knees, gathering what they could carry in arms or the folds of skirts. Villar had witnessed the event only once; that was all he could stomach. He had felt nauseated and decided that the Crow would be the first building to burn. Its operator, Brandon Hingus, would be the first executed. Maybe he meant well, but the result was the public humiliation of his people. Such a blight would need to be erased with extreme prejudice to expunge the ugly memory.

Despite the common-knowledge ban on most commercial venues, there were a few places mir were tolerated so long as they didn't make trouble. Public squares were generally safe, as were bridges—beneath which many lived. They were allowed to draw water from common wells even though the law clearly prohibited it. The mir were also allowed to enter Grom Galimus. They couldn't go past the Teshlor windows, the first pair of stained glass panes that illuminated the nave and depicted the ancient imperial order with images of grim armored warriors who appeared to watch so that not a toe crossed the line.

Still, mir were allowed to stand inside the doors, observe the services, listen to the choir, and then wait on the steps, hoping for handouts. So long as they were respectful and didn't block access, they were granted the privilege of silent begging. As such, it wasn't odd for a mir to trot up the marble steps and enter the giant doors of Grom Galimus.

Once more, no one looked, no one noticed, no one cared when Villar slipped inside for his first meeting of the night.

Villar had been a fraction late, but the bishop was more so, leaving Villar to stand between the two stained-glass Teshlors. No service was under way, and the vast interior was mainly empty. The only ones there were a few boys cleaning up and a few devoted faithful kneeling on the stone floor, praying to the statues of Novron and his doting father, Maribor. Despite his covert mission, Villar refused to dip his head or avert his eyes. He would not worship these gods, nor even pretend to. They were the gods of men. From either side, the Teshlors stared at him. Villar felt uncomfortable under their watchful, sunlit gaze—a gaze that suggested they saw more than a stubborn mir—but even as he waited, Villar noticed the light failing and their images fading with it.

Hard heels echoed. A robed figure moved through the gallery pillars. The bishop approached.

When he came into view, he silently waved Villar to a corner. They were still not past the knights, but Villar was also not near the doors.

"Is there a problem?" Tynewell whispered. The bishop positioned himself between Villar and the door, blocking the view of everyone except the boys cleaning up.

"No, everything is perfect."

"Then why are you here?"

"A Calian named Erasmus Nym will need access to Grom Galimus the morning of the feast."

Tynewell looked puzzled. "I have an early service. People will—"

"After the service. Midday is fine. He doesn't need long to prepare."

The word *prepare* made the bishop wince. "What exactly will this Erasmus person be doing? I won't allow him to desecrate the church. He's not going to sacrifice a goat on my altar." Tynewell's eyes widened. "Or a child."

Villar paused a moment, wondering where that had come from. He hadn't told the bishop everything. Villar didn't think it wise, and the bishop didn't want to know the details. The only thing Tynewell cared about was that every Alburn noble at the feast would die.

"Nym won't do anything other than what I have."

Tynewell thought a moment then asked, "And where will you be?"

"Someplace else. A place that I don't want Erasmus to know about."

"And what does this Erasmus fellow know about me and my involvement? Is having him use my church such a good idea? Will it point a finger my way?"

"No, this cathedral is huge, and you can't be expected to know what occurs in every crook and corner. I've already shown him where to go, and he didn't ask anything about others involved. I just wanted to let you know it would be him rather than me in case you happened upon each other."

"And no one else knows anything, right? You haven't bragged, have you? Gone off in some tavern about how the bishop has promised you a favor in return for arranging a murderous riot?"

"Mir aren't welcome in taverns."

"Be that as it may, the point is still valid. You haven't been drunk under some forsaken bridge boasting about how you'll be Duke of Rochelle when the bishop crowns himself king for lack of options, have you? If anyone discovers I'm involved, neither of us will get what we want."

"I don't drink."

Tynewell studied him carefully, then smiled. "Good. You know, I had my doubts about you. Relying on a mir—such a thing doesn't come easy, but I'm a man of faith. I believe that if you show faith in someone, that someone will prove themselves worthy. This is your opportunity. Succeed and you'll earn my trust and the rule of this city. Imagine that. You'll be a hero to your people. You'll live in the Estate and govern this region on my behalf. I will be king of Alburn—a bishop-ruler just like Venlin—and you'll be the first mir noble since the fall of Merredydd. You and yours will get their due, trust me."

Villar didn't trust him, but this was the only chance he, or any of them, had. The whole affair was a terrible gamble, and there was no way to be certain the bishop would honor his pledge to appoint him duke. But it didn't matter. Left to itself, nothing would change. Villar would rather die than face another day of eating the Duke of Rochelle's trash and watching the mir people beg for scraps thrown in the street. And either way, at least Villar would have the chance to fight back. The ability to kill those who had humiliated him and his people for generations would be a worthy reward. This was something Mercator could never understand. She had become domesticated, but Villar's heart was still free.

Leaving the cathedral, he stood upon the steps to watch the last of the daylight fade. He had plenty of time to reach his second appointment. He would, in fact, be incredibly early. Perhaps he should get something to eat first. He considered rummaging through the duke's garbage for dinner, something he'd have to do just one last time. He looked down at the Estate, a place that would soon be a place of honor rather than one of humiliation. That's when he saw them, the two strangers. The foreigners who had been asking questions about the duchess and poking around where they shouldn't. One was perched high up on the pediment at the far end of the bridge watching the Estate as if waiting for something.

Villar realized what it was, and he knew he wouldn't be getting dinner that night.

CHAPTER FOURTEEN
THE DRIVER

"What *exactly* are we looking for?" Hadrian asked, shifting his position again. The capstone he sat on was cold.

"The driver," Royce replied.

The two were on the west side of the East Bridge, where Royce hadn't taken his eyes off the front gate of the duke's estate since they'd arrived. Hadrian sat on the bridge parapet out of the way of traffic, looking like a lost boy who'd foolishly let go of his mother's hand and hoped she'd come back. Royce was above him, perched high on the massive end-pediment that announced the start or end of the bridge, depending on which way one was walking. He stood behind the statue of a winged beast, a giant, ugly bat-thing with horns and fangs. Royce and the sculpture made quite the diabolical pair as he clung to a wing, peering over the stone monster's shoulder. Occasionally the gate to the Estate opened. Someone would exit, or enter, and each time Royce became still and attentive. Then the gate would close, and he would settle back, disappointed.

They never did find a new place to stay. All livable spaces were occupied, even the open-air patches of dirt under bridges and behind stables. Royce had continued to search until the sun threatened to set, then he insisted on a hectic race to the Estate. They'd been there for more than an hour, and, so far, nothing had warranted the rush. Except for his two-word statement, Royce hadn't responded to any inquiries about their current vigil.

The day had remained reasonably warm, continuing the rumor that spring was just a few steps down the road. The morning had been sunny, but afternoon had invited clouds to the party, and more were showing up all the time. A variety of boats passed beneath them. Professional fishermen hauled in nets, heading upriver after a day on Blythin Bay. The waterway also played host to a series of trows that ran up- and downriver, dropping off one load of cargo at the harbor and picking up another to haul back upstream. Along the bridge, the flow of foot traffic, wagons, and carriages was picking up. With slumped backs and bowed heads, servants, traders, and laborers returned home, their way lit by a fading sun.

"There he is!" Royce said with urgency as he leaned forward, leering with the same malevolent expression as the statue to which he clung.

A small figure stepped outside the front gate of the ducal estate, gray-haired, partially balding. With his protruding brow and long beard, the dwarf looked like the quintessential depiction of his race. He glanced both ways before crossing the street and then entered the flow of traffic coming toward them.

"The dwarf?" Hadrian said.

"Shh!" Royce scolded as he climbed down. "Yes, that's the driver."

"How do you know?"

"I don't *know*, but he's the only dwarf to come out of the duke's residence, and I doubt His Lordship employs many."

He didn't look like a carriage driver. If Hadrian were to guess, he would've pegged the little guy as a gardener or a stable hand or, given the sack slung over one shoulder, perhaps a bearded child who was running away from home. The dwarf was dressed in a no-frills worker's tunic and belt, with wool pants and worn boots. He held a mud-stained cloak and a small sack tied at the mouth with twine. He struggled to work his way into the flow of the bustling people who jostled him as if he weren't there.

"I know you don't like dwarves, Royce, but that doesn't mean every—"

"The carriage's footboard was ratcheted up for someone his size, so, the driver was either a child or a dwarf. Everyone would have noticed a child driving a carriage, but look how people ignore the dwarf like he doesn't exist. Everyone blocks out what they don't want to see. And honestly, who wants to lay eyes on the likes of him?"

The dwarf walked past, and Royce slipped into traffic a few pedestrians back.

"He works at the Estate," Royce said quietly as they followed the dwarf across the bridge toward the plaza. "Not full-time, I don't think. Probably hired for some temporary task, stonework most likely. And when they needed a driver for the duchess, guess who volunteered?"

"That sounds like a lot of guesses."

"Either that, or an eight-year-old was hired to drive the duchess."

Hawkers took advantage of the evening migration by shouting invitations and waving welcomes to the mob. Their efforts were stymied by the bells in the tower of Grom Galimus, chiming six times. When the ringing finally ceased, the dwarf was through the plaza and heading up an alley that divided the cathedral from another large stone building. This sister building had a flight of steps leading to an imposing colonnade of marble pillars above which IMPERIAL GALLERY was chiseled into the entablature. Both buildings had gargoyles, none of which were missing.

The alley between the cathedral and the gallery was wider than the one in Little Gur Em, but it was congested. This helped their pursuit. Royce kept two rows back from their prey, which required slowing down to let others pass. Moving on little legs, the dwarf wasn't speedy. The sun was on the horizon, its dying light already lost to them in the stone canyons of the central city, where the buildings were so close Hadrian thought he might be able to touch the walls on both sides of the street with his sword tips.

The crowd began to thin as they followed a street that curved northeast. The buildings here were residential, shorter, less ornate. Hadrian spotted women on small wrought-iron balconies beating rugs, and numerous chimneys pouring smoke. The stone houses gave way to wood with stucco and timber uppers, and the number of stories lowered with each successive block. By then, the sun was gone, the hazy afterlight competing with streetlamps.

THE DRIVER

The street they followed spilled out onto another, where a long wall ran along the one shoulder. Eight feet high, the barrier was made of brick and topped with metal spikes. When the dwarf reached it, he turned and followed along its length until he reached a gate. The wooden double door was open, and the dwarf passed through. Royce paused to study the latch and hinges for a moment. They were simple iron drawbolts. The oddity was the presence of latches on both sides. The doors could be used to lock people in or out. With a hesitant glance at Hadrian, Royce continued after the dwarf.

Within the confines of the wall was a completely different world of tightly packed wooden shacks. The widest streets inside were the size of the narrowest alleys outside. Here, too, were cart vendors, but narrow as the streets were, the vendors nearly blocked them, causing pedestrians to squeeze around wagons and barrels. Royce and Hadrian had only traversed one block when Royce stopped. With concern, he looked up and down the street.

"What is it?" Hadrian asked.

"We're in trouble."

Hadrian looked around. They were on the cobblestones of a narrow block gripped between shabby shacks where laundry hung from the sills of open windows. Residents gathered in small groups, some in front of doorways, others at intersections around trash fires, warming themselves. The alleged driver of the ducal carriage had stopped at one of these and talked with those huddling around it.

"What's wrong? What do you mean?"

"Don't you see?"

Hadrian looked again but couldn't find a threat. "See what?"

"We stand out," he declared. "Literally. Everyone here is short."

Hadrian looked again. Royce was right. All along the street, not a single person was more than four feet tall, and nearly all the men had beards of considerable length that were frequently braided or bound with ribbon.

"What do we do now? Walk on our knees?"

Royce shushed him, guiding Hadrian into the shadow of a porch. The thief focused on the group at the intersection's fire, where the driver had paused to chat with five other dwarves. They mostly stood with arms folded across their chests, but on occasion, they would hold out their hands to the heat.

At that distance, Hadrian couldn't hear what they said, but he suspected Royce could. "What are they saying?"

"Arguing about the weather," Royce replied.

"How can you argue about weather?"

Again, Royce motioned him to silence, and Hadrian leaned against the grayed wall of the building where they sheltered. In the window, a sign hung. Maybe it said HELP WANTED or ROOM TO LET, but Hadrian couldn't tell. It wasn't written in any language he recognized. The window itself was oddly low, and the pair of rocking chairs on the porch looked to be for children.

This is like a miniature version of the world.

"I feel like a giant," he told Royce. He turned back to the ring of dwarves around the fire, where a heated argument was growing; two of the dwarves gesticulated wildly, thrusting fists over their heads. Even Hadrian caught the occasional shout of "Don't tell *me* what is and what isn't!"

THE DRIVER

"These people really take their weather seriously."

"Not arguing about the weather anymore," Royce reported.

"What are they talking about?"

"Don't know. Something to do with the Calians, mir, and the coming of spring. Our guy isn't too popular, either. Nor is he happy with them. And nobody likes the duke. And—" Royce tilted his head to listen. "They're holding a meeting, an important one in the Calian Precinct. Sounds like it has something to do with an alliance."

The streets were emptying, and windows shuttered as the night erased the day's earlier promise of coming spring. The cold of winter had returned, reminding everyone it wasn't yet finished. The driver hoisted his sack and bid a less-than-fond farewell to those around the fire. He headed off into the darkening streets. Royce waved at Hadrian, and together they followed.

The dwarf stopped at a tiny butcher shop. There he haggled in an unfamiliar language over one of three chickens that hung from the porch rafters. A great deal of pointing, scowling, and foot stomping accompanied the conversation. The bird under debate was so small and scrawny that Hadrian questioned whether it was a chicken at all. If not for the white feathers, he might have guessed a crow. In the end, the driver reluctantly handed over coins and took the pair of legs, swinging the chicken as he walked. Then he stopped at a wheelbarrow where what appeared to be an elderly husband and wife sold firewood. The driver picked out three splits as if he were choosing produce in a market. Burdened as he was with an armload of wood, his sack, and a scrawny chicken that he continued to heedlessly whip about with the swing of his arm, the dwarf continued until he came to a tiny shack. The wood siding had been weathered to a dark gray. The upper story jutted out over the lower, creating an overhang that shadowed the door. A light shone from inside, and without a knock, the driver entered.

The shack had two glassless windows. Tattered cloth covered both, but one covering was ripped, and through it Royce and Hadrian spied on their suspect. To Hadrian's shock, more than a dozen people were within. Children and elders, male and female, they all crowded into the small space of one room. The light came from a cook fire where a surprisingly cute dwarven lady took the bird from the driver. With children pulling on her apron, she held up the chicken, made some comment, and then kissed the driver on his nose. The two laughed.

Instantly feeling guilty for spying, Hadrian left Royce to monitor the dwarf while he found an abandoned crate to sit on near a rubbish pile. After Royce's commentary, he'd expected that the dwarf was on his way to some nefarious hideout, a creepy tower, or ancient ruin where Genny Winter was chained to a wall or suspended over alligators. Instead, he was snooping on the hard-working provider for a warm and loving family. Their poverty made the act of spying even more distasteful. Hadrian hadn't been invading merely a gathering but an event as sacred as a funeral. Most of the garbage pile he waited in consisted of wood chips and strips of bark, which made Hadrian think it might not be rubbish at all. In a household so picky about buying firewood, he couldn't imagine them discarding anything that burned.

Hours went by before Royce approached Hadrian. The thief had something small in his hands. "Not a stoneworker," he said, holding up an exquisitely carved wooden figurine of a rearing horse, polished and lacquered to a honey finish. Every muscle and the individual strands of hair in its mane and tail were rendered in startling detail.

"It's beautiful."

Royce nodded. "There's a shed around the other side filled with things like this."

"Why doesn't he sell them?" Hadrian looked over at the house. "I don't know what they pay him at the Estate, but I would think such craftsmanship would pay well. This is better than what I've seen in the shop windows."

Royce nodded while still looking at the carving.

"We spending the night?" Hadrian asked.

Royce shrugged, then pivoted abruptly.

Hadrian heard it, too. The front door of the shack clapped. The woodcarver, and alleged driver of duchesses, was on the move again.

With cloak on and hood up, the dwarf appeared significantly more sinister than before as he slipped out of the shack and set out into the night. This time he clutched a bread-loaf-sized box in his arms and presented the image of the quintessential villain of a hundred children's stories: Gronbach, the little bearded dwarf bent on evil. As the driver scurried through the shadows, Hadrian had no trouble believing the tales of a nefarious dwarf. The scene was fable-perfect, except he had also seen the earlier moments when a tired worker dragged himself back to his impoverished family and provided them a miserable excuse of a chicken. Kisses from a loving wife were never part of the Gronbach myth. He didn't even have a wife or children. In the fairy tales, he was a monster, and his reputation cast a shadow over all dwarves.

The little guy moved with more speed, darting up the maze of narrow streets. At one point, he broke into a trot, and Hadrian was certain he'd been discovered. But after a few yards, the dwarf slowed to a quick walk. If he had looked back, the driver would have spotted Hadrian, who stalked with his own hood up. The dwarf certainly would wonder about the tall man with three swords strolling late at night in a dwarven enclave, but he wouldn't see Royce. While the thief was much closer, he was slipping from shadow to shadow and appearing as little more than a flutter, a faint disturbance that could have been the corner of a firewood tarp blown by the wind. But the dwarf didn't so much as glance over his shoulder as he maintained a generally northeastern course, avoiding windows, doors, and firelight.

Convinced they were finally on their way to the sinister ruined tower and alligator pit, Hadrian was puzzled when the dwarf approached a figure at the entrance to a cemetery. The burial ground was a modest patch of headstones walled in by a tight congestion of stone buildings, one of which might have been a small church. The tombstones, however, were marvelous. Even at a distance, they revealed artistry. Dwarves were known for stonework as much as for kidnapping young women, and the statuary in that yard was more beautiful than any he'd ever seen. Most were depictions of people—the deceased, Hadrian assumed. These weren't the diminutive, malevolently hooded monsters of a host of cautionary tales, but the exquisite heroes of their own stories. Straight, proud, smiling figures looked up at the sky or down with empathy at those who might come to grieve on their behalf.

This is how they see themselves, he thought. Combining this sight with the scene in the shack, Hadrian began to wonder if there would be an alligator pit at all.

The dwarf walked directly up to the figure at the entrance, no hesitation, no greeting, either. The fellow waiting at the gate to the cemetery was tall, thin, and dark-skinned, with hair that was mostly gray.

Royce looked backward with apprehension, and in his gaze was a wealth of information. He wasn't so much looking for anything as telling Hadrian to be wary. One slaughterhouse wagon was more than enough. Not that another runaway cart would be the threat again. This tiny street was peppered with windows, doors, and a host of other obstacles: barrels, awnings, porch steps, and piles of garbage. Royce wasn't saying, *Watch out for another killer wagon* but rather, *I don't like the feel of this; keep your eyes open for a trap.*

The fact that Royce had exchanged so much information with a look disturbed Hadrian. There was no doubt he had *heard* Royce correctly on all counts, and Hadrian's utter confidence in that silent discourse only added to the anxiety that he was harmonizing with Royce's mind. While that was good for work, Hadrian couldn't shake the sense that it was bad for everything else—like his sanity.

Sticking close to the walls and staying out of the moonlight, Hadrian crept up to where Royce stood at the base of the three-story church—the only stone building in the neighborhood, which obviously predated everything around it.

" . . . ninety-eight swords, half as many shields."

"Why so few shields?"

"Shields aren't as important and are harder to store," the dwarf said. "We haven't stopped. Production has slowed, sure, but that's all. Don't forget we're the ones carrying the burden. The rest of you aren't out a single din."

"You're just scared," the Calian replied. "We all had great hopes the ransom would succeed, but the feast is the day after tomorrow. Spring is coming, my friend, and whether I'm the seed, the rock, or the sod, I fear the plow."

The dwarf nodded. "Time's up. A hundred swords is the best we can do." He held out the box. "But with this, it should be more than enough."

"I'm more frightened of what you hold than the swords." The Calian eyed the container as if the dwarf were waving a crossbow in his face. "Griswold, if it becomes necessary, will *you* use it?"

"This one is yours." The dwarf handed the box to the Calian.

He took it slowly, gingerly, and held it away from his body, as if a swarm of angry bees were inside.

"With that, I can ask the same of you. Will you use *yours?*" the dwarf asked.

"If it comes to it, what choice do we have? A hundred swords won't be enough, and Villar will use his. Giving him a monopoly on such power would be the pinnacle of stupidity. We have a responsibility to act as safeguards to one another. And then there's the sacrifices to think about. Not to mention what happens afterward."

"That's something we'll decide when we get there—if we get there. One can't start building a house without determining the size and shape of the foundation."

"Comments like that are what make others see only your height," the Calian said. "You're reinforcing false ideas. You're a woodcarver, for Novron's sake!"

The dwarf laughed. "I'm a woodcarver, but in no way is it for Novron's sake."

They both smiled. Then the Calian stretched his neck and peered up the road. Hadrian and Royce froze, but the Calian didn't see them. "Where is Villar?"

The dwarf gave his own casual glance. "He's usually the first one here, isn't he?"

"Do you think—"

Royce spun and shoved Hadrian out into the street. Off balance and bewildered, he staggered backward into the moonlight, catching the attention of the dwarf and the Calian. They both stared at him in shock and fear.

"What the—" Hadrian began just as the thief sprang to his side. An instant later, a massive block of stone struck the street where the two had been standing. It shattered, kicking up a small cloud of dust.

Looking up, Hadrian spotted a silhouette peering down from the roofline of the church. It withdrew from sight, melting into the darkness.

"Meet you back at the boardinghouse," Royce said quickly as he leapt to a windowsill. From there, he scaled the stonework to the church's roof where he, too, vanished.

Hadrian looked back toward the graveyard. The dwarf and the Calian were running away in opposite directions.

Hadrian had always considered himself a good runner, but that night he was handicapped by racing in the darkness of an unknown city. Weighed down by three swords while chasing a slender man with a solid head start didn't help, either. Unable to pursue both, and already knowing where the dwarf lived, he chose to follow the Calian. The good news was that his target appeared to be considerably older, and he still protectively held the dwarf's box.

The contents must be valuable or he would've dropped it before running.

The Calian cut through an alley Hadrian didn't know existed, pulling down stacks of empty crates to block his pursuer's progress. By the time Hadrian emerged from the debris-strewn alleyway, the Calian had gained a greater lead and was openly sprinting down the center of the next street. Hadrian didn't know what time it was, but he guessed it was after decent folk went to bed. Few remained on the cobblestone thoroughfares, and while all of them stopped to watch, none made any attempt to stop his pursuit. The Calian tried to lose him by cutting through more alleys, and he succeeded. Hadrian lost sight of his target; the man was gone. Guessing that the man would head for the same gate that marked the exit from the dwarven community, Hadrian ran for it. He was rewarded by a glimpse of the Calian racing out.

He headed south toward the harbor, sandaled feet striking the stone in rapid slaps. In the growing fog of the silent streets, Hadrian could hear the man long after he'd lost sight of him. This was the only noise the Calian made. Hadrian generated a multitude of sounds: clapping swords, the flap of his cloak, and the pounding of his boot heels.

Luckily, the Calian was slowing down, getting tired most likely. Darting into a series of dilapidated houses, he dodged a ladder and jumped a pile of manure that Hadrian slipped in. He didn't fall, but it was close.

They both ducked under a clothesline loaded with clothes someone had forgotten to take in. With boots still slick with muck, Hadrian ran past a cascading avalanche of busted crates, over an open sewer grate, around a brimming water barrel, and into a yard enclosed by a battered wooden fence. The Calian managed to leap the stockade-style wall, and for precious seconds, Hadrian lost sight of him again.

By the time Hadrian had cleared the fence, he'd once more lost his prey.

The barrier was merely a dividing line between one property and another—separating an alley filled with a stack of broken wagon wheels and one filled with dented buckets. The Calian could have gone left or right. Rather than running off blindly, Hadrian stood still, held his breath, and listened. He had no idea where he was anymore. They had raced up a dozen different streets. The architecture was back to four-story buildings with stone bases and timber-and-stucco uppers. Damp, salty air accompanied a growing level of fog, which reduced his visibility to half a block. His only clue was a familiar pungent fragrance, a pervasive incense burned in many homes in Calis.

Slap. Slap. Slap.

Off to his left.

He darted around the buckets and back out onto a street, another tiny affair. Again, he had a choice, and once more Hadrian paused to listen. He waited but heard nothing.

Is he hiding? Hadrian was exhausted after the long run. The old Calian had to be, too, or maybe he'd realized it wasn't such a good idea leading his pursuer back to his home. Or perhaps he had simply taken off his sandals. Slowly, carefully, trying to make as little noise as possible, Hadrian made a calculated guess that the Calian had continued in the same general, southerly direction, and he crept that way. Reaching an intersection, he found a lonely streetlamp illuminating three choices. Straight ahead lay the masts of ships, black against the starry sky. To his right, the dark edifice of the cathedral towered over rooftops and the bright-white fog. Its lower reaches were illuminated by the increased presence of streetlamps. To his left, there was only darkness.

I'd pick darkness, Hadrian thought and started down the dismal street. He'd only gone a few steps when he heard a wet tearing noise. In daylight, while surrounded by a crowd of smiling friends, the sound would have made him cringe, but in a strange, dark place of mist and twisting streets, it made him shudder. This wasn't a happy noise. Hadrian drew his short sword. The metal made a soft ring as it left the scabbard. Something moved. Hadrian saw little more than a shift in shadows, but the sound was a harsh sudden jerk, the sort a startled deer might make. There was a thrash—something knocked over—and then silence.

Hadrian guessed his prey was fleeing again and quickly rounded the corner. He tripped, and this time he did fall. He hit the hard alley floor with his left shoulder and knee, grunting with the pain that shot up his thigh. His knuckles struck the cobblestones hard enough to make him let go of the blade. Instinct made him roll to one side and snatch up his weapon as he did. He raised the blade in defense against the expected attack.

No one was there.

He was alone, lying on the ground in a dark alley, feeling foolish. Hand throbbing, knee aching, shoulder sore, he once more held his breath to listen. All he heard was the distant ringing of cathedral bells.

It's official, I've lost him.

Royce would never let him hear the end of this fiasco. *You couldn't even catch an old man?*

Angry and disappointed, Hadrian looked for what had finally tripped him up. It took several seconds of staring to understand what he was seeing. It failed to make sense in so many ways that his mind took a great deal of convincing to finally accept it.

Three steps back, the Calian was sprawled on the wet stone. Hadrian knew him by the burgundy wrap, the green scarf, and the box. These features provided the identity rather than his face, because he no longer had one.

CHAPTER FIFTEEN
BIRD HUNTING

Royce leapt from the roof of the four-story building and landed on the slate tiles of the structure on the opposite side of the street. He ran to the ridgeline and sprinted along it. A slender figure in a dark, hooded cloak ran with abandon ahead of him. Racing entirely across rooftops, Royce had pursued his quarry out of the congested dwarven district toward the center of town. At that moment, the cathedral's soaring tower began tolling ominous peals of cascading notes, providing musical accompaniment for the drama unfolding against the starry night sky.

With buildings tightly packed, the canopy tour had been without serious challenge. Still, Royce's prey had been impressive. He'd proved more than comfortable with heights. He was fast, agile, and clever in his maneuvers. The moment his quarry had decided to make his flight across the high ground, Royce experienced a giddy sense of victory. Rarely did a target act so agreeably. Rather than trying to disappear into the unfamiliar maze of city streets, this guy was like a bird trying to escape a shark by diving into the ocean. Royce's sense of jubilation was soon replaced with a rush of excitement at finding an unexpected challenge. This bird, he was stunned to discover, could swim.

Ahead was trouble. They were at the end of the easy jumps. Before them was another street-imposed gap, a wide one, and on the far side, the vertical wall of a much taller building.

Royce expected his prey to slow, to hesitate, to double back or climb down. Any of these would have granted Royce the opportunity to catch up to a lethal distance. Instead, once more his little bird did the unexpected. Reaching the end of the building, the figure didn't slow or pause. Instead, he made a running leap directly at the wall of the taller building. He missed the wall and smashed through a window, taking down a curtain. Royce was right behind, diving through the narrow opening of shattered glass. He expected his bird to be on the floor tangled in cloth and bleeding from cuts. All he found was the glass-laden drape and an open door creaking slightly.

Royce rolled to his feet, bolted out the door, and raced down a corridor into a very strange place. He almost ran into a knight before discovering it was merely pieces of armor stacked in the shape of a man. It even held a spear in one of its gauntlets. Royce found himself on an upper-story indoor balcony that circled a large four-story chamber. No one was in the building. This was a public business of some sort, and at that late hour, the place was dark except for the glow of streetlamps entering the windows. Below, were numerous displays: pedestals supporting statues, books, musical instruments, tools, even clothing on stuffed dummies. In the center stood a huge chariot and two stuffed white horses. Much of one wall was covered in a mural depicting the landscape of an impossibly grand city lit by a perfect summer sun. Paintings in lavish frames covered the other walls. Hanging from the ceiling were still more oddities. The most eye-catching was a massive creature that looked to be a dragon suspended over the center of the chamber by several chains. The thing was huge, but not real. It appeared to be made of painted cloth wrapped over a wooden frame.

Distracted by the bizarre nature of the place, which seemed to be some kind of curio shop, Royce gave up several seconds to his fleeing quarry. The sound of shattering glass pulled his attention back. He spotted the figure breaking a window on the far side and raced around the balcony to the broken opening. Outside was a sheer drop to the street; his prey had gone up.

The climb wasn't trivial. Several of the handholds were no more than fingertip-sized, but his bird had scaled the wall quickly. Before Royce was halfway up, his quarry was on the roof. A moment later a series of slate shingles flew his way. The first barely missed him, shattering on the stone to the left of his face. Royce had to duck the second, which he heard as it passed. More were coming.

With a lurch, Royce leapt up and caught hold of one of the grotesque downspouts. This one looked like an evil, sharp-toothed dog, snarling and extending a long serpent's tongue. He hugged the statue around its neck as another shingle clipped his boot. The impact stung. If it had hit his head, Royce would've fallen. The next shingle came, this one aimed higher. Royce managed to catch it as he dangled one-handed from the dog's head. His enemy boldly straddled the ridgeline. The rising moon was behind him, giving a silvery outline to his whipping cloak that snapped in the wind. With his adversary's hood up, all Royce could see was a nose, part of a cheek, and a chin.

I'm chasing myself.

Royce waited until his opponent bent down to pry up another slate before throwing the one he'd caught. Slate shingles weren't knives, and his throw was off. Royce had aimed at the hood, but it hit his target in the thigh. Despite the bad aim, he was rewarded with a grunt.

Royce pulled himself up on top of the dog's head, then sprang to the eave, catching the lip. Another strong pull and he was crouching on the roof. He scanned the ridgeline. The shingle-thrower had abandoned his attack and was back to running. He sprinted along the peak, then veered right, following a long gable. It acted like a plank extending off the side of a ship. By the time Royce reached the gable, his prey had made the long jump across the gap of an alley, which separated the strange shop from Grom Galimus—the same alley where, only hours earlier, he and Hadrian had followed the dwarf. His hooded bird landed safely on the far side, touching down on another gargoyle, its ugly head protruding out from the side of cathedral's buttress. Royce made the same leap, landing on the same stony head: a hideous lion with fangs that extended well past its lower jaw.

By then, Royce's twin was already climbing up the buttress's pier, a sheer column of stone.

They were already up five stories. Royce could see the plaza out front, where the massive statue of Novron looked tiny. What he'd thought to be a curio shop was the Imperial Gallery, whose roof he was now looking down at. Still, they were only halfway up the side of the cathedral.

Slab after slab, ornate divider after divider, Royce scaled the stone pier in pursuit.

Who is this?

Royce had never encountered anyone who could match his skill at climbing, his ease in high places, or his ability to see in dim light. This hood-and-cloak really could be his long-lost brother. With each foot they scaled together, Royce's respect for his adversary grew. Even if this guy wasn't connected to the job, Royce couldn't give up this chase.

I've got to find out who this is.

When he reached the top of the pier, Royce's rival swung around the little pointed cap and ran up the incline of the flying buttress. If the long, rising arm that held up the side wall had been a bridge, it could have spanned half the Roche River. Running up its slope, they both gained significant height. Reaching the top, they jumped a stone railing that protected a long balcony just below the eaves of the main roof. They were above the great oculus window, above the creepy statues of old men in draped robes who glared down with stern indignation, but above them still more gargoyles jutted from the edge of the roof—no two alike.

Royce's adversary raced down the length of the open walkway, which ran along one side of the churchlike battlements on a castle. At the balcony's end, the hood-and-cloak had only two choices: up or down. Stakes were literally higher now. The wind at that height was brutal, and unlike all the previous roofs, Grom Galimus's pitch was sharp as a miserly wedge of cheese. Royce trotted up, waiting to see which way his prey would choose. When his opponent went up, Royce found himself oddly pleased. This game of cat and mouse wouldn't end with a whimper.

Far too steep to walk up, the roof offered vertical ribbing that divided the sets of shale shingles. Royce's opponent used them to pull himself along the slick surface. What the roof didn't offer was a usable ridgeline. A tall fin of decorative metalwork crowned its peak. Royce's enemy shimmied higher, kicking the slates and creating an avalanche with his heels. Displaced shingles cracked, and the broken bits fell down toward Royce. Shifting left and then right between the ribs, he dodged the cascade. With each shift, he climbed higher until he, too, reached the ridgeline.

"You've run out of places to climb," Royce shouted above the rush of wind that snapped both their cloaks. "What now?"

His adversary's hood tilted up, assessing the bell tower. As far up as the two of them were, the tower of Grom Galimus went up half again as high. While not the height of the Crown Tower, it was nothing to scoff at.

"You'll never reach it before I get you," Royce told him as he continued to inch closer. "And what good would it do?"

His quarry turned to face him, and as he did, the wind caught the hood and blew it back. A pale face adorned with arched eyebrows accentuated a pair of angry, angled eyes. Swept-back hair displayed a broad forehead and ears that came to sharp points.

That explains a lot. In at least one sense, we are related.

The two faced off with cloaks snapping back and forth like cat's tails—two male tabbies having a deadly dispute over territory.

"Who are you?" the mir demanded with a harsh eastern accent, the words kicked out from behind clenched teeth.

"You don't know?" Royce was puzzled. "I'm the guy you tried to crush with a rock. Is that something you do to random strangers?"

"You shouldn't be in Rochelle. Our business is our own. Leave now and you can go in peace. If you continue to interfere, you and your friend will be added to the list."

The mir looked off to his right, searching for an escape and finding none.

"There's a list?"

Royce lunged forward, hoping to catch his prey's wrist. Just as quickly, the mir jerked away. He tried to switch his grip but missed with the other hand, his balance off, his footing lost. Down he went on the far side of the roof, sliding across the surface of the slates on his back like a kid riding a sled. He pushed out with his feet against the ribbing, trying to stop, but the momentum was too great.

Royce held his breath as he watched. Hanging onto the wrought-iron crown of the peak, it was all too easy to imagine taking that trip, the conclusion of which Royce already knew.

Coming to the end of the roof, the mir made a desperate grab for the railing of the balcony but missed it by more than a foot. His speed skipped him well away from the walls of the cathedral. There wasn't a scream. Royce appreciated that. He had no idea who had just died, but under different circumstances he might have made a valuable addition to Riyria.

Just as well, he thought. *We'd have had to change the name.*

Taking a more deliberate and far slower route, Royce descended to the balcony and peered over the railing. Below, lay buttresses. The dead man had most likely missed hitting them. Below that lay the river.

Royce climbed the rest of the way down, taking his time, not only because he'd seen the repercussions of a tiny mistake, but because he felt no urgency. He expected to spot the mir's body impaled on one of the gargoyle snouts or at the very least on the bank of the Roche River, but Royce had found neither. He walked the length of the riverbank, first south then back north, and saw no evidence of a body.

Could he have hit the river? Royce looked up at the slope of Grom Galimus's roof. Theoretically, it was possible. Still, the fall would have been painful and likely fatal.

Royce scanned the surface of the moonlit water for any floating, body-sized object. Nothing.

It was as if his bird had flown away.

Royce spent more than an hour searching the base of the cathedral and the banks of the river just to be thorough. Satisfied, he returned to Hemsworth House and walked up a deserted Mill Street just as Hadrian was walking down. Only those up to no good, or people with no place to go, would be outdoors at that hour. Royce had to remind himself that he didn't fall into either group, at least not that night. It felt strange, and yet it was an altogether too common reality as of late. Over the last few years, Royce had found himself acting within the limits of the law. They were making more money with less risk, yet it felt wrong, like writing with his left hand or walking backward.

The two met in front of the boardinghouse in a bank of fog. "Any luck?" Hadrian asked.

Royce shook his head. "Had a fun run. Got a squirrel's tour of the city."

Hadrian looked shocked. "He got away from you?"

"He took a tumble. Pretty sure he's dead."

They spoke just above a whisper. The fog demanded it. Royce always enjoyed a good fog. It reduced visibility while increasing the distance sound traveled. And since it usually occurred during the shifting temperatures of night or early morning, it proved a thief's friend and an assassin's weapon. Spring and autumn were the seasons for lowland mist, and rivers were its breeding ground. That night the river was working overtime, and the oil lamp in front of Evelyn Hemsworth's home served to do nothing but illuminate the white haze.

"Any idea who he was?" Hadrian asked.

"A mir," Royce replied. "Said we should leave or we were going to be added to a list."

"There's a list?"

"That's what I said."

"And why both of us? I didn't chase him."

Royce smiled. "Maybe he didn't want you to feel left out."

"Oh, well, at least someone thinks about me."

"What happened to the dwarf and the Calian?"

"They bolted in different directions."

"You followed the Calian, right?"

Hadrian nodded. "Chased him clear across town, almost to the docks."

"And?"

"He went around a corner. I lost him for a bit; then I tripped over his body."

"He was dead? Did you see who killed him?"

"Nope."

"Was his throat slit?"

"No, worse."

"How so?"

"His face was gone. Looked like it had been eaten."

Royce had excellent hearing. At that moment, he could tell a mongrel dog was padding its way along the alley one block up, but he still wasn't certain he'd heard Hadrian correctly. "Did you say *eaten?*"

Hadrian adjusted his scarf, tucking the ends inside the leather of his tunic. "Chewed up pretty bad."

Royce leaned in. "Is that new?" He gestured at the knitted garment.

Hadrian grinned and hooked his thumb, showing the blue-dyed wool in the hazy lamplight. "Like it? I was down in the Calian section of town. That place never goes to sleep. All sorts of merchants still selling everything imaginable. Honestly, you should go there. I'll help you shop. We could get you a nice new cloak, didn't see any polka dots but there was a sweet lemon-yellow one. You'd look good. What do you think?"

"You stopped to buy a scarf in the middle of the night?"

Hadrian shrugged. "An impulse buy. I just happened to spot it at the *fourth* cart I went to. Actually, I was hoping for a whole cloak, but this was all I could find. You should get yourself one."

"Why?"

"Because it's blue, and because I think having a face is a good thing."

Royce rolled his eyes. "Let's try to keep focused, shall we? What about the box? Let me guess; it was taken and you didn't get a chance to look inside?"

"Why would you assume that?"

"It's just the way these things always seem to go," Royce grumbled. "You either have a day when everything works out or one when nothing does. Following the dwarf turned up only that he has a family and likes to carve wood; the guy you went after led nowhere, and the phantom who tried to flatten us with a slab of stone killed himself, denying me the opportunity to check his body. With such a grand set of circumstances, I must assume the box also vanished, thereby putting the perfect finish to a miserable day."

"We know where the dwarf lives. We can—"

"He'll be gone, along with his whole family. You saw that place. They're as tight-knit as a sweater knotted out of human hair."

Hadrian looked at him with that appalled expression he so often wore when Royce talked about drowning loud dogs or eliminating witnesses. "A sweater made out of—"

"I'm just saying, it's going to take a lot of torture to get anyone in that neighborhood to talk."

"We aren't torturing anyone."

Royce rolled his eyes. "Well, I certainly wouldn't be taking you along if I was. But it doesn't matter, they would only lie. To get the truth I'd have to launch a complex operation where I could—"

"No torture, Royce."

Royce frowned. "So, to reiterate . . . the perfect finish to a miserable day."

"So pessimistic." Hadrian shook his head slowly, frowning. "I was thinking just the opposite. About how good the day turned out to be." He raised his hand, spreading his fingers. "Count with me." He held back a finger. "First, we managed to discover where the dwarf lived." He held back another. "Second, we found two more suspects he was colluding with, and where they were meeting." Another finger. "Third, we *didn't* get crushed by a block of granite." He bent another back. "Fourth, the fellow you were chasing fell to *his* death—not you. Nor did you kill him, so we are also not wanted for murder this morning. I consider that a plus even if you might not." He held back his thumb. "Best of all, I still have a handsome face." Hadrian shook his five fingers at Royce like a child waving an enthusiastic hello. "So you see, we had a very good day, and to prove it let me put forth the evidence of the box. It wasn't taken, Mister Grim. I found it on the ground beside the Calian. Apparently, all his assailant was after was the man's face."

"And inside?"

Hadrian's expression lost its buoyant sarcasm. "Rocks."

"Rocks?"

Hadrian rolled his shoulders. "Just a box of gravel. That's all that was inside. I dug through it, which I should get credit for. Especially given that I was in a dark, foggy alley next to a faceless corpse, but yeah, it was just gravel."

"So, the box wasn't taken, but it turned out to be empty for all practical purposes, and you claim that as evidence that we had a good day?"

"Still have a face, see?" Hadrian grinned at him.

"Yes, I see. I see very well, in fact, which is part of why I don't accept it as conclusive proof that things worked out for the best."

Hadrian scowled.

Royce reached Hemsworth's door, and as expected, it was locked.

"You just hate being happy, don't you?" Hadrian asked.

"I have no idea. What's it like?"

If Royce needed any more evidence Hadrian was wrong about the day, he found it the moment he popped the lock and opened the door to the boardinghouse. Inside, Evelyn Hemsworth stood before him. She was dressed in a beige robe, her hair wrapped in a floral-print scarf, her arms folded. She stared with a surprised expression that quickly soured.

"How did you get in?" she asked accusingly. "I *locked* that door."

"I guess I used the key you gave us."

"I gave you nothing of the sort."

"We rent a room here. How can you expect us to get in if you lock the door and don't give us a key?"

"I told you, I expect those under my roof to arrive during civilized hours. I don't approve of you slinking in at all hours like a pair of burglars. There's no legitimate reason for a body to be on the streets at this time of night. No reputable excuse. Now, as I did not—as I said—give you a key, how did you open that door?"

"You must have forgotten to lock it."

Evelyn took a menacing step forward, glaring at Royce with a stern-faced expression. She jabbed at him with her forefinger. "Don't get smart with me, young man. You know full well that door was locked, and that I never gave either one of you a key. Now, explain yourself."

Royce pointed at Hadrian. "He did it."

Hadrian's brows went up. "Did not."

Evelyn's eyes narrowed on Royce. "You're dancing on the edge of a very steep cliff, my boy."

"What happened to treading on thin ice? I only ask because I don't dance."

She ignored him. "I don't like these late-night shenanigans the two of you have been conducting. I also don't like being woken from a dead sleep by someone banging on my door!"

Royce glanced at Hadrian, who showed he was just as puzzled. "We didn't knock."

"Not you." Evelyn shook a hand at them. "The other one. Got me up by threatening to break down my door. Hammered on it with his fists, which was utterly futile. My husband was a tax collector, you see. He took precautions against home invasion. Would take a battering ram to break this door. So, after tiring himself out and getting frustrated, he tried to convince me he was your *brother*." She sniffed indignantly. "As if I couldn't tell the difference."

"I don't have a brother," Royce said.

"Well, if you did, I wouldn't let him in, either. Not at that time of night. I told him I didn't care if he was related to the duke. It was far too late to be banging on proper people's doors. If he had business with you, he would have to conduct it in the morning at a decent hour."

"What'd he say?" Hadrian asked this time.

"That he *knew* you weren't back, and he'd wait quietly in your room so I could go back to sleep."

"You didn't let him in, did you?"

Evelyn rolled her eyes. "What do you take me for? Of course not. The fellow was dressed up like a bandit in a dark hood and cloak, and soaking-wet as if he'd just taken a bath in his clothes. And he was a *mir*." She whispered this last bit as if it was a dirty secret. "Which is proof he was lying about being your brother. I certainly wasn't opening the door for a dishonest, drenched marauder. Do you think me a fool? That person was up to no good. Dangerous is what he was, and while you're under this roof, you're under my protection."

The bird is still alive? And he knows where we're staying.

Evelyn Hemsworth didn't look like any sort of bodyguard Royce would have picked, but there was no denying that she'd defended them from the most dangerous adversary Royce had encountered in years.

"So, he finally left." She leaned in toward Royce, her arms still folded, her eyes locked on his. "The two of you had better mend your ways. I can see you're falling in with a bad crowd. You both seem to be decent boys, granted a bit dim-witted and slow, but the captain of the city guard vouches for you, and—"

Royce and Hadrian both raised their brows.

"Don't look so surprised. When I heard you were picked up by the watchmen, I was planning on throwing you out into the street. But then I asked Captain Wyberg about it, and he said it was all a misunderstanding. He also said that you two"— she nodded rather than pointed in Hadrian's direction—"had served together. Still, this city has bad elements. And if you're not careful, you'll end up in trouble. We don't want that, do we?"

"No, ma'am," Hadrian said.

"And I won't be having any more late-night visitors banging on my door, will I?"

"No, ma'am," Hadrian repeated.

"And no more fiddling with my lock," she said to Royce. "Agreed?"

"Yes," he replied.

"Good." She nodded curtly. "And don't be late for breakfast. I'm making waffles."

CHAPTER SIXTEEN
LOOKING AWAY

Genny had a razor-sharp edge on four of the silver coins. The key was a bigger issue. It made more noise when she scraped it, and the metal was much harder. She also couldn't grind it just anywhere as she did with the coins. Those she scraped across the floor, and then covered the marks with the straw. The key, she had to file down carefully. Genny needed to grind away all the teeth except the top one. That meant she could only use rocks that protruded, providing an adequate edge. The rocks comprising the floor were flush and smooth. She was instead forced to scrape it against one of three stones that jutted far enough out from the wall. Luckily all three were hard and abrasive. And with nothing else to do, Genny managed to reduce her trunk key into little more than a cylindrical barrel with a single tooth at the end like a tiny, mouse-sized hoe.

LOOKING AWAY

After nearly two weeks, the key was close to done, and so were Genny's fingers. They throbbed, and her knuckles were a series of abrasions, two of which had scabs. Taking a break, she hid the key in the wall crevice. Then she lay down on the straw and sucked on her fingertips, staring at the ceiling. The underside was plaster. Parts of it had been painted. Most had faded; other sections had chipped and fallen. An old bird's nest was in one corner. She wondered how a bird had gotten in, then realized the door must be new.

Why am I still here? Why hasn't Leo agreed to the demands? Even if her life wasn't in jeopardy, what Mercator was asking made sense.

If the situation were reversed, she would have traded the duchy for Leo.

So why hasn't he?

Genny knew why. The answer to that question was too obvious, sort of like standing in a lush field and wondering about the color of grass. All she needed to do was look down, but Genny didn't want to. All her life she had looked, forced herself to see what others refused to accept. How much easier it would have been to welcome her role as a dutiful daughter, to blind herself to the facts and pretend everything was fine.

After her mother's death, her father gave up. Because he was a whiskey distiller, everyone expected Gabriel Winter to resign from life by becoming a drunk. Everyone thought he'd crawl into one of his casks, but that just showed how little they knew him. Her father didn't drink, never had. Even when he taste-tested, he spat. But there was more than one way to withdraw, and a man didn't need to be a drunk to become mean. People made excuses for him. Some even lied. And there were those who came right out and said that her life would be easier if she *looked away*.

"Get married," they told her. "Find a man and make a new home." But Genny knew that wasn't in her future, not back then. Even as a young girl, she knew spinsterhood was all but certain. Instead, Genny ignored all the advice. She looked, she saw, and she accepted the way things were—and then she decided to change them.

With the general abdication of her father, Genny took the reins of the business and rebuilt it. In less than a decade, Winter's Whiskey went from a cheap black-market product to a posh commodity. A few hidden stills that ran on stolen grain became the largest warehouse and distillery in the world, buying thousands of pounds of rye, oats, and barley. Genny even went so far as to purchase rights to farms from Count Simon, an unprecedented act since only royals controlled land. That could only happen in Colnora, which had always had its own rules. As long as the money flowed, the crown *looked away*. Genny made a habit of ignoring traditions, of pushing the boundaries that others observed but she saw as too limiting. With a loud mouth, a refusal to accept restrictions, an irritating habit of being right, and absolutely no concern as to what others thought of her, she ran naked and laughed at the fools who raced her in long robes. Success proved she was right, and that was all she needed.

This was the one lie she told herself. The only reality she chose not to *look away* from.

Genny convinced herself that saving her father would be enough. That and beating all those arrogant merchants who called her names. Hatred was another form of admiration, she concluded, and wealth was the measure of worth. The deception was hardly a choice. Love wasn't a commodity she could buy. Her blind eye was a simple matter of finding contentment within the bounds of the possible.

Then one day, a man, a duke, a short, portly, balding eastern noble smiled at her; and just like that, what was possible changed.

The situation was made unbearable because she genuinely liked him. Leo wasn't handsome or dashing; he was awkward and often silly. But when she was in the room, his eyes never left her. Many suggested he only pretended to care to get at her money. Her own father had told her that—he smashed a window with his bare hand, lacerating his fingers in the process to ensure she heard him. She did. Genny heard all of them, but for once, for the first time in her life, she chose to *look away*—to believe in a dream. She rationalized that her money, which was considerable, wasn't enough to make a dent in the coffers of a kingdom. The Duke of Rochelle made more in taxes on any given month than Winter's Whiskey did in a year. *He's not marrying me for my money,* she had assured herself. And in a way, that was true, which was why it was so easy to believe. In doing so, she understood what she never had before—why people decided to lie to themselves. Genny wanted to be loved, to be wanted, desired, cherished, not because of what she was capable of, but because of who she was, what she was. This was something she'd never dared dream of before, and Leo Hargrave was holding it out to her, begging Genny to take it.

She so desperately wanted the fairy tale to be true that she fell into the habit of *looking away*.

But he didn't come to her on their wedding night, or the night after, nor any night since. They slept in separate bedrooms. Leo didn't talk much. People said he was naturally quiet. She accepted this. Then when the whispers started, and even the servants began calling her the Whiskey Wench, Leo did nothing. He still smiled at her, gave Genny whatever she liked, complimented her, but the hugs were few, the kisses fewer. *He loves me, but not everyone shows affection in the same way,* she told herself. She needed to believe he felt the same way she did, because if he didn't, it would break her heart into so many pieces there would be no putting it back together.

Why am I still here? Why hasn't Leo found me? Has he even looked?

Tears welled up. She felt them coming hot and painful along with the truth.

Genny wasn't stupid. That was part of her problem. She had figured it out some time ago. Leo hadn't married her for the money. That was where everyone had it wrong. He had married her because he needed a wife. He needed one fast, and it didn't matter who.

It's not true, part of her still protested. But that internal voice was losing volume, smothered by facts that could no longer be overlooked. She was fighting a losing battle. Genny cried as quietly as she could. She didn't want Mercator to hear. It didn't work.

"Are you hungry?" Mercator asked.

"Is this a trick question?" Genny said, wiping her eyes and sniffling.

"I have bread. Would you like some?"

"I'd sleep with Villar for some bread."

"The bread isn't *that* good," Mercator chuckled.

Genny laughed with her.

Since that first real conversation about eating gold, the mood in her prison had changed. Mercator wasn't ready to fling open the cell door and set her free, but it was obvious she felt the abduction had been a mistake. The moment they shared was soft, gentle, comforting, fun. Strange how the flip side of tears was laughter. They could have been a pair of visiting friends up past bedtime, hiding from parents. Snickering as they shared secrets about boys, about clothes, about all the things friends were supposed to talk about. Only Mercator wasn't her friend. She had no reason to cheer her up.

"I'm sorry for disrespecting your husband," Genny said.

"Who?" Mercator asked.

"Isn't Villar your—"

"Oh, blessed Ferrol, no! How could you possibly think that he and I . . ." She faltered. "Villar is merely the leader of his clan, the Orphe. I'm the head of the Sikara. Ours are the two oldest and most respected mir families. We have no romantic relationship, and to be honest, I think he finds me repugnant."

"Well, he has no reason to feel that way. You are very kind."

"I was involved in kidnapping you, remember? How is that kind?"

"You offered me bread, and I know you don't have much. You didn't have to do that."

Mercator didn't say anything. There was no sound on the other side of the door.

"Oh, I see. Is that bread meant to be my last meal?"

"No!" Mercator replied hotly. "It's just bread."

Nothing was said for a moment, and the silence felt suffocating.

"There's still time," Mercator offered.

"And when the time runs out?"

Mercator sighed. "Honestly, I don't know."

"I suspect Villar does." Genny clenched her jaw. She felt lying to herself now was pointless, and yet there wasn't much point in not lying, either. The result was going to be the same, and it didn't matter one bit either way.

"Listen, do you want the bread or not?"

"No," Genny said. "Why waste it."

Silence followed, and lingered. No sounds came from the other side of the door for a long time, then Genny heard Mercator sigh again.

"What's wrong?" Genny asked.

"Now I don't want it, either."

"Don't be that way. You spent good money. You should eat it."

Another pause. Mercator shifted in the other room. Genny wasn't near the door, couldn't see her, but it sounded like she sat down, and none too gently.

"I don't like doing this, you know?" the mir said, her tone miserable. "You seem like a nice person. It's just like Villar to grab the only decent noble. It's just . . . I have to . . . we have to . . . something has to be done, and nabbing you was certainly better than the alternative."

"Which is?"

"Death. Many would die." There was a loud noise on the other side of the door, something clattering on the floor. "If only your husband would concede to the demands, this whole mess would be over. It's not like we asked for riches. We just desire the same rights everyone else already has. And you were already trying to do just that."

"So, you believe me?"

"I do now. I asked around. You really did attend a meeting of the Merchants' Guild, and you suggested the Calians and dwarves be allowed membership."

"You're being nice. I doubt anyone who was there described it like that."

"You're right. They said the Whiskey Wench had lost her mind. That the *bitch* was blackmailing them and would ruin the city as a result."

"At least I made an impression."

"You did," Mercator said. "So why hasn't the duke agreed? Why hasn't he demanded the guilds alter their charters? Doesn't he care about his people? Doesn't he care about you?"

Genny didn't answer. She couldn't. She honestly didn't know, and not knowing hurt so badly the tears came again. She cupped her face, trying to muffle any sounds, pushing them inward so that her body jerked with the agony.

"I'm sorry," Mercator said. "That was an insensitive thing to say."

A key turned in the lock, and the door to the cell opened. Normally, Mercator set her meals carefully, never coming close. This time she took a step into the room and *handed* her a bit of bread. "Eat it. Don't eat it. I don't care." She left, slamming the door and locking it behind her.

"Thank you," Genny said.

"Don't say that."

"I mean it."

"So do I."

Genny bit into the bread. This was the first real food she'd had in days. "Thank you just the same," Genny muttered softly.

"I can still hear you!"

"Sorry."

Mercator groaned.

Mercator looked up. The cloth drape that hung over the arched entrance in lieu of a door drew back. Villar had come to bother her again.

He was soaked and paused just inside to shake the water out of his hair. Slipping off his cloak, he snapped it twice to shake the wet off.

"Is she still alive?" he asked, looking at the closed door to the little chamber. This had become something of a ritual, being the first thing he said each time he entered.

Every church needs its rituals, Mercator thought.

"Yes," the duchess responded. "I'm still alive. And how goes your search for proof that you aren't the accidental love child of a whorish werebat and a horse's ass?"

This made Mercator chuckle. She put a blue hand to her face, trying to hide it.

Just as Villar always asked the same question, their captive always replied with a new retort—some of her responses quite creative. The woman had a surprisingly inventive mind.

Villar glared at Mercator. Then his sight shifted to the fresh dye on her arms, and his expression of disgust deepened. Mercator hated herself for it, but she pulled her sleeves down just the same. "Is it raining again?"

"No," Villar said, throwing his soaked cloak on the only stool in the room.

Mercator looked at him, puzzled, but he refused to explain.

"The feast is in two days, and the duke hasn't taken any action or uttered a public word concerning the demands. He's not going to concede. Humans don't care about anything except keeping others down so their position at the top is maintained."

Mercator toggled a finger between them. "We're both at least half human."

"Our lesser half, certainly. And you're—" He stopped himself and stared at her. An awkward moment lingered.

Mercator did nothing to help. She didn't say a word and stared right back, daring him to say more. Villar was less a book to be read and more a clear window one hoped the owner would drape out of common decency.

He turned aside. "The point is, compromise doesn't work. You can't say I haven't tried to be reasonable. I've given them a chance to avoid blood. But time has run out, and now we have to do things my way."

"You can't."

"We have to."

"You're suggesting suicide, and not just for those of us in Rochelle, but for all of Alburn, all of Avryn maybe. Even if we succeed, the backlash will be a generational tidal wave of hate and persecution."

"Are we not persecuted now? We're already drowning. What difference is a wave to those trapped at the bottom of the sea?"

She pointed at the duchess's door. "She agrees that things need to change. Maybe if we let her go, she could talk to—"

"She's lying, saying what she knows you want to hear." Villar threw up his hands. "You're so stupid! Do you hear yourself? Let her go? We kidnapped her, held her for weeks in a filthy cell. Do you honestly think that once she is safely back within the Estate's walls she'll lift a pinkie finger to help us? And don't forget, a man has died. Do you think they grant pardons for murdering the ducal cofferer?"

"You should never have killed him."

"She will point us out and cry for revenge."

"She's not like that."

"Maybe it isn't stupidity, maybe you're so indoctrinated into accepting their views that you've forgotten who you are. Ours was once a proud and respected people, and we can be that again. I've called for a meeting tomorrow, and I expect you to attend . . . and support my plan. You're the head of the Sikara family. Your great-great-grandfather was Mir Sikar and mine, Mir Plymerath. It's time that those who currently rule accept the truth about this region's past and give us the respect we deserve."

"Things will change, but not all at once," Mercator said. "You can't obtain respect at the point of a sword, not from people who despise us. Respect needs to be earned. Trust needs to be built up over time, over generations."

Although she argued against him, Mercator understood his hatred all too well and, even more, the damaging effects of ridicule. In many ways, she wanted to join in his outrage. They only disagreed over methods. Her outrage of principle was as acute as his. But after more than a hundred and twenty years, she had learned that wisdom was superior to passion, and that *the easy* and *the fast* never changed much; in fact, it often made matters worse. At a mere sixty years old, Villar hadn't learned that lesson yet. Knowing Villar, she wondered if he ever would.

"At this meeting you've called, will Griswold Dinge and Erasmus Nym support your plan? If they don't, will you reconsider?"

"No need, their people have suffered nearly as badly as ours." He stole a look at the locked door and frowned. "We can only achieve our goals by force. Change—real change—happens no other way. And you're wrong. The only means of gaining respect *is* at the point of a sword because power is the only thing people respect."

"So you respect the duke, do you? Because he has plenty of swords. And the king—whoever he turns out to be—will have even more at his disposal. If you shed blood, you'll be starting a war we can't possibly hope to win. No, not a war. That presupposes a conflict between reasonably able forces; this will be a slaughter." She fixed him with a steely gaze. "Do you know what a scapegoat is?"

"I know the term."

"But do you know what it really means, its origin? Ages ago, before the time of Novron, people lived in small villages. They were superstitious and easily frightened. Once a year they would take a goat and cast all their faults and offenses on it. Then they drove it out of the village to die in the wilderness. They did this in the hope that the gods would punish the goat instead of them. As it turns out, people haven't changed much." Mercator walked over and grabbed a blue cloth off the line and held it up in a fist. "They're still just as superstitious and ignorant as ever. The nobility of Alburn will use us as their scapegoat. They'll point at us and say, *There is the cause of our hardships, punish them.* Only they won't wait for the gods to deal out the retribution. They'll take it by their own hands."

"Would that be any different than how things are now? Our people are starving! I doubt Amyle will live to see another week's worth of dawns. Histivar—you pass him every day—he lives under a bridge! Under a lousy bridge! How can you stand there and suggest things can get worse?"

"Because they can. Right now, we are alive, and alive is better than dead."

"No, it's not. Not like this."

"You'll only get us killed. And not just here. You do this, and the repercussions will ring out all over the world. Our people everywhere will suffer."

"I don't care. Better to die than live and suffer in poverty and humiliation. Better still to take some of them along."

Villar snatched up his cloak, threw it back over his shoulders, and started toward the exit. "And one more thing." He paused, turning back. "You need to prepare yourself. When this happens, you have to do your part, too."

"My part?"

He nodded and pointed at the door that trapped the duchess.

Mercator shook her head and mouthed the word *no!*

"The revolution will start here." He spun and walked back out.

Mercator stood staring at the drape, but not seeing it. She felt cold. Mostly because her dress was soaked from working with the dye—mostly, but not completely.

"Are you going to kill me?" the duchess asked, her voice uncharacteristically soft, hesitant.

Mercator looked at the blue-black of her stained hands. Even to her, they looked like the hands of a monster.

She didn't answer.

CHAPTER SEVENTEEN
THE GATHERING

Breakfast the next morning was a surprisingly civil affair. Royce and Hadrian were on time, and Evelyn showed her approval with a slight nod before taking her seat. The meal was every bit as sumptuous as the morning before, but this time with waffles pressed into the shape of elephants. Evelyn didn't bother asking either of them to do the benediction, but Hadrian and Royce waited patiently for her to do so, and showed respect by bowing their heads.

"These waffles are excellent," Hadrian said, mostly to break the silence, but also because it was true. Evelyn was an incredible cook, and he was wondering if she did indeed employ an army of fairy helpers.

"Thank you," she replied. Then, as if in acknowledgment of their fine behavior, she scrutinized Royce, who not only had risen early to wash and shave but had also elected to leave his cloak in their room. "That's much better breakfast attire. I approve."

"Thank you," Royce replied with equal propriety.

Then Evelyn narrowed her eyes at Hadrian. "Is that a new scarf?"

Hadrian sat up and smiled. "Yes, do you like it?"

"It's blue."

"Popular color in Rochelle, I've discovered."

"Only among idiots."

This brought a surprised smile to Royce's face, but shocked Hadrian.

"Your front door is blue," Hadrian pointed out.

"I didn't paint it," the old woman said. "That was my late husband's doing. He had some fool notion it would protect us from a monster."

Hadrian looked down at his scarf, disappointed. He had expected the old woman to appreciate his adoption of the local style. Why he cared remained something of a mystery, but perhaps his desire to please her stemmed from the loss of his mother. Hadrian couldn't remember much about her. She had died when he was still young, but he imagined Evelyn was what mothers were like, or supposed to be: stern, correcting, fault-finding, and great cooks. Her disapproval, as ridiculous as it was, bothered him more than all of Royce's scoffing. Her mention of the monster, however, opened a door too tantalizing to let close without a peek. Hadrian gave up trying to win approval for his choice in fashion and asked, "You don't believe in the Morgan?"

THE DISAPPEARANCE OF WINTER'S DAUGHTER

Evelyn's brows rose as she delicately tore a pastry in half. "Yesterday you didn't know basic history, but today you're steeped in local arcane folklore, are you?"

"We're trying to educate ourselves," Royce offered.

Evelyn wiped a crumb from the corner of her mouth, then sniffed. "Well, you won't do it by listening to gossip and ghost stories, gentlemen. The Morgan is nothing more than a silly old legend. Honestly, I would think two grown men would know better. But of course you aren't the only ones. Tomorrow, you'll see. If you go to the Feast of Nobles, the whole lot will be attired in a bewildering spectrum of sapphire, cobalt, ultramarine, navy, turquoise, cyan, cerulean, and azure, all in an attempt to ward off a monster straight out of a children's tale." She focused on the scarf. "I think a man who carries three swords ought not fear a ghost."

"What exactly is this ghost story?" Royce asked.

"You won't like it. There's more of that icky history stuff you're not fond of."

"Make it short, and I'll try and stay awake."

She tilted her head down and peered up at him. "You washed this morning, so I'll let that go." Evelyn paused to refill her teacup, set the ceramic pot down with a petite *tink,* and then picked up her cup with both hands. She sat back, watching the steam rise. "Yesterday, if you recall, I mentioned a fellow by the name of Glenmorgan. He was the brute who, back in the year 2450, conquered all the other petty little mongrel lords and called himself the new emperor, a title the church later changed to steward. He's also the one who set up his capital in Ervanon and forced the Church of Nyphron to do the same. Well, he had a civilized son, but the boy didn't live very long. His grandson, Glenmorgan the Third, was different. While still young, the child demonstrated he was just as barbaric as his grandfather, and he ran off to fight the goblins in Galeannon. To his credit, he won that battle, which was thereafter known as the Battle of Vilan Hills. At least it was until recently when another battle was fought, and now that original engagement goes by the less significant title of the *First* Battle of Vilan Hills."

"I was in the second," Hadrian mentioned.

Evelyn lifted her chin and peered at him over her cup. "Under whose banner?"

"Lord Belstrad."

"You fought under the banner of Chadwick, Warric's first regiment in the coalition force commanded by Lanis Ethelred? That was the conflict that turned back the Ba Ran Ghazel's second serious invasion of Avryn. The one where Sir Breckton, Belstrad's eldest son, had the rightful glory stolen from him by Rufus of Lanksteer. The northman's ill-advised and downright ludicrous charge into a ravine won him the title of Hero of the Battle despite costing the lives of nearly all his men. Would have killed him, too, if the Ba Ran Ghazel hadn't been just as dumbfounded by the stupidity as everyone else."

Hadrian blinked, his mouth hanging in surprise.

"Close your mouth, dear. This is Rochelle, and more than mere goods flow through these ports. Here, we are fond of our history. My late husband was a particular maven of all things antiquated, and his passion became mine." She took a sip of tea. "As I was saying, Glenny Three won the First Battle of Vilan Hills. The celebration took him across the bay to Blythin Castle, the onetime stronghold of the exiled empire and Nyphron Church—at least until they built Grom Galimus. Glenny spent the next few days drinking and basking in the praise of his nobles. When it came time to leave, they had a surprise waiting for him. The old families didn't like the idea of a strong emperor who wasn't sanctioned by the church. They were afraid the true Heir of Novron would be forgotten."

"They killed him?"

She shook her head. "Heavens, no. Just as they are now, the nobility of that time were notorious cowards. They shied from murder. Instead, they locked Glenny Three in the bowels of Blythin Castle. Rumor says the granite cliff the castle sits on is riddled with ancient tunnels where the Seret have carved out a vast number of oubliettes. They sealed him in, walled him up, and walked away. As you can imagine, betraying your emperor after he'd just saved the empire from disaster generated a fair degree of guilt. So here in Rochelle, the city nestled in the shadow of Blythin Castle, there arose a ghost story to accommodate that shame. The tale tells that Glenny was upset with his fate, and being a bundle of ambition that even death couldn't squelch, he turned into a monster and found a way out of those tunnels. Now he creeps down here to Rochelle in search of the nobles who betrayed him. They're all long dead, but Glenny doesn't know that, you understand, and when it sees someone that *looks* like one of them, *the Morgan* has his revenge. And it's bloody; it's always very bloody."

Evelyn took another sip, set her cup down, and reached for her pastry.

"And the color blue?" Hadrian asked.

Evelyn flipped her hand in nonchalant dismissal. "Blue wards off evil, of course. That's why proper baby boys are always covered in it, to protect them from demons and evil spirits. Superstitious fools are willing to pay the exorbitant cost to protect their precious darlings."

Hadrian considered this. "What about baby girls? Aren't parents concerned about them, too?"

"It's not a matter of concern. They don't need protection. Evil spirits aren't interested in them." Evelyn made no attempt to hide her caustic sneer. "They're females after all, entirely unimportant. No self-respecting demon would waste its time with a girl, so inexpensive pink is just fine."

"Where are we headed today, my faithful hound?" Hadrian asked as Royce, having donned his cloak once more, darted off at a brisk pace up Mill Street, heading away from the river. Once again, Hadrian struggled to keep pace with his partner as he moved swiftly uphill.

While Hadrian maintained his belief that the two had been lucky the day before, there was no denying their efforts had yielded little progress in finding the duchess. They knew the whereabouts of an Estate-employed dwarf who might, or might not, have been the driver of the duchess's coach. They also knew that the aforementioned dwarf was in nefarious contact with a Calian who was now dead, the victim, it seemed, of the five-hundred-year-old reincarnation of a betrayed emperor. Then there was the phantom who had tried to crush them with a rock, whom Royce had thought was dead, but wasn't. This elusive mir had survived a high dive from the cathedral roof into the Roche River well enough to pay them a visit, but failed to leave his name or address.

"Back to dwarf-land?" Hadrian asked.

"No," Royce replied. "Today we're going to a funeral."

"A funeral? Whose?"

"That's what I hope to discover." Royce stopped when they reached the first cross street. A brisk wind gusted down its length, blowing a tumbling basket past them. "Which way leads to this wonderland of Calian shopping you love so much?"

"It's down near the harbor, in Little Gur Em, close to where we ate yesterday."

Royce set off down the street, staying on the walk to avoid the wagon traffic. "I'm betting the Calian with the missing face had a family, and families have a tendency to bury members when they die. If we see a funeral—a procession, a gathering at a graveyard or home—odds will be good that we'll have found the faceless man."

Traffic increased as they headed south toward the bay, where the salty air mixed with the smell of fish. Men wheeled laden carts uphill and empty ones down toward the docks. Others carried hods, or toolboxes, or ladders. Several in the loose-fitting dress of sailors staggered out of doors, squinting at the sun as they dragged themselves back toward the ships. Others milled about in a daze with no clear purpose. They wandered without an evident destination, looking with child's wonder at the buildings, shops, and carts. Hadrian realized that they acted much as he did, and in that instant, he understood that these were visitors to the city, there to witness the historic crowning of the new king.

Hadrian studied the streets and building shapes, trying to recall his trip from the night before. He looked for anything familiar, but it was significantly different in daylight. Recalling a neighborhood of dilapidated houses, he turned down a narrow street and found what he was looking for: an avalanche of busted crates, an open sewer grate, and a familiar clothesline stretching overhead. Clothes had been taken off the cord, and the ladder was missing, but the dollop of manure was still there, complete with the slide mark from his boot.

"Getting close," Hadrian said. After a wrong turn, he doubled back and found the shabby wooden fence. With no one watching, they jumped it together. Back in the land of dented buckets, Hadrian found the intersection, verifying his memory by looking down the street and seeing the spires of the cathedral. The crossroads, so ominous the night before, was laughably mundane in the daylight. He turned his back on Grom Galimus and walked only a few steps before being rewarded with a stain of blood leading to an alley.

The bells of Grom Galimus were chiming as Royce bent down, studying the ruddy blemish. He scooped up some pebbles, chips, and shards of rock recently scattered. He sniffed them.

"What's it smell like?" Hadrian asked.

"Gravel," Royce replied.

"From the box," Hadrian said. "I probably spilled some when checking it last night."

Royce nodded and stood up. He looked around and sighed.

"Nothing?" Hadrian asked.

"Other than the fact the body is gone, I have nothing."

After that, the two proceeded to imitate the rest of Rochelle's visitors who wandered the maze of streets. Royce and Hadrian explored the back areas—those residential sections where chickens wandered free; where hanging rugs formed all the privacy available for roadside privies; where naked children played in puddles, and gatherings of mothers watched the two of them with suspicious interest. Royce made a methodic search, up one row then down the next, with an eye to the impoverished homes. They looked for crowds, for groups dressed in black, for weeping huddles of those who might be mourning the loss of a loved one.

After hours traipsing through trash and garnering unfriendly glares, Royce stopped. "I suppose it's possible he didn't have any family or friends."

"Someone took his body away," Hadrian said.

"Maybe the guards or neighborhood elders? Can't have the children playing with dead bodies, might give them sicknesses and a true understanding of their genuine worth to society. Maybe we should head down to the harbor. That's where they probably dump bodies. This city looks like the sort to have a cadaver-sluice. Our Calian conspirator is likely halfway to the Goblin Sea by now."

"He had to have somebody who cared about him," Hadrian said.

"Why?"

"Everyone has someone."

"No, they don't." Royce focused on a scraggly little pug-nosed dog that was rummaging through a pile of rotting fish bones and tangled netting. "Think about all the stray dogs out there, the ones like that, the mangy wretches no one wants, the sort that people throw rocks at to drive away. They don't have anyone, and people like dogs, right? Man's best friend, isn't that what they say? There are a lot of stray humans, too." Royce continued to watch the dog with sympathetic eyes. There was something odd about the mutt. The dog wasn't a stray. It had a collar. A blue collar that—

"You're not a stray anymore, Royce."

"What?" Royce turned with a puzzled look.

"I'm just saying that if you died, I'd bury you. And if not me, Gwen would." He laughed. "By Mar, Gwen would build a tomb for you and paint it blue."

"I wasn't talking about me."

"Sure. I was just saying."

"Perhaps you should try not *saying* anything."

When Royce looked back, the dog was gone.

The light of another day began to fade as they returned once more to Little Gur Em's merchant square; the bells of Grom Galimus chimed.

"I don't know." Royce sighed. "Maybe we should look for the dwarf. He might not have relocated. If I put a knife to his throat, or better yet his wife's, he might . . ." Royce paused. Looking around at the crowd, his expression became puzzled.

"What is it, boy? What do you smell?"

Royce glared.

"Sorry." Hadrian grinned.

Royce nodded toward the people moving around them.

THE DISAPPEARANCE OF WINTER'S DAUGHTER

There were three young girls carrying cloth-covered baskets of baked goods. A man with a saw looped over one shoulder walked past and tipped his hat. An elderly couple strolled hand in hand, shuffling along as slowly as a pair of lazy snails, looking both romantic and cute. Most were Calian, a few were dwarves, and several were mir.

At first Hadrian saw nothing odd, then as he watched he saw it. Where earlier, people were going, coming, and milling about, now everyone—*every single person,* right down to the children—was heading east.

"They weren't doing that a minute ago?" Hadrian asked.

"The bells." Royce nodded in the direction of the cathedral. "They just rang."

"Hurry up or we'll be late," a Calian woman said as she ushered children out of her home. She caught sight of them, offered a cautious smile, then looked away and shooed her boys along.

One by one, the shopkeepers and cart vendors closed their doors and covered their wares. After locking their treasures away, they, too, headed away from the setting sun.

"Where do you think they're going?"

The two stood in the square and watched as it emptied of people, draining like a leaking bucket until only a few stragglers remained. As the light faded and night crept into the city once more, Royce and Hadrian followed.

THE GATHERING

࿇

Pursuing the parade east, Hadrian noticed they were leaving Little Gur Em and entering a decidedly less inviting part of town. In all his wanderings and late-night chases, Hadrian hadn't been here. Based on the way Royce was looking about, he hadn't, either.

Like the fringe of an old coat, the eastern edge of the city frayed. Rochelle had been bigger once; now the forest worked to reclaim stolen land. Grand homes and shops abandoned to decay had been uprooted by trees bursting through foundations, popping roofs, and throwing branches through windows so that the forest appeared to wear the houses. Streets had lost stones; the gaping holes reminded Hadrian of missing molars in an ancient mouth, while the tufts of yellowed grass that spurted in doorways were the unwanted hair of the aging. Wind blew shredded curtains, tattered awnings, and loose boards, which made a hollow, lonesome sound that echoed down the cavity-plagued road.

The procession took several routes, but all of them concluded at a stone ruin that might have once been a warehouse. Large enough to have been used to construct sailing ships, the building had four intact walls and half a wooden roof. None of the windows retained any evidence of glass, and the stone exterior showed only a speckled stain of paint where a mural had once decorated a wall. Conversations had been few, but as the many groups and individuals transformed into one tight crowd, soft murmurs rose. Royce and Hadrian drew their hoods up as they slipped inside. The sun was gone, the land dark. A single bonfire shimmered brightly at the front of the building, casting giant shadows on chalk walls.

Hadrian had no idea what he was seeing or was about to see. In many ways, the confluence of people reminded him of a church service, but he couldn't understand why a religious meeting would be held at night in such a fearful place. Something seasonal like a Wintertide or Summersrule observance, he guessed, as a cold wind shook the branches of a tree, clacking a branch against the broken roof. This was winter's last night, and the season thrashed with a spiteful anger.

Royce clapped Hadrian on the arm, and with a slight tilt of his head, he indicated a small figure near the fire. With the dwarf's hood pulled back, Hadrian recognized Griswold, who stood on a wooden crate alongside a taller figure. That person wore his hood up, his face hidden.

"Seventeen days," the hooded one next to Griswold said loudly. He turned halfway around and then repeated it. "Seventeen days ago your leaders embarked on an ambitious plan on your behalf. The disappearance of the Duchess of Rochelle was our doing. We took her to apply pressure on the duke, to get him to grant rights for those who have none. Our demands were reasonable, easily granted, and completely ignored. For seventeen days we sought a peaceful solution, but tomorrow is the Spring Feast, and we can't wait any longer."

Even the low murmuring stopped. The interior of the ruined building grew silent.

"We all wanted a peaceful solution, but injustice cannot be defeated by good intentions. Prejudice cannot be reasoned with. It cannot be beaten back without a cost. We must rise. Blood! That's what it takes. Blood must be spilled. The noble houses wear blue, but they should fear red. The crimson of their own lives. We need to show them we will no longer silently withstand their degradations. Seeing the color splattered on the walls, on the cobblestones, and on their pretty blue jackets will get their attention."

"Oh, it will certainly do that!" a mir said. Dressed in a deep-blue kirtle, the woman had equally dark skin, her hair nappy as any East Calian. She walked up to stand next to Griswold and the hooded speaker. A full head shorter than the one she interrupted, she was small and slight, but she stood tall, chin-high, eyes bright. "It will also terrify them. And not just the aristocracy of Rochelle, or even the three great houses of Alburn. I've already spoken to Villar about the folly of his proposal. If you listen to him, if you take up arms, you'll be declaring war and gain the very fervent attention of both the nobility and the church. And I'm talking about not just here, but all across Avryn. Not one of those kings, dukes, earls, or marquises will abide such a filthy house. They'll scrub the streets clean and use gallons of *our* blood for the washing. For every drop of theirs we draw, they'll demand a barrel of ours."

"Mercator Sikara, everyone," the tall one said, holding his hands out and introducing her to the crowd, but his tone wasn't inviting or welcoming. Hadrian suspected everyone already knew who she was. Villar shook his head. "What would your grandfather think of you? Of your fears? Of your willingness to abase yourself. Would he approve of you offering your people the *illusion* of safety through complacency? I don't deny that sacrifices will be made, but anything worth having comes at a price. We have had our heritage stolen from us. All of us." He pointed at Griswold. "Once proud Belgriclungreians have been shuttered into ghettos, locked in on festival nights, and forced to *lock themselves in* during their own celebration days to avoid being victims of violence. Calians, once the noble merchant-citizens of the imperial province of Calynia, whose city of Urlineus was the last to surrender its imperial banner, are now forced to beg for the right to buy and sell on the streets of a city that considers itself the last echo of the imperium. A city that should welcome them the most! And the mir . . ." He paused, shaking his head.

He took a breath as if it was far too much to go on, but somehow he managed to continue. "*Mir* . . . that was once a term of respect, a title of an honorable heritage. Those of us who can trace our lineage back to the imperial province of Merredydd know that we were once proud and admired members of the Novronian Empire. Mir Sikar sat on the Imperial Council beside Mir Plymerath, both of whom personally knew, and fought beside, the living Novron. But now . . . now . . ." He faltered and gestured up at the walls around them. "Now we barely exist, denied even the right to dwell in a house, the freedom to conduct a business of any kind, and the dignity to provide for ourselves and our loved ones."

"That voice is familiar," Royce whispered.

"The one in the hood?"

Royce nodded.

"Living in the past is no way to create a future," Mercator said.

"It's from the past that we find our future," Villar declared.

"I wish he'd lift his head high enough so I could see his face," Royce said, peering up.

THE GATHERING

Hadrian was acutely aware that all the people in attendance, other than the two of them, were dark-skinned Calians, short dwarves, and easily identified mir. Anyone getting a good look under either of *their* hoods would know they didn't belong. Given that they had stumbled into something akin to a pre-revolution rally, Hadrian preferred not to be noticed. Spies were always given the same reward, whether it was handed out by kings or insurgents, and three swords wouldn't be enough to fight off hundreds of furious people.

"You're asking us to commit suicide." Mercator threw up her hands, her voice growing shrill in frustration.

"I'm asking for us to stand up for ourselves, to be brave," Villar countered. "We outnumber our oppressors. We can defeat them. We can take control and make our own rules."

"Our numbers are greater only *in Rochelle,*" Mercator argued. "Outside this city are thousands, maybe tens of thousands of people who would like nothing better than to see every one of us dead, and they'll respond to this attack. Well-equipped and well-trained armies will have no qualms about putting down our little insurrection. And do you think it will stop there? No! The aristocracy of every kingdom will purge their homes of the *unwanted.* Today we are seen as merely a nuisance, but after tomorrow we'll be a threat. If you do this, you doom not just ourselves, but every mir, Belgriclungreian, and Calian across the face of Elan. You'll launch a universal war that we have no hope of surviving, much less winning."

Villar's voice showed disgust and an end of patience. "You have all heard Mercator's words before. And as I said, I tried things her way, and at great personal risk. I was the one who kidnapped the duchess. And what did the duke do? Nothing. He has ignored our demands. So many of you have suffered, so many have asked why we don't stand up for ourselves, why we don't fight. Tomorrow we will. On the first day of spring, the nobles from every corner of Alburn will be at the feast. It's our best chance, a perfect opportunity. They're not expecting a revolution, and they won't be protected by thick breastplates, nor will they be carrying swords. But *we* will! The dwarves have secretly prepared nearly a hundred weapons, ready to be handed out. The Calian soothsayers have confirmed that tomorrow is a turning point for this city, and it will be if the mir, the Belgriclungreians, and the Calians all join forces and attack the Feast of Nobles tomorrow at midday. Listen to me now, and we won't ever have to listen to the nobles again. I ask for your support, by a show of—"

Villar finally lifted his head high enough that the light splashed his features, and both Hadrian and Royce got a good look at the person beneath the hood. A triangular face, black hair, angled brows—a mir, and an angry one. There was a cold hate in the pull of his lips and an intensity in his dark eyes as he scanned the crowd, seeking to speak directly to everyone gathered. Royce had also tilted his head to get a better look, and in that same moment the two recognized each other.

Lowering his head, Royce whispered, "It's him. The guy I chased last night."

Villar shouted, "Grab that man!" and pointed at Royce.

"Time to go," Royce said. They struggled to retreat but ran into a mass of bodies.

Villar continued to shout. "Get him! Both of them! They're spies for the duke!"

The phrase *spies for the duke* did the trick, and instantly Hadrian felt uncountable hands.

Royce reached under his cloak.

"No, Royce, don't!" Hadrian yelled.

His partner hesitated and in that moment was equally besieged by a dozen men who swarmed until they had him in a firm grip. Royce glared.

The crowd was filled with innocent people, the elderly, women, and children. Any hope they had to get free would require killing—lots of killing, and even then they might not get away. That sweet old couple Hadrian had seen on the way to the rally stood four rows back, still arm in arm, looking upon them with fear. Beside them, a beautiful blond girl, a mir, stared at him wide-eyed in shock. The rest of the crowd was confused and frightened. These people weren't soldiers. They were a host of Griswolds. People who came home from a long day with nothing more than a miserable excuse for a chicken. And even so, their meager offering garnered a kiss from a grateful wife. None of this would matter to Royce.

"There's too many," Hadrian said.

"What are you talking about, Villar?" Mercator asked, "Who are these men?"

"They have been searching for the duchess. Asking questions and hanging out with the captain of the duke's guard. Just last night I came upon them spying on Griswold and Erasmus. I chased the little one. And the large one murdered Erasmus Nym."

"Nym's dead?" someone asked, but was ignored.

Hadrian tried to pull free, but it was hopeless with so many pressing in from all sides. Someone put an arm around his neck, tilting Hadrian backward and off balance. He felt them take his swords.

Hadrian and Royce had been turned to face the front of the room. Mercator, whose arms were two-toned as if she were wearing black gloves to her elbows, stepped forward. "Is what Villar says true?" Hadrian was encouraged by the sincerity of the question. She, at least, hadn't made up her mind.

He looked to Royce, who refused to answer. Hadrian offered as charming a smile as the chokehold allowed and focused on her. "Yes and no."

Mercator wasn't amused.

"No, I didn't kill anyone. Yes, we have been looking for the duchess. No, we aren't spies of the duke; we've never even met the man. Yes, I know the captain of the guard, we served together years ago."

"I was there," Griswold said, "I saw you chase Nym last night, and now my friend is dead."

"Well, yes, I did *chase* him, but we got separated, and when I found him again, he was dead. But I *swear* I didn't have anything to do with it."

"He's lying, of course," Villar said. "I'd lie, too, if I were in his place. He's only trying to save his own skin."

"And why are you looking for the duchess?" Mercator asked.

"My friend and I were hired by her father, Gabriel Winter, who's worried about the disappearance of his only daughter; he feared for her life."

"See! He admits it," Villar said. "They know we kidnapped her. They know what happens tomorrow. Let them live and we die. We need to kill them; throw their bodies in the Roche; let it take their stink to the sea."

"No!" a voice in the crowd yelled, the girl with blond hair and blue eyes. "Leave him alone." She pushed through the crowd to face Hadrian. "I know this man, and I won't let anyone hurt him."

Royce looked at Hadrian and Hadrian looked back, his face mirroring the confusion.

"Seton?" Mercator asked, pushing forward toward the girl. "What are you talking about?"

"This is *the rasa!*" The blonde pointed at Hadrian and stared at Mercator with big eyes.

Mercator continued to appear puzzled. "The rasa?" Her eyes widened. She studied Hadrian closely. "Are you sure? How can you be . . . how could he be . . ."

"I'm positive," Seton said. "I could never forget his face, his three swords, those eyes."

Hadrian, on the other hand, had clearly forgotten hers. She was vaguely familiar but only because he thought she looked a bit like Arbor, the shoemaker's daughter from Hintindar whom he'd been in love with at the age of fifteen. But this girl was a mir, and Arbor must still be living in Hintindar, married and with children by now. Hadrian had no idea why this young woman was defending him, or why she called him a rasa. Given his position, he wasn't about to deny anything she said.

Villar pivoted. "What's this all about?"

"This is Hadrian Blackwater," Seton said. "Seven years ago, he saved my life."

CHAPTER EIGHTEEN
THE RASA

She didn't say any more. The beautiful blonde mir—who literally and figuratively stood between Hadrian and Royce and death, looked uncomfortable as she faced Mercator with pleading eyes. Villar shifted impatiently. He likely wanted them dead, their bodies jammed down a sewer shaft, and while Hadrian obviously preferred to avoid that future, he was also curious to understand why this girl was so adamant about saving his life.

"Seton," Mercator said gently. "You have to tell the story." The blue-stained mir looked out across the crowd. "I know this isn't the—I'm sorry, but you're going to have to explain."

Seton nodded but still struggled to find her voice, and when it came, her words started faint and so low that Hadrian strained to hear. "I was living in the village of Aleswerth a few miles north. That's where I was born. Lord Aleswerth had defied

King Reinhold. I don't even know about what or why, but one day the king's soldiers arrived."

"Louder!" someone in the back shouted.

"We can't hear you," someone else said.

Seton's embarrassment showed, but when she resumed her story, her voice was louder, and as she spoke it grew even more so. "Everyone was called into the castle. We were told that anyone left outside the walls would be slaughtered. I didn't think they would let me in, but I guess with my hair covering my ears they didn't notice I was a mir, and I slipped in with everyone else." She paused and swallowed hard.

"The battle went on all day and on past sunset. I hid behind the woodpile. Then in the middle of the night, the gate burst open. They set fires everywhere, and men in chainmail carrying swords ran through the courtyard, killing everyone. They didn't . . ." She stopped, her eyes searching the dark for the words. "They didn't look human. They looked like monsters, cruel and horrible. One was worse than all the rest. He was tall, powerful, and covered in blood. Among my people there are legends of vicious creatures called rasas: terrible fiends, part elven, part beast, wholly possessed of evil. That's what he looked like to me."

She paused, regained her composure, and then continued. "He charged in swinging this incredibly long sword. Lord Aleswerth's men attacked him from all sides, strong men, good men. I was certain they would kill this savage invader. Instead, they all died, their blood adding to his gore. He cut them down, cleaving off arms and legs, beheading, and in one case, he cut a poor man nearly in half, slicing him from the shoulder to hip."

As she spoke, her eyes focused on Hadrian, squinting as if she peered into a painful light. "He killed the horses, too, the ones the lord's knights rode when they came at him. This man— this rasa—took down mounted knights with no more difficulty than a butcher slaughters a lamb. Before long, they were stacked around him, bodies in a pond of blood."

The crowd was quiet as she spoke. Only the faint crackle of the campfire broke the stillness, the sound and the flickering light adding to the imagery she conjured.

"When all the soldiers were dead, the invaders came for the women. I was discovered. They liked my hair and how young I appeared. In the dark, they thought I was human."

She paused, her face tense, her sight dropping to her own feet. She took another breath. "I could smell the beer on their breath. The battle was over, the celebration begun. Everyone was drinking. I held onto the hope that I might survive, that if they continued to think I was human, they would let me live. I feared they would . . . would . . . but they didn't want me for themselves. Instead, I was dragged to the rasa. The blood-soaked man was in the middle of the courtyard beside a barrel of beer, his giant sword still in one hand, a cup in the other. He was drunk.

"The soldiers threw me and three other girls down at his feet. 'To Hadrian Blackwater, the hero of the battle, go the spoils,' they yelled. 'Pick your favorite, Blackwater.' He picked me."

Seton paused there and began to cry. "I was terrified. After seeing what he'd done to the knights of Lord Aleswerth, I was certain this man was capable of unspeakable horrors. I knelt in the dirt, made muddy by the blood of so many, and I waited. All around me was fire, smoke, and screaming. My stomach was so bound in knots that I vomited. I didn't care if he killed me. I just wanted it to be over. I couldn't . . . I couldn't . . ."

It took her a moment to find her voice again, and when it returned she looked directly at Hadrian, as if she were speaking only to him, like they were alone. "Then he did something so unexpected, so unfathomable, that I thought I hadn't heard him correctly. He said, 'I'm sorry.' The rasa's voice wasn't what I expected. It was soft—soft and gentle, and sad. I thought he was speaking to me. I thought he was telling me that he regretted what he was about to do, but he never moved. He just kept saying it, repeating those two words. I realized he wasn't talking to me at all. He was looking at the pile of bodies. Staring at it, he drank and repeated his apology. Finally, he did look my way. He acted as if he'd just noticed I was there. I was sobbing, and he stared. I thought my life was about to end. When he reached out and grabbed me, I screamed."

"And then?" another from the crowd asked, a woman who glared at Hadrian with hate. "What did he do?"

"He . . ." Seton lifted a hand in Hadrian's direction, reaching out. "He held me. He held me tight, but gently. I was still terrified, expecting the worst at any minute; he, too, was crying. Then he let go. A couple of other soldiers came up. They saw he wasn't doing anything with me, and they tried to pull me away. Said they didn't want *the blond bitch* to go to waste. He told them *no*. They weren't happy with that, but he said if anyone touched me—*anyone*—that he would kill them and their horse."

"And their horse?" Hadrian asked. "I really said that?"

Seton nodded. "You did."

Hadrian started to remember now. It was seven years ago, not long after he had joined Reinhold's army. Most of the memories from that night had been mercifully washed away with beer, but some returned to him in nightmares or came in flashes triggered by fire and screams. The last time was when Queen Ann of Medford died, when Castle Essendon went up in flames.

"The next day," Seton went on, continuing to look at Hadrian. "I was alone. Just me and the ruined castle walls. The army of the king had gone, and so had the rasa who had protected me. I searched. I looked everywhere. Not a single person was left except me. I later heard folks who said the king was teaching his nobles a lesson. I only learned one thing—that I, too, would have died if it weren't for this man. This man who scared me so much that I vomited out of fear. He protected me. I'm the only survivor of the infamous Sacking of Aleswerth Castle, and I walked out with my life, dignity, and virtue all intact. And all because of him. Now, for whatever reason, fate has seen fit to swap our places, and so help me Ferrol, I'll fight anyone who tries to harm him." She peered into Hadrian's eyes, and added, "And their horse."

Seton took Hadrian's hand, kissed the back of it, and rubbed it along her cheek. "Thank you," she told him, and lifting his fingers to her lips, gently kissed each one. "Thank you, thank you."

Hadrian couldn't imagine that a young mir, even given her gift for storytelling, could dissuade a mob bent on killing two outsiders threatening their existence, and yet the demeanor of the crowd had markedly changed. Whoever this girl was, she held significant status in this underground society of theirs, one that exceeded her apparent age.

"They still must die," Villar demanded. "Seton, you'll have to step aside."

The blonde, who had appeared so shy and gentle until then, sharply spun to face him. "You want him dead? Fine, but don't ask others to do it for you." Seton pushed one of those holding Hadrian aside. "Let go!" She pulled on the fingers of another man. The others released their grips, and she pushed them back.

"There! Go ahead, Villar. *You* kill him, but by your own hand. Show us the way to your bloody revolution. Be the first to draw blood. Go ahead. Don't let my foolish little story worry you. The man is unarmed. Surrounded. Go on!"

Villar stared at her, not Hadrian. In his eyes smoldered a seething hatred.

"Do it!" The girl's voice rose to a shout.

"We don't have to kill them," Mercator said. "We only need to keep them from informing the duke or his guards of our intentions. If we vote for revolution, our actions will make what they learned here moot. If we take no action, then there is no crime, and no one will believe a crazy story of murderous plots from two foreigners."

"They know about the duchess," Villar reminded them. "The duke will kill us for that."

Mercator nodded. "Yes, *us*. You and me. No one else. Her abduction was our doing and our responsibility. Even so, they have no proof, and it'll be our word against that of outsiders."

"But if we kill them, then we—"

THE RASA

"He's right here, Villar!" Seton exploded again. "No one is stopping you. Go ahead." She took a step toward him, staring him down. "You tell us that we must fight. You say we have to stand up for ourselves, but what you really mean is we have to die—to die for you, for your pride, your hate. You want us to sacrifice ourselves so you can have a better future. That's not leading, Villar, that's exploitation. You want any of us to listen to you? To follow you? To risk our lives for your vengeance? Then give us more than words. Risk your own life first. Take his life *yourself*—or shut up."

Villar was shaking. Sweat glistened on his face in the torchlight. Hadrian thought he would attack her, hit the girl, make her stop. Instead, without a word, Villar turned away, pushed through those watching, and disappeared into the crowd.

"Griswold, can you get some rope?" Mercator asked. "We can—"

In the drama, nearly everyone had forgotten about Royce, who hadn't said or done anything. Those holding him had relaxed their grip, likely believing they were in charge of *the quiet one*. They discovered their mistake when one cried out in pain and another doubled over as the thief twisted free of all the rest. In a flash, Alverstone appeared, followed by gasps and a sudden retreat of those closest to him. "Sorry, don't like ropes."

"Royce." Hadrian spoke in a measured voice, the same one he would use when calming a spooked horse. "Don't . . . don't do anything that you'll . . . I mean . . . that *I'll* regret."

"Would be more productive if you told *them* that." Royce spun, blade out, and everyone took another step back.

"We aren't going to hurt you," Mercator said. She was one of the few moving toward him, but not quickly.

Smart woman, Hadrian thought.

"Not going to tie me up, either."

"We can't just let you walk out. If you were to tell the duke—"

"Who said anything about walking out?" Royce fanned the dagger as he moved closer to Hadrian. "We came for the duchess, Genny Winter. You're going to give her to us."

Mercator stopped and folded her arms, staring at him. "Or what? You'll kill us all with your dagger?"

Royce frowned, glanced at Hadrian, and sighed. "Why does everyone jump to that conclusion with me?"

Polka dots, Royce, Hadrian thought. *Polka dots.*

"Look," Royce told her, "I don't care for being locked up *or* killed. Big surprise there, right? And I'm guessing you'd prefer that we don't reduce your gathering's population by even a single life, true? Given her story"—he indicated Seton—"I suspect you understand it'll cost you at least that if you force the issue. So, let's try something else. How about a trade?"

"We have the duchess, I get that," Mercator said. "But what do you have that we could want?"

Royce smiled. "The duke."

No one returned Hadrian's swords, but neither did they attempt to tie the two up. Mercator left the crowd in the main meeting hall with a promise to update everyone before morning. Then she sent a runner to fetch someone named Selie, convinced

Griswold to come along, tried in vain to discourage Seton from doing the same, and chose a dozen of the larger Calians and mir to act as guards. Then the entire entourage escorted Royce and Hadrian across the street.

They entered a small dilapidated building with a partial roof, broken windows, and a mostly intact wooden floor. A well-worn path had been cleared through the debris down the stairs to the cellar. Four stone walls without a single window, six wooden chairs surrounding a rickety table, and the stub of a candle melted onto an overturned cup made up what Hadrian suspected to be the headquarters of the revolution.

Mercator took a seat and gestured for Royce and Hadrian to join her.

Seton looked at the dozen men and mir who were trying to look as tough as possible. "You don't need them."

"Not all of us share your unwavering faith," Mercator told her.

"It's not faith. I'm just saying . . ." Seton smiled shyly at the guards. "No offense, but if Hadrian wanted to kill us, they wouldn't be able to stop him."

"He doesn't have his swords," Griswold said.

"I know."

Mercator puzzled on this a moment. As she did, an older, dark-skinned woman entered in a rush. "Mercator? I was told you needed me."

"We do." Mercator motioned to the open chair. "This is Selie Nym, Erasmus's widow. She will be acting in her husband's stead as a representative to the Calians, agreed?" She looked to Griswold, who nodded. "I'm sorry to impose on you at a time like this, Selie, but we have an emergency."

The widow shook her head. "Don't go to worrying about me. This is bigger than an old widow's problems. Erasmus would never forgive me iffen I didn't pick up his part in this."

Mercator folded her hands on the table and took a breath. "Okay, we're listening."

Royce straightened up and faced the three. "Hadrian was telling the truth. We were hired to find and, if possible, rescue Genevieve Winter, the Duchess of Rochelle. If she's still alive, we can help each other."

"She is, but it doesn't matter; her husband doesn't care what happens to her. Or he does, but not enough to meet our demands."

"Or there's a third explanation."

"Which is?"

"That he doesn't know anything about your requests, and he thinks his wife is dead."

Mercator's brows knitted, her eye shifting in thought. "That's not possible . . . is it?" She looked to Griswold, who only shrugged.

"How were your demands relayed?" Royce asked.

"We wrote them down and left a note in the carriage the night she was taken."

Royce shook his head. "Maybe it got lost in the debris, or it blew away, but in any case, the duke knows nothing about the note."

"What makes you say that?"

"We've been investigating her disappearance, remember? And Villar was right about us meeting with Captain Wyberg of the city guard, but he didn't say anything about finding a note.

And Leopold had the guard searching the city, and none of them knew about any demands. In fact, Wyberg thinks she was most likely killed by some rival for the crown." Royce leaned in. "If you could prove to the duke his wife is alive, and make your case for reforms, he might agree in exchange for her return. Your original plan can still work, which means there would be no reason for the revolt tomorrow. Isn't that what you wanted?"

Mercator's eyes showed a momentary glimmer of hope, but then it vanished. "Except there's absolutely no way to get to the duke. I can't enter a shop to buy a loaf of bread at midday, so there's no way anyone is going to let me into the Estate at night, especially to have an audience with the duke."

Royce looked at Hadrian. "I'm guessing the captain could get us an audience, right?"

He nodded. "Wyberg could manage it, and he owes me favors much larger than this."

"So, all we need is proof that his wife still lives. If we had that, I think he would listen to what you have to say. Then, if I could persuade him to agree . . ."

"Royce can be very persuasive," Hadrian explained.

The thief nodded. "I have a lot of money riding on this job, so trust me, I'm motivated."

"You want *me* to speak face-to-face with the duke?" Mercator gave a little laugh. "That sounds incredibly risky. What's to stop you from handing me over and saying, 'This is the kidnapper!'"

Royce shook his head. "If we did that, you'd have the duchess executed, right? The duke would lose his wife, and I'd be out a fortune. Where's the benefit in that?"

The Disappearance of Winter's Daughter

Technically, Royce could make even more money if he let them kill her, then gathered up the heads of those responsible and carried them back to Gabriel Winter, but Hadrian imagined such a debate was for another day and a different crowd.

Hadrian watched Mercator. She was no fool; nor was she one of the typical meek elves he so often saw on the streets of Medford. While appearing not quite middle-aged, she had a demeanor that suggested otherwise. Her eyes surveyed them with a careful judgment born of wishful thinking but tempered by years of disappointment.

Mercator looked to the widow Nym and Griswold, both of whom shook their heads.

"These boys have no skin in the game that they're setting up." Selie said. "We're betting the house and they're tossing in a copper din."

Mercator nodded. "She's right. Your *fortune* doesn't stack up against the gamble we shoulder in this proposal. I need greater assurance. Lives are at stake, mine being the least of my worries. But the two of you—the architects of this grand plan—have no serious risk."

Royce faltered, searching the ground for ideas.

Hadrian noticed Seton was still watching him. She wanted a solution almost as much as he did. His time in the east had always been a dirty stain on his life, but she'd showed him there had been at least one pinprick of light. Another one would be nice.

"I'll stay," Hadrian declared.

"What?" Royce and Mercator asked together.

"I'll spend the night here, under guard, as insurance. Royce can escort you to the duke. If he betrays you, has you killed or whatever, then your people can kill both me *and* Genny Winter."

Griswold pointed at Seton. "According to her, that's not too easy."

"But unlike Royce, I'll let you tie me."

Mercator looked surprised at the offer and nodded. "I could agree to that."

"Yes," Griswold nodded. "That seems fair."

"No, it doesn't," Royce said. "In fact, that sounds *really* stupid."

"Why?" Hadrian asked. "Do you plan on betraying anyone?"

"No, but . . ."

"But what?"

"I don't like working under pressure, okay? And what guarantee do we have that they won't . . ."

"Won't what?" Hadrian asked.

"Won't kill you anyway?"

Hadrian looked at Seton. "I have a protector."

The blonde smiled. "Yes, you do."

"I'd be happier if it were someone a little taller," Royce said.

"Does everyone agree?" Hadrian asked.

Griswold nodded.

"Selie?" Mercator turned to the Calian. "What do you say?"

"Old Eras, he never did like the idea of fighting. Couldn't even bring himself to argue with me. Just said, 'Selie, there's no reason to be that way,' and he was usually right, too." Her lips shifted as tears slipped down her cheeks. "People got the wrong impression because he was always haggling, but he just liked the sport of it. Couldn't understand why folks refused to get along. He would've wanted to find a peaceful solution." She looked around to nodding heads. "We agree to this."

Mercator gave a single nod. "So it's decided. Let's pray to each of our gods that this will work. We're going to need all the good fortune we can get."

CHAPTER NINETEEN
LIVING PROOF

The key was done.

Genny finished it more out of habit and a sense of accomplishment than anything else. She had no idea if it would work, and only a mild desire to test it. Curiosity was the only driving force now. Escaping felt almost counterproductive. Better to be killed and retain a thread of hope than live and discover the truth. In a choice between the murder of her body and a murder of her spirit, she suspected the former might be best. At least she wouldn't be forced to suffer needlessly. Besides, if it worked, the key would only open the collar. The shackle around her throat was held fast by a warded padlock, but the door's lock was a tumbler, and she didn't know anything about those.

She rubbed the key with her thumb. "You did a good job, old girl," she said aloud, and she wasn't just referring to the key.

The Disappearance of Winter's Daughter

She was alone again. Mercator and Villar were both off to the meeting, which meant that Genny didn't have long to live. If they decided the way Villar wanted, Mercator would return to perform her final task. Genny wondered if she would follow through with it. While she'd never killed anyone, Genny imagined it wouldn't be an easy thing to do, but it was clear that no point in Mercator's life had been easy. The mir hadn't said a word, but that last argument with Villar, how he looked at her, and what he didn't say told Genny everything she needed to know.

Mercator would kill her. She wouldn't like it, wouldn't want to, would probably apologize and possibly cry as she dragged a knife across her throat, but she'd do it. Mercator was a survivor, and her sort did what they had to.

Genny looked at the key. She thumbed it, feeling where the rest of the teeth had been, noting how smooth it was. Her old trunk key was now a skeleton key. The problem with warded padlocks, like the one that held the collar, was that they only had a few configurations for the obstructions, or "wards," that made it impossible to turn any but the correct key inserted in the hole. With so little space in each mechanism and so many unique locks to make, some were bound to be identical, which meant keys for one could open others that used the same design. Worse, almost all warded locks left the first notch unobstructed so that a universal key—a skeleton key—could be used. This was handy for when a key was lost, or when someone had hundreds of locks to deal with and didn't feel like carrying hundreds of keys.

Genny had learned this after discovering a consistent discrepancy in her inventory. Her warehouse in Colnora had a fine-looking warded lock, big and new, but a locksmith explained how useless the thing was to anyone who knew the first thing about how locks worked. This was bad news in a city that was home base to the Black Diamond Thieves Guild. She replaced the lock with a far more expensive and elaborate version, and the thefts stopped. Genny thought nothing more of the matter until she woke up with a collar locked on her neck and an old chest key in her purse.

How many noble duchesses know how to pick a lock? How many have potential skeleton keys in their wrist purses? So what are the odds Mercator and Villar used an irregular ward lock? Genny felt her odds were good, but getting the collar off was only half the battle. The other was the door.

Mercator opened it for every meal. The mir wasn't very big, but Genny had never been in a brawl. She didn't know how well she would fare, and she honestly didn't want to find out. That's where the sharpened coins came in. If she could . . .

But why bother? I gave all my love to a man, and received only lies. What do I have to look forward to now?

Genny decided to stop *looking away* and face the unpleasant truth that some people, no matter how hard they try, never get what they desire the most.

She tossed the key, letting it skip across the stone into the corner.

Genny heard someone. Quick steps rushed up and flew into the room on the other side of the locked door. She held her breath. This was it. Whoever had come was there to end her life.

The door would open and she would see a knife, or a sword, or a—

"Can you write?" Mercator asked.

Genny was confused.

"Do you hear me? Can you write?"

"Are you talking to me?" Genny asked.

Mercator was moving around outside the door, shuffling loudly. She appeared to be in a hurry. "Of course I am!"

"Don't take that tone with me. How am I supposed to know? I'm locked in a room."

Mercator paused, took a breath, and began again. "My apologies, but I'm in a bit of a rush. And you should be, too, if you want to get out of here."

Get out of here? Is this a trick? Doesn't make sense. Why trick me?

"Yes, I can write."

"Wonderful! I need you to do something for me, and for yourself."

Genny slid to the door and peered out the central knothole. Outside, Mercator flipped over piles of wool. She was searching for something in a mad dash.

"I need you to write a letter to your husband."

"Are you serious?"

"Yes." Mercator found a feather and cut the end of the quill with a small knife.

"Why, I'd love to, dear. Can I tell him where I am, and give him your best wishes?"

"Do you know where you are?" Mercator set the knife back down, then reconsidered and stuffed it in her belt.

"No."

Mercator found a sheet of parchment and grabbed it up. "Then I suppose not."

"What *do* you want me to say?"

"Tell him what we talked about; ask him to do what is right; and mention something that only you two share, so he'll know the message came from you."

"Wait. What? Leo doesn't know I'm alive?"

"There's a rumor to that effect."

"A rumor? You don't know? Why don't you know? By Mar, are you serious?"

Mercator opened the door and set the parchment and quill before Genny. "We think the duke never received our first note and that's why he hasn't done anything. But if you can convince him . . ."

If that's true . . . does that mean . . . could Leo love me after all?

Genny's heart leapt as she took the paper and quill. Then she hesitated.

No . . . she thought. *It doesn't explain everything else: him keeping his distance, our separate beds, his failure to defend me.*

"Leo doesn't love me," she told Mercator, an admission that brought tears. "He married me so he could be king. This won't change anything."

"You don't know that."

Genny bowed her head and sniffled. "Yes, I do. I pretended he cared, but it's not true." She set the quill down and wiped her face with the back of her hand.

Mercator sat down opposite her. "Maybe you're right. Maybe he doesn't love you, and only married you to better his chance for the crown. Makes sense. But he *still* needs you if he's to become king. And if he's crowned, then you'll be a queen."

"I don't care about that. Never have."

"You should."

"Why? Why should I care? If he doesn't love me, if this has all been a charade, if all he wanted was a crown—"

"It could save your life."

"I'm not sure I want it saved. If the only person who ever said they loved me, doesn't . . . I'm not sure life is worth living."

Mercator's tone lowered, her eyes growing stern, nearly angry. "It's not just your life at stake." She changed from hectic jailor to disapproving teacher scolding a petulant student. "If the duke doesn't agree to reforms, there will be an uprising followed by a retaliation. Hundreds will die, maybe thousands." Mercator picked up the quill. "I don't care if the duke doesn't love you, and right now you shouldn't, either. You have the power to save lives. Your Ladyship, isn't that worth pretending he loves you for at least one more day?"

Genny looked down at the parchment and sniffled. "As pathetic as it sounds, you're the closest thing I have to a friend in this city. Call me Genny." She sniffled again and reached out and took the quill. "I need ink."

"I don't have ink." Mercator said, then smiled and looked at her arms and hands. "But, *Genny,* I think I can manage something."

CHAPTER TWENTY
JIGGERY-POKERY

Royce waited in the shadows between two stone giants, torturing himself.

Standing in the dark, narrow street dividing the imposing Imperial Gallery from the immense Grom Galimus, he watched people carrying lanterns and moving through the sprawling riverfront plaza, celebrating a festival of rebirth. The populace danced and sang in joyous abandon as they said goodbye to winter the way a squirrel waved farewell to a frustrated dog thwarted by high branches. They wore bright colors and waved streamers of green, blue, and yellow. Giddy as children, they were oblivious to the dangers around them. They were prey. He'd grown up in a city like this: old, dark, and decrepit. Royce was a panther in the grass, gazing out at a watering hole after a drought, but he wasn't there to hunt. He was waiting for Mercator.

THE DISAPPEARANCE OF WINTER'S DAUGHTER

As unpleasant as it was to ignore the temptation to act when the revelers were such ripe pickings, they weren't the source of Royce's agony. What needled him was the way the stakes of their job had risen while the payout hadn't. What Royce suffered was the contradiction that was Hadrian Blackwater.

While he hoped that his friend survived the night, he also felt, in a purely theoretical way, that Hadrian deserved to die. The fool had willingly surrendered to a mob of revolutionaries. A group that believed he had killed one of their own. That was stupidity taken to an art form, like giving up higher ground or leaving an enemy alive. And yet, this was only a symptom of a larger, more perplexing issue, that irritated Royce like an infected splinter. He couldn't ignore that their lives had been saved by a random act of kindness that Hadrian had once shown to a total stranger.

From Royce's perspective, the best insurance for a long life was murder. Potential threats—even remote or indirect—had to be eliminated. Not broken, not reduced, but burned out of existence. Royce left no hatred to smolder, never granted revenge the potential to return to roost. He wouldn't have violated the blond mir, either—the very idea was repugnant—but given the circumstances, he imagined he would have seen her dead. When you're part of a force that wipes out an entire town, you don't leave *anyone* alive. Not even a young girl.

Back in his Black Diamond days, when Royce was a member of the infamous thieves' guild, he had been one of three assassins the BD employed. The other two were his best friend, Merrick, and Jade, Merrick's lover. Jade had been a young girl, too, and just as sweet as Seton, but she had become one of the most feared assassins in the known world. Not despite her gender, but *because* she was female. Men always underestimated her.

Was Jade a mir, too? Thinking back, he couldn't help wondering. *Not all mir have elven features.*

Since meeting Hadrian, he'd recognized that the man *was* unnaturally lucky, but that thought, that excuse, was too consistent an occurrence. It had become less a rationalization and more of a truism, which irked Royce.

If it had been me, if I had saved her life, Seton would have spent the last seven years training to kill, and one by one she would have seen to it that each of the duke's soldiers who took part in that raid died a horrible death. Then, when I showed up, she'd be overjoyed to find the one guy that got away. My reward would have been a vivisection.

But it had been Hadrian, and he received a tear-filled oratory of appreciation and an advocate for his defense.

That was the problem with life; it often failed to be consistent. Nothing could be relied on. Royce was positive that if he dropped a rock enough times, he'd eventually see it fall upward. He was also certain that this event would coincide with the worst possible moment for it to occur. What others saw as miracles, Royce perceived as dumb luck. Still, there was a problem with that, and its name was Hadrian Blackwater.

By all accounts, the man shouldn't have survived childhood. Maybe he had caring parents who watched over their son— yet another example of the universe showing preferential treatment. Still, after he left home, he should have died within a week, a month at best. Ridiculous skill with a sword can protect someone from only so much.

THE DISAPPEARANCE OF WINTER'S DAUGHTER

Tonight is a good example. We both should have died, but we didn't. Why?

This was the puzzle that frustrated Royce, the embodiment of the sliver. It challenged his very clear and proven worldview.

Aside from Hadrian's professional soldiering, during which he apparently killed the equivalent of a small county's worth of men, he was unusually kind, empathetic, and forgiving. Everything in Royce's life had convinced him that those three idiosyncrasies were synonymous with swallowing brews of arsenic, cyanide, and hemlock all in a single gulp. Even if the result wasn't suicide, such attributes should result in massive handicaps when trying to survive in a world that claimed to value such qualities but in reality punished people who possessed them.

Except in Hadrian's case, it hadn't, and by virtue of being with him, Royce had been rewarded. The worst part was that Royce couldn't pass it off as a rock falling up. This wasn't the freak singular occurrence. Four years earlier, the idiot had made the worst mistake of his life by staying to save Royce when they were on top of the Crown Tower. Hadrian had the opportunity to escape, but he had stayed, performing a suicidal defense on behalf of a man he hated. Anyone else would have paid for such an error with their life. Not Hadrian Blackwater, and again, by virtue of being with him, Royce had lived, too. Then there was Scarlett Dodge. She was another person Royce would have killed if Hadrian hadn't been with him, another example of a good deed rewarded. Royce and Scarlett had once laughed at Hadrian's naïveté, his moronic integrity. But given how things turned out in Dulgath, Royce didn't find it funny anymore.

Jiggery-Pokery

Once could be explained as a fluke. Twice was a coincidence. But three times? Three times was a pattern, wasn't it? And if it is, what does that pattern reveal?

Royce pushed the thought away. It didn't expose anything. Weird stuff happens all the time, doesn't prove or disprove anything. *Even a rock will eventually fall upward, right?*

He was making too much out of nothing. Something he criticized others for doing. People spot a goose heading south in early fall, and they expect an early winter. They see a squirrel amassing nuts and convince themselves the winter's snows will be deep. All this from an overeager goose and a greedy rodent. One thing doesn't dictate the other. Hadrian was lucky, that was all. Except . . .

I don't believe in luck.

Luck, as it was understood by most people, was some supernatural force that benefited one person more than another. An incomprehensible, impetuous power that blessed certain people without reason, and would abandon them just as inexplicably. *What a load of nonsense.* Luck was a word insecure or envious people used to explain events they didn't understand. What they didn't realize was that everything had a certain probability. Those people described as *lucky* were merely individuals who increased their odds of success either by their actions or lack thereof. A man who lives on a mountaintop but isn't hit by lightning isn't lucky, he simply didn't go outside in a storm. People made their own luck. This, too, had been an axiom that Royce had believed. Now these two established principles were slammed against each other, and he didn't care for the new landscape the collision left behind. The pattern was wholly strange, an alien thing that challenged all he knew to be true, everything he'd learned. If Royce didn't know better, he would almost conclude that—

Mercator appeared, moving through the crowded plaza. She had added a blue shawl to her attire and dropped part of it over her head. *Does she own anything that isn't blue?*

She entered from Vintage Avenue, but that didn't mean anything. Royce had known Mercator for only an hour and already he knew she wasn't stupid enough to travel in a straight line from where Genny Winter was being held. The best he could determine was that the Duchess of Rochelle was somewhere in the city or on the outskirts—somewhere Mercator could have gotten to and back in less time than it took Grom Galimus to chime twice.

It took her several minutes to cross the plaza. Because this was the night before the big feast, it seemed everyone was out. Royce watched as Mercator threaded her way through the crowd, looking for anyone who might be following. She seemed unobserved, and Royce met her in front of the cathedral.

"That didn't take long. Are you certain you have ample evidence? You realize we won't get a second chance at this. If he isn't persuaded that she's alive, this whole thing fails."

Mercator presented Royce with an understanding smile, the sort an adult would offer a child who has just said something stupid. "This will do the trick." Mercator drew out a folded parchment.

"A letter?" Royce was disappointed.

"Were you expecting a finger?"

Behind Mercator, not far from the fountain, a Calian man was juggling flaming torches that made muffled *whump* sounds each time they spun.

"To be honest, yes. A fresh-cut finger shows the victim was recently alive. And there is the added bonus of indicating the seriousness of the kidnapper."

Mercator continued her patient smile. "You've done this sort of thing before, haven't you?"

"Hadrian and I weren't hired for our looks."

"Nor for your intelligence." The insult was presented without malice, making it sound more like constructive criticism.

Royce was never one for criticism, constructive or otherwise, and certainly not when it came to his area of expertise. The presumption of this mir was astounding if she thought she could educate him on blackmail and coercion. She looked to be the type to spend most of her days scrounging garbage for food or begging for handouts in the street.

A ring of people in colorful clothes held hands and danced in a circle as a trio of fiddlers played in the center. All the dancers were red-faced, from either the exertion or drink—likely both. Royce found it hard to believe that he and they were the same species.

"The duchess wants us to succeed," Mercator said. "Given that her life weighs in the balance, and since she knows her husband better than either of us, it's sensible to assume she is far more capable of providing us with the means of convincing him to act. Wouldn't you say?"

Royce didn't answer. As simple as that concept was, he reran it twice through his head looking for an error. He couldn't find one beyond the possibility that the duchess might encode a message only Leo would understand, which would convey her whereabouts. This, however, seemed unlikely.

"What?" Mercator asked.

"Nothing." Royce shook his head.

"You're shocked. I can see it on your face. You didn't believe it possible a mir could think."

Royce shrugged and gave a glance at the revelers laughing and dancing as if they were mad from fever. "Don't take it as a slight; I'm usually shocked that *anyone* can think."

"But how much harder to accept from me, a mir *and* a female. You assumed I was incompetent, didn't you?"

She was right, and such an admission wouldn't have troubled him a year ago, but a year ago he'd thought he was human. Discovering he was also a mir made it difficult to think that those with mixed-blood were inferior. Difficult, but not impossible. The fact that he didn't exhibit elven features allowed Royce to believe his blood was only slightly tainted. This was a weak, impractical argument, but prejudices were a form of fear, and fear was often senseless. Groundless anxieties permitted ludicrous rationalizations. At least they did in the quiet, controlled spaces of his own mind. Such carefully crafted constructions tended to fall apart when facing the reality of a blue-stained mir who showed no evidence of inferiority.

"Yes," he admitted.

No offense or anger surfaced on her face. Instead, she nodded while maintaining that understanding smile. "So, what now?"

"We're waiting on Roland Wyberg. The captain of the city guard is supposed to meet us here. He wasn't at the guardhouse, but I told one of his men that I'd found the duchess, and he anxiously volunteered to fetch him, *immediately*. I hope he didn't lie or exaggerate."

"You didn't mention me, did you?"

"No, but would it have been a problem if I did?"

Mercator sighed. "It could. People have a lot of preconceptions about my kind. We're not what you think, you know. We didn't cause the destruction of the empire. We aren't lazy or stupid, nor are we abominations. We don't carry disease, aren't cannibals, don't steal babies or worship Uberlin. We're the same as everyone else, except more destitute because the rest of society hates us. They keep us dirty and desperate, then condemn us as if we chose our circumstances. The irony is that long ago we were considered superior to humans. I'm guessing you didn't know that. The term *mir* comes from the word *myr,* an Old Speech word that originally meant *son of.* It was also an honorific, like *sir* added before the name of a knight. If you put those two things together, you must conclude that we are descended from pretty good stock. It was only after the fall of Merredydd, a province of the old empire that was governed by mir for mir, that the term became derogatory."

"No offense, but all of that contradicts history as I understand it."

"That's because the history you know is wrong. History isn't truth. You're not too foolish to recognize that, are you?"

The dancers moved away as acrobats tumbled into the center of the square, encouraged by applause. Men in tight clothes jumped and rolled and climbed onto one another, creating human ladders of various designs.

"And how do you know *your* history isn't a lie?" Royce asked.

Mercator grinned. "I'm older than I look, a lot older. That's one of the things about mir. We live a long time. Not so much as elves, I suspect, but longer than humans. My mother lived to be four hundred and fifty. She could remember Glenmorgan and his *Second Empire.* Age gave her the wisdom to conclude that our long life was a gift turned into a curse by a world filled with ignorant hate and bad timing. My grandfather Sadarshakar Sikara was born in 2051 and lived for five hundred and sixty-seven years. Can you imagine that? He remembered the birth of Nevrik, the Heir of Novron, and the appointment of Venlin as the Archbishop of Percepliquis, and he witnessed the fall of that grand city. He was in Merredydd at the time, a province established for the *myr* who chose not to live with humans."

She leaned in, placed a hand to the side of her face, and whispered, "Rumor has it the *myr* were a bunch of bigots." She laughed as if it was a joke, but Royce couldn't tell if it was ironic or just silly.

"If you're the descendant of such an esteemed family, why do you look so . . ." Royce hesitated.

"Calian?" Mercator glanced at her hands and nodded as if she'd expected the question. "When Merredydd fell to barbarians, Sadarshakar brought his family here to what was then called Alburnia. Few survived, and Sadarshakar took a Calian woman as his wife. The situation didn't improve, and my mother married a Calian man." Mercator drew back the shawl off her head and pulled on her nappy hair. "Which makes me arguably more Calian than mir. A highly respected combination, I must say." She laughed again, managing to find humor in every tragedy.

Royce could understand that, at least.

"Fact is," she said, "I learned history from someone I trust . . . my grandfather, who witnessed the events firsthand. That's how I know. Tell me . . . Royce, is it? How do you know about the history of your people?"

"I actually don't care," Royce said. "All of this clearly means a good deal to you, but it doesn't mean anything to me. Doesn't matter whether your version is true or not. I'm here to do a job, not debate ancient history. Now, if you want to talk about something, I'd love to hear where the duchess is."

Mercator shook her head. "Sorry. She's the only good card I still hold. But she's safe and unharmed, as this letter attests. I'd like to keep it that way. I've grown to like her. She's . . . different."

"It was worth asking," Royce said. He gazed out at the plaza once more, trying to decide if he was pleased or irritated with the number of celebrating people. They complicated everything, which was both good and bad. "We probably—" Royce saw movement where there shouldn't have been any.

The plaza was still a swirl of activity—dancers spun, acrobats tumbled, jugglers tossed, spectators clapped, and children ran—but overhead, nothing should have moved. Too dark for a bird. Too big for a bat. Royce looked up at the front of Grom Galimus. The great doors were huge but dwarfed by the massive bell towers on either side. Above those doors stood a row of sculpted figures of robed men. Then came the oculus of the great rose window. Next, a colonnade of pillars and arches, and above that, and still only halfway up, was a pediment upon which perched a series of gargoyles.

"What's wrong?" Mercator asked, craning her neck, trying to see what he saw.

"Thought something mov—"

They both spotted it then. The third gargoyle from the left flexed its wings.

"I'm not from here," Royce said. "Is that normal?"

"Of course not. It's—oh no!"

The gargoyle's head turned. Like so many others, this figure was monkey-like with powerful hunched shoulders, the wings and face of a bat, and saber-like fangs. As it looked down at them, Royce noticed that the eyes had been sculpted to look decidedly evil, but he guessed that was how he'd have seen them, regardless of what the artist had carved—because the gargoyle looked right at him.

Royce expected it to shove off the side of the cathedral, spread its wings and dive. Instead, the beast began to climb down the front of the church, moving awkwardly at first but gaining balance and skill as it descended, until it moved with monkey speed, leaping from pediment to column.

"Run!" Mercator shouted at Royce.

"Why did you kill Nym?" Griswold Dinge asked Hadrian. The dwarf sat across from him in the little room.

With Nym dead, Selie preparing for his funeral, Villar gone, and Mercator off to meet with the duke, the dwarf—the last of the civic leaders—had apparently pulled guard duty. Hadrian was glad Erasmus Nym's widow wasn't there, as he was certain Seton's story didn't absolve him of that accusation. If anything, it cast more doubt, and he'd preferred to deal with an angry dwarf rather than a grieving widow.

"He didn't kill Erasmus," Seton affirmed faithfully.

The three sat cozy and close in the stone cellar, which was littered with rat droppings. Griswold had bound Hadrian's hands behind his back. As an added precaution, he held a naked dagger. His manner wasn't overtly threatening, but the menace was there.

"She's right. I didn't kill the Calian." Hadrian smiled, but his charm had no effect on the dwarf.

"Oh yes, even though you were right on his heels during your pursuit, someone else came out of nowhere and took his life. Do you expect me to believe that?"

"I honestly have no idea what killed him," Hadrian said.

"Don't you mean who?"

"Seemed more like a what. All I know is he was dead, and his face was gone. It looked like it had been chewed away. I only knew it was him because of the clothing and the box he had been carrying. Didn't seem like a typical murder to me."

"He didn't kill Nym," Seton asserted again.

"And how in the bloody name of all that is holy do you know that? He spared your life; so what? He also butchered a pile of men; you said so. Your own words show he's a killer, no innocent little lamb here. And *his* story about Nym missing his face is beyond belief."

"No, it's not," Seton said, "and it's not because he spared my life that I believe him."

This caught the dwarf's attention and he turned, revealing a little gold earring piercing his left lobe. *Decoration? Mark of a sailor? Wedding gift?* Hadrian knew so little about the small folk that he felt not only stupid but ill-equipped to help himself, much less his cause.

"So what makes you think he didn't kill Erasmus?"

"Killings where people are mutilated the way he described have happened before." Seton said. "That's the reason the nobles wear blue."

The dwarf shook his shaggy head. "Bah! The nobles are skittish. The streets are dangerous. Not every person butchered in the alleys is a victim of—"

"I'm not talking about the recent murders." Seton's voice lowered and grew several degrees more serious. Her eyes supported the shift in tone, growing solemn. Hadrian found it odd to see so much darkness in a face that looked so young. "I'm talking about Throm Hodinel."

Griswold squinted his eyes. "Who now?"

"Throm Hodinel. He was the curator of the Imperial Gallery. Some said he was a relation to the Killians, a distant cousin or something. I saw his body the day they found it at the feet of the statue of Glenmorgan. And his face was a mess. They had to identify him by his clothing because . . ." Seton hesitated, her eyes focusing on Hadrian as if he knew the answer.

"Because his face had been chewed off," he answered.

Seton nodded. "Actually, it wasn't just his face; a large portion of the man had been eaten. But yes, his face was gone. So were a good number of his bones."

"Sounds like wolves," Griswold said.

"Inside the gallery?"

The dwarf stared at her skeptically. "I've never heard this story."

"It happened before your time."

The dwarf tilted his head and studied her more intently. "How old *are* you?"

She grinned at him. "Throm Hodinel died fifteen years before you were born."

This raised the bushy brows of the dwarf. Griswold looked to easily be in his forties, maybe older. Seton wasn't a teenager, wasn't human, and if what she said was true, she was decades older than Hadrian. Adding these truths to the embarrassing fact that he hadn't initially recognized her, Hadrian realized that while he had misjudged women before, this time marked a whole new level of stupidity.

"Throm Hodinel wasn't the only one," Seton went on. "Every few years someone dies the same way. It's almost always a noble, or someone suspected of being an illegitimate child of one of the old-world dukes, usually male, and always within a few miles of Blythin Castle. The murders happen at night or around dusk in a heavy fog, and in every case, the victims are eaten. Some are only eaten a little, others are almost completely devoured, but their face is always gone."

"You're speaking about the Morgan. Villar told me that was a myth," the dwarf said.

"Villar doesn't know everything."

"Where *is* Villar?" Hadrian asked.

"Don't know." He spoked the words slowly, not looking at either of them. The statement caused the dwarf to frown, and his considerable brows knitted the equivalent of a full sweater.

THE DISAPPEARANCE OF WINTER'S DAUGHTER

"Is something wrong?"

Griswold looked up but didn't answer.

"Griswold, what aren't you telling us?" Seton asked.

"Riots are a bloody business. If something went wrong, if our people were in jeopardy, we wanted protection. We needed a backup plan. So we could intercede, if necessary. But only if necessary."

"Is that what the three of you were meeting about?" Hadrian asked.

"For the most part, yes. But I also needed to give Erasmus his supplies."

Hadrian nodded. "The box. I found it with Erasmus's body, but it only contained some rocks, just gravel. The way he carried it, you'd think it was dangerous."

"In the hands of a skilled dwarf, dirt, stone, metal, and wood are all dangerous."

Hadrian felt that rope ought to be included on that list, as his wrists were starting to ache and his hands throbbed. In binding him, the dwarf had exhibited a level of skill that his people were known for when creating stonework or anything mechanical.

"I don't understand," Seton said.

"Of course you don't. How could you? It's old magic. Older even than you. Older than Rochelle, older than Novron."

"What are you talking about?" Seton asked.

"Do you think only mir hold the claim to ancient secrets? For all your age, our collective history goes back far beyond yours. Before Novron and his empire, before the mir, before humans, the Belgriclungreians lived and thrived. I'm talking

298

about the days when only full elves and dwarves roamed the lands, when Drumindor was the world's greatest forge. There was a time when we had a king, an age of greatness, an age of wonder. They say it was Andvari Berling and King Mideon who did it, but the magic predates even them. It goes back to the gods of the ancient giants, to the ones known as Typhins. They were prohibited from having children of their own, according to legend. But they found a way to bring forth life from earth and stone. A magic they used to create the giants themselves. My people discovered that secret, but because it was outlawed by the gods, it was forbidden. Only once was it attempted, and that was during the War of Elven Aggression when King Mideon saved our people. Elves had used their magic to crush the Tenth and Twelfth Legions on the Plains of Mador, and then Mideon called on the legendary Andvari Berling and asked him to crack the forbidden scrolls and make a weapon that could defeat the elves. Some say Andvari never succeeded; others claim he did, but that something went terribly wrong. They claim it was his failure, rather than the attack of the elves, that actually defeated the Kingdom of Mideon and laid waste to Linden Lott."

"What did King Mideon ask this Andvari to make?" Seton asked.

"The only real magic our people ever had."

"Which is?"

Griswold paused a moment. Then a twinkle flickered in his eyes and he leaned in and whispered, "A golem, a protector made of stone."

No one in the plaza had noticed the gargoyle come to life. All eyes were on the acrobats, the dancers, or the juggler. Mercator nimbly raced through the oblivious crowd. For someone who claimed to be old, the Calian mir moved as well as the acrobats they dodged. She and Royce ran through the ring of dancers, breaking the chain of clasped hands, causing a disturbance. Like rambunctious children running through an adult party, they turned heads and provoked shouts. Royce was reminded of his youth. Fleeing had been a daily occurrence back when he survived by picking pockets in the squares of Ratibor. Just as wind was a bird's ally, crowds were his. They provided cover as well as opportunity, but just as too much wind could kill a bird, too dense of a crowd could jam him up, lock him in, and give his pursuer the chance to catch up. Being able to read a mass of people, to see the patterns and guess the timing, had made the difference between getting away and losing a hand.

Royce was older now and out of practice, but it didn't take long to rediscover the familiar skills and remember old techniques. Mercator did a fine job of finding and exploiting holes as well. Anticipating openings, she managed to stay out ahead. She looped the fountain, heading for the steps of the gallery. He wasn't sure what her plan was, but then Royce wasn't certain about the extent of the danger. Seeing a gargoyle come to life was disturbing, but the fact that Mercator felt the need to flee was the real worry. *Why,* was something he could ask her later. As it turned out, *why* was answered sooner than expected.

Jiggery-Pokery

People pointed at something behind Royce, then the screams started, and finally he understood why Mercator was making for the steps of the gallery. The plaza was like a river where a dam had burst upstream. He needed to reach the safety of the bank before the rush of the flood. Whatever the gargoyle was doing, it had caused a panic, and the once happy crowd turned into a mindless mob as people began to push in a frantic attempt to get away.

A man bowled over a woman and her daughter, causing him to trip and fall to the ground, where he, too, was stepped on. The juggler and the dancers were consumed in the tidal surge. Royce and Mercator reached the marble steps of the gallery just as the wave burst. She wasted no time running to the big bronze doors. Royce finally saw her plan and was once more impressed by the level of strategic forethought. And she was a mir.

If she knew, she could say the same about me, couldn't she?

The gallery wasn't as big as Grom Galimus, but it was still large and almost entirely made of stone. There weren't any ground-floor windows, and its doors opened *out*. Royce and Mercator would only have a few seconds to get inside. The swell of the crowd fleeing whatever mayhem had ignited their stampede would realize what Mercator had: The gallery was protection from this storm. If Royce and Mercator were inside when that happened, the bottleneck would inhibit the gargoyle . . . *brilliant*.

"Locked." Mercator pulled angrily on the door. "You can open it, right?"

"How'd you know?" Royce knelt at the door, making a quick study of the basic lever-tumbler mechanism.

The Disappearance of Winter's Daughter

"Anyone expecting a severed finger seems the sort to have a background in theft."

Royce inserted his curtain pick into the keyhole. Lifting the lever, he popped the latch. Although the process had taken only seconds, the crowd moved faster than Royce had expected; a mass of revelers-turned-stampeding-herd pushed up behind them. Unable to pull the door open wide, the two barely managed to slip in before the pressing weight of the mindless crowd slammed it shut again. Part of Royce's cloak was caught, and he freed himself by ripping it in half.

The two looked back at the pair of bronze doors, backing slowly away, listening to the muffled cries of the terrified crowd that grew louder as the seconds passed. The interior of the gallery was tomb-quiet and dark, but Royce knew the building and remembered the room. He'd been there only the night before. This was the rotunda with the murals and paintings, odd artifacts on pedestals, and that big chariot with the stuffed horses yoked to it. The strange beast he'd seen from above he now saw from level ground. This was the proper viewing position for everything, and from there the dragon hoisted overhead was suitably terrifying.

"What is that thing outside?" Royce asked.

"A golem." Mercator's eyes remained fixed on the doors as the two backed away. The fear on her face did nothing to convince Royce that they were safe. "Dwarven sorcery, old, deep, evil magic."

"That thing was a statue a minute ago. What is it now?"

"Still a statue—in a way."

"It *was* after us, right?"

"Still is."

"Can it get in here?"

Mercator looked up at the broken window in the upper colonnade where the night before Royce had chased Villar. "I think so."

"Maybe you'd better tell me exactly what a golem is. I hate getting visits from total strangers."

&

Sitting in the chair was aggravating the pain in his arms, so Hadrian switched to the floor where he could stretch out his legs. Seton helped him, brushing away a pile of rat pellets.

"What does ancient dwarven magic have to do with you, Erasmus Nym, and Villar?"

Griswold reached up and ran fingers under his beard, his lower lip jutting out. He paused there, and Hadrian thought he might not say anything. "We doubted our forces would be enough to prevail against the duke and the city guard. We needed more. We needed what Andvari offered King Mideon."

"I'm guessing that's knowledge you can't pick up just anywhere," Hadrian said.

Griswold nodded and addressed Seton. "Do you know about the Night of Terror?"

"That was centuries ago," Seton said.

Griswold scowled at her. "And I suppose you were there?"

"Before my time. Even before Mercator's, I think."

"One cold night, mobs came into Little Town—that's what they called our ghetto back then—and set our houses on fire. Everyone was dragged into the street for a beating. Almost a hundred of my people died on the same night that the rest of the world calls Wintertide. Strange way to celebrate the rebirth of the sun, don't you think? In the aftermath, the elders found a way to protect us. At that time, the city was under construction, Grom Galimus only half built. My people did the stonework. Cheap, skilled labor is what we were. The archbishop commissioned many sculptures, and we were happy to oblige. Right under his nose and with his blessing, we created weapons that we could call on in time of need."

Griswold smiled. "Surely you've seen all the fanciful downspouts and carvings, malevolent faces that spit rainwater out to the streets?"

Hadrian nodded.

"Those were our creations. Every one of them sculpted by my people. We made them fierce and grotesque as a means of embodying what they are—monsters. The archbishop thought they were fanciful—funny, he called them. What he didn't know was that each one was sculpted ritualistically, and the shards were saved so that we could use them when necessary. If the day came when we were threatened again, we could breathe life into these decorations and send them to fight for us." Griswold's glare hardened. "The nobles have their soldiers, and we have ours. Ours sit upon their perches high above the city, awaiting the day when all debts will be paid in full."

"You can be really creepy, you know that?" Hadrian asked.

"What exactly *is* a golem?" Royce asked. "Is it alive? Can it be killed?"

"I'm not an expert on dwarven magic," Mercator said, "but I know golems are sculptures brought to life. Creatures that are supposed to retain the characteristics of the material they were made from."

"This one is made from stone." Royce stared at the bronze doors with their detailed reliefs, nine framed images that told the life story of a grand city. "How do you harm stone?"

Boom! Boom! Boom!

The gallery echoed with the sound of drumming on the doors by what could have been a huge hammer. They both watched as the elegant images were distorted by dents, the metal puckering where it was struck.

Mercator and Royce backed up.

"Can't burn it. Doesn't have any blood, so slitting its throat is useless. Pretty much nothing sharp will be helpful . . ." Royce was thinking out loud as he scanned the chamber for a weapon. "What *is* this place?"

"The Imperial Gallery," Mercator said, bumping into a bust of a balding man. The sculpture toppled, fell, and shattered on the marble floor. She stared aghast at the ruined artwork. "The noble houses brought a lot of this stuff with them after the fall of Percepliquis. They keep the best pieces in their homes, and the rest is displayed here."

"I don't suppose there's an ancient weapon around that kills stone gargoyles?"

Mercator flashed him a scowl that he guessed had more to do with the beating on the door than his poor attempt at humor.

Hadrian would have appreciated it.

Royce found a pair of hammers set on a display pedestal, one large, one small, both old and crude. He felt the weight of the heavy one, thinking it might be useful. "Why is it after us?"

Mercator stared at the door. "It's being controlled by Villar."

"How do you know?"

"He's one of the few people who know how. Erasmus Nym is dead, and Griswold is busy guarding your friend. It has to be Villar."

"So what does he want with us?"

"I don't know." Her eyes darted back and forth in thought, then they widened. "Wait, you said no list of demands was found in the carriage?"

"No one but you appears to know anything about a list."

Mercator placed a cupped hand over her mouth in disbelief. "The list wasn't overlooked or blown away; he never left it. Everything makes sense now. Villar didn't kidnap the duchess to seek concessions. He never wanted a peaceful solution. He was only placating me, pretending. And now—"

The bronze door ruptured. A stone fist punched through. Claws reached in and began ripping the hole wider. The metal screeched as it tore.

Mercator stuffed Genny's note into Royce's hand. "Take this to the duke."

"What are you going to do?"

She looked back at the doors and Royce couldn't tell if she was scared or angry. *Both maybe.*

"Stop him, I hope. He's driving that thing, running it like a puppet. He can see and hear through it, so I can talk to him, reason with him."

JIGGERY-POKERY

The golem pushed in farther, and Royce dropped the hammer and sprinted for the stairs. The extra weight would only slow him down, and speed was what he needed now. He took the steps three at a time. Four flights up, he glanced back.

Mercator remained in the middle of the main room next to a statue whose plaque read GLENMORGAN THE GREAT. The gargoyle had opened the hole to the size of a window, and it was pulling its body through, emerging like some hideous insect splitting a pupa sac.

"Villar!" Mercator shouted. She had both hands up, palms out. "Stop! You don't have to do this. I've talked to the duchess. She's on our side and wants to help."

The creature appeared to be listening, or maybe it was merely having trouble getting through the ragged opening it had made. The bronze had left deep scratches across its stony skin.

"I know you want your war, Villar. You think it's the only way, but it isn't. Genny can get the duke to change the laws, and they will force the guilds to change their rules. The duchess was already working on it. The very night you kidnapped her she was on her way back from . . ." Mercator stopped. "Oh, my Lord Ferrol." She staggered as if from a blow. "You knew, didn't you? You knew all along that she was working on a solution. That's why you did it. You wanted to stop her. You needed to stop her."

The gargoyle cleared the door. Using its feet and the knuckles of its hands, the thing scrambled monkey-like across the room. It slowed down as it neared her.

Mercator shook her head in disbelief. "Villar, how could you?"

The golem hesitated for a moment, and Royce thought she had a chance, then the thing sank both sets of claws into her body. Royce was no stranger to violence. He'd seen—he'd performed—brutalities that many would label gruesome, even sick. He was as used to bloodletting as a butcher, and yet what he witnessed in that artifact-filled chamber unsettled him. It didn't so much vivisect Mercator as tear her open like a cloth bag with poor stitching. Royce heard muscles shred and her bones make a greenwood-splinter sound. The Calian mir whom Royce had only begun to know, and thought he might like, died in an explosion of blood that splattered the statue of Glenmorgan and stained the perfect marble floor.

The gargoyle showed fangs and pointed teeth, grinning its delight. Then, as tears of blood ran down stone skin, that grotesque monkey-face tilted up. No more encouragement was required. Royce resumed his rapid climb.

The window on the top floor was his goal, his exit, the broken one Villar had shattered the night before.

Reaching the top floor, Royce once more spotted the suit of armor standing against the wall, still holding its long spear. Behind him, the gargoyle was climbing the steps. Royce listened to the *crack* of stone on marble as if someone were clapping rocks together.

Glass from the window still lay on the floor. Outside was the wall, the leap to the cathedral, and a trip across rooftops that Royce had made once already. Except this time, he would be the prey, the one who would slide down slate shingles and fall into the river. Maybe he, too, would survive. *No . . . that sort of thing happens to other people, not me.* He wasn't Villar, and he wasn't competing with a mir. With Royce's luck, the thing would embrace him in a bear hug, they'd hit the river, and he'd be dragged to the bottom.

. . . supposed to retain the characteristics of the material they were made from.

Remembering what had happened to the bust that Mercator had knocked off its pedestal, he grabbed the spear. Jerking it free of the armor, he positioned himself near the balcony's railing. *Hope this works,* he thought even though he suspected it wouldn't.

I'll still have the window, he consoled himself. *If I survive that long.*

Royce held the spear low, not in front, not braced against himself, just at his side. He didn't want to slam the beast head-on. Royce was certain if he tried that, the gargoyle would splinter the spear—or more likely drive it from his hands. He didn't want to stab the thing. He wanted to do what Hadrian had once achieved when facing an indestructible foe. *Worked once, might work again.* But theory and reality were often distant relatives. After seeing what the golem had done to Mercator, Royce was less than confident. Watching a person being torn apart had that effect.

I don't have Hadrian's luck.

The gargoyle's head rose above the steps as it climbed. Its wings spread wide like the hood of a snake before a strike. It spotted Royce, and its eyes widened, the mouth displaying more teeth. Stone teeth, stone face: Every inch of it was craggy and coarse and covered in rivulets of blood. The creature broke into a charge.

The spear didn't give the monster the slightest pause. It didn't try to dodge, didn't shift or slow. The gargoyle appeared bemused, even joyful. Royce couldn't have had a more accommodating enemy, and he imagined the golem felt the same way. As they came together, Royce planted his rear leg and held tight to the pole, then as they collided, he gave ground to prevent the gargoyle from jarring the spear from his hands. The impact was nonetheless powerful, and the tip broke. Royce fell back, dodging to one side while pushing against the stone beast, acting as a lever instead of an impediment. The golem's course altered, only two feet to one side, but it was enough.

Shoved off balance, all its weight slammed into the balcony's railing. A man would have hit the balustrade and slid or bounced off.

. . . supposed to retain the characteristics of the material they were made from. It may have wings, but stone can't fly.

The heavy body of the charging gargoyle shattered the rail, and over the edge it went, crashing through the suspended body of the dragon, shattering the whole exhibit and sending it all to the floor four stories below.

A bang, deep and solid, echoed off the walls, bouncing back and forth twice.

Shatter, you miserable figurine! This half thought, half wish filled Royce's mind as he peered over the edge. He hoped to see a burst of plaster, as when Mercator had overturned the bust. Four stories down lay a mess of broken dragon parts and the torn body of Mercator, her blood draining through a large crack in the checkered marble floor that marked the impact crater of the golem.

JIGGERY-POKERY

The gargoyle hadn't been pulverized. The creature was on its knees in the center of the cracked floor.

No, not Hadrian's kind of luck. Royce then noticed that the golem hadn't escaped unscathed. Part of it was missing. Its left arm lay on the floor a few feet away. The gargoyle looked at it mournfully. Then the fanged monkey-face once more fixed its stare on Royce. This time it added a hiss.

Great, I've made it angry. Well, angrier.

The golem ran for the stairs, and Royce raced for the window. Already knowing the route was his one comfort. The map was still engraved in his mind, which allowed Royce to move with speed and confidence. Poking his head out, he saw the street below. The avenue throbbed with a mass of people, some of whom wore uniforms and held torches. Bodies lay in a line, marking the golem's path to the gallery.

Ducking past the remaining broken shards and out the window, Royce climbed up the wall. He wished he'd brought his hand claws, but he hadn't had them the last time and had managed just fine.

But I was the hunter then. Being the prey is a different matter.

Royce had been chased before. He never cared for it, and usually the hunt ended when he managed to gain enough distance to turn around unseen and don the role of huntsman once more. That wasn't going to happen this time.

How do you harm stone?

He'd broken its arm by dropping it from a height.

Perhaps taking a tumble from higher up?

Reaching the roof of the gallery, he looked back. Nothing but a single sheer curtain fluttered, blowing out through the broken window by an errant wind. *Is it possible the thing lost interest?*

The answer came when the window's remnants burst outward and fell, along with portions of the frame and a few stones of the wall. More screams erupted below. Arms went up. Fingers pointed. Men shouted, "Up there! There it is!"

The gargoyle wasn't as nimble as it had been when descending the cathedral—climbing was clearly harder to manage with only one arm. Brute force now replaced grace. It fearlessly launched itself up from the sill, one clawed hand creating its own handhold, gouging out mortar like soft dirt. Rear claws did the same, then punched up again—stone muscles propelling it amazing distances in single thrusts.

Royce didn't like the ease with which it followed nor the power it displayed. Mercator's death remained fresh in his mind, and he didn't want to be anywhere near those claws. Taking a cue from the previous night, he pulled slate shingles free and threw, hoping he might make the golem fall. Royce's aim was better than Villar's, and he struck the beast three times: once in the head, twice in the body. The slates shattered. The gargoyle didn't notice.

How am I going to make it fall again? The question was pushed aside as he realized it didn't matter—not yet. He needed to get higher. Royce resumed his flight.

Running out along the gable, he jumped the gap between the gallery and Grom Galimus, landing on a stony lion's head. Below him, he heard the crowd cheer with excitement. As he scaled the cathedral's pier, Royce realized how futile the effort was. Even if he got away from the golem, reached the duke, somehow convinced him his wife was alive, and persuaded the man to concede to Mercator's demands, Hadrian might still die. The issue of Nym's death hadn't yet been addressed. If Hadrian's luck provided him the means to slip free of that noose, Royce just might kill him anyway.

They were up six stories now.

Is that enough? No, I need to go higher.

After Royce reached the flying buttress, obtaining additional height was no longer an issue. He ran up its angled length, and the world below dropped away as he climbed several stories as quickly as ascending stairs. Reaching the high balcony just below the cathedral's eaves, Royce saw it as a death trap. Too narrow to pull another spear stunt, even if he had one. Up there the golem would have all the advantage. Facing the thing on the steep roof of Grom Galimus wasn't to Royce's liking. The peak was equally dangerous for both. The battle odds would be even: each had a good chance of falling. Royce was never pleased with a fair fight, but fair was better than certain death. They were about two hundred and fifty feet up, and he guessed his odds of surviving a fall, assuming he could hit the water, were one in a hundred.

Villar had managed it. Hadrian could probably pull it off as well, but I don't have his kind of luck.

Royce saw it as a last resort.

Reaching up, he grabbed the eaves, scowling at the row of gargoyle faces that glared down at him. Each one, he now realized, was grinning. *I really hate these things.*

Royce was breathing hard, his clothes stuck to his skin, and as he pulled himself up, he realized his muscles were weakening. *Stone,* he guessed, *doesn't get tired.* As he reached the roof, the wind greeted him with a familiar blast of cold air. He replied with a grunt and a scowl as he was forced to remember that spring, while very near, hadn't yet arrived. The chill sent a shiver through him and whipped what was left of his cloak over his shoulder.

Below, he spotted the golem racing up the buttress, wings extended like an acrobat's balancing pole. When crouched and seen at a distance on the walls of buildings, the gargoyles appeared small. Up close, the creature was eight feet tall.

This isn't going to end well.

Royce shimmied up the ribs to the fence-like peak of the roof where he would make his last stand. His options were limited. He could try to climb the bell tower as Villar had considered doing, but there was no more benefit in it now than before. He could climb down the other side of the cathedral and hope the golem would follow and fall the way Villar had. Already tired, Royce knew if anyone fell it would most likely be him. Each step inched him toward exhaustion while the gargoyle showed no sign of weakening.

The thing lost its arm! If I lost one after falling four stories, I'd quit. It hasn't even slowed down!

Royce had to make a move while he still had the strength. The golem was one-handed now and needed both feet to stand on the roof, so it couldn't rip him apart as it had Mercator, the thing would have to resort to slashing, biting, or crushing. But without a spear, without a weapon, fighting the golem would be suicide, except . . .

Royce pulled Alverstone from the folds of his cloak. Moonlight gave its blade a luminosity that was pleasantly eerie. Royce had few possessions; the dagger was his most prized for two reasons. The first was that it had been a gift from a man who'd shown him kindness and saved his life. The only one to do so—until Hadrian acted the fool on the Crown Tower. The second was that the blade was remarkable. He had no idea how it had been created. The weapon had somehow been forged in secret in that infernal pit that was the Manzant Prison and Salt Mine. The one good thing to come out of there. *No*, Royce corrected himself, *not the only good thing*. The dagger wasn't the real gift he'd received; it was but a symbol, the embodiment of something more. The gleeful, thieving assassin who entered that salt mine wasn't the same as the one who'd crawled out. As Royce straddled the peak of Grom Galimus waiting for the arrival of the golem what he held in his hand wasn't a dagger; it was what it always had been—hope.

He didn't wait long. The gargoyle leapt onto the roof and once more grinned with delight to find his prey waiting.

With his other hand holding on to the decorative iron fins along the roof's peak, Royce braced in a crouch, facing into the howling wind.

Is this the craziest, stupidest thing I've ever done? That this was even a question made him suspect the idiocy of his past life choices.

Using the stone claws on its feet, the gargoyle pinched into the slate, creating firm footholds as it walked up the steep slope.

A gust of wind hit its wings, staggering and nearly toppling the beast, but the creature folded them away and continued its climb.

This is what Villar had seen last night. An unstoppable predator. Irony, oh how I hate thee.

Royce maintained his perch along the line of the peak. When the first attack came—a wide swipe from the remaining arm—he shuffled back along the length. All this did was grant the gargoyle room to take position on the ridgeline with him. With only one arm, the golem couldn't both attack and hold on to the fins. Still, it had claws on its feet and, of course, fangs. Royce couldn't forget the fangs. Mercator's blood was already drying, aided by the brisk wind. An ever-present, sinisterly sculpted smile revealed zigzagging teeth as pointed as spear tips, the invention of an artist with a sick mind and no concern for realism. The gargoyle moved forward with the confidence Royce lacked.

Facing the monster, guarding from attacks, Royce shuffled backward blindly, knowing he would eventually run out of roof, and do so without warning. He was a sailor walking a plank backward.

Royce dodged a swipe from the golem's foot. In the process, he backed up too far and found the end of the roof. He fell, catching himself by grabbing the decorative ironwork.

The golem pressed the advantage, rushing forward. With Royce dangling and nearly helpless, the sensible thing for the golem to do would have been to crush his hand and let him fall. Instead, it grabbed his wrist and jerked him up. The golem's grip on his wrist was exactly what Royce expected, vise-strong and cold. This was the end of the fight, but while the golem had but one arm, Royce had two. As the golem jerked Royce up, it had no defense—likely didn't feel a need for it.

How do you harm stone?

The golem had no reason to fear a delicate dagger. Royce had slim hope himself, despite knowing the weapon was endowed with an extraordinary blade that cut wood like hot iron cut wax. Once, it'd even cut a link of iron chain. Alverstone was hope in the face of despair, and Royce hoped very hard as he jabbed at the gargoyle's chest.

Rather than turn, deflect, or snap as it should have, the dagger's blade punctured the stone. Not deep; it didn't have the opportunity. The golem screamed, recoiled, and in that instant of shock, the heavy stone creature was thrown off balance. Falling from its precarious perch, the golem let go of Royce in the hope of grabbing support.

Released from bondage, Royce fell. He hit the roof's surface, started his slide, and without thought used Alverstone the way he so often used his hand claws. Royce stabbed into the slate with the blade. It penetrated, caught, and held, leaving Royce hanging from the dagger, as beside him the golem tumbled.

The gargoyle's weight worked against it. It managed to grab an edge but tore it free. The onetime statue fell, rolled, and picked up the sort of speed one expects from a rock rolling down a steep roof. It bounced, jumped, and finally fell, this time on the plaza side. The gargoyle's wings spread, but stone wings did nothing to slow its fall.

THE DISAPPEARANCE OF WINTER'S DAUGHTER

Royce didn't see the impact. The edge of the roof blocked the climax. He heard it: a loud *crack*. Screams and shouts followed. They were short-lived, the sort that came from the surprise of a falling stone, rather than the fear of a living golem.

CHAPTER TWENTY-ONE
THE DUKE

The bronze doors of the Imperial Gallery—one with a massive hole torn in it—were open by the time Royce reached the street. A skittish crowd remained in the plaza, and given the way they scuttled back at his approach, they had watched his upper-story jiggery-pokery. That was most certainly what Evelyn would have made of his chase across the rooftops if she'd been in the crowd. Royce considered for a moment whether she'd been one of those people the gargoyle had injured in its murderous march across the plaza. No one would have fared well before the golem's onslaught, but an old woman would lack any ability to get out of the way. His teeth clenched in anger. He didn't know why. He hated that old woman.

He took a breath before entering the gallery, and then another. He'd just survived a race with a golem and felt he deserved to take a moment. His back was sore, and his wrist ached where the stone monster had held onto it, but at least it wasn't broken. Not exactly Hadrian's luck, but better than his normal lot.

Few spectators had found the courage to venture inside. Those who did hugged the wall nearest the exit. A handful of men dressed in the uniform of the duke's city guard made a semicircle around the bloody mess in the middle of the rotunda. Most stood awkwardly, shifting their weight, unsure where to look or what to do. Three others pulled back the broken remains of the fallen dragon, revealing the extent of the gore. Everything within twenty feet of Mercator's body wept blood. The remains bore as little resemblance to a once living person as did a slab of bacon. A young man in a crisp new set of clothing clapped both hands over his mouth; when that didn't work, he ran for the door, brushing past Royce in his dash to the street.

As a general rule, Royce disliked everyone. Strangers began at a deficit that required they prove their worth just to be seen as neutral. Mercator had jumped that bar in record time.

And a mir to boot, he thought. *How remarkable is that?*

Royce couldn't help feeling he'd blindly brushed past greatness. An opportunity had been lost, a treasure squandered. That was how he framed it in his head, as an abstract business failure. But looking at Mercator's blood and the blue-stained lumps of meat that had once been the most remarkable mir he'd ever known, Royce clenched his fists.

A shriveled-up biddy and now a mir. I'm becoming soft. This is all Hadrian's fault.

"You there!" one of the guards shouted. "Grab him!"

THE DUKE

Not twice in one night, Royce thought as he took a step back, dipping into a crouch.

The guard wasn't a fool. He recognized the body language, which must have looked like a badger raising its fur, teeth bared. The man didn't rush him. Neither did anyone else. Instead, the guards fanned out.

Royce heard movement behind him. Turning, he found himself face-to-face with Roland Wyberg, just coming in through the torn bronze door. "Well, it's about time," Royce said. "C'mon, we gotta go."

"Go? What are you talking about? Where's Hadrian?" Roland asked, puzzled. He looked at the hole in the door then at the bloody mess in the center of the room. "What in Novron's name happened here?"

"I saw this man running across the rooftops chased by . . ." The guard faltered.

"Chased by whom?" Roland asked. His stare extended to everyone in the room, finally settling on Royce.

"Not a who, a what," Royce replied. "One of the stone gargoyles from the walls of Grom Galimus."

"A *gargoyle?*" Roland asked, pronouncing the word with distinct incredulity.

Royce nodded. "A stone statue, normally content to sit on a ledge outside the cathedral, decided to climb down. It took a particular dislike to myself and"—his eyes tracked to the blood pool—"a mir named Mercator Sikara."

Roland stared. He opened his mouth. It hung there for a moment, then he closed it again, his eyes shifting helplessly. "I—I don't know what to make of that."

"Luckily, I do," Royce said. He pulled out two parchments. "Here, this one's for you. It's from Hadrian, explaining why you need to take me and Mercator to the duke and insist on an audience. Although now we'll have to settle for just me."

"And the other?" Roland pointed at the parchment but made no attempt to take it.

This guy is a lot smarter than I gave him credit for. And that's good because whether either of us likes it or not, we're about to become a team.

"This?" Royce held up the letter from Genny Winter. "If we're lucky, it's a weapon we can use to prevent a slaughter tomorrow."

Roland continued to look puzzled; then realization dawned. "The Feast of Nobles?"

"Exactly. We need to see the duke. Right now."

Governor's Isle was an odd name for the ancestral residence of dukes, but Royce guessed it had something to do with all that gibberish Evelyn had blathered on about. The place didn't look anything like a ducal castle. The Estate had the typical ugly wall surrounding the grounds, but it appeared out of place, newer and more slapdash than anything inside, all of which was extraordinarily precise. Brick paths wound through open lawns and alongside trimmed hedges. One led through a small orchard and garden to a stable, a coach house, barracks, and a kitchen built separate from the main structure, all constructed from a smooth rock with no visible mortar.

The Estate itself was a rambling country home built of the same precisely cut stone—something the elite of Colnora might have referred to as a grand villa. The house was three stories high with gables and a centered portico complete with stone pillars. Royce counted five chimneys and twenty-nine glass windows facing front, including a round one set at the portico's peak. At the very top, the ducal flag flew just below the colors of Alburn. The entry path formed a circle before the front doors, and fine gravel lined a neatly edged lawn, well-trimmed hedges, and early purple flowers that Royce couldn't identify. The style was relaxed, opulent, and open, nothing like the homes of western nobles, which skewed toward the dull and solid—with an emphasis on solid. In places like Warric and Melengar, a duke's residence was barely discernible from a stronghold. Even successful knights lived in gray stone citadels with narrow, glassless openings. But this place . . .

If the wall was a relatively recent addition, Royce struggled to imagine how the Dukes of Rochelle could have lived in an open, defenseless house. The idea was both incredible and unfathomable. *The lack of walls suggests an absence of enemies, but no ruler fits that description. Had the ancient governors been so ruthless that sheer terror replaced the need for walls? Perhaps in place of stone battlements they had encircled the island with posts laden with corpses. Or . . .* An odd, alien thought popped into Royce's head, one that was as unlikely as his walking alongside the captain of the guard into a ducal estate. *Could there have been no need for walls because it was a more virtuous world? The sort of place where Hadrian would have fit in?* Royce pondered all this as he walked past the yellow-flowering forsythia bushes, listening to his feet crush the gravel. *Hadrian is one of those people born too late, and I? Am I born too early?*

Royce wasn't surprised that obtaining an audience in the dead of night was difficult even for the captain of the duke's guard. Wyberg had to browbeat the soldiers at the gate, who complained about his lack of an appointment. At the front doors, Roland had to remind the pair of men about his rank in order to gain entry to the foyer.

Looking up, Royce spotted an open third-story window. He could have already entered the duke's bedroom by then, though the meeting might not have been as cordial with that approach.

Inside, the Estate continued to impress. The duke's foyer was ballroom-sized and decorated with sculptures and paintings instead of swords and shields, the normal ornaments for any serious lord intent on projecting a sense of power. Royce was genuinely impressed by some of the art. When he'd visited such places in the past, the homes were always dark, and he was in too much of a hurry to notice the furnishings. The place was elegant, but he wouldn't want to live there. The residences of the rich always felt cold.

"Duke Leopold does not meet with his *soldiers* in the middle of the night," said the duke's chamberlain, a portly, balding man who displayed a well-worn frown beneath a neat mustache. While unarmed and unimposing, he was proving to be a worthier adversary than the gate or door guards. With thumbs hooked on the breast of his robe, chest thrust out, he stood blocking the way. "We have a hierarchy to handle problems."

"Exactly, and I'm captain of the guard," Wyberg declared.

"But did His Grace request an audience?"

"No, this is an emergency."

The chamberlain's frown deepened. "Aren't *you* supposed to handle emergencies? Why does the duke have you in charge, if not to provide him the luxury of sleeping at night? As you can see, the sun is down. We don't bother him with trifles when he is sleeping."

"Trifles!" Roland burst out. "I just said—"

"Tut-tut!" The chamberlain placed the palms of his hands together then tilted the tips of his pressed fingers toward Roland. "This is what you will do. Tomorrow morning—and not *too* early—you can come and make an appointment to speak to the ducal clerk. Given the feast, I'm sure he'll be too busy to receive you, but if it truly *is* an emergency"—he looked at Wyberg skeptically—"he'll get you in to see the duke's secretary, who will evaluate your request and determine if it warrants an audience. If it does, your request will be passed on to the Ducal Council of Attendance, which will review His Lordship's itinerary and try and find time in the schedule for you. Now, doesn't that sound like a better way to go about this? I'm sure whatever the problem is, you can manage it for a while."

"This can't wait!" Roland exploded.

Royce stayed out of the confrontation. He had entered behind the captain, acting as Roland's shadow, and soundlessly moved about the foyer, feigning interest in the art. With all of Wyberg's outbursts, the chamberlain only gave Royce a cursory glance, then ignored him altogether. Royce inched behind the chamberlain, slipping beyond his peripheral vision. Spotting a painting of a stag in a river valley, Royce moved toward it. While it wasn't the best art in the room, it was near the corridor. Moving over, he leaned in to inspect it further.

"I must see the duke tonight!" Wyberg shouted and thrust his arms out in a rage. "You have no idea what's going on! If I don't—"

"Calm yourself!" the chamberlain snapped, throwing up his hands and cringing as if he felt Wyberg was about to attack.

Royce took that opportunity to slip into the unguarded hallway.

Wood paneling, tiled floors, and an arched ceiling complete with painted designs in the ducal colors greeted Royce as he trotted down the corridor, moving fast—far faster than if he were burgling. It felt odd. This was wholly without precedent, and Royce wasn't certain how to proceed. *What do I do if I spook a servant or, worse, a guard?* He guessed his normal solution might not be the best choice in this instance. He was there to *talk* to the duke, not kill him or his servants. He was acting blind. Moving boldly through a lit house, unannounced and unwanted, was strange when doing so with none of the normal tools he used in such situations.

This is more like something Hadrian would do. The man is becoming a serious liability.

As he searched the vast estate for clues to the duke's whereabouts, Royce reviewed the pros and cons of continuing his partnership with the man who didn't seem to live in the same world. He genuinely liked Hadrian, although at that moment he wasn't able to bring to mind a single reason why. *But is liking something a good enough reason to offset the risks? I like Montemorcey wine, but too much will kill me.* The more he thought about it, the more similarities he found between them. *They both impede my ability to think sensibly, resulting in bad judgments, and too much of either gives me headaches.*

Still, the best argument was also the worst. *Hadrian was wrong. I do have a unicorn in my world, and the damn thing goes by the name of Hadrian Blackwater. He's a mythical beast impossible to believe in, even when he's right in front of me.* Royce had never had the need to believe in anything before, but that was the effect of the unicorn on a mortal man. It made him consider things he thought impossible. Because if unicorns were possible . . . what else might be? In that way, Hadrian was less like Montemorcey and more like Alverstone. Perhaps that was why Royce could never throw either of them away.

Finding another stair, Royce took it, guessing the duke slept on the highest floor. Reaching the top, he found the residence to be more inviting. Deeply stained wood and tapestries softened the hard edges. Small tables topped with bouquet-filled vases added a dash of personality through spring blossoms. Expansive windows framed with thick green drapes invited moonlight in and made the house feel more like a home—a three-story one with a footprint the size of a large island and filled with priceless art. Royce passed an open door and spotted a chambermaid turning down a bed. She didn't see him, and Royce slipped quickly past.

A boy in a white tunic, who carried a tray of porcelain cups and plates, did see him, but the lad didn't say a word—just walked right past.

I've been doing it all wrong, Royce thought. *Apparently, I can saunter into any mansion, lift what I like, and stroll right back out.*

He looked at the corridor of closed doors and considered his next move. *Should I knock?* The idea felt absurd.

Royce heard a noise behind him and spun to find the chambermaid stepping out, holding a pile of white linens. She, too, saw him; he was certain she had, but the maid—like the boy—didn't raise her eyes to the level of his face. As she turned to leave, Royce had an insane idea. It was the sort of crazy notion that Hadrian would propose.

"Excuse me," Royce said, feeling ridiculous. "Where might I find the duke?"

As soon as he said it, Royce knew he'd made a mistake. He wasn't Hadrian, and such things only worked for him. *Maybe if I was wearing polka dots . . .*

"I believe His Lordship is in the library, sir," the maid replied. "He's having trouble sleeping again, sir."

Royce stared at the woman, dumbfounded.

Apparently, mistaking his bewilderment for an unfamiliarity with the Estate, she added, "Around the corner. First door on the left, sir."

"Ah . . . thank you," he replied.

She nodded and walked off with her armload of sheets.

What sort of place is this? Yes, please. Right this way, sir. The duke is right in here. Have at him, sir. Slit his throat. Would you like tea with that? Royce shook his head while watching her vanish down the steps, then remembered why he was there.

The door to the library was open, and Royce walked in. What wasn't windows was bookshelves, though there weren't many actual books. Most of the shelves were filled with painted plates, potted plants, intricately carved boxes, models of sailing ships, and even skeletons or stuffed figures of small animals set in poses. A large map hung from the ceiling above the fireplace's hearth, where a meager fire halfheartedly burned. The duke stood at one of the windows, looking out at the night sky. He was a balding, plump man, the sort that might have been strong and stocky in his youth, but years and wealth had transformed him. He was barefoot, wearing only a long nightshirt that exposed the gray hairs on his calves.

"My lord?" Royce ventured, trying his best not to sound like a thief. The duke failed to react and continued to stare out the window. Royce inched forward as if sneaking up on a skittish rabbit that might bolt. "Duke Leopold?"

The man turned. "Oh," he said. "I see." He nodded some understanding that eluded Royce. Perhaps he thought he was there to retrieve dishes or turn down the bed.

The duke lifted a decanter filled with an amber liquid and poured some into a crystal glass. He held up the decanter in offering.

Royce shook his head.

"Do you mind if I . . ." He didn't wait for approval, and drank, then took a deep breath. "I'm ready."

"For what?" Royce asked.

"You're here to kill me, right?"

Royce was stunned.

"You look surprised."

"I ah . . ."

"What else could you possibly be doing in my residence unannounced this late at night just before the crowning? And your cloak and hood—well, it just screams *killer*."

THE DISAPPEARANCE OF WINTER'S DAUGHTER

At least someone is awake in here. That's what separates the duke from the chambermaids—paranoia.

"Not going to get any complaints out of me," Leo said. "Honestly, you're doing me a favor."

"I'm not here to kill you."

The duke looked over with an expression that could only be described as annoyed. "No?"

"No."

"That's disappointing." He turned. "So, who the blazes are you, then? And why are you here?"

Footfalls rushed up the steps.

Royce pulled the parchment from his belt and held it out. A moment later soldiers burst into the library. They would have to wait.

"To give you this."

The duke stared at the parchment, puzzled. "What is it?"

"A letter," Royce said as a guard stepped toward him. "From your wife."

He waited in what they called the parlor, but Royce saw it as just another overly polished medium-sized room with too much art and too few chairs. He was left to himself. No guards watched, the door was open, and he hadn't been shackled or tied. No one had even tried. This was a good thing for everyone involved. After reading the letter, the duke had ordered his thugs to let Royce go. Then Leo Hargrave had merely asked him to wait. Royce appreciated that it hadn't been an order. He'd actually used the word *please*. Nevertheless, waiting wasn't something

THE DUKE

Royce was fond of, especially as the night was short, and there was so much left to do if Hadrian was to be extricated from the pickle barrel he'd jumped into. Roland had been ordered to wait as well, but then he was called up for questioning, leaving Royce alone. That had been some time ago.

The Estate had many paintings. In that room alone, there were eight. Only one caught his eye: the portrait of a man who was unmistakably Leopold. The work was exquisite, and Royce felt uneasy, as if the painting were an actual person in the room with him. The sensation was so pronounced that he went over to inspect it. His eye caught the artist's signature: SHERWOOD STOW. *Should have known.*

Royce had no idea what Wyberg was telling the duke, and that made him uneasy. Just being in an expensively appointed room filled with carvings of elephants and deer, not to mention a silver tea set, made him jumpy. He didn't stay in places of this sort, but he did often visit, and he couldn't help noticing how easily the carvings would fit under his cloak or avoid calculating what a small fortune they would bring on the black market. The room was chilly despite the fireplace because no one had bothered to light it. This left Royce sitting on the velvet-and-wood chair, feeling the cold seep in and wondering why he was still there.

He thought I was here to kill him. If this job had turned out the way I had expected, I would have been.

Royce pictured two different paths running side by side, so close, yet so different. He'd come to Rochelle to kill Leopold. That's what Gabriel Winter had wanted. *Make that goddamn duke and all those working for him bleed. Turn the Roche River red for me, for me and my Genny.* Royce had arrived on that road, but somehow he'd gotten off it. Now he was on another path, but the duke had assumed he was still on the first. Royce felt as if he'd performed sleight of hand, so subtly that the world itself had been duped.

I was duped, too.

Even as he sat in that cold, empty room, he could see himself on the other path. *I would have stood behind the duke as he stared at the stars and slit his throat—careful to catch his glass so it didn't shatter. That reality feels more authentic than this one. That's what I should have done. That's what I was supposed to do.*

Royce found it surreal that he should be standing beside that path, looking down and seeing a history that didn't happen. His trajectory had altered course, just a smidge, a tiny tilt, but it was enough to change events from bloodbath to letter delivery.

Were you expecting a finger?

Royce had been expecting a whole lot of fingers and even more heads. Instead, he sat in a luxurious room, waiting on the ruler of the city to . . . he had no idea. That was the problem with this new path. Royce didn't know where it went. He'd never gone this way before. Just as he was deciding that waiting on a duke was about as smart as listening to Hadrian, the duke showed up.

The man was dressed, but not in the finery Royce would have expected for a ruling noble. Wearing a crisp shirt, waistcoat, and casual trousers, he looked more like a modest merchant. He was followed by half a dozen men, who were better dressed but appeared worse for wear. Whereas *they* looked as if they had just woken up, *Leo Hargrave* beamed as if born again. Bright and smiling, he strode up to Royce and nodded.

"So, old man Winter hired you," Leopold said and studied Royce's face for his reaction.

Royce didn't give one.

"He hates me, you know. You're in the Black Diamond, right?"

Royce remained silent, his sight shifting briefly as Roland entered. For better or worse, Wyberg was his advocate, his lifeline out of this, and it was reassuring to see he was still there. This way when the bastard betrayed him, Royce wouldn't need to hunt him down to slit his throat.

"Doesn't matter," the duke said, and then chuckled. "And you can relax. Right now, you're my best friend, and I owe you." Leo shivered. "Why is it so cold in here? Did they leave you so ill attended? Idiots." The man scowled, then lifted the parchment in his hand, grasping it as gently as if it were a newborn. "My Genny is alive."

"She won't be if you don't—"

"I know," Leo said. "It was all in the letter. Grant the dwarves the right to work. Give the Calians the right to trade. Bestow on the mir the right to exist. Not something I can simply change overnight. Guilds are powerful things but Genny . . ." He shook the letter again. "Never a dull moment with her around and never a moment's peace. The woman was already working toward those ends. She was fixing the problem that is Rochelle. She's a businesswoman, you see. Rochelle is a horrible tangle. This city is choked with regulations and procedures, layers upon layers of protocol, and ages steeped in narrow-minded intolerance. She doesn't know anything about such things. Had no idea of the impossibility of the task. That's the way with her, you know.

Don't ever tell that woman she can't do something. She'll take it as a challenge. In this case, she came up with a plan where the existing members of the merchant and trade guilds will receive a percentage of the money earned by the Calians and dwarves. She also indicated that if they refused, I should raise taxes on trade goods. Nothing speaks to businessmen like money, or someone threatening theirs. And as it turns out, the daughter of a Colnora merchant baron is fluent in such matters. She was getting close to an agreement, but then she disappeared."

"I need to get back," Royce said. "I need to bring proof you're planning to do something."

"Yes, I know. Genny mentioned an uprising. Lovely handwriting." He grinned. "She has these pudgy little hands, but her penmanship is beautiful. Years of keeping books, she told me."

"What proof can we provide?" Royce pressed.

The duke gestured at his companions. "These gentlemen are leaders of the city's merchant and trade guilds, the ones Genny met with. They are quite eager to assist, especially after I explained that if my wife dies, I'll charge them as complicit in the murder and execute every last one of them." Leo focused on the sleepy men and glared.

"The king will condemn the murder of prominent merchants," one of the men said.

"What king?"

The man looked uncomfortable.

"Don't worry," Leo smiled. "I will definitely hold a trial immediately following your deaths in order to get to the bottom of this conspiracy. And while we are doing that, you can voice your concern to his late majesty King Reinhold when you see him."

I like this guy, Royce thought. "Guess we'd better get going."

"Captain Wyberg will go with you. Good luck . . . Royce, is it?"

He sighed and nodded.

"Royce," the duke said to himself as a curious, thoughtful look came over him. "I've heard that name before."

"Let's go," Royce told Roland and quickly headed for the door. He didn't want to discover what revelations the duke had uncovered.

CHAPTER TWENTY-TWO
THE MORNING AFTER

With nothing else to do, Hadrian had fallen asleep. He woke to the first light of dawn spilling down the wooden steps from the shack above. The three of them were still huddled in the stone cellar. Griswold sat where he'd always been, hunched up with knees high, his long beard pooling on his lap, demonstrating the patience and unruffled composure of a rock. He still had the dagger, out and ready. Seton had curled up beside Hadrian using him as a pillow, her hair creating a pool of blond across his lap. He guessed she'd done it for warmth, or perhaps as a precaution against treachery while she slept.

No one can steal me away without waking my protector.

For Hadrian, who was cold, cramped, and couldn't feel his hands, the beautiful mir was a wonderful comfort. In the newborn light that gave everything a spotless purity, she was something more than beautiful, more than a woman. In the same way, the first snowfall of the year was more than snow; both were transcendent.

She's so light, like having a cat sleep on me. Hadrian had always felt that cats were picky, untrusting things. Being fragile, they had to be. Whenever a cat sat on him, Hadrian felt special, as if the animal approved, and their acceptance was some sort of gift. *Makes a body feel worthy of something to have a cat trust you that much.*

Hadrian didn't feel worthy. *I did one good thing. How quickly does a pure drop of rain disappear in a muddy lake? How many did I kill that night? I don't even remember.* In her story, he was a monster who came to slaughter and maim. Hadrian had few illusions about those days, and his memories only got worse the farther he traveled east where civilization was little more than an inconvenient philosophy. Still, he'd never really seen himself as evil.

But I was. Maybe I still am.

He looked down. Her eyes were closed, her body rising and falling gently, silently. Maybe she was a hundred years old and had witnessed and even participated in atrocities of her own. Maybe she had closets full of horrible regrets. Who didn't? But in that forgiving light, she was as innocent as a newly budded flower, and she was his savior.

Cats don't sleep on monsters, do they?

Noises turned Griswold's head and woke Seton. They all listened: voices coming from outside. The sound soaked through the walls of the overhead shack and dripped down through the gaps in the floorboards, conversations impossible to clearly hear. Identities were equally vague. Men and women were all Hadrian could reliably discern. Not many, two or three perhaps, but they were coming closer.

The dwarf climbed to his feet. "Either your friend's back or time's up. If he's betrayed us . . ." He pointed the dagger at Hadrian, an old, dull blade. *Is it the same one he uses to carve figurines?* After seeing him with his family, after looking at the beauty he created out of wood, Hadrian found it hard to believe Griswold could kill. But Hadrian had been wrong before.

Maybe in a society of stoneworkers, wood carving is an indication of insanity. Griswold might be the sort of crazed killer that no one suspects. Hadrian had met a few of those. Young soldiers, usually the quiet ones that he worried might not be up to the task, revealed a different side on the battlefield. Normally constrained by social pressure, they felt a sense of freedom in combat that they never encountered in daily life. Killing, the ultimate taboo, became a necessary relief to the building pressure to conform. After the fight, they went back to their shadow life, but the taste of blood worked like an infection. They were the ones who volunteered for missions but fell into trouble after the war. Killers hiding in plain sight; pots boiling with sealed lids. Griswold might be like that.

Hadrian felt Seton stiffen as if she'd had the same thought, and then the mir got to her feet as well, her eyes on the dagger.

"That was the deal he made," Griswold told her.

The noise grew louder. Then footfalls hit the floor of the shack, thumping on the ceiling above.

"Hadrian?" Royce yelled.

Griswold shuffled away from the stairs and toward Hadrian.

"No!" Seton moved with surprising speed, thrusting herself between them and raising her hands, putting up the defense Hadrian couldn't.

Griswold's expression was grim, not gleeful. And Hadrian was pleased to see it. *At least he doesn't want to kill me—or maybe it's just her he regrets killing.*

"Stop!" The order came from the stairs where Selie Nym descended. "Griswold Dinge, you put that dagger away! Right now, you hear?"

"Why? What's happened? Where are Mercator and Villar?"

"Mercator Sikara is dead," the Calian woman said.

This did nothing to improve the dwarf's attitude, and his expression went from grim to angry.

"Was it the small one who did it?"

Royce joined her at the bottom of the stairs and Griswold took a tighter grip on the dagger. Hadrian got to his feet.

The dwarf let out a heated growl. "What happened to Mercator. I don't see—"

"That's right, Griswold, you don't see anything!" The widow was furious. "Mercator Sikara was murdered. And it's all your fault!"

"My fault? Don't be ridiculous. I've been here, with them, all night."

"Mercator was torn apart by *a golem!*"

She could have hit the dwarf with a bucket of water and gotten the same response. He stopped not only his movement toward Hadrian but even his breathing. A fortunate turn for Griswold, as by then Royce was past the widow, and Alverstone was out and ready to say hello.

"Drop the dagger or lose the hand," Royce ordered in the sort of voice that allowed no hesitation or argument.

Griswold let his blade fall and backed away, but his eyes were still trained on Erasmus's widow, still aghast.

"Damn it," Royce cursed, kicking the blade away and frowning at the dwarf. "They never pick the choice I want."

The dwarf had backed up all the way to the wall, retreating from more than Royce. "I don't understand. How could a golem kill Mercator?"

"You tell me, you little bearded excuse for a mole rat!" The widow was filled with fury. "Erasmus had always been against using those things, those evil, disgusting creatures, and now . . . now . . ." She took a deep breath to compose herself. "Who have you taught that evil sorcery? Do you see what price has been paid? Mercator is dead and so is my Erasmus!"

"He killed your husband!" Griswold pointed at Hadrian.

"He didn't." Seton looked at Selie in desperation.

The widow patted Seton's cheek. "Honey, do you think I would believe anything coming out of his mouth? Erasmus's face was damn near chewed away. What happened to my . . . to my . . . that wasn't done by any man."

"I—" Seton began.

The widow was done with her but not with Griswold. "You're the only one who knows . . . the only one who . . ." The widow put her hands to her hips, her eyes narrowing to the sort of slits archers used when targeting small prey. "Hundreds of people saw a golem in the plaza last night! That stony monster climbed down the side of the cathedral, smashed into the gallery, and tore that poor woman apart. First my Erasmus, now Mercator. All because—"

"It wasn't me. I was here with them." He gestured toward Hadrian and Seton.

"But you showed others. You're the only one who knows how. Who else did you teach that vile black magic to? Who else can raise a golem?"

Griswold bowed his head. "Just three of us, only three. I had to, you see, as a kind of safeguard. A way to ensure no single person, no one sect had more power than the others, and so each race would have equal power. I was one, your husband another . . ."

She glared. "Who was the last?"

"Villar," Royce said cutting Hadrian's bonds free.

The dwarf's eyes indicated agreement.

"Mercator figured it out," Royce said. "He never left any note with demands. He used Leopold's lack of action to fuel dissent and his bloody little war. He was trying to stop us from getting to the duke. Mercator tried to talk him out of it, but it didn't go so well."

"Did you get into the Estate? Were you able to see the Duke?" Hadrian asked.

Royce nodded. "And he has Wyberg and a group of guild leaders in the meeting hall right now. They're discussing the duke's intentions and what changes will be coming. Looks like Mercator accomplished that much at least. There won't be any revolution." He looked at Hadrian. "I told Roland we'd take care of getting the duchess back to the Estate."

Hadrian's fingers suffered the dreaded pins and needles as blood flowed back to them. To his surprise, Seton, whose face was streaked with tears, took his hands and rubbed them.

With his hands returning to normal, Hadrian clapped and rubbed them together. "Let me get my swords, and we'll get going. So, where is she?" he asked Royce.

"Don't know." He looked to Griswold.

The dwarf began shaking his head, though Hadrian doubted the dwarf was aware of it. He had a lost, horrified look, as if he'd just woken up with blood on his hands. "I don't know. No one does."

"What do you mean *no one?*" Hadrian asked.

"The duchess was the mir's responsibility, and only Villar and Mercator know where they took her. But the duchess isn't the real problem."

"Then what is?" Hadrian asked.

"If Villar doesn't want reforms and is only after bloodshed and violence, then . . ."

"Then nothing. He has no mob to follow his—"

"He doesn't need anyone's help. You don't understand," Griswold interrupted, his face white. "He knows how to create a golem. You have no idea how much damage they can do."

"Think I have a pretty good idea," Royce said. "Had one chasing me most of the night."

"Trust me it can be much worse."

"But why?" Hadrian asked. "Why would Villar be so bent on violence?"

Royce shrugged. "Frustration, revenge, hate. He blames others for his lot in life. His father never appreciated him.

The weather has been cloudy. Take your pick. People have an inexhaustible supply of excuses to wreak havoc."

"In this case, however, Villar has a once in a lifetime opportunity," Griswold said. "He can raise an unstoppable monster and later today, all the nobles of Alburn, the very people Villar blames for his misfortunes, are going to be gathered in one place. It'd take no time for him to tear through that crowd."

Hadrian shook his head. "Villar's last golem had to have made an impression. It'll keep everyone away. People are probably fleeing the city as we speak."

"We're talking about nobles vying for the crown," Royce said. "No one is going anywhere."

Selie Nym nodded. "It's Villar that we have to find." She turned to the dwarf. "Maybe you don't know exactly where he is, but you know something—some way to narrow the search."

Griswold nodded. "To raise a golem, you have to be on consecrated ground."

"What does that mean?" Royce asked.

"It has to have been blessed, sacred. Otherwise, you're committing suicide."

"How so?"

"Raising a golem requires trapping a demon and forcing it inside a statue. They don't like that, and the first person they'll kill is their creator. Golems can't step on consecrated ground, so that's the only safe place to raise one. If they can't reach the summoner, they're forced to act as his puppet."

"Does that have something to do with the boxes you were handing out? Do they have to spread it around or something?" Hadrian asked.

"No, the boxes are filled with the residue, the waste bits and chips, that were chiseled off the statues when they were created. Using them, the summoner can animate the statue related to its corresponding bits. The plan had been for Erasmus, myself, and Villar to raise golems to aid in the uprising. I was going to use the church near the graveyard. The place where you saw me give Erasmus his box of gravel."

"So, where else can this be done?" Hadrian asked. "Will any graveyard work? Any church?"

"That's the thing. There aren't many places in Rochelle that meet the requirements. It's not like anyone can throw salt around and say some magic words. The site must be on a focal point." Griswold looked at them and sighed again. "It's hard to explain if you aren't a dwarf. Even hard for some of us to understand. So many of the old ways have been lost since we were scattered to the winds by the empire." He cupped his hands. "It's like this. There are places—natural places—in the world that are centers of power. You've heard of Avempartha, right? That's an example. Drumindor is another. Power rises to the surface in places like that, and people have built structures on them to harness that strength, sometimes without even knowing why."

"Grom Galimus?" Royce said.

Griswold nodded. "That's where Erasmus"—he looked at the widow and cringed—"was going to raise his golem. Villar was going to be somewhere else."

"Where?"

"I don't know. He wouldn't tell anyone."

"How long can a summoner control his golem?" Royce asked.

"It comes down to a force of wills. The summoner needs to conduct the actions of the golem. You see through its eyes and direct its movements. But it hates being used, so the whole time you have to concentrate and be mindful about the amount of time the connection is in place. Keeping control for too long is dangerous."

"How so?"

"Hang on too long, and you lose your soul and become permanently trapped inside the golem. It becomes immortal and nearly indestructible."

"Yeah, okay," Royce said. "That's worse. How long does that take?"

"Generally, we try to not hold the connection for more than a few hours, but a golem can do a lot of damage in that amount of time. Best way to stop the summoner is to force him to sever the connection."

"And how do you do that?" Royce asked.

"Distract, threaten, or kill him."

"So the connection is broken if the summoner dies?"

"Yes."

"Sounds like a plan to me." A smile grew on Royce's lips.

"I think I would prefer stopping him *before* he makes another one," Hadrian said, moving to the steps.

"What are you going to do?" Griswold asked.

Hadrian shrugged. "We have a tendency to make this stuff up as we go."

The Disappearance of Winter's Daughter

⁓

A mir had been waiting at the top of the stairs and handed Hadrian his weapons without saying a word. After Hadrian strapped them on, he jogged to catch up to Royce.

"What's the plan?" he asked as they walked down a roadway. He knew it was called Center Street only because the name was neatly stenciled on a wooden road sign that the birds loved more than the residents did, as evidenced by the white streaks on the placard and pole. The street, as far as Hadrian could tell, tracked due west toward the plaza. He knew this not due to any growing understanding of the city but, because he could see the spires of Grom Galimus straight ahead. The tallest building by far in the city, the cathedral could always be seen rising above the other roofs.

"Not sure. I'm thinking."

The two were as alone as they could be that morning in a cramped city that was coming alive with the rising sun. Griswold, Seton, and Selie Nym had remained to aid Roland with quelling the rebellion.

"Happy first day of spring," Hadrian offered along with a yawn as they walked by a shop where the owner flipped over a sign, presumably for the first time that year. It had read DRIED HERBS but now announced FRESH FLOWERS.

Royce gave him a sidelong glance. "Don't do that again."

"You have something against spring? When did that happen?"

"Don't offer yourself as a hostage."

"Oh, that." Hadrian yawned again. He hadn't gotten much sleep, and it was starting to drag on him.

"Don't *Oh that* me," Royce reprimanded, sounding eerily like Evelyn Hemsworth. "This is *not* a laughing matter. You put me in a box."

"*I* put *you* in a box? See, I saw it as me putting myself in one."

"You did both. In our line of business, associations are liabilities. Loyalties are points of weakness. They get you killed. If they had captured you, locked you up, that would have been fine. But you—"

"How would that have been fine?"

"I would have just killed them." Royce said this in such a matter-of-fact tone that Hadrian failed to question the boast.

If it had been anyone else, Hadrian would have passed it off as bombastic bluster, but Royce wasn't bragging, wasn't exaggerating to make a point. He was serious, and to him this was a practical matter. A basic trade rule, like not shoveling manure into the wind.

"But when you volunteer to act as collateral," Royce went on, "that puts me in a tight spot. The stakes go up, and I can't walk away if things take a nasty turn—like this one did."

"Is this your way of saying you care about me?"

Royce continued his Evelyn Hemsworth impersonation by displaying an I-can't-believe-you-really-exist expression. "This is my way of saying you're an idiot, and the next time you do something that stupid, I'll let them kill you."

Hadrian smiled. "You really like me, don't you?"

"Shut up."

The Disappearance of Winter's Daughter

"I feel bad now," Hadrian said. "I didn't get *you* anything for Spring Day."

Royce walked faster, shaking his head as he moved forward.

The sun was barely up, but already the day displayed all the indications that it would be glorious. The sky was blue, the sunshine bright, the temperature warmer than it had been in days. Birds built nests under the eaves of shops as owners threw wide winter shutters, letting the birdsong in. How rare that the first day of spring lived up to expectations. That sentiment was on every face as people crept out of dark homes to celebrate the holiday of rebirth. Mothers dressed their children in fine clothes, delivering stern ultimatums and handing out rules against doing anything beyond standing still. Young women burst out of doorways, resembling budding flowers as they twirled their dresses of bright yellows, pinks, and greens, full of excitement that they might attract the attention of a handsome bee or two.

The usual vendors were not present in the plaza. Even they had taken the day off. In their place, musical bands were in the process of setting up while men who moved awkwardly in waistcoats, capes, and shiny-buckled shoes set up banquet tables or roped off squares for dancing. One area suffered from an odd break in the boundary where several shattered paving stones created a nasty crater. Hadrian noted that even though the steps of the gallery had been cleaned, there was still a rusty tinge on some of them, and one of the beautiful doors had been battered and torn. The tragedy of the previous night had been mostly erased by the morning light and the new season, but just like winter, the hardships couldn't be entirely forgotten. The people in the plaza moved around the crater and avoided the steps to the gallery. Still, they were unwavering in their efforts to celebrate the spring. Surviving was often a matter of moving forward. Moving forward was a matter of putting yesterday in the past, and all of it began with putting one foot ahead of the other, remembering how to smile, how to dance, and especially, remembering that laughing wasn't disrespectful; it was essential.

Hadrian's attention was pulled away by the grand procession underway as ten men carried a massive garland-festooned post across the bridge. The Springpole, streaming ribbons of various colors, was headed to the plaza, where it would be erected for the opening dance. Hadrian's home village of Hintindar put up a Springpole every year as well, though not nearly so big. He imagined every town did. Rochelle planned on celebrating on a scale Hadrian couldn't imagine. Feeling the energy and anticipation, he wanted to join in, help put up the pole, roll out the barrels, and find a partner for the Rabbit Run and the Blossom Ball. But they still had work to do.

As if realizing only then that he was walking, Royce stopped. He took in a long breath and let out a sigh of frustration.

"What's wrong?"

"I've got nothing. Villar is the only one left who knows where the duchess is." Royce looked around at all the congested buildings. "He could be anywhere!"

"No," Hadrian said. "He has to be somewhere special, someplace sacred."

"Sure, okay, but what is considered special or holy in Rochelle? Do you know? Because I don't. This is the problem with taking jobs outside our neighborhood. Even Griswold, who I'm guessing has lived here his whole life, only knew about two places. And if Erasmus was using the cathedral and the dwarf the old church, then where was Villar going? Griswold would have mentioned other sites if he knew any."

"Villar knows of at least one more, obviously," Hadrian said. "He's a mir, and mir live for a long time, right? So it might be something ancient. Something everyone else has forgotten about."

"How does that help?"

"Maybe we just need to find someone who knows a lot about the ancient history of Rochelle." Hadrian smiled. "Can you think of anyone like that, Royce?"

Royce's eyes widened. "Oh, you are kidding me."

CHAPTER TWENTY-THREE
A Prayer to Novron

Like the rest of the city, Mill Street had been transformed. The quiet thoroughfare of dignified stone homes was festooned with whimsical decorations. Nearly every house had garlands of spring flowers and pastel-colored ribbons in loops beneath windows. Some homeowners extended the loops beneath two windows, creating smiling faces with flowered lips and crisscrossed-glass eyes. Here, too, groups of residents gathered in small clumps, chatting on a street devoid of its normal traffic. Five men in tall hats spoke in the middle of the road. A larger group of women in hoop skirts gathered near the lamppost, which had been trimmed with a spiraling green ribbon. One bent down to pet a little pug-nosed dog.

"Where have you two been?" Evelyn burst out the moment they entered the house. With arms tightly folded, she stood beside a table of uneaten food. "Just when I thought you'd been tamed, you prove that wild animals can never truly be domesticated." She looked at the grand banquet she had prepared, as if she might cry. "But even a wild animal . . ." She waved at the table. "It's food after all. Even a cave-dwelling beast will make a habit of being on time for a feast."

"Our sincere apologies," Hadrian said. "We were unavoidably detained."

"Whose prison?" she asked.

Royce wiped his feet on the doormat and removed his cloak. Hadrian took off his sword belt. They needed her cooperation and couldn't afford to irritate Evelyn any more than she already appeared to be.

"Did the duke catch you, or was it some underworld thug who locked you up?"

"What makes you—"

"Oh, honestly." She scowled and grabbed her skirt while stepping to the head of the table. Royce moved quickly and pulled out the chair for her. She frowned. "If I look that simple-minded to you, I suggest investing in canes to help you walk like all the others Novron punished with blindness. The only surprise about you two is that my silverware hasn't gone missing, which, incidentally, is the only reason you are still here. I have friends in the duke's court. My husband was very popular there, you know. In a way, he, more than the duke, paid their salaries. I would have seen both of you in chains if so much as a toothpick had been pilfered."

"I didn't even see the toothpicks." Royce glanced at Hadrian. Hadrian shook his head.

Evelyn tilted hers and peered sternly at the both of them. "At this point, there is nothing either of you can say to redeem yourselves. I told you no jiggery-pokery, did I not? No shady business. But here we are. I'd throw you out now, but I can't stand wasting food. So, sit down and eat your last meal under my roof. Immediately afterward, please gather your things and leave. I'll have no more to do with either of you."

"But—" Hadrian started.

She shut him down with a raised hand. "No! No, I don't want to hear your excuses! Just eat and get out. The eggs are ruined, and the pastries are likely hard, but that's your fault."

They settled into chairs. Hadrian reached to uncover the food plates but Royce stopped him.

"What are you waiting for?" Evelyn asked, annoyed.

"We haven't given thanks." And before Evelyn could reply, Royce bowed his head. "We thank you, Lord Novron, for the food Mrs. Hemsworth has made for us, and apologize for being late. We weren't in a prison. Well, Hadrian was, sort of, but only because he volunteered to risk his life to save the Duchess of Rochelle. She's still alive, by the way, but being held prisoner by a murderous mir—the same one who brought the stone gargoyle to life and hurt all those people in the plaza. Oh, and it killed Mercator Sikara, a mir who was only trying to keep peace between the Pitifuls and the nobles. More would have died if I hadn't managed to lure the thing to the top of Grom Galimus and cause it to fall, shattering on the plaza. Despite all this, we would have still been on time except we haven't yet found the mir holding the duchess, and we're in a bit of a hurry because he may kill her at any moment. Oh, yeah, and he's intent on unleashing a great deal of bloodshed later today. So, Lord Novron, we've been a tad busy. We hope you understand and forgive us for our tardiness."

Royce looked at Evelyn, who stared at him incredulously.

"May we prove worthy of your kindness." She concluded the prayer with wide eyes that looked back at Royce, dumbfounded.

Hadrian gave her a big smile as he uncovered the food and scooped spoonfuls onto his plate, then passed it on to Royce.

"Are you . . . was that true?" she asked.

"I wouldn't lie to Novron," Royce told her through a mouthful of eggs, which were not at all ruined.

"Who *are* you?"

Royce glanced at Hadrian. Normally this was where his less experienced partner would put them in jeopardy, openly admitting everything because someone had gone to all the trouble of asking. Hadrian, however, kept himself occupied with the meal. Neither of them had dined the night before, and Hadrian was fond of repeating the military axiom: *Never pass up a chance to eat or sleep, as you don't know when you'll get another opportunity.*

Royce turned back to Evelyn Hemsworth, who waited with a cringing expression, a look that was half dread and half curiosity. She wanted to know, and at the same time she didn't. Royce used the moment it took to chew and swallow to mentally sort through the most reasonable replies. None worked for this. After his acrobatics, and his admission that they were seeking to save the duchess, he couldn't exactly pretend they were traveling merchants or agents for such. He toyed with the idea of saying they were undercover Seret Knights, but Royce was certain Evelyn knew more about the Seret than he did. He also considered refusing to answer at all, but that wouldn't do. They needed her help, and while his message of grace had blunted her anger, she was many leagues from trusting him.

With all other options eliminated, and this being an absurd situation, Royce tried something utterly ridiculous. He once more borrowed from Hadrian's example. "We were hired by Gabriel Winter of Colnora to come to Rochelle and find Genny Winter, his missing daughter. Mister Winter thought she might have been murdered. What we discovered was she hadn't been killed but kidnapped. She was taken by a loose coalition of the city's underprivileged, who hoped to influence the duke's policies by a route that avoided a full-scale revolution. However, it turned out that not everyone wanted to avoid the insurrection. A mir named Villar intends to use dwarven magic to create another stone golem to kill everyone at the Feast of Nobles today."

Royce waited for the explosion. He expected Evelyn to demand that they leave, or to see if she would shout for the city guard, calling for their arrest. At the very least, she would loudly deny everything he said. He also expected a good helping of disbelief concerning the raising of golems. Royce had arguments ready, but they weren't good ones. The truth was a poor weapon when fighting faith, but he was prepared to do battle nonetheless.

"Oh my blessed Novron!" she exclaimed in shock. Her hands came down, two wrinkled fists pounding the table, soundly ringing the porcelain plates. "Then why are you just sitting here?"

Royce and Hadrian looked at each other, surprised.

"You . . . you . . . believe me?" Royce asked.

"It makes perfect sense, doesn't it?"

"It does?" Royce looked at Hadrian, who had a mouthful of pastry and could only shrug.

"Absolutely," Evelyn said. "And besides, everyone saw you and the golem wreaking havoc through the gallery and across the cathedral. That's hard to argue with. So, shouldn't you two be out looking for this Villar fellow? If what you say is accurate, he's been recruited to murder every noteworthy noble in Alburn."

"We are," Hadrian said. "We didn't actually come for breakfast."

She watched him chew a huge mouthful. "No?"

"We need to ask you about Rochelle," Royce said. "We're looking for any special places, ancient churches or something that might be considered deeply sacred."

"Grom Galimus," she replied instantly.

"Besides that," Hadrian managed to say after he swallowed.

Evelyn thought a moment. "Well, there is supposed to be an ancient burial ground up in Littleton. Dates back to the early imperial age. I've never been there. Littleton, or 'Little Town' as it was once called, is the dwarven ghetto. Not a safe neighborhood, you understand."

"We've been there," Royce said. "But that's not it, either. There has to be another place, maybe something related to mir?"

Evelyn pondered while pouring tea for herself. Royce and Hadrian watched as she deposited two cubes of sugar and stirred. "I'm sorry. I can't think of anyplace else like that. Of course, you could visit the gallery. That's what I'd do."

"Already been there, twice," Royce said.

"And from what I've heard, I shouldn't send you a third time lest the entire place be destroyed, but there are old maps. One in particular hangs on the third-floor wall. It's very big and believed to have been drawn by the original surveyors who laid out Rochelle. You might find what you're looking for on it."

Royce and Hadrian pushed away from the table.

"Good luck, gentlemen," Evelyn said.

Royce stopped and looked back. He reminded himself he hated this strict, authoritarian, erudite woman, but with no success. Had life seen fit to give him a mother, Royce suspected she really would have been something like Evelyn. Anything less would have been useless. "You might want to leave," he told her.

"Leave?" Evelyn said. "Leave what?"

"Get out of the city."

"Are you suggesting I flee?" She signaled her indignation with a raised eyebrow.

"Look, Villar harbors a good deal of resentment against those he feels suppressed his people. You're pretty much the face of that fellowship. Everyone knows about your hatred for mir, and if you're—"

"I do not!" she snapped. "Why would you say such a thing?"

"Because we learned about your room for rent from one."

Hadrian nodded his support. "A young mother living on the street just a block down from here with her child. Said she could knock on your door all day, but you'd never take her in."

"I can assure you, she never came here. I don't see how she could conclude such a thing if she never bothered to so much as knock."

"When the Dirty Tankard refuses to let you a room," Royce said, "it doesn't seem too likely that the wealthy widow on Mill Street is going to invite you into her parlor."

Evelyn looked at the rug with a thoughtful frown.

"Would you have let her a room?" Hadrian asked. "A mir with a child in her arms?"

Evelyn hesitated. "I let you two in, didn't I?"

Royce nodded. "And what does it tell you when you compare two shifty foreign men to a homeless mother and her child? I'm just saying, if we can't stop Villar, there's a good chance he might seek vengeance in places like Mill Street. Leave. Stay. It's your choice, but if I were you, I'd disappear for a while."

Evelyn folded her arms with her normal self-righteous indignation. "Well, I think we can be quite thankful that I'm not you. Now get out of here."

Royce picked up his cloak and a pastry. Hadrian grabbed his sword belt, strapping it on as they headed for the door.

"Wait!" she called to them as they started down the hill toward the gallery.

"What?" Royce asked.

Evelyn once again hesitated as she stood on the stoop, then said, "Don't be late for breakfast again, or I really will throw you out." With that, she stepped back inside and slammed the door shut.

No one stopped Royce and Hadrian from entering the Imperial Gallery. The two didn't draw attention even when they climbed the steps and slipped through the bent gap in the bronze doors. Inside, the grand hall was a mess, debris everywhere. What looked to Hadrian to be a giant scaffold lay strewn across the floor. The snapped wooden beams were splintered and wrapped in cloth that had been ripped and torn. The thing had a papier-mâché head like an alligator and huge leathery bat wings. Little more than thin material stretched over bowed sticks, it reminded Hadrian of toys he'd watched kids play with in Mandalin. They would run with playthings tethered to strings until the wind blew the toys into the sky. *Maybe that's what this is, a giant wind toy.*

Under the ripped cloth and broken timber were shards of broken vases, the remains of chalky, white busts of dignified people, and toppled pedestals. Tears of blood, dried drips on statues and paintings, had yet to be addressed. He surmised this was where Mercator had been killed—*torn apart*, Erasmus Nym's widow had said. There had been an uncharacteristic look of revulsion on Royce's face, but such sights weren't unfamiliar to Hadrian. In Calis, men were ripped apart by bulls or torn to shreds by lions, both in the name of entertainment, and while arenas always had sand-covered courtyards that could be raked, the walls were dyed a ruddy brown from the layers of splatter. Gore on a grand scale was one more love letter addressed to Hadrian from an unwanted past. They were stacking up.

The gallery had an odor. Hadrian knew what death smelled like, and it wasn't that. At least, it wasn't the stench of decomposing bodies, nor even blood; but it was similar. The scent reminded him of rotting straw, or a stagnant pond, a musty, almost spicy fragrance of decay.

Hadrian had an urge to look around. The gallery was filled with so many strange and wondrous items set out as exhibits. Weapons both refined and crude. A large bow hung on the wall beside a spear and a series of swords, two of which bore a close resemblance to the one on Hadrian's back. There were shields, cups of painted clay, woodcarvings, sets of armor, musical instruments, furniture, cloaks, hats, lamps, rakes, and still-corked bottles; even a window, complete with its frame, hung on the wall. He only managed a glance as Royce led him in a rush up the stairs to the third floor.

The marble steps bore sharp chips and cracks and indents the size and shape of large feet. *The golem?* Hadrian wondered. Looking down, he placed his own feet in the same spots. The golem would have dwarfed him. A giant stone beast wasn't something he wanted to fight.

The map wasn't as easy to find as it should have been. The thing was huge and took up one whole wall, but it didn't look like a map. The ones Hadrian had seen comprised fine lines of iron gall ink on parchment. This was a tapestry. A massive wall hanging with needlework so fine it must have taken years to complete. The artwork was colorful, filled with shades of green for the forests and blues for the ocean and rivers; in the fields were dazzling splashes of yellow, pink, and purple wildflowers.

The perspective of the image was as if the viewer were a bird flying at a slight angle so that buildings and hills had depth and dimension. The coast was easy to recognize, as were the Roche River and Governor's Isle, but little else was familiar. The map showed a bridge linking the banks and the island, but there was no building on the isle itself. Instead, cows grazed on what looked to be a pasture. The plaza wasn't on the map, either, nor Grom Galimus. Instead, a little clump of trees marked that spot. There were roads, but few followed the same paths as the modern ones. Mill Street was nothing but a path that led to, not surprisingly, a mill. The city center was located farther to the east, centered on the smaller stream that today ran through Little Gur Em and the Rookery. A dock was there, not far from the modern one, and several small homes clustered up the slope. The town was tiny, rural, and more a village than a city. The focal point of everything, in the exact middle of the tapestry, was a round building east of the Rookery. It possessed a dome like Grom Galimus but was significantly smaller. Pillars held the roof up, forming a circular, open-air colonnade that stood on a raised dais.

"What's that?" Royce asked, pointing to the same building Hadrian was puzzling over.

"A church?"

"Doesn't look like any church I've ever seen."

"A temple?"

"To whom?"

Hadrian peered at the map, but there was no writing. He shrugged. "How old do you think this map is?"

"It obviously predates the city, or maybe this was the start of it. The graveyard and Grom Galimus aren't shown, so . . ."

"So, what? Imperial times?"

"At least; maybe even earlier."

"What does it mean?" Hadrian asked.

"It means we should have dragged Evelyn here, because I have no idea."

"But that"—Hadrian pointed to the temple—"that looks like something special, right? Something . . ."

"Sacred?" Royce finished for him.

Hadrian nodded. "Do you know where it is?"

Royce shook his head. "Up on a hill. Looks like if we go to the Rookery, head east, and search for high ground, we might find it."

"How long do you think we have before Villar attacks?"

"The Feast of Nobles is midday, right? That's when it's held in Colnora and Ratibor."

"Same in Hintindar and Medford."

Royce looked at the windows. "So, we still have a few hours if Villar sticks to the plan to catch all the nobles at the feast."

"What are the odds of that?"

"At this point?" Royce scowled. "We should hurry."

Hadrian agreed but was disappointed. "We should come back here. I'd love to look through this place."

"Absolutely not," Royce said. "We are *never* coming back."

"Be careful," Hadrian warned him. "My father used to tell me: *Never say never on any endeavor; it sounds like a dare to gods that don't care. If the likes of us prosper, fail, or falter; it matters not while they roll with laughter on an altar, at our miserable, sad little lives.*"

Royce looked over and smiled. "I think I would have liked your father."

CHAPTER TWENTY-FOUR
HAUNTED

Oswal Tynewell concluded what he knew to be his final service as the Bishop of Alburn. By the end of the day, his title would be different—his world certainly would be. Standing on the raised altar, he watched the people leave. They spilled out like water swirling through a funnel. Choked by the big doors, they clogged into a crowd. The exodus took longer than usual because the high masses always drew greater crowds. Usually, the cathedral never got close to full. Grom Galimus was a monster of a church, his grand flagship that sailed the stormy seas of iniquity. There simply wasn't enough faith in the city to satisfy its belly. Normally such an idea distressed him, made him feel he wasn't succeeding in his role as spiritual leader. That morning, he couldn't have cared less about *that* role, and he wished for a smaller flock. *Or at least a faster one.*

The Disappearance of Winter's Daughter

He wanted them out, all of them gone so he could shut and bolt the doors. The time had arrived, and Oswal was uncomfortable watching his sheep as they went to slaughter. Not so distressed as to stop or warn them, of course. He felt merely a disquiet, the sort of unease one faces when delivering a white lie. That's what it was, a positive wrapped in a negative, a good intention shrouded in wolf's clothing. He would benefit the most initially, but everyone would make out in the long run. They would all see that in time.

Oswal knew this was true. He accepted it without reservation, but that hadn't always been the case. At first, Oswal had ignored his calling. *Grom Galimus has a voice,* it was said. She spoke to people who took the time to open their hearts and listen. When first appointed, Oswal believed this to be a metaphor that dovetailed neatly with the strange and inexplicable creaks and groans of the old cathedral. He knew better now.

Thinking back, he was surprised it had taken a whole year.

He'd been working in the office and had left his feathered quill in the bottle. The wind from an open window had blown the inkwell over, ruining hours of carefully worded letters to his fellow bishops—the sort of mindless drudgery that was a grind to get through. The whole pile of silly, pointless reports had been soaked, making them illegible. He'd cried out in despair. Smashed his fists on the desk and wept. He sobbed like a child, not merely for the loss of the letters, but the need for them in the first place.

What has my life become? he had thought.

It wasn't merely the letters, it was everything. He was the Bishop of Alburn, curator of Grom Galimus, but he saw his future grow clear out of the mist. His life would be no more than a handful of ledgers and reports, the same as his predecessors'. *How can this be?* he'd thought as he cried into the ink-stained desk. *I always thought I was chosen—destined for more. How could I have risen to this seat merely to keep it clean and tidy? Something has to happen.*

And something did. That was the night he first heard the whispers, the voice of Grom Galimus. Only it wasn't one voice, it was two, and they called his name.

The last of the faithful funneled out, including the boys and the ushers who were all eager to join the festival crowds, and Oswal personally shut and locked the great doors. This left him alone in the church. *No,* he thought, *I'm not.* The Calian had to be around somewhere, but he didn't want to know where he was or what exactly he was doing. He refused to involve himself further in the details of the day's events. A blind eye was best.

My part in this is done.

He returned to his office, slipped inside, and locked the door. He didn't want visitors. Or more precisely, he didn't want any *more* of them. Tynewell was never alone in that office.

He removed the miter from his head and set it in the case, careful to pull the tails up before closing the cabinet doors. After slipping off his high vestments and hanging them up in the wardrobe, he poured wine into a silver chalice and sat down in his undershirt. Kicking his slippers off, he threw his hairy legs up on the desk and drank. He paused and raised the cup.

"To a better future, gentlemen," he said, hoping they didn't notice how his hand shook.

But of course they do. They see everything, don't they? No sense denying it. They know what I am.

THE DISAPPEARANCE OF WINTER'S DAUGHTER

"I suppose you two never had doubts as you piloted the waters of your own lives, did you? Never had . . ." He almost said *fears* but caught himself. "Concerns. Well, we all know I'm not either of you." He turned to Novron, who was forever holding up either the exact same silver chalice Oswal now held or its sister. He gesticulated with his goblet so that the wine spilled. "After all, I'm not the son of a god like you are. You have to admit that's a pretty big advantage. Not really fair, when you think about it. And I'm certain things were easier in your day. Fewer people to deal with at least, less bureaucracy. And you had the Rhelacan. I don't have any magic weapons at my disposal to sweep aside my enemies."

His words were forceful, loud, and confident; no humble self-effacing blather allowed. That was how he had to talk to Novron. The emperor couldn't hear him otherwise. Then Oswal gestured at Venlin, a bit more slowly, but the wine still spilled down his knuckles. "And you! What are you crowing about? What competition did you have? You were revered, and already the undisputed head of the church, and you had an army that would"—he paused to lick the wine from his fingers—"take turns cleaning your sandals with their tongues if you told them to. So don't look at me like that. I have it hard—harder than either of you." He swallowed a mouthful of wine. It was much better than the watered-down service vino. "I have to claw my way." He held up his empty hand. "Do you see these fingers? Worn to a nub, every one. And these feet!" He sat back and held the bottoms out to the painting. "Sore from the bloody balancing act I've been doing. I'm a lion tamer trapped in a cage with a dozen hungry beasts. 'Up! Up!' I yell, but do they listen?"

HAUNTED

Oswal settled back and breathed, letting the chalice rest on the arm of the chair. Outside the window, he could hear laughter, shouts, and musicians' instruments being tuned up. *Such children,* he thought. *They have no idea what's about to happen.*

He didn't worry so much about his flock. They were docile things. But the Alburn aristocracy, the wealthy merchants and clerks, and the military were another matter. He couldn't run the kingdom without them. If they refused to recognize him as ruler, which they would if they suspected his involvement in the massacre, or if they found a suitable surviving noble, he'd have a civil war on his hands. A war that he had no army to fight. All he had was faith. That, too, could be taken away.

"What will the patriarch do? Will he recognize me as the rightful ruler of Alburn?"

Of course! Venlin said, his smooth delivery two parts velvet and one part barrel-aged whiskey. Venlin was the intellectual of the two, the brilliant confidant and adviser, the shrewd politician. *That old recluse granted you complete freedom to choose the best successor to Reinhold. He did so because you know each of the candidates personally. Who better to select the most devoted, the most pliable, the best ally. You're doing that. He can't get upset because you did what he asked.*

"But it's probably not how he expected me to do it."

Novron scoffed. *Are you serious? Doing what people expect gets you nothing and nowhere. Honestly, man! How did you rise in the ranks with that attitude?*

"I should have asked permission, shouldn't I? I mean, it feels like such a deception."

Novron shook his head and addressed Venlin. *Talk sense into him before I throw him out the window, will you?*

367

THE DISAPPEARANCE OF WINTER'S DAUGHTER

Venlin sighed. *It doesn't matter if it's a lie or not. If it helps you sleep, then wrap it around you each night and smile. If you had asked for consent, or even floated the idea past Saldur when he was here, you know he wouldn't have liked it. Better to seek forgiveness than ask for permission. What you count on is that the world will come to see the truth in time. At first, it sounds crazy; worse, it sounds conceited and self-centered. But you were granted the choice to anoint whomever you saw fit, and Oswal, you're going to do just that. There isn't anyone in the running who isn't a shortsighted, self-centered idiot. And, of course, all the candidates will be dead.*

Novron parroted back Saldur's words, *Well, whoever you pick, best keep in mind that he actually has to rule a kingdom, you know?*

That was why he had to pick himself, but Saldur wouldn't see it that way, and Maurice Saldur was typical of the church. Oswal was the Bishop of Alburn, but somehow Maurice Saldur was more influential. How that was possible was hard to determine. Perhaps it was location. He was Bishop of Medford, and that was but a short carriage ride to Ervanon.

I didn't actually chat with the patriarch. I've never seen the man.

Oswal was certain this had to be a lie. While he was busy writing letters, Saldur was handling affairs like the disappearance of the *Eternal Empire*. Even after botching his own efforts to replace the ruling family of Melengar, Nilnev had given Saldur another chance. He hadn't even trusted Oswal to take care of his own king.

They all have it better than you, Novron told him. *And Saldur isn't your problem. Garrick Gervaise, lord of Blythin Castle, is the ox you'll need to yoke or slay.*

Oswal nodded. He was about to defy the intent, if not the letter, of the patriarch's orders while living in the shadow of the Seret's base and ancestral home. Blythin Castle was less than a day's ride up the coast to the east, and the castle commander wasn't a philosophical man. Reason and logic, to Garrick Gervaise, were sinful things. Oswal knew that convincing the black knight to support him wouldn't be easy. Garrick wouldn't see Oswal's initiative as a positive development. After all, Garrick saw his job as regulating the clergy, and crowning oneself king would certainly attract close scrutiny. Handling Gervaise would be his most dangerous battle.

If only he would attend the feast.

Oswal settled deeper into his chair and drained his cup. He felt exhausted, the sort of fatigue that hits only after all the work is finished.

"Is it finished?" he asked.

For now—your part at least, Novron said. *All the pieces are in motion.*

He got up and searched for the bottle to refill the chalice.

"I don't *want* to kill them, the nobles, I mean, but it's best to eliminate one's competition." He held his cup away from the desk as he poured so as not to spill on anything important. Although his hands had stopped shaking, his head felt a tad loose, and he had a vague sense of it floating like a bubble on his shoulders. This was only his second cup, but he had hardly touched the breakfast tray. He couldn't eat then, but he thought he might now. *I'd better, or at the rate I'm drinking I'll pass out before the feast.*

Would that be so bad? Novron asked.

You do need an excuse not to attend, Venlin said. *You can't trust Villar to contain his violence to only those dressed in blue.*

CHAPTER TWENTY-FIVE
KEYS AND COINS

By the time Villar woke up, the sun was high. Light streamed in through the drape that Mercator had hung in place of a door. The old one had likely rotted away centuries ago. The new drape was—like everything else Mercator touched—blue. The long dyed cloth fluttered lazily, letting in varying degrees of brilliant sunlight, changing the shadows in the room. For a long moment, Villar lay on the floor, feeling the pleasant flower-scented breeze and watching the light war with the darkness. Sunbeams ricocheted up the wall, exposing the dye-stained pots and dust motes. Then the breeze exhausted itself, the cloth fell flat, and the room returned to its dull darkness. Outside, birds sang and bees hummed. *A perfect spring day,* he thought with detached judgment, as if he weren't part of it but rather some distant observer.

That aloof perception lasted no more than a minute. It took that long for the pain to catch up with his sleep-muddled mind. When it did, the observer became the tortured. Villar felt terrible. He always did the morning after. His head throbbed, his body ached, and his muscles were drained. He continued to lie there, breathing slowly, letting the blood bang at his temples. It would subside in a little while, always had in the past. That's when he realized this wasn't like the other times. He'd stayed with the golem longer than usual because the little hooded foreigner was fast and agile and saw him coming. That was odd. No one had ever seen him before. But that wasn't all that made this time different. Villar felt pain in his chest. It, too, throbbed, but it also burned, and that didn't make any sense at all.

Grunting as he engaged stiff muscles, he rolled to his side, his elbow and hip hurting where they pressed against the floor. He had lain down on a blanket, one of the blue-dyed ones that Mercator had stacked all over. *Should have used more than one. Should have used all of them, made a thick comfortable cocoon.* He'd learned never to run a golem while standing or even sitting. Too easy to become disoriented and fall. When in the golem and on the hunt, the experience was so vivid it was easy to forget it wasn't his body running, jumping, and fighting. Everything was so real.

Villar didn't know his safety point—how long he could maintain the connection without going too far. Griswold had warned him never to remain for more than two chimes of Grom Galimus, but that was only a rough estimate; he didn't think the dwarf really knew. Villar speculated that the cutoff point would be different for each person. Not everyone's strength of will was the same. It stood to reason that an individual with a strong sense of himself could maintain the golem longer. The real concern, as Villar saw it—and perhaps this tied in to the idea of losing one's soul—was that in the heat of things, it was easy to miss the passage of time, and everything else. Still, Villar was confident he hadn't gotten anywhere near two chimes. And for the first time, it wasn't he who had severed the connection. The connection had vanished all by itself.

No, not by itself. The golem had been destroyed, and I was nearly killed. That's what happened, but how?

When he possessed a golem, he wasn't actually there. The golem acted on his commands, but no matter what happened to the creature, Villar was safe because he was miles away. The whole process worked much like a dream. Dreams, no matter how awful, were safe; they had no power to penetrate the real world. He thought hard. Trying to remember. Then it came to him. The gargoyle had fallen off the cathedral and hit the plaza. The moment it struck the ground, the connection snapped, releasing whatever demon he'd trapped in the stone, but because the gargoyle fell rather than Villar, that was all that should have happened.

Then why do I have this pain in my chest?

Thinking perhaps the pain was imaginary, a lingering, vivid memory, Villar reached up and touched the spot that hurt. Running fingertips lightly, he found that his shirt was stiff, stuck painfully to his skin. Gritting his teeth and emitting a pained grunt, he pulled the tunic off. With the agony of ripping off a scab, he tore the cloth free of his skin. *Thank Ferrol, I don't have hair on my chest.* On the shirt, a large rusty-red stain radiated out in a circle from a small slice in the garment. Touching his bare chest, he felt a very real wound.

I was stabbed. I was stabbed? How could that have happened?

The wound wasn't deep. It had cut the skin but was stopped by the sternum. Judging by his shirt, however, the injury had caused more than its fair amount of bleeding.

After the two strangers had broken into the meeting, Villar had left and waited outside. He'd watched as the hooded foreigner and Mercator set off together. The two had a plan to contact the duke. If they succeeded, everything could unravel. If they convinced Leo to intercede, no one would support the revolt. He couldn't allow that. When the two went separate ways, he considered killing the foreigner but wasn't certain he could. The prior chase across the rooftops had made him second-guess his chances. Instead, Villar came up with a better plan, an easier and ultimately far more enjoyable one. He would use a golem.

He'd followed Mercator back to the temple and waited for her to leave again. The ancient ruin had been the perfect place to keep the duchess. It existed at the three-way intersection of the remote, the secluded, and the inaccessible. No one ever went up there—too much trouble and too many brambles along the way. This had long been Mercator's secret craft shop, and all her dyed cloth was worth a small fortune. She'd used this place as a safe haven and wisely never told anyone about it.

The ruins made an excellent place for him to store his supplies as well. Over the previous months, Griswold had provided him several boxes of gravel, keys to various statues stationed around the city. He had plenty to choose from. And of course, he had his hearts, a reagent he had to provide for himself. They were not nearly as plentiful as the gravel. He had been down to his last two, but that problem could be easily rectified. He'd have the golem collect several more before breaking the connection. It was worth risking a heart to stop the foreigner and Mercator from reaching the Estate.

KEYS AND COINS

Once Mercator left, he entered. In his haste, he didn't bother with his usual safeguards. This wasn't the main event, merely a brief interlude. He'd be safe enough; only he and Mercator knew about the ruin, and she wouldn't be coming back. He made the bed and began the ritual.

Originally, he had only planned to stop Mercator. Yes, he would kill the foreigner, but Sikara need not die. Keeping them from reaching the duke was the important thing. But then she figured out he'd been working against peaceful solutions since the beginning. If she told the others, they would turn on him—all his hard work ruined. And of course, the mir didn't need two leaders; he could be both the duke and the representative for the mir people. Besides, her Calian blood made her an *abomination*.

He'd borrowed the term from the bishop, but it fit. The mixing of elven and human blood was bad enough. Somewhere in his own distant past, one of Villar's ancestors had made that mistake, but the Sikara family hadn't merely succumbed to a necessity—they wallowed in the deep end. Villar's great-grandfather Hanis Orphe traveled to Alburnia with Sadarshakar Sikara after the fall of Merredydd. The two had a falling-out when Sadarshakar chose to marry a dark-skinned Calian. The tribes diverged at that point, the Orphe being more steadfast and the Sikara more accommodating. Further relations with the Calians led to the dilution of the Sikara bloodline, and Mercator was the obvious result of this weakening. She was more Calian than anything else. She lacked dignity, and commitment, and barely looked like a mir.

Villar rolled to his feet and moved to one of the pots of clean water. He sniffed it to be sure. Grabbing the corner of a large blanket, he soaked it and gingerly scrubbed at the wound while he gritted his teeth. Most of the blood wiped off easily enough, but around the cut, it had hardened, and he didn't feel like messing with it.

Turning, Villar looked at the door to the little cell.

He had forgotten all about the duchess. The woman had been quiet. She hadn't even greeted him with one of her usual insipid quips. Usually, the duchess just couldn't keep her mouth shut, and it was such a large, loud mouth. She was their prisoner, their captive, but she failed to act her part. A helpless, captive woman was supposed to be quiet, tearfully sobbing in the corner, or begging for life, praying to her god. But not this one.

He had wanted to kill her the night before. The ritual required concentration, and he couldn't afford any interference from her; nor could he risk her giving away his secret should anyone come looking.

Villar had planned on killing her for months. Now with Mercator's death and the feast imminent, he'd finally get his chance. He couldn't rely on her staying quiet again. Villar looked for a knife, turning over crates of wool and throwing aside mounds of linen. He went through barrels that stank of vinegar and shook out rags. Nothing.

Seriously, Mercator? How did you work without a knife?

Then Villar remembered she'd had it with her at the gallery when the golem . . .

No, not the golem, it was me, and I do regret what happened.

Her death was a loss; the mir needed to rise to the greatness the past proclaimed them to be, and after the feast, there would be so many seats left unfilled. As duke, he would have campaigned for her to be appointed Duchess of Rise. She might be a mongrel, but she was still the descendant of the famed Sikar. Villar liked the idea of making Alburn a mir kingdom just as Merredydd had been. She could have had a part to play in the restoration of their heritage; her death was a waste.

Villar took one last look around. Seeing no sign of a knife, he clapped his arms against his sides in resignation.

I'll just have to strangle the bitch.

As a golem, he'd killed dozens. That's how he got the hearts, those hard-to-obtain ingredients. At first, he'd tried without success to use animal hearts.

Then Ferrol smiled on him and intervened, reversing his fortune.

It had happened on the last hot day of autumn. Villar had watched six children playing at the storm drain where the Rookery and Little Gur Em butted up to the city harbor. Villar had gone there to watch the ships load—or so he'd told himself. What he was *really* doing was searching for a victim, some new immigrant without family or friends. Someone small, weak, and bewildered by the big city. A youth whom he could easily overpower.

The sky was cloudy as the evening heat invited late-day thunderheads to form. The kids had pulled back the heavy metal lid of the cistern and were taking turns jumping into the stone reservoir, using a rope to climb out. They obviously had done this all summer. The rope was bleached, and its edges frayed where it rubbed against the sharp side of the cistern wall. The children didn't notice, nor did they appear to care, about the rain clouds blanketing the sky. Villar considered chasing them away for their own good, but one thing stopped him. The group of kids was a mixed lot: two Calians, one dwarf, one mir, and two humans. If it had been simply a group of mir, he would have ordered them out. Even if dwarves and Calians had been with them, he might have said something. But the presence of the humans enraged him. Villar couldn't bring himself to warn them off.

As the sky darkened, one of the humans left, as did the dwarf and the two Calians. The other human and, much to his dismay, the mir lingered. The two continued to play as if there was nothing wrong with their twisted friendship. Revolted, Villar was driven to leave. He was walking away when the rope snapped. Screams followed by cries for help echoed up.

No one else heard.

"By Mar! Thank Novron!" the human said as Villar peered over the edge. "Can you lower more rope?"

Can you lower more rope? Villar could still hear that voice in his head. The kid didn't say *sir,* he didn't say *please,* just *can you lower more rope?* A common human child, ordering him to obey with the same sense of disregard and entitlement as a noble. The little brat expected Villar to do as he was told. Why wouldn't he? How many times had the kid seen adults do the same? How many times had he seen grown mir smile and bow as they surrendered their dignity.

The two children were treading water in the cistern below. Without the rope, the interior sides—sheer and slick with algae—made the site a death trap.

"You really shouldn't be playing in here," Villar said. "It's dangerous. That's why there's a cover over this. And it's about to rain. This thing fills up fast in a downpour."

"It's okay." The little human smiled at him. He had red fleshy cheeks, the sort mir never had, the kind gained from an abundance of everything. In that smile, a sickening confidence bloomed, an absolute assurance that the world would always take care of him. He hadn't the slightest fear, not the hint of a doubt that Villar would save them. "If it rains, the water will lift us up and we can just climb out."

He was right. Even without the rope the two might survive—if it rained hard enough.

They thought he was joking when he closed the lid. The laughs stopped when he secured it with the metal rod the kids had originally removed. With the top closed and the growing roar of rain, no one heard them. Villar regretted that one was a mir, but that was what came from associating with the wrong crowd.

Villar was back before dawn to collect his prizes, and neither Dinge nor Nym asked where he had gotten the hearts.

Turned out mir hearts worked better—at least for Villar. The human heart resulted in a vague, hazy, intermittent connection. The mir organs formed a clear coupling. The novice summoners speculated that the more similar the heart was to the individual conducting the ritual, the better the connection. Villar became responsible for obtaining hearts for Erasmus and Griswold as well. He spent one heart to gain two or three, four if he was lucky. The dark, twisted streets of the Rookery were ideal for killing the unobservant. Not only did hearts of the underclass work better, hunting them had another advantage: Few cared about the death of young mir, Calians, or dwarves. This point was driven home as more and more children died while the city guard did nothing. The poorly run investigations aided Villar's efforts in provoking people to revolt. Witnesses, when there were any, were ignored or told tales related to the Morgan myth.

Villar glanced at the blue drape across the doorway of the old ruin. He could tell by the sunlight on the cloth that it was nearly midday. The feast would be starting soon. Erasmus was dead. If the foreigner was able to deliver the cow's note to her husband, and if he agreed to changes, Griswold would sit the party out. So would the others. They didn't have the courage of conviction that he had. The citywide uprising he'd hoped for wasn't going to happen, but a single golem—the *right* golem— let loose at the right place and time could still do the job.

So, before he could crack the next box of remnants and set up his ritual, he needed to take care of one other thing. It was time to kill the Duchess of Rochelle.

Genny didn't like the way Villar looked. She never had, but now he was worse. Something had happened, something bad. He had blood on his chest and a cold expression on his face that suggested he'd suffered more than a bad night's sleep. Then he started tearing the place up, and she knew.

She'd guessed something wasn't right the night before when he arrived alone. Villar had never before visited when Mercator was out, and it scared her. Never once did he call Mercator's name. He knew she wasn't there. Genny had almost asked about the letter, but kept her mouth shut. The sense that this isn't right, that something had gone wrong, shoved her heart to her throat.

Instead, she had watched as he opened a box and checked the contents: something the size of a shriveled apple, gravel, some leaves. To this, he added a few strands of his own hair. Then he closed the box and set the whole thing on the cook fire.

Villar took a seat on the floor and spread out a blanket as if he planned to take a nap. He waited for the box to burn, until it was mostly consumed. When the wood became ashen white, he lay down and started talking, chanting words Genny didn't understand. A cloud belched forth from the smoldering box.

Villar's eyes were closed as he continued, and she watched bright-white smoke snake up from the box, then stream out the doorway as if it had a mind of its own and places to go. Villar stopped muttering and appeared to fall asleep. Five minutes later she saw him jerk and twitch. His eyes remained closed, and it seemed like he was having a bad dream. He lay like that for some time, and then his eyes flew open, he gasped in shock, and lay panting.

"How?" he said, and then fell asleep.

She waited for a long time. Then curiosity overwhelmed her, and she took a chance and tried talking to him, but he didn't hear.

That was when Genny knew she had to get busy. She took out the coins and the key and set to work. She didn't know how long she had, so she worked with haste. She had tested the coins on single hairs, and they cut just fine, but when it came down to the wholesale hacking of locks, they proved a lot duller than she would have liked. Listening to the deep breaths of Villar just outside the door, she pulled out as many hairs as she cut.

The Disappearance of Winter's Daughter

She wanted to believe Mercator was alive, but the fact that Villar was here and Mercator wasn't made that a hard sell. As long as Mercator acted as her jailor, Genny believed she might survive. Now that there had been a changing of the guard, it was time for her to execute her plan. Like all jailbreaks, it was an all-or-nothing shot. She would either escape or die. That kind of pressure made it hard to hold her fingers steady on the coins.

This isn't going to work! This is crazy. What am I doing?

Something. I'm doing something, and something is oh so much better than nothing. I may die, but I'm not just going to sit here and give up. It's a chance, damn it! So quit thinking and cut!

Turned out there was no rush. Villar slept through to the morning.

When he finally woke, he was in a bad mood. He washed, then began looking around, going through Mercator's things, and Genny had a sinking feeling she knew what he searched for.

Villar came to the door of the cell. He grabbed the latch, but it wouldn't move. Mercator had asked Griswold to make locks for the door and the collar. They opened with keys; keys he didn't have.

No knife. No key. Mercator is dead and still causing me grief.

Villar turned over crates once more and threw aside folds of linen and wool. His frustration turned to anger, and he began smashing things in his search. He even kicked the suspended pot, knocking down the tripod of metal poles, which clanked and scraped across the stone.

Villar went through the barrels and shook out rags.

Keys and Coins

Why is this so hard? Did she keep the key with her, too? Why would she take it? Why not leave it in easy reach? Hang it on the wall—

He saw it then. A shiny key was dangling from a hook just to the side of the door. Why he hadn't seen it before he had no idea, except he wouldn't have expected Mercator to act in such a rational way. After the missing knife, he had assumed she wouldn't be sensible about the key. By the time he snatched it off the hook, Villar's blood was up. He was ready for murder. Still, the idea of actually strangling the noble bitch, of touching her, was awful. Then he remembered the metal poles. Better to beat her to death. *I can do that!*

Returning to the pot and it's stand, he saw a blade in the bottom of the empty container—a small one, not much bigger than a paring knife. Mercator had left it where she used it the most. With a grin, Villar took it. Holding the little knife in one hand and the key in the other, he returned to the locked door. He was so enraged his hand shook, and he had a hard time putting the key in the lock. He was forced to put the knife under his arm as he used two hands to steady the key.

Watch it not work.

He turned and felt the tumblers engage. The bolt slid free.

Ha! Finally, something went right!

Pulling the door back, he spotted the duchess. The lazy bitch was still asleep on the floor. She had one of Mercator's blankets over her such that only her head was visible, and only the top of that. He could see the chain looping from the wall to the collar, which was lost below her long sandy locks of hair. That had been Mercator's idea. She needed to be able to feed the cow, and that meant opening the door. Without a chain on the big woman, she'd be able to overpower Mercator the moment she popped the lock. Chained up by the neck, she was helpless.

He took a step into the room, then stopped.

Something wasn't right—a lot of things in fact.

The figure underneath the blanket was too small. He could see her hair peeking out from where her head should be, from where the chain led, only there was no bulge, no head—just hair. For an instant, he thought all the days of starving had magically shrunk her to the size of a skinny dwarf, but that wasn't possible.

A kick revealed all: One blanket was laid over straw and another bunched up to look like a body. There was a pile of cut hair, and the collar—the empty collar.

He turned and caught sight of her bolting out the door. She had waited just to its side when he entered. Out she went, trying to slam the door closed behind her—trying to lock him in! The old bovine was no match for a mir. Villar kicked the door wide, throwing her flat on her back.

She screamed, thrusting her hands out to ward him off.

"Time to die, you fat cow!"

CHAPTER TWENTY-SIX
HAGGLING

"Explain something to me, Royce," Hadrian said as the two struggled up the slope. "Why did Maribor create picker bushes?"

"Did he?" Royce asked, fighting through a thicket of fallen deadwood, high grass, and a wicked snarl of the thorny bush Hadrian was taking issue with. "Thought he was just the god of men, not flora."

"Oh, you might be right. Bet Evelyn would know."

"With any luck, she's long gone. I don't think we're going to find this place." Royce paused to wipe his face with his sleeve.

That was when Hadrian knew it was hot. He, of course, was soaked with sweat. His shirt stuck unpleasantly to the center of his back. Worse, the material of his pants clung to his thighs, making it hard to move. Royce rarely perspired, but that day his hood was back, his forehead slick and shiny, his hair sticking.

Two days before, it had felt like it might snow, but now summer appeared to have leapfrogged spring. Trudging uphill across sodden grass and through brambles as formidable as castle walls didn't help.

"I get the strong feeling we're wasting our time," Royce said, waving a hand before his face to clear away the mini-storm-cloud of tiny black bugs. He turned and looked behind them to where the city of Rochelle spread out below. "It wouldn't be this far out, would it?"

Hadrian shrugged. "We're coming into a forest now." He nodded at the staggered line of pine and spruce that grew just up the slope. The trees were gathered in small groups as if chatting about their neighbors, but farther on, they marshaled en masse, forming a dense forest that covered the base of a coastal mountain. "Was there a forest on the map? Do you remember?"

Royce shook his head. "No, but these trees are, what, thirty, forty years old? Probably been cut for firewood for generations. That map goes back hundreds of years. No telling what this place might have looked like then. The only positive thing is that it does make sense for Villar to be out here. The seclusion is ideal. I can't imagine too many people coming up this way if they didn't have to."

Hadrian took advantage of Royce's pause, and plopped down in the grass. At least the puddles left by the previous days of rain were cool. He scooped up a handful and wetted the back of his neck. Then he lay back and stared up at the blue sky and white clouds. "Beautiful day. Doesn't seem right."

"What doesn't?" Royce asked, scanning the way ahead and not looking pleased.

"That such awful things should happen on such nice days."

"You'd rather be up here in the rain?"

"I was thinking more about the people down there. You saw them this morning, all dressed up in their finest clothes. Been a long, dark winter. They just want a little happiness. And on the first good day in months what happens? It's not fair."

Royce gave Hadrian a puzzled look. "That's so odd."

"What?"

"Here we are, fighting brambles and slick, muddy slopes while trying to find a madman before he massacres hundreds, and your thoughts are focused on how unfair it is for the people having a grand time at a festival?"

"Why is that odd?"

"Why wouldn't you think about us struggling in this heat against these thorny vines while breathing in these tiny black flies? Isn't that unfair? Why can't we be eating pork and dancing with ladies on such a fine day?"

Hadrian chuckled.

"What? Why is that funny?"

"It isn't. It's just I have this image in my head of you dancing. Can't get past it."

Royce frowned. "I'm just saying it's strange that you feel sorry for them rather than us."

"Well, I do feel sorry for *you,* if that makes it better."

Royce clapped his hands together before his face, trying to kill some of the swarm that plagued him. "Why?"

"Because you can't understand why it is I would feel sorry for them. Makes me think your world is very small."

"Oh," Royce said, sounding disappointed. "I thought you were going to say something else."

"Really, what?"

Royce made a *pfft* sound, spitting as if the flies had invaded his mouth. He stepped back from the brambles, waving his hands before his face as he retreated. "Miserable little horrors. Why do they do that? Fly right into our mouth, eyes, and nose. It makes no sense. They can't like it; I certainly don't. There's no benefit to be had, and yet into my mouth they go."

"What was it you thought I was going to say?"

"Oh." Royce washed a hand over his face. "I thought you might be on the verge of apologizing for volunteering to be a martyr last night."

"Apologize? Are you kidding? I saved us."

"Is that how you see it?"

"Is there another way?"

"You put me in a very unpleasant position."

Hadrian sat up to face him. "Oh, I'm sorry. Were you the one tied up all night while a dwarf played with a knife, reminding you about his intention to slit your throat? 'Cuz I thought that was me."

Royce was struggling, trying to extract something from his tongue with two fingers, a fly no doubt. He got something, peered at it in disgust, and gave it a flick. "You're supposed to be learning from me. You can't do that if you don't listen."

"Learn from *you?*" Hadrian said. "I think you've got that backward, pal. Arcadius teamed us up so I could teach you."

Royce, who had moved on to cleaning his eyes, paused. "Did you just call me *pal?*"

"Yeah. It means friend—literally brother."

"I know what it means."

"So it's just your hearing that's going? If you want to talk about *odd*, that would certainly qualify. You have the most disturbingly acute ears of anyone I've ever met. Seriously, I don't know how you sleep at night. The crickets must drive you insane."

"It's not the crickets . . . it's *definitely* not the crickets."

Hadrian smirked. "I would think that this job would have convinced you of the virtues of being a decent human being. Look at Roland. My friendship with him has helped us, not just once but twice. Being respectful to Evelyn has reaped huge rewards. And we lived last night because a long time ago I acted honorably."

"Was that the same night you helped slaughter a town?" Royce asked. "And it wasn't that long ago, was it? You're not that old."

"Because of nights like that, I *feel* old."

"So, which was it?" Royce asked. "Were you saved because of a kindness extended to a girl? Or were you in jeopardy in the first place because you and your compatriots killed most, but not all, of the people during that battle?"

"It's because I protected Seton."

"Are you sure? What would you have protected her from if the town hadn't been sacked? And if you hadn't been so proficient with your sword, the other soldiers might not have granted her to you. Which makes me wonder, what actually made the difference, your kindness or your cruelty?"

"Why is it you choose to see the darkness in everything?"

"Because it's there, and ignoring that fact invites peril."

"But light is also there, and recognizing it allows happiness."

"What good is being happy if you're dead?"

"What good is being alive if you're miserable?"

Royce paused, and for a moment Hadrian was certain he had won. Royce was stumped, but then he tilted his head.

"What's up, boy?" Hadrian asked. "You hear something?"

"Wasn't funny the first time," Royce said.

A moment later a woman's scream came from up the hill.

I'm not just *going to kill her.* Villar realized this with the perfect clarity that accompanied every mistake he had made while the noble cow hid to the side of the door. She had plotted to lock him in. He imagined her literally as a bovine with black and white spots. In his mind's eye, he saw her standing on her back legs; a massive tongue licking the broad pink nostrils of her nose, waiting with hooves up and together, like a begging dog, hoping he would fall for the bait. The moment he opened the door, the second he rushed in so blindly, focused on her decoy of blankets and straw, was the same second she slipped out.

He almost fell for it.

The hair and the chain.

His mind had registered those two things as incontrovertible evidence that she lay on the floor near the back wall. How could he conclude anything else? If her neck wore a collar attached to a chain secured to a wall, the odds were strong the rest of her was there as well. His eyes and his mind had joined together in a conspiracy to betray him. If the room was bigger or the cow smaller, the ruse might have worked. The realization of how close he'd come to a fatal mistake was frightening.

As she lay on the floor screaming, Villar felt his heart pound from the near miss. He took a second to breathe, to calm down. Then he adjusted the grip on his knife.

She scuttled away, kicking out with her legs like a crab. When she rolled to her knees and started to stand, he grabbed her.

The duchess was no dainty woman, no slender flower. She equaled his height and outweighed him by twenty pounds. With a sharp lurch, she slammed her body against his, knocking him back against the wall, nearly throwing him to the floor. The assault also knocked the duchess off balance, and she went down to one knee.

He was after her an instant later, but the old cow threw everything she could find at him, including two of the heavy urns. One hit his hand, knocking the knife free. He grabbed it up just in time to see the duchess making for the door.

He was on her then, catching her in the middle of the room. One hand latched on to her butchered hair, pulling her head back, while the other brought up the knife. She continued to twist and kick until the knife reached her neck.

"Stop!"

Villar looked up as the two foreigners burst into the temple.

The smaller one had that white knife, the one that had stabbed the golem and somehow cut his chest. The other—the big one Seton had called the rasa—held two blades, one in each hand.

ॐ

"Kill her and you die," Royce shouted.

A portly woman whom Hadrian assumed to be the Duchess of Rochelle was on her knees, panting, sweating, her head pulled back. Villar stood behind her, his left hand holding a fist of the woman's hair, his right holding a dagger near her throat.

"Help me," Genny Winter cried.

Irritated by the outburst, Villar pulled her head further back, causing the duchess to cry out once more.

"Drop your weapons," Villar said.

Royce made a sound like he was clearing his nose. "Why?"

"Do it or I'll kill her!"

Royce glanced at Hadrian. "Didn't I already explain that if he kills her, I'll kill him?"

"You did."

"So, what is this idiot doing? Threatening us with suicide?" Royce asked.

"He's under the impression you care about her life."

"Really?" Royce chuckled.

"It's an easy mistake. You did order him not to kill her, and, besides, he doesn't know you."

"Okay, sure, but even if I were someone else—I mean, why would anyone surrender? Would you? Even if that person cared if she lives, Villar is still at a disadvantage. It's like trading pieces in chess. Sure, we would lose her, but then he loses the entire game. On the other hand, if we surrender, he'll kill all of us and we get nothing. No one would take that deal. It's stupid. Not to mention I'm going to get paid whether she's dead or not."

HAGGLING

Hadrian focused on Villar. "That's his way of saying we aren't going to put our weapons down, but if you kill her . . . well, I'm sure you got the rest."

Villar hesitated, the knife unsteady at the woman's throat.

"You need to make a deal, boys," Genny said, her voice steady. "Villar made you an offer, so now you counter. That's how haggling works. So, now it's your turn. What do you propose?"

Royce shook his head. "Don't have to counter."

"Yes, you do!" the duchess cried. "You want me to live, or we wouldn't be having this conversation, right? Of course, right. But we're at an impasse. So, you need to deal. Got it?"

"Whose side are you on?" Royce asked.

Her eyes widened in surprise. "My own, obviously. I want to live. Now listen." She allowed herself to swallow; in the small room it made a sound they all heard. "I don't want to die, but that's beside the point because bizarrely this has nothing to do with me. It's between the three of you. You don't want him to kill me, and Villar doesn't want you to kill him. That's good because you both have something the other wants. Everyone can win here—even me."

No one said anything as all three waited.

"Okay, good. How about this. Villar lets me go, and you let him go? How does that sound?"

Royce smiled. "Fine with me. Go ahead. Let her go."

"There, you see?" Genny said.

Villar shook his head. "You think I'm an idiot? The moment I let you go, they'll rush me. This won't work! It's stupid. We can't make a deal. And if I'm going to die then I'm taking—"

"It's not stupid!" Genny shouted as the blade pressed against her skin. "I can make any deal work. It's what I do. Now shut up and listen to me."

"I'm not letting you go so long as they can chase after me the moment I do."

"Fine, fine. No problem. This will be easy."

"It will?" Hadrian asked.

"Absolutely," the duchess replied. "Villar? How would it be if these nice gentlemen and I got into the cell and you locked us in. That way, you're free and no one can harm you."

"What's to stop him from—" Royce started.

"Shut up!" Genny shouted. "Whoever you are, please just be quiet."

"His name's Royce, and I'm Hadrian Blackwater."

"How nice. Now Royce, Hadrian, please shut up and let me handle this, will you?" She forced a smile. "The two of you will keep your weapons—that way, you won't be at Villar's mercy. Locked in a room, sure, but *safely* locked in a room."

"That's not a very—" Royce began.

"Shush, I don't want to hear arguments or counterproposals. We have a deal on the table. Will you agree?"

Royce looked at the door, huffed, then said, "Fine."

"Hadrian?"

"Yeah, sure, why not."

"Villar? You want to live, and so do I. This is a fair trade, a better-than-equitable exchange. My life for yours. Will you take it?"

Villar didn't reply.

HAGGLING

"Lower the knife and let me move back while these two enter the cell. Then I'll get in. You can lock the door and just walk out."

He still didn't answer, but slowly, the knife moved away from Genny's throat. She waved for Royce and Hadrian to enter the cell. "Gentlemen, if you please?"

Royce looked disgusted but stepped in. Hadrian went so far as to sheath his swords before entering. Then Genny Winter followed the two of them. Villar shoved her forward into the room, slammed the door shut, and turned the key that he'd left in the lock.

The moment the door sealed, Genny threw her arms around Hadrian and kissed him. "I love you!"

After the embrace, she started toward Royce, whose dagger was still out.

Hadrian pulled her back. "I wouldn't do that if I were you. Royce isn't much of a hugger."

"Well, gentlemen, you have my eternal gratitude, but who in Maribor's name are you? And what are you doing here?"

"Your father sent us to rescue you," Hadrian said.

"He *hired* us to discover *what happened* to you," Royce corrected as he moved to the door. He knelt before the latch.

"And you did both! You're my heroes. I'll knight you, or make you earls or something."

Hadrian smiled at her. "I think only kings can do that."

"Kings!" the woman burst out. "Leo! I need to find my husband. I need to show the bishop I'm still alive so Leo can be crowned king."

"Should have thought of that before locking us in a stone room," Hadrian said.

"I did," Genny replied. She pointed at Royce, who had just managed to pop the lock and open the door.

Royce immediately raced out like a dog released from a cage after being teased by an arrogant squirrel.

"You knew he could pick locks?" Hadrian asked the duchess.

"I knew he wasn't the type to allow himself to be confined in a cell unless he was positive he could get out. Business is like a card game: You have to judge people quickly and play the odds."

Hadrian looked out the open door. Royce was already so far away they could no longer hear him. At that moment, the only sound came from the breeze and birds.

"Look, I have to help Royce find Villar," Hadrian said. "You need to stay here. Safest place, really. I know you want to go down to the feast, but right now that's not such a good idea. We'll be back after we find Villar. Then we'll escort you back to town."

"And if you don't return, shall I stay here and starve? Or should I wander through the wilderness until I die of exposure?"

"Look, we *will* be back, I promise. But if it makes you feel better, town is straight that way." He pointed at the door. "Just keep heading down the hill, and you'll run right into Rochelle. Just don't go until we get back."

"Why not?"

"It could be dangerous."

The duchess scoffed. "I'm not some fragile debutante. I'm sure I can manage a hike downhill to town."

HAGGLING

Hadrian glanced outside. *I'm never going to catch up with Royce now. I didn't even see which way he went.* "Look, I'm wasting valuable time. You just have to trust me on this. If we can't find Villar, if he gets away, there's a chance he might create a monster and attack the feast."

Genny Winter blinked.

Hadrian saw the confusion on her face. "It's called a *golem,* a monster made of stone." The explanation sounded absurd even to him. "Villar made one before. If he does it again, he'll slaughter everyone at the feast. So you don't want to go there, understand?"

Her hand went to her mouth. "Leo!" she whispered, and her eyes darted toward the door.

"Look, I know you're worried, but there's nothing you can do. Truly, you need to stay here. Don't leave. Keep yourself safe."

With that, he ran out in pursuit of Villar and Royce.

CHAPTER TWENTY-SEVEN
THE SPRING FEAST

G enny had never been in the best of shape, and being trapped for over two weeks in a small cell, eating next to nothing, had only made matters worse. The moment Hadrian left she bolted toward the city and was soon sweating rivers and heaving for breath. Blood pounded in her head; her chest burned; and she'd only run fifty feet.

Three times she stumbled; twice she nearly fell.

Run, feet! Run!

Her whole focus was on the ground before her.

Don't fall. Don't fall. Don't fall. Rock! Don't fall. Don't fall. Tree!

On and on she went, only vaguely registering the blur of green and brown and the warmth of a hot sun baking her skin, something she hadn't felt in days. The heat was nice, but it made her perspire. By the time she hit pavement, she was soaked, struggling to see through sweat-filled eyes.

THE SPRING FEAST

She had come down out of the trees and fields and entered the broken ruins of the Rookery. She'd seen the place before, but only from the window of a carriage and only the part of the destitute neighborhood that bordered Little Gur Em near the harbor. When she emerged from the forest, she was in the shattered heart of this neglected corner of the realm. Grass grew up through the cobblestones and the entrances to buildings. Last year's leaves remained in corners where the wind had gathered them. The old buildings with their empty windows and missing doors looked hollow, cadaverous. Some were missing walls. Rotting plows and the rims of broken wheels rusted on the street or in the yards. Despite the neglect, Genny spotted yellow and purple wildflowers sprouting everywhere, even on the roofs of some buildings. She loved flowers, and seeing them again made her smile to the point of crying.

I'm alive.

Genny found she couldn't get enough air, as if the world were suddenly in short supply, and her chest burned from the effort of trying. Blood flushed her face; she could feel it hot and full, and her heart continued to pound a loud beat. *When did running become so difficult?* When she was younger, and a whole lot thinner, she used to run everywhere. Never once had her head felt like a cork in a shaken bottle of sparkling wine.

When did that change?

The answer came quickly and in the form of another question. *When was the last time I ran? When I was a child. When I was thin. Now I'm . . . little wonder Leo doesn't love me. No one could possibly love this.*

Tears added to her torment. She ought to hate Leo, but at that moment what she wanted most was to see his face and know he was safe. All she could remember were the laughs they shared. He was so comfortable to be with, never making her feel ugly or awkward, never hurting or belittling her. Even Genny's father had a tendency to condescend, to trivialize her feelings. Leo actually listened, or did a damn fine impression of it. He never told her *no*. Never tried to rein her in or told her to behave. Thinking about it, she wondered if his refusal to protect her from ridicule was less evidence that he didn't care and more a sign of respect that she could handle herself. And they agreed on so much; at times it felt as if they were the same person.

Genny slowed down. She was out of the Rookery, somewhere between Littleton and Little Gur Em. This was the trade and business district, filled with warehouses and workshops . . . and strangely few people.

Everyone is at the festival.

Leo was most certainly there, seated as close as possible to the bishop, trying to impress Tynewell and sway his favor. *If I'm not there, will he be disqualified? Will someone else be chosen?*

For Maribor's sake, how pathetic am I being? What does it matter who wears the crown? I nearly died, but I'm still alive! I'm free! I'm married to a goddamn duke and live in a lavish estate! What's there to complain about? So what if he doesn't love me. Who cares? I love him, and I'll keep on loving him.

Bishop Oswal Tynewell stood behind the many panes of glass that formed the great rose window directly above the front doors of Grom Galimus. Eight stories up, he had a perfect, unobstructed view of the plaza below. The dancing had stopped, and the rope dividers had been removed. Everyone advanced to take their seats at one of twenty tables set up in four rows circling the statue of Novron. Oswal marveled at the accuracy with which they were placed. No one down there could see the spacing the way he could. The fourth row on the right side was off a little, and it irked him for no reason he could fathom. The banquet tables appeared tiny from his vantage point, though he knew each seated twelve, and that meant more than two hundred nobles were gathered. From where Oswal stood, they appeared as little colorful dots—bright-blue specks.

The rest of the city's citizenry, as well as the throngs of visitors, were forced to stay back behind rope barriers that outlined the plaza. Those who, until recently, had been dancing and singing on the paving stones before the cathedral became sweaty spectators of the momentous event that they expected to reveal itself soon.

The event will certainly be momentous and absolutely worth witnessing—just not too closely.

Not everyone was there. Some of the lesser nobles, such as those who had resigned themselves to monasteries, hadn't come. Also absent were women who were old and unmarried. Inviting them would have appeared strange, if not openly suspicious. Monks and spinsters were nothing for Oswal to be concerned about. None of them could be considered serious contenders for the throne.

Oswal's immediate concern centered on the fact that food was being brought out, yet nothing had happened. If the servants pulled the lids off the plates—if they began serving without his presence—there would be concern. Already heads were repeatedly turning to look at the door of Grom Galimus. Everyone was waiting for his entrance. Waiting for him to give his speech and explain who the new king of Alburn would be, or at least how the person would be chosen.

Oswal had no intention of coming out. The church was one of the few safe places in the city. At least that was what Villar had told him, and he ought to know. That mir was dabbling in powers best left untapped, but if doing so got the job done, who was he to argue with results? Still, magic could be unpredictable, and Tynewell didn't want to leave his survival in the hands of those who might not be able to control the evil they were planning to unleash.

While the Novronian Empire had once employed wizards, magic had also been the source of its destruction. As such, after the fall of the great capital city, magic had been eradicated from the world by edict of the church. Only the truly evil practiced the forbidden art. Its use was grounds for both excommunication and execution. That Villar planned to employ the dark art was further evidence of his vile character. Oswal shivered at the thought of his association with the mir, and yet what else could he do? To obtain what he wanted, some rules needed to be bent and some lines needed to be crossed. Oswal felt that so long as he closed his eyes beforehand, he could step over those lines and still absolve himself of guilt by way of ignorance. Besides, no one could tell him that the sinking of the *Eternal Empire* was virtuous. Sin was often the bridge to salvation.

Time kept ticking, and still nothing happened. No revolt, no attack from magical creatures. Oswal pondered what excuse he would give when at last he was forced to emerge. Perhaps he could put them off, saying he still hadn't decided. No, that wouldn't work. The kingdom had already gone five months without a king. A contest. He would have to go with that, but what sort? One that was impossible to achieve might be good. It would buy him time to—

From outside the window and through the many panes of glass, came the sounds of shouts. At first, they were merely cries of surprise. Then they turned to exclamations of fear.

In the plaza below, faces looked up and fingers pointed at the great marble statue of Novron that graced the center of the square. Some seventeen feet tall, the sculpture was a marvel of artistry, a source of inspiration, and a point of reverence, but never before had it elicited cries of fear. Oswal couldn't understand the source of the panic until he realized that Novron, who for generations had looked across the plaza to the cathedral, was now looking down at his feet.

A moment later the statue shifted, twisting its torso and drawing forth its sword.

A miracle!

Oswal stared in stunned wonder. *The god Novron has come to life!*

Many of the nobles believed similarly as they remained in the square, moving away but not fleeing. A few even went so far as to approach the giant figure. Floret Killian, for instance, who was dressed in his long velvet gown of solid blue with a matching cape, was the first to advance. The attire was so inappropriate for the weather, but so apropos for a man to be crowned in. Perhaps Floret saw this animated statue of Novron as a machination of the church—maybe he thought it was the test their bishop had arranged to find Alburn's next king: Fleeing from it might prove a lack of faith. Surely the bishop knew Novron would attend in person, and he would be the one to anoint the next ruler. Why else would the bishop insist that *all* nobles in the kingdom be present? Why else would he wait so long to declare the identity of the new ruler? Yes, of course, Maribor had told the bishop that his son would make an appearance at the Spring Festival and he wanted to ensure that everyone would be on hand to view this miracle.

Then the marble Novron began killing people.

One of Novron's giant sandals came down on Floret's side and crushed him against the paving stones. From that point on, the statue left red prints wherever that foot landed. With the other leg, Novron kicked Killian's two sons across the plaza. Oswal was certain from the stain on the marble shin that they had died the moment the leg hit them. This was merely the preamble. Once Novron was off his pedestal and had his feet firmly planted, he began swinging the sword. A good eight feet in length, the huge marble weapon hewed through swaths of people, all conveniently clumped together. With each successive stroke, the once immaculate statue turned scarlet from the spray and splash of blood.

Oswal clutched his throat in horror. He stood transfixed by the speed of the massacre. He was appalled. That a mir had chosen to defile the most sacred symbol of the church as his instrument of murder caused him to hit the panes of the rose window with his fists.

How dare he!

THE SPRING FEAST

His horror at the shrieks of the dying and the soon-to-die was overpowered by outrage at the humiliation being wrought upon the faith by a mir using the image of Novron as a tool of destruction.

This is intolerable.

Revolution was one thing. Dark magic another. But this, this was an inconceivable perversion. He had to do something. He jogged to the stairs and raced down. Tynewell had no thought as to what he would do when he got to the bottom, but his indignation was overwhelming. He tripped on his own robes and fell the last three steps, but he refused to feel the pain.

Grabbing up a wrought-iron candlestick, he ran from his office to the massive front doors. There he stood, puffing from exertion, leaning on the iron stand and staring around at an empty cathedral while outside the screams continued. He didn't dare open the doors. Instead, he peered out through the windows at the massive animated statue wreaking havoc on the plaza. And just when the bishop felt it couldn't be worse, another towering statue arrived.

Villar didn't notice the arrival of Glenmorgan, which was odd given that the onetime ruler of the Steward's Empire stood a good twelve feet tall, and his boots crushed cobblestone to gravel. Villar was preoccupied—giddy—by his delight in crushing the life out of Alburn's rulers using their own god.

The statue of Novron was huge, and so different from the smaller gargoyles he had been used to. It moved slowly, reacting on a delay, but it was powerful beyond belief. And he liked the view. The statue was so tall he could see everything—everything except Glenmorgan. That revelation reached him in the form of a tackling blow.

Villar wasn't actually in the plaza; he was remotely operating the golem just as he had done with gargoyles so many times before. And while both Novron the Great and the statue of Glenmorgan—who normally stood on a pedestal in the center of the Imperial Gallery—slammed into a stone pylon that commemorated the war heroes of the First Battle of Vilan Hills, Villar didn't feel a thing. He also didn't feel the repeated blows Glenmorgan hammered him with. He did, however, see the chips of marble broken from his chest by Glenmorgan's fists.

Griswold! With Erasmus Nym dead, only the dwarf had the knowledge and ingredients to raise another golem. *He's trying to stop me.*

Villar rolled away, pushing back to his stony feet.

Glenmorgan refused to let up and grabbed him from behind. Leaping on Novron's back, he threw an arm around the emperor's neck and squeezed.

Griswold might be a dwarf, a member of the race who had unlocked the secrets of the golem, but he lacked experience at running one. They had let Villar do all the work, all the prior murders in stone form. They had been lazy, and now the dwarf would pay the price. Griswold fought like a person, an easy mistake. Villar had done the same his first few times. Only neither one was flesh, and stone doesn't breathe. Choking was pointless. Crushing and falling, on the other hand, was devastating.

THE SPRING FEAST

❧

Before she arrived, Genny was met by a stampede. Hundreds of gaily dressed people fled from the plaza. Ladies in spring gowns and men in hose and buckles ran as if Uberlin were in pursuit.

A woman in a light-blue dress with white lace cuffs waved harshly at her. "Run!" she cried. "Novron is killing everyone!"

She might as well have said Grom Galimus was dancing a jig for all the sense that made, and Genny didn't even slow down. Not that she was moving all that fast. Her one bit of luck was that everywhere she had run that day had been downhill.

"No! No! Go back!" A man holding a fanciful hat in his hands waved at her. "Everyone is being killed down there!"

Genny did slow down then. The man's words hadn't retarded her speed, but the smear of blood across the side of his face gave her pause. That streak of gore made her take his warning seriously, and yet it still didn't stop her. She continued down Center Street to where it joined Vintage Avenue. From there she had an unobstructed view of the plaza. Two giant stone statues were locked in battle, one on the other's back with an arm around its neck. Below them was a horrific display of colors. Like blueberries in strawberry jam, bodies lay on the blood-soaked paving stones of the plaza.

Genny continued moving forward.

Leo?

She scanned the bodies. They were a ghastly mess, and she didn't think she would be able to identify him in that tumbled macabre mass, but she thought she might spot the vest. It was so bright. Then Genny remembered she hadn't bought it. But even if she had, she wouldn't have had the chance to give it to him. They took her before she returned home.

I wish I had given you something. She cried once more.

If any doubt hid within the shadows of her heart that she still loved Leo Hargrave, it was washed away by those tears.

Even if Leo doesn't love me, he is a good man, a kind man. I couldn't love anyone this much if that wasn't true.

Something blue moved.

A man near her edge of the plaza struggled to crawl. One of his legs was twisted unnaturally and he hauled himself away by the strength of his arms, leaving a trail of red in his wake. Overhead, the giants staggered, their massive stone legs bashing the paving stones so hard they shook the Spring Day decorations off the walls. The statue of Novron was struggling to throw off the statue of Glenmorgan and in the effort, four feet repeatedly bombarded the plaza, threatening to crush the desperate man.

Genny's heart leapt at the possibility that it might be Leo, and she rushed forward into the red sea beneath the stone-footed hailstorm. She quickly realized it wasn't him. This man was younger, thinner. She didn't stop. Even if it wasn't Leo, it could have been, and she wanted to help him just as she hoped someone was helping the man she loved. Without even looking at the statues, and gasping for every ounce of air she could haul into her chest, Genny grabbed hold of the man by the shoulders of his tunic and pulled.

In her younger days, the Duchess of Rochelle had hauled, rolled, and stacked casks of whiskey along with the men. The cripple on the plaza was lighter than any cask she had ever hauled. She dragged him away from the carnage with speed, if not gentleness. Genny wasn't certain where this extra burst of energy came from. It didn't matter. She had it and was going to make use of the newfound strength. She pulled the survivor out of harm's way.

Then the ground shook, and there was a great *crack!*

Novron had managed to lift Glenmorgan, flip him over his shoulder, and slam him down hard on the plaza's pavers. While the emperor god had been chiseled from solid marble, Glenmorgan had been sculpted from lesser stone. The huge ruler of the Steward's Empire, who had once stood in the center of the Imperial Gallery, broke. Just to be certain, Novron brought his foot down and shattered his adversary, scattering the pieces across the plaza.

Genny had dragged the wounded man a short way up Vintage Avenue. But it wasn't far enough. The giant marble monster was finishing off the wounded, crushing them under his massive feet. He would notice them before long.

The wounded man knew it, too, and she felt him cringe.

Vintage Avenue was one of the finer streets in the city and equipped with storm drains. The large pipes ran under the street and flushed rainwater to the nearby river. Their mouths were as big as barrels; a normal-sized man could wriggle in and disappear.

"Crawl into that drain, and get as deep in as possible without falling in," she told him. "I'll be right behind—" She heard the slam of stone on stone. Looking back at the square, she realized the golem had spotted them. The giant statue began its uphill charge. "Damn," she cursed.

They couldn't both shimmy into that drainpipe in time.

"Tell Leo I love him," she said, and ran away from the wounded man. As she did, Genny flailed her arms and shouted, "Villar! You son of a whorish werebat! I'm still alive, and you're still ugly."

She wasn't committing suicide, although she realized it might have looked like it. To the wounded noble, she probably appeared to be sacrificing herself to save him. In reality, she had a plan. Her strategy was to catch Villar's attention and lure the golem away, granting the nobleman time to escape. This was an easy decision and a simple choice, given that Genny had concluded she couldn't possibly fit into even a barrel-sized pipe. The second part of her plan was less thought out. She hoped to make it to the carriage shop across the street in time to find shelter for herself. This latter part wasn't likely, not by a long shot.

So maybe this wasn't such a smart idea after all.

The reality of her situation crystallized when her exhausted legs finally gave out. With muscles screaming from fatigue, Genny stumbled on the uneven cobblestones. Then she fell face-first in the street as the giant statue of Novron closed in.

CHAPTER TWENTY-EIGHT
HIDE-AND-SEEK

Royce followed a dirt path outside the ruin, looking for clues. He wasn't certain what he hoped to find; a dropped note penned by Villar saying *I went this way* would have been helpful. Hadrian had eventually exited the ruins and circled them twice before wading into where the hawthorn bushes were thick. Royce had no idea where the duchess was—still in the cell if she was smart.

Villar might have returned to the city or gone deeper into the forest. Both plans had advantages and drawbacks. The city was downhill, but the terrain was mainly open. The forest was closer and offered cover. *Which way did he go?*

Hadrian emerged from the brambles. "Find anything?"

"Nope," Royce replied.

The two met back at the ruins.

THE DISAPPEARANCE OF WINTER'S DAUGHTER

The search was extra credit, and it wouldn't result in any higher payment. Royce was only looking because Villar had nearly killed him on not just one but two occasions. He didn't like loose ends, and Royce made a point of not letting those that opposed him live.

He scanned the domed building. *Such an odd place.*

The roof was the most striking feature, forty feet high and massive. Royce was no engineer, but he couldn't imagine that creating a dome out of stone was an easy task. The only other one he'd seen was on the top of Grom Galimus, and he wasn't certain what that was made of—looked like gold but probably was just painted that color. This roof was assembled from solid, hand-cut rock—no mortar—each stone precisely fashioned.

What is this place? Too small for a cathedral, monastery, or church, too elaborate for a house. It appeared to be a temple of some sort, like an overgrown chapel.

"You want to give up, don't you?" Hadrian asked.

"Not giving up. We found Genny Winter, even saved her life. I bet Gabriel will pay us extra for that. Job is done. Besides, Villar could be anywhere."

"Pretty good bet he went to Grom Galimus," Hadrian said as the two entered the temple. "Villar doesn't seem like the type to just give up."

"Not our problem, we did—"

They both halted abruptly only a few steps inside the ruined temple.

The first thing Royce noticed was the smell. The interior had an awful odor akin to—

"Smells like someone roasted a dog in here," Hadrian whispered. The whisper said more than the words. Hadrian had come to the same conclusion Royce had.

Royce took another step and peered into the cell. The room, the whole temple, was deserted, but if that was true ... "Where's the duchess?" he whispered back.

"I'm guessing on her way back to Rochelle," Hadrian replied. He had one hand on the handle of his short sword as he carefully moved toward the fire.

What had been a nearly extinguished pile of faintly smoking ash had come back to life. Flames continued to lick a mostly consumed stack of wood. Royce glanced behind him at the doorway they had entered. He looked at the floor near the wall and found it bare.

"There was a box here," Royce said. "I saw it when I came out of the cell."

Hadrian nodded. "Like the one Griswold gave Erasmus. I think that's what's burning."

Royce stared at the fire. "Villar didn't run away . . . he doubled back."

"That's crazy. We were just outside, looking for him. That's a huge gamble."

"All his stuff is here. He had to come back. He waited for us to leave; probably figured we would go back to Rochelle and look for him at the cathedral, just like you said. When we ran out, he rushed back in. Not a bad idea, considering it's the one place we knew he couldn't be."

Royce and Hadrian began a systematic search of the debris but found nothing. "So, where is he now?"

જી

Genny expected to be crushed.

She thought the stone Novron would stomp her like a bag of grapes, but instead, the god emperor's head cocked to one side as if listening; then it abruptly turned and charged east between the gallery and the cathedral. It didn't quite run— Genny wasn't certain something that big and heavy could—but the long legs gave it the speed of a horse. She watched it leave, dumbfounded.

Where's it going?

"Genevieve?" the man she had pulled clear called out from the mouth of the drainpipe, looking like a groundhog peering out of its hole.

Genny rolled to one side. She wasn't getting up. That was *way* too much effort. Instead, she crawled over the cobblestones. She recognized the blood-smeared face of Armand Calder, Earl of Someplace. She didn't know him well, had only seen him once, during her wedding. She seemed to recall he might have kissed her hand. He was a lesser lord, no one of great account in the world of Alburn politics.

"Hullo, Army, how you doing?" she responded with a ridiculous smile. "Hanging in there, right? You're gonna be fine. Might not be dancing for a while, but you'll be up and about in no time; trust me, I'm going to see to that."

Armand shook his head. Either it was the pain—which looked considerable given the condition of his leg that had been facing the wrong way when she'd found him—or the terror had finally caught up, but she saw tears in the Earl of Someplace's eyes.

"It just came to life and started killing everyone . . . *everyone*." He shuddered as he spoke.

Everyone. The word hurt to hear, yet hope, like a wisp of smoke in the temporary absence of a breeze, lingered.

"What about . . ." Genny stopped herself. She needed to know. "Have you seen my—"

"Leo wasn't here," Armand stated.

Luckily, Genny was already on her hands and knees. Even so, she nearly collapsed. "Are you saying . . . I mean . . . are you sure?"

The news was too wonderful to accept. Genny so desperately desired to believe Armand that her need made her hesitate. *I'm only hearing what I want to hear.*

"His spot, the chair next to Floret's, was empty all morning," the earl told her.

"Are you sure?" Genny replied. "We're talking about Leopold Hargrave, Duke of Rochelle."

"Yes," Armand nodded. "Your husband."

"But Leo—he . . ."

"He never showed up," Armand said. "Guess he didn't want to be king as much as the rest of us. Lucky him."

Genny's body was still begging for air from all her exertion, but at that moment she held her breath. "Do you know where Leo is?"

"He was out looking for you. Everyone was talking about it."

Genny breathed. "Army," she said, crawling the rest of the way to the Earl of Someplace. "Army, you sweet, sweet man." She helped pull him out on the cobblestones and covered him with a discarded cloak, tucking the edges around his neck. "You hang on. I'm going to take care of you. I'm going to see you get through this. I swear by every god there is that I will."

She meant it—every word. Genny decided then and there that she would defend Armand Calder with the last beat of her heart, for he had given her a gift beyond value, beyond imagining, beyond her wildest dreams.

Leo wasn't just alive. Leo loved her.

They were beneath the dome in a generally round room with the fire pit in the middle. The interior was a mess of overturned crates, urns, and scattered piles of wool, of which there was a surprising amount. Royce and Hadrian had dug through the clutter: several tall clay pots stained with tears of blue dye, an overturned wooden tub, mounds and mounds of raw wool. But no Villar.

Royce heard something outside, a distant thumping sound like someone running. He darted out, certain that Villar had broken from cover and was making a dash for it, but the sound was louder than the pounding of hooves. It sounded like—

"Royce?" Hadrian poked his head out of the doorway and then joined him. "Royce, what is that?"

Peering between the oak tree and a spruce, Royce saw the sun glint off something brilliantly white, something moving toward them at the speed of a galloping horse. As it cleared a gully, Royce got a good look.

"Royce, is that . . . ?"

"The statue of Novron from the plaza," Royce finished for him.

They could both see it clearly as it traveled through the open, it's long legs stomping with ease across the same fields and thickets they had just struggled up. The god's chest was marred: Chips of marble had been chiseled away. Other than that, he was perfect as only an artist could create: broad shoulders, narrow hips, lean muscle. This was exactly how Royce expected Novron to look. Not surprising, given that Royce's understanding of the god had been formed by various statues like this that he'd seen in and around churches. This one had been the best of those, the most realistic—in many ways, too realistic. Seeing it move felt less strange than knowing the life-like statue was only stone. As the statue grew nearer, Royce saw dark stains on its legs, as if the Son of Maribor had been stomping grapes for wine.

"Don't suppose it's just out for a stroll, eh?" Hadrian said, even as he drew his two swords.

"What are you going to do with those? It's stone. You'd do better with a hammer and chisel."

"Don't have those."

The statue crashed through a copse, kicking the trees into a cloud of splinters. A branch too heavy for Royce to lift landed twenty feet away. Novron was close enough for him to see the marble god's expression. The normally stoic, proud, and noble features were twisted in vicious rage.

Royce pulled Alverstone out of the folds of his clothes.

"Oh, okay," Hadrian said. "A dagger is *sooo* much better."

"A very *sharp* dagger," Royce replied. "When I was on Grom Galimus—"

"Grom Galimus! Sacred ground!" Hadrian burst out. "Get back inside!"

They ran through the doorway.

Having fought the gargoyle, Royce knew all too well the impossibilities of combat with *living stone*. He had managed to do some tiny damage with Alverstone, but Hadrian was right: A dagger wasn't a match for a giant. The fall from the roof of Grom Galimus had destroyed the golem, but that wasn't going to happen this time. Novron the Great looked a whole lot more dangerous than the stone monkey with its useless wings. But the thought that they could hide inside the ruin and wait out the golem like a summer downpour felt like little more than wishful thinking.

"Not going to work," Royce said as outside they heard, and felt, the rumble of the charging marble giant.

"Why do you say that?"

"The golems-can't-tread-on-sacred-ground thing can't be true. I fought the gargoyle on top of Grom Galimus," Royce said as if admitting some terrible sin. He had to shout to be heard over the hammering of the statue's footfalls as it closed the remaining distance. "Doesn't get much more holy than a cathedral."

Royce and Hadrian waited, each with a wincing expression.

Nothing happened. The footfalls ceased.

Through the open doorway, they spotted a pair of marble legs. They stood still like a pair of birch trunks.

HIDE-AND-SEEK

Hadrian looked at Royce and smiled.

Royce shrugged. "Maybe because I was on the roof it wasn't literally sacred *ground*? Or perhaps only the altar is sacred." He didn't think the golem's restriction would be that specific, and yet he couldn't come up with any other reason why Villar's Novron wasn't crawling through the door to kill them.

"It's not reaching in the doorway, either," Hadrian said. "Just standing there. Maybe it can't enter the interior space?"

Royce bent down and peered out at the legs. "We can't stay here forever, but I'm thinking the God of Man might." Giant Novron also bent down and peered in at them.

"Remember what Griswold said? There's a time limit. The person animating the golem can't keep the connection too long or his soul will get stuck permanently, making the golem an immortal, indestructible terror."

Royce sighed. "And anyone willing to stick around to roast a child's heart while we were outside searching for him is bound to be the type to go down with his ship, the *HMS Revenge*. So, waiting for Villar to break the connection might not be such a good plan."

"Probably not. Good news is that the duchess is safe."

"Yes . . ." Royce said with a sour look. "By all means, let's thank Maribor for that."

"Why not thank Novron. He's literally right outside."

Royce frowned. "If only—" he started to say, then stopped as a new thought distracted him. "Villar has to be on sacred ground to summon that thing, right?"

Hadrian nodded.

"And if he leaves it, the golem would kill him."

"Theoretically."

"So he must still be here."

The ruin wasn't a big place. There were no adjoining rooms except the cell, no cabinets or curtains to hide behind. Just the big dye pots, piles of wool, and the cook fire. Nevertheless, Royce moved around the space, nudging the blankets and looking inside the pots, which were huge but still far too small for even a mir to hide.

Where? Hadrian silently mouthed.

Royce shrugged in frustration. He looked back down at the crates and the piles of wool. He had to be close. He wasn't in the room with them, which meant . . .

Villar had led Royce on a merry chase across the rooftops of Rochelle. That tour of the city wasn't random. The mir knew where he was going, what transom led to what windows, what ledges could be leapt to, and what streets were narrow enough to cross at a running jump. He'd been that way before.

Villar has a thing for roofs.

Royce looked up and pointed at the dome.

Hadrian's eyes widened. He shook his head. "Can't be. The golem is out there. Why doesn't it just climb up and kill him."

"Can't reach him."

"But you said the gargoyle—"

"The gargoyle was small. Well, smaller. And Grom Galimus had all kinds of ornaments and handholds. I don't think Novron can climb up the smooth walls of this temple. Villar, on the other hand, would have no problem."

"Probably been up there this whole time—that's why we haven't found him," Hadrian whispered. "Now what?"

Royce didn't answer.

"The only way to stop that thing is to kill Villar. One of us has to get up there." Hadrian looked out the door. The legs hadn't moved. "And that means the other has to distract the god." Hadrian sighed. "You're the expert climber, so—"

"There you go again!" Royce snapped.

"What?"

Royce shook his head in disbelief. "Didn't we just talk about this? About your stupid habit of playing the hero? That's not grape juice on its legs."

"No . . . no, it's not." Hadrian's voice lowered. "But time's running out, and I don't see another option, do you? I can't climb up these sheer walls, but you can."

"Obviously, you should be the one to distract that thing, but that's not the point!" Royce snapped.

"What is the point?"

"You don't have to be so eager. You should try to persuade me to be the bait out of self-preservation." Royce took a step closer to the door, to the marble legs. They were massive.

Hadrian smiled. "You think if I go out there I'm committing suicide?"

Royce nodded.

Hadrian shook his head. "I'm not. I have complete confidence. I'll be fine."

"And what makes you think that?"

"Because there are unicorns in my world."

"There aren't any stupid unicorns, Hadrian."

"Yes, there are, I'm looking at one right now. And I know you're a very fast one." Hadrian pulled off his cloak. "Ready?"

"Villar probably heard all of this," Royce told him.

"Then I have nothing to worry about."

Royce held out Alverstone "Take this. It hurt the gargoyle before."

Hadrian shook his head. "You'll need it more than me, little unicorn. Ready?"

"Don't ever call me that again, or when this is over, assuming you're still alive, I will kill you."

"Deal."

Hadrian threw his cloak out the doorway.

A marble foot came down, crushing the garment. Hadrian dived directly between the pair of white polished legs. His plan was to somersault to his feet and run. But the green grass beyond the door was an illusion. The turf lied about the rocks beneath its blades. Hadrian slammed his shoulder against a hidden stone the size of a saddle horn, making him cry out in pain and killing his forward momentum.

A moment was all he had before the golem turned and another foot came down.

Hadrian log-rolled downhill, feeling the ground jump with the golem's second failed attempt. Finding his feet, he ran for the thickets. The golem chased after him. Hadrian wasn't certain it would. If Villar had heard their conversation, there was a good chance he might ignore the self-proclaimed decoy. Either Villar hadn't heard or suspected the verbal planning was a ruse. Or maybe he simply didn't care. In any case, Hadrian had the statue on his heels, a marble god he had no hope of outrunning and couldn't fight.

Hadrian plunged into the mass of thickets, hoping to slow the golem down. The thorns slashed him, tore his clothes, and cut his cheek just below his left eye. Like a rabbit chased by a wolf, he clawed his way into the underbrush, aiming for thicker branches and better cover.

Behind him, the ground shook. Branches snapped, and vines were ripped clear. Thorns didn't bother the god emperor.

Royce didn't waste a moment.

The instant the golem turned its back, he was out the doorway. A strong leap gave him a fingertip purchase on ancient decorative molding. After that, he relied mostly on cracks— small ones to be sure, but there were many to choose from. He pulled himself up as fast as he could. Everything was working perfectly. Too perfectly. No plan ever unfolded so nicely.

Why did the golem chase Hadrian? Villar must have heard. He knows I'm the real threat. Unless . . . I'm not.

Royce cleared the rim of the roof and ran up the curve to the peak of the dome. The roof of the temple was empty.

Villar wasn't there.

Stones!

Hidden beneath the brambles and old tree roots, Hadrian discovered a graveyard of tumbled slabs. Once part of the temple, these stones had fallen away and collapsed upon one another like playing cards. Three mostly buried slabs formed a hole that Hadrian crawled into.

A deep cave would have been nice, a tunnel even better; what he found was little more than a pocket.

Better than nothing.

Peering out the opening, he watched the world grow brighter as saplings and brambles were ripped away by Novron the Great. The god was digging down toward him.

Villar wasn't on the roof, but he had to be nearby. Royce climbed back down and reentered the temple. Hadrian couldn't survive much longer.

Royce stood in the little room, frustrated. Villar had to be there somewhere, but he couldn't find him and Royce was almost out of time.

I told you there were no unicorns!

Royce looked at the smoldering coals of the fire.

But the world is filled with vicious, merciless killers.

Then he noticed the heaping piles of wool.

I should know . . . I am one.

Hadrian squeezed himself as deeply as he could into the stone burrow. The slabs were massive, far from trivial impediments, even to a seventeen-foot marble god, but Hadrian was reminded about Villar's resolve as the golem grabbed the first stone and heaved it clear, tossing the giant granite block like a bag of grain. The second slab followed the first, leaving Hadrian exposed, his cozy refuge destroyed.

He scrambled to his feet. There was no fighting the thing; all he could do was run and dodge. Hadrian watched Marble Novron, hoping he might be able to evade whatever attack it made. If he could, he'd try running again. The golem raised a fist to smash him with, but its arm didn't come down. Hadrian waited, but Novron continued to stand there, perfectly still. Its eyes were blank, vacant . . . like a statue.

Royce had been quick, just quick enough.

Inching away from the marble god, Hadrian moved back up the slope. He found the ruined temple engulfed in flames. Black smoke and orange tongues of fire licked out the doorway. Royce was out in front of the door, dagger in hand, watching the place burn.

"What happened?" Hadrian asked.

"Villar wasn't on the roof," Royce replied, not taking his eyes off the doorway. "And I sort of got tired of looking. How about you, where's your playmate?"

"Standing over in the thickets looking a lot like a statue." Hadrian peered into the smoke and flames. "You think Villar's dead?"

Royce shook his head. "Not yet."

"No? Then why isn't the golem moving?"

"Only a guess, but I think when the smoke reached him, Villar panicked and broke the connection."

"You know where Villar is, don't you?"

"I can't prove it, but I think so," Royce said. "If he wasn't on the roof, the only place left is underneath."

"Makes sense. It would have been hidden," Hadrian said.

"What would?"

"The tomb. That's what this place is, a monument or crypt to someone. This one was secret, so the entrance to the burial chamber is disguised. Villar set his box to burning, then crawled inside to run the golem."

The two watched the fire grow. The inferno was thirty feet away, a distance required due to the heat. When the fire spread to the undergrowth, they retreated farther.

"How did you figure out it was a tomb?"

Hadrian pointed at one of the fallen slabs the golem had thrown, now only a few feet away. On it was chiseled a passage of text:

FALKIRK DE ROCHE

FIRST DISCIPLE OF BRAN

REST WITH MARIBOR

"Any idea who that is?"

Royce shook his head. "Must have been someone important, but I suppose given enough time, even really important people are forgotten. It could have been—" He stopped, and then pointed. "There!"

Something moved just inside the doorway. It slowed, then collapsed before getting outside.

Royce nodded. "Now he's dead."

HIDE-AND-SEEK

ೲ

After the killer statue had inexplicably run away, Genny took a few minutes to catch her breath. When the marble monster didn't return, she found two boys cowering in the carriage shop. They looked like good kids, the sort to help a woman who could barely get to her feet. They said they were Wardley Woffington's sons. After a good deal of coaxing, which ended when one recognized her, Genny convinced them to come out. Once they did, she ordered them to build a stretcher and carry Armand Calder to a physician, which they managed with the skill of those desperate to have some normal task to concentrate on.

After that, Genny walked—very slowly—down the hill. She had no idea where she was going or why. The plaza was a gory scene, but maybe someone else might need help, and . . . it was downhill. She reached the river's edge, but got no farther than the start of the paving stones when everything finally caught up to her, and she broke down and sobbed.

She wasn't alone.

People began to spill back into the square from all corners. They came across the bridge, down Vintage Avenue, from Center Street, even through the alley between the gallery and the cathedral. All the faces were the same—shock, horror, bewilderment, sadness. No one could do much more than stare and cry. Hundreds of men, women, and children, most of whom were dressed in the blue clothes of the wealthy and noble, lay dead alongside those who had served them at the feast. Out of that sea of morbid faces emerged an oddity.

Genny saw him through blurry eyes. A portly fellow with a salt-and-pepper beard was dressed in a poorly fitted metal breastplate and carrying a sword. He dropped the weapon and ran toward her, his arms spread wide. He crashed into her, his embrace so tight she could barely breathe. His bushy beard pressed hard against her cheek.

"I thought I'd lost you," he said, and when he pulled back to stare at her face, as if to assure himself it was really her, she saw tears of relief.

"I thought the same of you." She gestured at the plaza. "But you weren't here. You were . . . looking for me?"

"I was." Leo stared into her eyes, his lips trembling. "I thought you were dead. For more than two horrible weeks, I lived with that pain. Then I got your letter. I gathered my men and have spent the entire night and all of this day digging through every hovel, shop, and barn looking for you." He started to laugh then covered his mouth and shook his head. "I was coming back because I heard about the attack and . . . and . . . and here you are. I don't know how, but you are. Genny, my love, where have you been?"

Genny lingered on those two words: *my love.* "Leo, tell me, *do you* love me?"

The duke's brows shot up. "What a question! Didn't I just get done telling you—"

"I need to know. Do you *really* love me?" she insisted, grabbing him by the arms and holding him fast.

"How can you ask such a thing?"

"Because everyone says you married me for my money or the crown."

"That's not true." His voice was stern, his eyes growing dark and stormy.

"Then why? Why do we sleep in separate rooms? Why on our wedding night didn't you come to me . . . that night or any other. Why have you been so distant?"

The storm faded and Leo looked down. The expression on his face shifted to pain and embarrassment.

It is true. He doesn't—

"I'm an old man, Genny. Set in my ways. I don't like too many people; even fewer like me. Living here, surviving in this place, it teaches you not to trust anyone. You learn early that people only take—they never give. *Loyalty* is a word that means 'What can I get from you, and for how long?' I've had to guard myself, and I have, but it makes for a lonely life. But you're different, knew it the moment I met you. So bright, cheerful, smart, and open. You never asked how many servants I had, or how big my holdings were. That was so odd."

She smiled.

"You never really asked anything of me, except which whiskey I liked best, and what was my favorite food."

"Rye for the drink and apple-braised venison to eat," she confirmed.

He nodded. "I was drowning, Genny, and empty at the same time, and you were a lifeline, one I never thought I'd find. You gave me a reason to live when I didn't have one. I needed you . . . but you didn't need me. You were rich, beautiful, smart—what could I offer you?"

Beautiful?

"And what am I? Selfish, that's what. I shouldn't have asked you to marry me, but I couldn't help myself."

Genny's eyes widened. "You regret your proposal?"

"I wanted to marry you," he assured her. "I just thought you would refuse. The question was my way to end our relationship before it went too far. But you said yes."

"I don't understand, Leo. What are you talking about?"

"You should be queen and so much more. But I couldn't provide any of the things you deserve. Many thought I was the front-runner for the crown, but I knew better. Rochelle is such a mess, and if I'm not able to properly administer my own finances, why would the bishop put me in charge of an entire kingdom?"

"Leo, my love, I don't care about being queen. It's you I want. Only you."

"Is it? Is that all? What about children, Genny? And you'd be such a wonderful mother. Your children would grow up to be strong, determined, and honest. I can never give you that. I can't give you children. I can't give any woman children. To be honest, I can't do much of anything. Swords are dangerous things, and in battles men have lost eyes, arms, and legs. I was wounded years ago, in a nameless battle at an insignificant creek. A handful of monks nursed me at a little monastery. I never told anyone, and neither have they, for which I was grateful, but I should have told you. It was wrong for me to accept your hand in marriage knowing I couldn't be a *real* husband." His beard wriggled as his lips folded, his mouth quivering. "It's just that I fell so deeply in love with you, Genny. And I was going to tell you. Even if it meant you'd leave me. I lied, but at least I didn't tether you to me forever. The bishop will grant an annulment since the marriage was never consummated."

"You do love me," Genny said as tears fell.

"With all my heart, dear girl. That's why I want you to have your freedom."

"I don't want freedom."

"You don't? What do you want?"

"I want a goddamn double bed!" She grabbed hold of that bristly face and kissed him hard. His arms closed around her again.

CHAPTER TWENTY-NINE
WINTER'S DAUGHTER

"I suppose you two were involved," were the first words out of Evelyn's mouth as she poured her obligatory morning tea.

"Indirectly," Hadrian replied.

The lids came off the food. That morning's thank-you to Novron had been a mere communal bowing of heads. As usual, the breakfast table was impeccable and laden with a feast fit for kings, emperors, and at least one pair of very quiet thieves.

Evelyn didn't look at either of them, focusing instead on the amber stream spilling into her porcelain cup.

"The Seret will be coming soon. Such a thing happening in their own backyard must be addressed. They're not known for being prudent. It's likely they'll seek justice, and it won't matter who they choose to hold responsible." She looked up. "A pair of no-account foreigners would be tops on their list. I think it best if the two of you returned from whence you came."

"You're kicking us out?" Hadrian asked.

"Yes," she said simply and with an ever-so-curt nod. "I am." Evelyn set her spoon down sharply and frowned. "Truth is, I've already rented your room to someone else. So, please pack your things and be out by midday, thank you."

Hadrian stared at her and smiled. "You're concerned about us, aren't you?"

Evelyn glared back. "Don't be ridiculous. You're abominable people, and I'll not have you spoiling my house with your unsavory ways any longer. There, you wanted the truth, you have it. Stop smiling. I'm not doing this for you. I'm not. Stop it."

A knock at the door ended the one-sided debate as Evelyn stood up and, with an exasperated huff, marched to her home's entrance.

"Hullo!" a loud voice bellowed.

"Oh good gracious." Evelyn gasped. "Your Ladyship!"

Royce and Hadrian abruptly stood. Leaving the dining room, they entered the foyer at the same time as the Duchess of Rochelle who was dressed in a long black gown, black shawl, and a matching wide-brimmed hat, the sort that demanded special care when moving in tight spaces. Large though she was, her presence was twice as big. She commanded attention like a loud bee in a small room. Her face, round and happy, beamed a smile that made crescent-moons of her eyes.

Evelyn smoothed a lace doily that was already perfectly placed. "I'm so sorry. I had no idea you were coming. Please forgive this terrible mess!"

"Oh, nonsense, my good lady!" the duchess said. "I'm the one who should be apologizing. Dropping in unannounced at this hour and after such a tragedy. I wouldn't be the slightest bit surprised if you turned me away. Kicked me to the gutter. A fine woman such as yourself would expect that I know better than to act so abominably."

"I . . . I . . . ah . . . Evelyn stammered, lost.

"She's met her match," Royce whispered to Hadrian.

"But you see, I do have a reason, and while it might not be readily apparent, nor may you find it entirely important, I assure you that to me it most certainly is. And being the duchess of this city, that counts for something, doesn't it? Of course it does. So, I do hope you'll pardon this intrusion."

The large woman pushed deeper into the home, sweeping the hem of her gown to make certain it wasn't stepped on. As she moved clear of the doorway, Hadrian spotted an elegant carriage waiting on the street and a surprisingly large contingent of armed soldiers, including Roland Wyberg, working as the woman's security detail.

"I'm looking for two—" The duchess spotted them and smiled. "There you are, aren't you?"

She said this as if she expected some sort of answer, but neither Royce nor Hadrian had any clue how to respond. The pause took only a single beat as her smile widened. She spread her hands toward them. "My saviors."

She crossed the room and enveloped Hadrian in a hearty embrace; no bear could do better. Apparently, she didn't remember his comment about Royce and hugging, for she took hold of him as well. Royce went rigid, enduring the embrace as best he could.

"Our pleasure, Your Ladyship," Hadrian replied.

"To you, dear boys, I'm *Genny,* your most grateful damsel in distress. I thought you would like to know. My husband sent men up the eastern slope to look for any signs of Villar. They found the ruins, burned and destroyed, along with two bodies."

"Two?" Royce asked.

"Villar and the original inhabitant, Falkirk de Roche, a first-century monk after whom the river and city were named. De Roche was in a tomb under the dome. Villar, on the other hand . . . well, I'm guessing it was Villar . . . was burned beyond recognition. They also found the inanimate statue of Novron. That monster killed nearly every noble in the city. Armand Calder and I came within a heartbeat of becoming two more Spring Day casualties."

Evelyn, who still hadn't found her tongue, continued to stare.

"Now then, if I know my father, my rescue wasn't his only request. I'm sure your remuneration is contingent upon returning me to his side. Well, that's *not* going to happen. My husband loves me and I him, and I'm not going anywhere." She held out a sealed parchment, and Hadrian took it. "So, here is a letter for my father, explaining that I'm safe and couldn't be happier, and that he should pay you the full amount he promised. But just in case he doesn't see it that way . . ." She turned and bellowed, "Wentworth!"

A little man with his hair in a ponytail rushed forward and held out a purse. Royce took it.

"Inside, you'll find seventy-five gold tenents to hold you over and pay for expenses. I'd give more, but it's no longer just my money, you understand. My husband and I are going to get the city's finances in shape, and we have to watch our expenses. Still, I wanted to make sure you weren't left empty-handed. So please accept this along with my undying gratitude."

"Thank you," Hadrian said.

"Oh no, dear boy, thank *you*! If not for your intervention, I'd be dead, my husband would be heartbroken, and Alburn wouldn't have such a fine new king!"

"Has the bishop crowned your husband?" Evelyn asked.

"Ha-ha! No, no. Rochelle will just have to be content with us here. My husband took himself out of the running when he didn't show up at the feast. Apparently, finding me was more important than a crown. No, the bishop chose Armand Calder, the only noble to attend the feast and live. He might walk with a limp for the rest of his life, but it looks like he will make a complete recovery. He seems like a decent sort, which is good, and he likes me, which is better. Alburn is in need of many changes, and I think King Armand will listen to my ideas about reform. Did you know Mercator Sikara?"

They both nodded.

"Remarkable lady. She died trying to get my letter to Leo, didn't she?"

"Yes," Royce said.

The duchess nodded. "That poor woman. All she wanted was a better life for her people." The duchess raised her hand and shook a finger. "I'm going to ensure the mir are treated better—in Rochelle if no place else. Leo and I are going to make this city a beacon for the rest of the world. A safe haven for the mir, the Calians, and the little bearded folk. When people see the prosperity that harnessing so many talents can produce, they'll surely want to emulate our success. Well, I really must be going. So, thank you again, Hadrian Blackwater and Royce . . . Royce. I'm sorry, but I didn't catch your last name. What is it?"

Royce sighed. "Melborn."

Evelyn glared. "I thought your names were Baldwin and Grim!"

Returning from the stable that had quartered their animals, Hadrian led their horses down Mill Street. He'd felt guilty about not checking in on Dancer all week. The stable hand had complained, saying he should have been warned if they were going to *abandon* their horses for so long. In truth, the man was probably more disappointed when Hadrian showed up. Any hopes he might have had of selling a set of orphaned animals had vanished, and now he would have to *settle* for the ridiculously steep caretaking fee that he imposed. Dancer showed no signs of ill treatment or ill will, nuzzling Hadrian's shoulder as they walked.

Returning to Hemsworth House, Hadrian found Royce waiting on the stoop out front, surrounded by their gear like a man washed up on a deserted island.

"What did you do now?" Hadrian asked.

"Nothing," Royce said, standing up and throwing Hadrian's saddlebag at him. Royce hooked a thumb over his shoulder. "The new occupant is here, and Evelyn wanted me and our things out so we didn't upset her."

"Her?"

"Yep." He wore an odd smirk, part surprised, part amused. "The new guest is that mir mother who told us about the place."

Hadrian put his little finger in his ear and made of show of wiggling it before pulling it out and saying, "Sorry, sounded like you said Evelyn let the room to a mir."

Royce nodded. "Don't know how she did it, either. Tracked the mir down somehow. I suppose she's lived here her entire life and knows this city pretty well. Old woman is full of surprises."

Royce tossed his own bag on his horse, but before tying it, he lifted and hooked the stirrup on the horn, double-checking the cinch.

"Seriously?" Hadrian leaned on Dancer, shaking his head in disgust. "You had to check? You don't think I know how to cinch a saddle?"

Royce didn't even look up as he ran fingers along the strap, checking its tension. "No, I don't."

"Trust. You have to learn to trust people, Royce."

He dropped the stirrup without making any changes. "No. I don't."

They finished lashing bags to their mounts. The animals stood impatiently, stomping hooves to express their desire to be on the road. Along the street the milkman was back to delivering his jugs, and a flower girl was going door-to-door with a basket of fresh-cut purple pansies. Only a day later and the city was back to old routines.

Hadrian pulled himself up onto Dancer and grasped his reins, but Royce hesitated. He had his things secured but remained staring up at the window of what had been their room.

"Forget something?"

"The rug."

"What rug? Oh, wait . . . you're not serious!"

"It's just that it would definitely fit nicely through that window and hit the street with hardly a sound." Royce looked up and down the thoroughfare. "There are never any constables on this street. I bet we could sell it in Little Gur Em for five gold, maybe six."

"I'm leaving." Hadrian started to urge Dancer into the traffic, then stopped.

"What?" Royce asked. "You're having second thoughts about the rug, aren't you?"

Hadrian gave him a sharp look. "No." He pointed across the street at a little pug-nosed dog sitting on a patch of recently turned earth. "Must be a stray. I've seen that dog around here a lot. I wish I had some food."

"It's not a stray; it has a collar," Royce said and continued to stare. Then his eyes narrowed and a stunned looked filled his face. "That's not possible."

"What's not?"

Royce abandoned his horse and crossed the street.

Royce famously hated dogs, and, thinking he might harm the animal, Hadrian leapt off his mount and raced over, catching up just as Royce bent down to study the little mangy pup's collar.

"I can't believe it."

"What?" Hadrian asked.

"It's Mister Hipple."

"No! That's not possible. You don't mean . . ."

Royce nodded. "Lady Martel's dog. The one who sounded the alarm at Hemley Manor and nearly got poor Ralph the guard killed. How could that dog possibly be here?"

Hadrian looked around at the unkempt field filled with crooked posts. "This is a cemetery, a paupers' graveyard. Maybe this is Lady Martel's grave."

"Lady Martel wouldn't be buried in a pauper's grave in Alburn. She's the wife of a wealthy Melengar lord."

"But didn't Puck say something about the diary belonging to a monk named Falkirk?" Hadrian asked.

"No. He said the diary was *written* by someone named Falkirk, and that she *got it* from a monk."

"Whoa, that's really weird. Wonder what she's doing here, and how she died." Hadrian looked at the dog, sadly. "That's one loyal pet. I've heard stories about things like this. The dog gets so attached that it waits on its owners' grave for them to come back. Some end up dying because they just can't leave."

Royce didn't say anything. He merely stared at the dog and the grave.

"Maybe we should take Mister Hipple with us," Hadrian said, bending down and reaching out.

The little mongrel with the flat face and folded ears snapped at him. "Or not."

They returned to their horses and climbed up.

"Perhaps Evelyn will adopt him," Hadrian said hopefully.

"Or maybe he'll be crushed under the wheels of a milk wagon. I'm not sure which would be the worse fate," Royce added.

The streets were just as congested as on the day they had arrived, but this time the current was all in one direction, out. Like Royce and Hadrian, everyone was leaving the city, heading home. At the bottom of the hill, they found that the plaza had been cleaned. The sound of hammering announced that the door to the gallery was being worked on, and the bells of Grom Galimus were chiming on time, but no vendors had set up shop. In their place, flowers had been laid out in bunches around the empty pedestal where a seventeen-foot statue of Novron once stood. Wreaths, candles, and lovingly drawn portraits were mixed in with the bundles of recently gathered blossoms. The odd thing—no delineation existed between the memorials for servants and nobles. No line separated the privileged from the poor. Grief blended them all together, ignoring differences as readily as death had.

"Don't understand how all this connects," Hadrian said as they waited to cross the bridge to Governor's Isle behind a trio of wagons filled with families. "How could reading the diary of a several-thousand-year-old monk get Lady Martel and Virgil Puck killed? Maybe some ancient ghost wants his book back. Which brings up another mystery."

"What?"

"Who killed Erasmus Nym?"

Royce shrugged. "I suppose a golem got him."

Hadrian shook his head. "Only Villar, Griswold, and Erasmus knew how to raise them. You were chasing Villar across rooftops when Erasmus died."

"So, it must have been Griswold."

"Nope. He'd run away from the cemetery. Besides, the two of them were friends. He'd have no reason to kill him."

"I have a friend, and I think about killing him all the time." Royce said with a straight face.

"Oh, so you admit it now. We're friends?"

"I never said anything about you. Don't be so presumptuous."

The wagon ahead of them began moving, but slowly. They were at the edge of the bridge where the big gargoyle pediment Royce had perched on was still guarding the entrance to Governor's Isle.

Hadrian looked around at the congested city of towers and grotesque statues dominated by the cathedrals and bridge spires. Even in the daylight, with the many shadows cast by the tall buildings, the old city felt dark. Who knew what other secrets it kept to itself.

Royce turned sharply around in his saddle and looked behind.

"What?" Hadrian asked, looking back as well, but he saw only the city and more throngs of people.

"Nothing."

"What is it?"

Royce gave a second glance back and sighed. "I just thought of something."

"What?"

"Why Lady Martel might have been buried in an unmarked grave. It's because her body wasn't claimed. No one identified her."

"I think that's obvious. If they'd known who she was, her body would have been sent back to Hemley Manor."

"And why do you think that was? I mean, why didn't anyone identify her?"

Shock crossed Hadrian's face. "You don't mean . . ."

Royce nodded. "What if Lady Martel didn't have a face?"

Hadrian grimaced and pulled his blue scarf tighter.

Crossing the river, they started up the far hills, heading west. When they reached the crest, they turned back for a final look. From that distance, the city, nestled in the valley surrounded by the mountains and the sea, appeared quaint, even romantic.

"What's that up there?" Royce pointed to what appeared to be a fortress down the coast.

The castle was nothing but an outline on the top of a distant mountain, but even from that far away it appeared intimidating, dangerous, powerful.

"Blythin Castle," Hadrian said. "I think that's where they imprisoned Glenmorgan the Third, and it's now headquarters to the Seret Knights. Creepy place. Wanna go look?"

Royce pulled up his hood. "No. Let's get home. I'm never coming back here."

Hadrian laughed. "Never say never on any endeavor . . ."

"Quit it."

"It sounds like a dare to gods that don't care . . ."

"I mean it."

"If the likes of us prosper, fail, or falter . . ."

"You are seriously annoying me now."

"It matters not while they roll with laughter on an altar . . ."

Royce kicked his horse and trotted off up the road.

The Disappearance of Winter's Daughter

Hadrian looked back once more at the city. He thought of Seton and the night he first met her amidst the smell of blood and the cries of widows. He remembered his father who'd made him butcher a chicken, the first life he took. And he thought back on his years of war and slaughters within the arenas of Calis. "At our miserable, sad little lives."

Royce was right. They were never coming back here again.

AFTERWORD

Well, there you have it. Another adventure with Royce and Hadrian. I hope you enjoyed coming along for the ride and meeting some new characters along the way. If this was your first trip with the pair, I hope you'll check out some of their other tales. Like the other Riyria Chronicles, this book was written to be a standalone . . . a self-contained story that doesn't require any prior knowledge of Riyria and wraps up nicely so you don't have to read the next book. I think I delivered on most of that intention, but I want to spend just a moment talking about a few things.

So, Virgil Puck, Lady Martel, and Falkirk de Roche walk into a bar . . . sorry, sometimes my mind just goes places whether I want it to or not. But seriously, this book definitely has a very loose thread, and I want to offer some further explanation. So, here goes.

For those who read *The Death of Dulgath,* you may recall it starts with a simple job to steal a diary from Lady Martel. Royce is caught by a small dog called Mister Hipple. When I originally wrote that scene, I had no plans for it to evolve into anything more than what it was . . . a fun, simple incident to start out the book—a way to reacquaint (or introduce) the reader with our duo known as Riyria. Anyway, in that book I happened to mention that Lady Martel denied the diary was stolen and claimed there hadn't been a break-in. I wrote those words mainly so I didn't have to send Royce back to kill ol' Ralph, the guard who had happened upon them during the heist, but that diary job also planted a seed. In *The Death of Dulgath,* Royce wonders why Lady Martel would deny the theft of the diary. I wrote this as an inconsequential matter, but then thought, *Wouldn't it be cool if the diary was more than just a diary?* And if it was, what would it be?

If the series had ended with *The Death of Dulgath,* the diary could be exactly what it started out as: a prop to start the book. But when I decided to write *The Disappearance of Winter's Daughter,* I was drawn back to that little support and considered what it could mean in the grand scheme of the Riyria tales as a whole. Hence it took on a new life. A life I couldn't possibly—nor did I wish to—bring to full closure in this book, but one that I wanted to at least begin to address. So, yeah, I did open a window without closing it . . . but in my defense, it was a very small window, and nothing in the cliff-hanger category. After all, the story of *The Disappearance of Winter's Daughter* has been resolved. Genny is safe, the duo's been paid, and the villain is dead. Case closed. If you never hear anything more about this sideline, you can just consider it for what it was, a little aside that never went anywhere. Literature is filled with such things, and so is life.

So, why bring it up at all? For the same reason I create any thread that spans multiple books: It'll greatly enhance the next story. Weaving threads was a hallmark of the Riyria Revelations and one of the things I enjoyed the most when writing the books. Getting just a taste of this, or that, or the other thing, and then contemplating where various clues might lead, was a huge part of the fun. When you get to the next book and Easter eggs start appearing, it's hugely rewarding. In short, a little bit of tease will make the next book so much better than if I didn't lay a foundation.

Does that mean there *will* be another Riyria book? This, too, must remain one of those irritating loose threads of literature and real life, because I won't make promises I don't know I can keep. With each year, my time grows shorter, and the books I want to write multiply. If people indicate that they are tired of the pair, I won't release another. If that happens, I might put out a freebie (either a short story or a behind-the-scenes piece), explaining this and other mysteries. But if there is still a desire for more, I have the start of a thread that I can knit into a scarf.

Okay, one last thing I want to mention, and this is only for people who have read the Riyria Revelations. If Genny and Leopold seem vaguely familiar, they should. You ran into the Duke and Duchess of Rochelle in the fifth book: *Wintertide* (which is the first half of the omnibus edition titled *Heir of Novron*). They ended up helping out Royce and Hadrian, and now you know why they were so willing to do so. After Riyria saved Genny's life and reunited the pair, the duke and duchess are forever in their debt, and I was glad that the opportunity arose to describe how that debt came into being.

Okay, I think that's all I have to say, except to once again thank you for your support of my writing, and to remind you that if you want to drop me a line, please do. My address is michael@michaelsullivan-author.com.

Acknowledgments

I've said it before, but it bears repeating: It takes a great many people to produce a work of this nature. Given that I write for a living, you'd think I'd be able to fully express my appreciation, but words fail me at times like this. *Thank you* just isn't enough, and the depth of my gratitude rivals that of the Mariana Trench.

As always, my first thanks go to my wife, Robin. Of all the books in recent memory, this one saw the largest number of changes due to her alpha feedback. Not only did she point out problems, she offered solutions that were both insightful and ingenious. Our "discussions" were often loud, and always passionate, but they came from the same place . . . both of us wanting the best book possible. I think we worked through it rather well. The book has a more satisfying conclusion than the one I originally penned, and if you were a backer of the Kickstarter or a member of the beta crew, you know just a little about how hard she works. What you didn't see is all the effort she put into the book before it reached anyone else. Her structural, line, and copyedits have made it better than I could have produced on my own, and we all owe her a debt of gratitude.

Speaking of editing, I also want to thank the amazing copy editors for their incredible talent: Laura Jorstad and Linda Branam. Both have edited multiple books for me. Laura worked on *Hollow World, The Death of Dulgath, Age of Myth,* and *Age of Swords.* Linda has helped out with *The Death of Dulgath, Age of Myth, Age of Swords,* and will be copyediting *Age of War.* Only a small group of people knows the difference between what I originaly wrote and the work that's released. They save me from looking stupid, clean up my messes, and act with the professionalism of people at the top of their game. I'm honored and grateful to have them on the Riyria team.

Which segues nicely to the beta readers! More than twenty-five people provided feedback, including rating the chapters and answering survey questions. When all was said and done, we had more than 2,100 rankings covering over 525 chapters! Thanks to Robin's hard work, the book was in really good structural shape when it went out. Still, there was room for improvement, and the beta readers contributed tweaks to a number of key scenes. They even caught a glaring loose thread that neither Robin nor I saw, and I was able to properly tie it up. There isn't enough space to go into full detail, but we hope to write a *Making of the Disappearance of Winter's Daughter* e-book (something we did with *The Death of Dulgath* and *Age of Swords*). If we do, it'll be free for anyone who is interested in the behind-the-scenes aspects of this book. Just drop me an email at michael@michaelsullivan-

ACKNOWLEDGMENTS

author.com to get a copy. Please put "Making of . . ." (and include the book's name) in the subject line, and we'll get it right out to you. Our thanks go out to every one of the beta readers, some of whom didn't wish to be acknowledged publicly. Here are the ones who did: Amy Lesniak Briggs, Michael Jay Brunt, Jeffrey Carr, Craig Cato, Beverly Collie, Buffy Curtis, Marie-Louise Faering, Cathy Fox, Sheri L Gestring, Julianne Gaston, Chris Haught, Craig T. Jackson, Toby Johnson, Evelyn Keeley, Stephen Kafkas, Sarah and Nathaniel Kidd, Frank Kincell, Jamie McCullough, Elizabeth Ocskay, Christina Pilkington, Slobodan Rakovic, Beth Rosser, Melanie Sanderson, Jeffrey Schwarz. Laurie Swensen, Scott Vout and Sarah Webb.

In addition to the beta readers, we added a gamma reader to our process. What are they? Think of them as the last line of defense. They're people who get the book after all the beta changes have been edited, when the book is in its final state. Their job is to find any nits that managed to escape other eyes. This book's gamma reader was Chris McGrath and not only did he find a number of typo and grammar issues, but he also pointed out a number of beta-like things that we were able to address before the book went to print.

Okay, on to others that I just can't leave out. Once again, we utilized the amazing artistic talent of Marc Simonetti to create the book's cover. If you aren't familiar with his work, definitely check it out. Not only has he created covers for six of my books, but he's also developed stunning work for Patrick Rothfuss's Kingkiller Chronicle, George R. R. Martin's Song of Ice and Fire, Brandon Sanderson's Mistborn series, Terry Pratchett's Discworld, and dozens of others. Some of my covers that he's been responsible for are the French editions of *The Crown Conspiracy, Avempartha,* and *Nyphron Rising.* For the English market he's created covers for *Hollow World, The Death of Dulgath, Age of Myth, Age of Swords,* and *Age of War.*

The audio book rights were acquired by Lee Jarit at Audible Studios. Lee has always been a huge fan of my work, and he did an amazing job with shepherding the release of *The Death of Dulgath.* Before production of *Winter's Daughter,* he was promoted to a new position, and we came under the care of Kristen Lang. I can't lie—the loss of Lee as our internal advocate was a heavy blow. But after meeting Kristen, we knew she'd take good care of us. She even signed my next series (codename: The Bridge Trilogy), and we're all excited about that project. Anyway, getting back to *The Disappearance of Winter's Daughter,* Kristen did an amazing job nurturing the book through the process and making sure the marketing folks at Audible.com were going to give it a great send-off. I'm writing this before that happened, of course, but I'm confident it'll have an amazing launch.

Okay, almost done . . . and I did warn you it takes a lot of people. Last, but certainly not least, is the phenom that is Tim Gerard Reynolds. This is our twelfth book working with Tim, and no matter how many times I thank and praise him, the words still fall short of how Robin and I feel about him and his talent. Thank you, Tim. Thank you, thank you, thank you. May your star continue to rise, but please try to find time to record my stuff!

As you can see, my team is well established and has been with me a very long time. Most of the collaborators are the same people used by my traditional publishers, whom I've

ACKNOWLEDGMENTS

hired for this project. When I find good people, I treat them right, and continue to send business their way. I hope they are as happy with how this book came out as I am. I think we did good . . . er . . . I mean *well*. Sorry, Linda and Laura, I just couldn't help myself.

Works by Michael J. Sullivan

Novels
The First Empire
Age of Myth • *Age of Swords* • *Age of War* (Spring 2018)
Age of Despair (Early 2019) • *Age of Hope* (Mid 2019)
Age of Novron (Early 2020)

The Riyria Revelations
Theft of Swords (The Crown Conspiracy and *Avempartha)*
Rise of Empire (Nyphron Rising and *The Emerald Storm)*
Heir of Novron (Wintertide and *Percepliquis)*

The Riyria Chronicles
The Crown Tower • *The Rose and the Thorn*
The Death of Dulgath • *The Disappearance of Winter's Daughter*

Standalone Novels
Hollow World

Anthologies
Unfettered: The Jester
Unbound: The Game
Unfettered II: Little Wren and the Big Forest
Blackguards: Professional Integrity
The End: Visions of the Apocalypse: Burning Alexandria
Triumph Over Tragedy: Traditions
The Fantasy Faction Anthology: Autumn Mists